WAITING FOR THE MOON

Kristin Hannah

BALLANTINE BOOKS • NEW YORK

A Ballantine Book
Published by The Random House Publishing Group
Copyright © 1995 by Kristin Hannah
Excerpt from *Between Sisters* by Kristin Hannah copyright © 2003 by Kristin Hannah

Published in the United States by Ballantine Books, an imprint of The Random House Publishing Group, a division of Random House, Inc., New York, and simultaneously in Canada by Random House of Canada Limited, Toronto.

Ballantine and colophon are registered trademarks of Random House, Inc.

www.ballantinebooks.com

Library of Congress Catalog Card Number: 95-90426

ISBN 0-449-14909-9

Manufactured in the United States of America

First Edition: November 1995

OPM 50 49 48 47 46 45 44

Praise for Kristin Hannah

ANGEL FALLS

"An all-night-reading affair—you won't be able to put it down . . . [*Angel Falls* will] make you laugh and cry."
—*The New York Post*

"A tearjerker. . . about the triumph of family . . . Perfect reading for hopeless romantics."
—*Detroit Free Press*

"One of the premier voices in women's fiction . . . Hannah deftly explores love in all its variations and manifestations."
—*Romantic Times*

ON MYSTIC LAKE

"Superb . . . I'll heartily recommend *On Mystic Lake* to any woman . . . who demands that a story leave her in a satisfied glow."
—*The Washington Post Book World*

"Marvelous . . . A touching love story . . . This page-turner has enough twists and turns to keep the reader up until the wee hours of the morning."
—*USA Today*

"Excellent . . . An emotional experience you won't soon forget."
—*Rocky Mountain News*

By Kristin Hannah
Published by The Random House Publishing Group:

A HANDFUL OF HEAVEN
THE ENCHANTMENT
ONCE IN EVERY LIFE
IF YOU BELIEVE
WHEN LIGHTNING STRIKES
WAITING FOR THE MOON
HOME AGAIN
ON MYSTIC LAKE
ANGEL FALLS
SUMMER ISLAND
DISTANT SHORES
BETWEEN SISTERS
THE THINGS WE DO FOR LOVE
COMFORT & JOY
MAGIC HOUR

To the best brother in the world, Kent. This one's for you.

To Tom and Lori Adams, friends and hosts extraordinaire, who first told me about the Shakers.

And always, to Benjamin and Tucker.

Prologue

THE COAST OF MAINE, 1882

He was an old, old man, and he thought he'd seen it all. For seventy-one years he had fished these icy waters of the Atlantic, as had his father and his father before him. He'd braved the angry sea as it crashed and howled along his beloved coast, gone out in his small, flat-bottomed dory into the sleeping blue giant when the fog was so thick he couldn't see his own hands. But he'd never been afraid out here until today.

The woman scared him.

He glanced at her from beneath the snagged brim of his cap, trying to hide his interest. He needn't have bothered. She seemed to have forgotten his existence.

He tried to think of something to say to her, to this strange, fey beauty who sat like a silent Madonna in his rocking, scarred little boat, a dozen old lobster traps in need of paint clustered around her.

She sat slumped over, beaten somehow, her pale hands clasped against the rough brown wool of her cloak, her sad gaze fixed on the sharp line of the horizon.

Blue water slapped the dory, sprayed over the high sides, and puddled on the floor at her feet, but she didn't bother to move her scuffed boots out of the wetness.

He waited for her to say or do something. But she just sat there, staring, staring. Long, wavy strands of reddish brown hair whipped along her pale cheeks, caught on the fullness of her lower lip. The odd, nearly transparent white bonnet that hid her chignon fluttered with the breath of the wind.

"That's Purgatory," he said at last, pointing at the craggy, lonely crown of granite that pushed up from the sea, its cliffs ringed in the white foam of a pounding surf.

She nodded silently.

He maneuvered his small craft toward the island, his eyes narrowed against the bright sun. The island wavered and danced before his gaze, seeming one moment to disappear amidst the swelling tide of the sea, then to thrust up again like a proud fist. It was the last rampart of land, this place; beyond it, the Atlantic stretched into the distant horizon. As they neared the lonely island, the pounding hammer of the surf became louder. The swells crashed against the stone cliffs, sending spray higher, higher.

"I'll go around to the bay side, miss. 'Tis a quieter place to land."

"No," she said sharply, in a voice unexpectedly throaty and full. A barmaid's voice from an angel's face. "I'll get out on this side. It doesn't matter now."

"But, 'tis rough, miss—"

She turned to him then, and there was nothing sad or lonely or lost in her eyes now, there was simply determination. Cold and hard and uncompromising. "Shall I get out and swim, sir?"

For a moment, he couldn't respond.

She sighed and began gathering her skirts.

"No! Th-There's a slight cove to the starboard. I can manage a landing there, but 'twill be bumpy."

She laughed, a hollow, empty sound that frightened him. "It will not bother me, I assure you."

He drew his gaze away from her eyes and scanned

the rocky shoreline. He knew from experience that he could manage a landing alongside one of the rain pools that gave the westernmost tip of the island a deceptive look of calm, but it wouldn't be easy. And it wouldn't be safe.

He shouldn't do it. Should tell her to go hang herself, *he* was the captain of this boat, such as it was

He turned to tell her as much, met her gaze, and fell into her sadness. Fifty years of his life fell away in that look; suddenly he was a young man again, and he couldn't let her down.

"H-Hang on, miss," was all he said, then he focused his full concentration on beaching the dory.

The sea fought him, tried time and again to push him back, but the old man fought harder, repeatedly maneuvering his craft toward the rocky outcropping at the western edge of the island. For a split second, the water hesitated, drew back, and the boat surged forward. He heard the whining scrape of the wooden hull as it slid across the smooth granite and bounced to a stop.

The woman didn't move.

"Miss?"

Slowly, so slowly, she looked up, and he saw the tears she made no effort to hide. "I shall be damned," she said softly, her throaty voice catching on the curse.

Then, with a dancer's grace, she rose to her feet in the precariously balanced boat and stepped onto the firm curl of granite. For the first time, he noticed the small drawstring bag that hung from her pale wrist. She slid the purse from her arm and eased it open, withdrawing a handful of wrinkled dollars and a ring.

"Here," she said, shoving her fist toward him.

The money flapped in the breeze. He frowned. "You can pay me when we land safe on the mainland, miss. And anyway, that's far too much. . . ."

She looked beyond him and gave a small, involuntary shudder. Reluctantly he turned, followed her gaze with his eyes. She was looking at Dead Man's Bluff, a forty-five-foot concave cliff of stone. Then he looked back at her.

"If you don't take the money from me now, I shall open my fist and let it go."

He licked his chapped lips, completely at a loss. "Fine."

He surged toward her fist and grabbed hold just as her fingers loosened. His old, gnarled hand closed around hers, and he felt the warm, damp heat of her flesh. And suddenly they were connected.

She drew her hand back sharply.

He slowly opened his hand. Atop the money was a plain, unadorned band of gold. " 'Tis a wedding ring," he said quietly, meeting her gaze.

The smile she flashed was thin and strained. "Those in the world would call it such."

He blinked, lost in the need to say something, anything, that would reach her. Nothing came to him except a soft plea. "Come back with me, miss."

"Do not worry overmuch about me, sir. Take your wife on holiday with the money, give her the ring as a token of love—that is, I believe, its purpose, after all." For a moment, her smile softened. "You have children, yes?"

He nodded. "Three daughters in Portsmouth."

"Children." She said the word with a quiet, subtle reverence that tugged at his heart. "Go see them. Hold them . . . tell them how much you love them."

Before he could think of anything to say, she drew back and pulled the misshapen hood around her head. "Good-bye."

Head held high, body stiff, she picked her way across the slick, rocky outcropping of stone toward the cliffs. He watched her get smaller and smaller, a pale, dark shadow against the bright sun, moving up the scrubby embankment and over the granite shelving, to the top of the island.

Frowning, he tented a hand across his forehead to cut

out the sun's glare. He wondered briefly what she needed to see out there on that lonely point. She'd said she was an artist and merely wanted to see the view, but he didn't believe her. For a second, he lost sight of her. Then, as if by magic, she reappeared, a slender slash of darkness against a deep blue sky. Her cape billowed out behind her, filled by the breeze.

She stepped closer to the edge of the rock.

And suddenly he knew what she was going to do.

"Jesus, Mary, and Joseph," he whispered.

She brought her hands to her throat, and in seconds the cape was free, twisting and dropping through the sky, buffeted by the wind before it landed in a bubbled heap on the turbulent surface of the water. Then it was gone.

"Miss!" he screamed with all his might, but it was useless. The wind erased his feeble, old man's voice, swallowed it as easily as the sea had taken her cloak.

She moved closer to the edge and ripped off her silly white cap, tossing it into the air. Her hair tumbled down, whipped out behind her.

And she jumped.

Horror washed through him in a wave so cold, so all-encompassing, that for a second he couldn't move, couldn't even breathe.

She wanted to die. The truth hit him like a cold, hard slap . . . and he had helped her do it.

He jerked around and tore for the dory, diving in. Pain shot up his knees as he hit the plank seat and yanked his oars into place. Furiously he rowed into the surf and spun the long, narrow craft around. Two old lobster traps slid into one another with a thumping scrape and plopped into the water, sinking. Cold water smacked the side of the boat, splashed his face, stung his eyes.

"I'm coming, miss," he yelled. With strong, sure strokes, he powered through the two-foot swells, searching frantically until he saw her. A dark shadow on the surface of the water.

He fought the tide and forced the dory forward. She lay there, facedown, floating on the swell like a broken doll. He flung the oars into the center of the boat and twisted around, reaching down into the icy, swirling water. He grabbed a handful of her hair, wrapping the long, wet mass around his knuckles. Breathing deeply, gathering his old man's strength, he pulled her into the boat.

She lay as if dead, her hair and throat veined with slimy, yellow-green kelp, her arms limp and flung out from her body.

Gently he peeled the curtain of hair and seaweed from her face.

Oh, Jesus . . .

A roiling knot of nausea clutched his gut.

Her beautiful face was unrecognizable. Blood trickled from her left ear, puddling beneath her head in a bright red pool. It was horribly red next to the pale blue-whiteness of her skin. The whole left side of her face was bruised and bloodied and scraped, as if she'd hit a submerged rock with her head.

With shaking hands, he leaned down to her, listened for the whisper of her breath.

She was breathing. Shallowly, desperately, but it was the sweetest sound he'd ever heard. She gagged and spit up seawater.

He let out a huge sigh of relief.

Moving slightly, he twisted around and slipped a hand behind her head, positioning her more securely on the plank seat. She gagged, her body spasming slightly at the movement.

When he drew his hand back, it was covered in blood.

His whole body started to shake. He wrenched off his shirt and tied it around her head as tightly as he could manage to stem the bleeding.

"What now?" he cried to God, to the sea, to himself. *What now?*

Old Doc Mather couldn't handle a case like this.

Who could? Her skull was cracked and she was probably going to die. No one could save her ... no one could make this crazy, beautiful woman whole again.

Crazy.

The word was a gift from the God he'd prayed to for seventy-one years.

He knew where she belonged.

Chapter One

Dr. Ian Carrick removed his small, wire-rimmed spectacles and set them down on the desk. Rubbing the bridge of his nose, he let out an exhausted sigh. Sheets and sheets of expensive paper covered with inky scribblings lay sprawled in front of him and on the floor, heaped in disorderly piles. His microscope sat at his elbow, hunched over like an old man, the slides in readiness beside it.

He leaned back in his chair and sipped at his scotch, glancing down at the mess of papers before him. The title blurred before his tired eyes. *Blood refusion in the treatment of carbonic oxide poisoning.*

"Fascinating," he said bitterly.

He didn't know why he bothered. No one in New York cared what he had to say anymore. His last paper on the causes of puerperal septicemia had been largely ignored by everyone except his friend Dr. Halstead.

He grabbed his glass and got to his feet. Paper scattered beneath his feet, skidded out of the way as he moved away from the desk. At the window he paused, glanced outside at the storm gathering force along his forbidding, rocky stretch of coastline.

Wind and rain hammered the roof, shook the old windows of the house, and moaned through cracks in the siding. Misshapen shrubs and spindly pines curled around the perimeter, their serrated edges backlit eerily by the bluish light of a nearly full moon.

He threw the window open and leaned out. Stinging rain hit his face, blurred his vision until all he could see was the shifting darkness of the yard and the half-light of the moon. Wind yanked his long hair, brought it against his cheek in a wet slap. Below, the surf capsized against the rocks, soaked the few trees hardy enough to creep along the shoreline.

It was the kind of night that used to spur him on, used to encourage him to do wild, crazy things like jump on his horse and ride ... or get in his boat and row ... or cajole a lady into his bed.

The kind of night that used to fire his soul and fuel his energy and make him think he was a god.

He drew back, closing the window, wishing to hell he had another bottle of scotch. Anything to end the cursed loneliness ...

He squeezed his eyes shut and leaned heavily against the wall. Draining the cheap glass, he let it slip through his fingers, heard it hit the hardwood floor with a satisfying crash. Running a hand through his hair, he stared out at the shifting sea, watched the painted tips of the waves break against the black rock of his beach.

Once, he'd never been alone. Memories of that life were becoming hazy, dulled by the dark isolation of his existence now, but he could still recall that he'd been in constant motion, talking, laughing, drinking, making love. He remembered that life as a staccato series of images—rich clothing, Baccarat crystal, naked flesh. He'd moved from elegant party to glittering ball with the jerky, fleeting motion of a butterfly, desperately seeking something he could never name. Always in the limelight, always the center of attention. So rarely alone. He'd thought then that he was urbane, sophisticated, bored by everything save the all-consuming passion of his medicine. But he'd been wrong.

Hell, he hadn't even known what boredom was in

those halcyon days, or what horror was, even though he'd looked at death every day for years. He hadn't understood horror or regret until the day his life ended in a spray of blood and betrayal and dishonor. If he'd known then what he knew now . . .

A knock at the door saved him from his dark thoughts.

He straightened, pushed away from the wall. "Come in."

The door opened slowly, just a crack at first. "Dr. Carrick?"

He rolled his eyes. "No, it's Mr. Hyde."

"Yes . . . right, sir." The door eased open, and his plump, gray-haired housekeeper waddled into his sanctuary, bearing a tray of steaming food. The familiar smell of baked beans and ham wafted in with her. She squinted, moved slowly forward. " 'Tis rather dark in here, Doctor."

"Yes, Edith, it is."

"Of course, you like it that way."

"Yes, Edith, I do."

She bustled into the room, her tray held like an offering. As she reached the desk, her foot caught on the edge of the Oriental carpet and she was flung forward. Without thinking, Ian reached out for her, grabbed her fleshy arm.

He knew it was a mistake instantly. His hands seemed to burst into flames at the touch. He staggered and snatched his arm back, but it was too late.

The vision hit him hard. *Edith yanking a half-empty bottle of whiskey from her husband's gnarled fingers . . . her screeching shout, "Get that whore out of our bed." The bitter, wrenching sound of her sobs . . .*

As if from far away, he heard her quiet gasp. The tray clattered onto his desk, sugary brown sauce dripped over the braided silver rim and bled onto a piece of paper.

And then the pictures were gone. "Damn it," Ian

hissed, fisting his hands to stop the shaking. The pulsating heat in his fingertips faded.

Poor Edith looked as if she might retch. "I-I'm sorry, Doctor. I stumbled ... I didn't mean ... Sorry." She spun in a rustling twirl of heavy fabric and ran for the door, slamming it shut behind her.

Ian closed his eyes and sagged forward. A dull, thudding pain beat at the base of his skull, deepening with each shallow breath he took.

How long could he go on? he wondered for the millionth time. How long could a man exist, closeted away in a murky darkness, touching no one, never being touched?

That first year after the "accident," he thought he'd go mad with it, thought the damned psychic ability would simply swallow him whole and he would fade away.

Nothing so dramatic had happened, however, and after a while he'd stopped expecting it to, stopped expecting anything at all. He'd simply gone on, living, breathing, sleeping, eating.

Pretending ...

He had died on a Sunday. The Sabbath.

When Ian looked back on it now—which he did with morbid regularity—he remembered that it had been such an ordinary day. So damned ordinary. Sunny and bright, the air crisp with the coming of winter.

It had started like every other day back then, with a blinding sense of purpose and an overwhelming optimism. He'd performed an appendectomy, which even his colleagues advised against.

As always, the doubt spurred Ian on, challenged him. That day he'd gone even further, causing an outbreak of dissension among the other doctors at New York Hospital. He'd done the unheard-of—he'd worn gloves and demanded the same of his assistant, and even worse, he'd forced Dr. Jones, his superior, to put out his cigar during the operation.

It had caused quite a scandal, of course, but the surgery was a brilliant success. There was no sign of the postoperative infection that would kill the man in less than a week.

Not then. Then, there was only the adoration of his peers. It rang loud and long in his ears, filling his soul, making him think that he could do anything, that he could conquer worlds.

Or, at least, one very alluring woman.

He sighed, feeling the familiar pang of regret. How was it that a whole life could spiral down to one moment, one wrong decision?

He'd gone over it a thousand times in his mind, asking himself endless, useless questions that had no answers. Why had he gone to see Charlotte? Why not any of the too willing women who held vigil at his front door?

But no, in his self-centered, blind arrogance, he'd gone to Charlotte, the one woman who'd rejected him. The one truly innocent human being he'd ever known.

He'd knocked on her door in the middle of the night, carrying an icy bottle of champagne and a dozen roses. Her husband had been gone—as Ian had known he would be.

She tried to resist him, tried valiantly, but the quiet country miss, made beautiful only by unattainability, was no match for Ian. He smiled and cajoled and seduced with an ease born of practice, making the young woman forget the vows she'd made with her sixty-year-old husband.

You're so lovely, Charlotte. . . . Does he tell you that? Does he kiss your luscious lips and breathe in your perfumed scent and lick the sensitive flesh of your breasts? Does he worship your body, Charlotte, as I do? Does he really see you . . . or are you simply the mother of his

*children, the keeper of his house? Ah, Charlotte, come
to my bed, let me love you. . . . You are so beautiful. . . .*

The moment he got her into bed, he'd stopped caring
about her. Nothing about Charlotte touched him, or
filled the void that had been in his soul since childhood.

He'd wakened after a brief and fitful sleep, unable to
recall how it had felt to kiss her. Wincing, desperate to
sneak away without a word, he'd rolled onto his side,
reached slowly for his clothes.

He'd dressed quietly and turned to leave.

Then he'd seen the shadow in the doorway, the flash
of silver from the gun. After that, the memory took on
the shimmering, inconstant feel of a dream. Images, one
after another.

You bastard, Carrick. I'll kill you.

The gun, blazing in the dark room like a small
orange-yellow burst of the sun.

A stunned moment of utter surprise, a jolt backward,
then pain, exploding in his chest, seeping like fire
through his veins. Vision blurring, balance gone, falling,
falling . . .

Dead. A brilliant, white-hot light enveloped him, as
seductive in its warmth as his lying words to a woman
had ever been. He drifted in the light, floating, wanting
never to let it go, never to know the freezing chill of
life again; the disappointment, gone; the frustration,
gone. Only the light, the searing, promising light.

Damn it, Ian, fight with me. Don't let go.

The words had come at him from somewhere, cutting
through the lethargy. He'd blinked, looked down, and
there was his body, naked, stretched out on a sheet-
covered table, surgeons with dirty hands peering around
him like insects, poking, prodding. Blood was a bright
red blur on his chest, dripping down the bedding, pool-
ing on the filthy floor. The gunshot wound was a serrated, gaping black hole in the middle of all that
redness.

Someone was pounding on his chest. He could see

the hammering blows, see his body convulse, but where he was, there was no pain, nothing but a vague sense of anxiety.

As the uneasiness grew, the light flickered and dimmed. Some dark, secret fear slipped through his mind, wound cold and chilling through his blood. He wasn't ready. There was something left for him to do. Something . . .

He felt his life slipping away from him, shimmering just out of reach, and he was afraid to die.

Let me live. Let me live. He screamed the words, shaking with his need to say them, though nothing came from the dead body on the table.

Please, God, I promise . . . He panicked. What could he promise to the God he'd disregarded for most of his life? What would give him another chance? He could think of nothing, nothing but his own desperate, worthless need. *Please . . . let me live.*

With a thrusting, powerful crunch, he was back in his body. Pain vibrated through his chest, filled him to overflowing. Tears squeezed past his eyelashes and streaked down his face.

His heart is beating again. Thank God. Chris, hand me that scalpel. I'm going to find that damned bullet.

After that, confusion; people touching, reaching, wrapping, grasping. Then nothing.

Nothing until the next morning when he woke up, steeped in pain, to a room filled with sunlight and dust. The vague sounds of coughing, of quiet shoes moving down an empty corridor. White beds. The soft scent of gas from the jets on the wall.

He tried to sit up. The first person he saw was a nurse, bent over his bed, peering down at him. Behind her, a cluster of men in white coats. The nurse touched him, a breezy, nothing little touch of her fat finger on his brow, but it had been enough.

Images hit him with the force of a blow. *The nurse huddled in a dark corner, shooting morphine into her veins . . . her gasping breath as the drug moved through her blood . . . the trembling smile of her release.*

Ian pushed her away from him with a growl, told her to stay away from morphine if she was going to touch him.

The nurse gasped, stumbled backward, her eyes rounding with horror as she looked at Dr. Halstead and the other men in the room.

After that, a whirl of sound and color: Halstead's angry voice, wrenching the nurse's sleeve up, seeing the needle marks, the bruises on her pale arm.

Ian squeezed his eyes shut, trying to ignore the throbbing in the back of his head and the strange heat in his hands. He thought it was a fluke, a hallucination caused by his own medication.

But the visions came again and again with every accidental touch, blinding him, overwhelming him, until he'd sunk back into his sheets, shaking and terrified.

The news spread like wildfire. *Dr. Carrick can read your mind . . . Dr. Carrick can see the past. It's a curse, a gift. Magic . . .*

People had come from as far away as California and Florida, clutching scraps of fabric, old timepieces, tintypes of loved ones. They came by foot, on horseback, in wheelchairs, all hoping for a miracle from the infamous Dr. Carrick, pouring their fear like an insidious drug into his veins, killing him quietly with each question, cutting him to the bone every time he failed them.

Help me, help me, help me.

At first he tried to help the pathetic souls who sought him out, he tried and tried, and failed and failed. His "gift" was a malicious, hurtful joke; he could know people's secrets, but he couldn't help them, couldn't find their lost loved ones by touching bits of fabric or perform miraculous cures. He couldn't even practice medicine anymore—the heat in his hands, the headache behind his eyes, and the images, always the images, kept him moving farther and farther away from people until finally he didn't go out at all.

As soon as he was well, he ran from the hospital, but it didn't help. Incomprehensible visions barraged him, smote him every time he walked in a room, with every accidental touch. Nothing stopped them, not gloves, not alcohol, not drugs; he knew, he'd tried them all.

Nothing stopped them except isolation, the end of all contact.

And so he was here, standing in his cell, looking out at the windy, stormy night, wishing once again that he'd never seen Charlotte, never showed up on her doorstep.

Remembering . . .

Ian turned away from the window, held his throbbing head in hands that felt slick with sweat. Eyes closed, heart pounding, he paced the small, dark room, feeling more and more like a caged, hunted animal with every step.

A timid knock roused him from his pain.

"Come in." He growled the words, harsher than he intended. Always harsher than he intended.

The door pushed open and a slim, red-haired woman slipped through the opening. Her small, bare feet made a whispery sound on the wooden floor as she shuffled forward. It took him a second to focus on her, a second more to recognize her. "Maeve?"

She nodded, a swift bob of her head, and took another step toward him, her hands twisted in a pale, nervous ball at her waist. Fear tightened the edges of her mouth, wrinkled the flesh of her forehead.

"What is it, Mother?"

"Ian." She said his name in that soft, swaying voice of hers, her lullaby voice—the one he'd always ached for as a child.

He stared at her hard, tried to see if she was lucid or demented this evening, but his head was pounding too painfully to think clearly. She knew his name at least. That was something. "What is it?"

"Th-There's a woman here. . . ." Her lilting voice trailed off. She looked momentarily confused, as if she'd forgotten what she came to say, and he had his answer.

Demented. "Who is it—Dolley Madison?" he said, unable to keep the bitterness from his voice.

"No, Ian. I'm not crazy tonight. There's a real woman downstairs. A lobsterman brought her in. She's . . . hurt."

The word brought him up short. "Hurt?" A pale heat fluttered in his stomach, and he knew instantly what it was: hope.

As quickly as it came, it crashed. His mother was insane; there was no hurt woman downstairs. "Of course, Mother. Hurt women come to insane asylums all the time."

Maeve moved toward him, and for the first time, he noticed the clarity in her hazel eyes. She was lucid now. She wasn't in a world of her own.

"This isn't an asylum, it's my home, and she needs help, Ian. You are a doctor."

Ian stiffened and turned away from his mother quickly.

He stared out the window, watching the storm. Maeve knew he couldn't help the woman. "I'm no doctor. Not anymore." He glanced around for a bottle of scotch. He needed a drink desperately, but his fingers were shaking so badly, he didn't think he could hold a glass.

"Oh, Ian . . ."

Once, the sad disappointment in his mother's voice would have ripped his heart out; now it caused nothing but a mild regret. "Send her away."

"You could—"

He spun to face her. "I want to help her—sweet God,

I'd give my arm to do it, but I can't. You know I can't. Now, go."

"No." There was an unexpected strength in her voice. "You need to help her, and she needs your skill to save her life."

"How? How can I treat her? The moment I touch her—"

"I-I'll be your hands."

He froze, too stunned for a second to respond. "You'll what?"

She gave him a look so drenched in promise, so filled with love, that for a second he almost believed her.

"Trust me . . . just one more time, Ian."

He wanted to back off, to return to some dark, hidden corner of this hellish house and drink until the wave of bitterness and disillusionment passed, until he'd beaten back the horrifying ray of hope. But it was too strong this time; the need was too seductive. *I'll be your hands.*

He could not possibly refuse.

The inmates stood around the sofa like a cluster of restless, buzzing bees, their hushed voices droning in fragmented, nonsensical whispers. Ian gave them a disgusted, cursory look, seeing them in a glance. Andrew, the disturbed eighteen-year-old man who routinely tried to kill himself; Johann, a disowned aristocrat dying from syphilis; Lara, a fifteen-year-old retarded girl with the mind of a child; a middle-aged woman who thought she was Queen Victoria; and Dotty, a seventy-year-old former Civil War spy who only spoke in whispers and codes and spent her days hidden in a broom closet, talking to invisible allies.

The bland gray wool of their winter wardrobe created an impenetrable barrier around the woman who lay in their midst.

His step slowed. He felt an instant's unwillingness to enter their ranks. When they were apart from him, when he was closeted in his hidden room, he could tell himself they didn't exist. But here, now, he was faced with the truth of their sorry lives, and it filled him with the same sinking sense of despair as always.

The irony of it wrought a bitter smile. Once he had been feted by society's upper echelon; now he lived among that very society's rejects in the house of lost and damned souls.

"Get out of the way." He hissed, striding forward.

There was a sharp, collective indrawn breath. *He's here.* The words floated through the darkened room, carried by several hushed voices. People moved instantly, parted like the Red Sea before their Moses.

Ian tried to ignore their upturned faces, and the reverence in their eyes. He wished they wouldn't look at him at all. For years he'd taught them not to touch him, never to touch him, but still they looked at him with that naked, blatant adoration, as if he were the god he once believed himself to be.

He walked around the sofa and knelt beside the body stretched out on the white brocade. She lay corpselike and still, her hair a tangled, matted heap, a strand of kelp twined around her throat. Blood trickled from both ears and from her left nostril, leaving a streak of bright red against the already bruising flesh of her cheek. He couldn't make out her face; it was bluish, battered, scraped beyond recognition. He couldn't tell if she was fifteen or fifty beneath the bruises.

Maeve appeared beside him in an instant, offering the expensive leather bag he hadn't used for years.

"Does she have a pulse?" he asked.

There was no answer.

He looked up sharply. "Mother, you brought me here. Do as I say. I need you to be my hands."

Maeve inched toward him and bent down. Then she did the unthinkable—she touched him. Images blasted through his brain in a miasma of pain and sorrow and regret; he saw her standing, alone and willowy, at his father's grave site, felt the devastating emptiness of her life. His headache came back, blinded him for a heartbeat to everything except his mother's despair.

"You have hands, Ian. Healing hands." She drew back, leaving him shaken and confused. The medical bag thunked to the floor beside him. "Use them." And then she was gone, melted back into the crazy people who had become her family.

Ian let out a shuddering breath and glanced up. The inmates stared at him in frank, breathless anticipation.

He wanted to bolt suddenly, to simply run.

You need to help her, Ian.

"I need a drink," he whispered, staring down at the pathetic shaking of his hands. He hadn't voluntarily touched anyone in so long. It was too bloody painful. What if he relived her accident? One touch, and he could be thrown into her agony, and still be no closer to saving her life. And what if she died while he was touching her? The thought of that pain blistering through his own psyche made him feel physically ill.

"Ian?" his mother prompted him.

Ian steeled himself, trying to blank out his mind, preparing for the pain. When his hands stopped shaking and his breathing normalized, he reached for the woman again.

The inmates gasped softly. He felt their circle tighten around him.

It was a meaningless touch, that first one. A nothing little trailing of his fingertip along the bloody curve of her throat. A test.

Nothing came to him.

Ian's heartbeat sped up. Something was wrong. He had touched her—briefly, yes, but that never mattered before—and he'd felt nothing.

Hope slipped through a crack in his armor, weakening him. He tried to fight it, but it was too strong. In sudden, blinding clarity he thought: *Maybe for once it won't happen.*

He tried to bury the unrealistic prayer beneath a mountain of cold rationality. It *always* happened.

"Ian, is she alive?"

He heard his mother's voice, but it seemed to come from a million miles away. His heart was hammering in his chest. Sweat had broken out along his brow. He wiped the beaded moisture and swallowed hard.

Barely breathing, he took hold of her wrist. His fingers curled around the slim, pale flesh. He felt the lightning-quick shiver of her pulse, the cool softness of her skin.

And nothing else. He knew nothing about her except that she was alive. At the realization, he felt a shameful stinging in his eyes.

"Ian?" Maeve prompted.

"She's alive."

"Will she die?"

"I don't know." With those words, the old power, the old strength of purpose, overwhelmed him, sweeping aside the isolation of the past six years. Finally, a person—a woman—whose mind was closed to him.

A mystery. Sweet Jesus above, a mystery.

He sat upright. "Prepare a bed on the second floor. Get boiling water and alcohol." He looked up. No one moved.

"Now."

The inmates scattered like insects.

Seconds later, Maeve reappeared and handed him a glass of scotch. Ian stared at it for a second before he realized that he'd asked for alcohol.

Queen Victoria was right behind his mother with a teapot. "Does milord have a cup?"

And boiling water.

He forced back a shout of frustration. "Andrew!" he hollered.

The reed-thin, sallow-faced youth stepped from the shadows, his eyes wide. "Y-Yes, sir?"

"Can you assist me?"

The young man swallowed convulsively. "I'd be honored, sir."

Ian looked pointedly at the man's wrists, still bound in white bandages from last month's suicide attempt. "Can I trust you with a knife?"

"He never tries the same death effort twice," Johann drawled from his place beside Maeve. "He might actually succeed if he did."

Andrew winced. "You can trust me, Dr. Carrick."

"Good. Here's what I need: lots and lots of bandages, several sharp knives."

When Andrew turned and ran from the room, Ian surged to his feet and started barking orders like the doctor he'd once been. "Johann, get Edith and bring her here. Tell her I need willow bark and paraffin and laudanum. Mother, I need several bottles of alcohol. Not a drink. Bottles."

Maeve smiled brightly. "Yes, son."

"Victoria . . ."

The old lady rapped him on the nose with her fan. "That's Your Highness to you."

He gritted his teeth. "Your *Highness*, bring me some sheets and a bucket of ice from the icehouse."

She frowned, looked worriedly to her left. "My footman—"

"Now!"

The queen blanched and ran for the icehouse.

Ian ignored little Lara and hurried back to the sofa. Taking the unconscious woman in his arms, he looked down at her, wondering fleetingly what she looked like beneath the broken, battered skin.

He eased the kelp away from her throat and let the slimy strand fall to the floor.

"Fight with me, princess."

She didn't move, barely breathed, but she was still alive, and there was a chance he could save her.

A chance.

He felt a rush of adrenaline. Just like the old days.

Chapter Two

◦❧◦

Ian rammed a dusty bottle of carbolic acid underneath his arm and raced to his bookcase, pulling out one long-unused volume after another. He scanned the texts quickly for any help, but there was precious little written about head injuries. When he had all that he could find, he ran downstairs to the woman's bedchamber.

Maeve, Queen Victoria, and Andrew were all there, breathing heavily, their arms heaped with supplies. Weak light from a bedside lantern splashed the trio, cast their elongated shadows on the white plaster walls.

Queen Victoria sighed. "This ice is deuced heavy. I say—"

"Drop it and get more, Your Highness. You, too, Mother. We're going to need a lot of ice and more clean sheets. More!"

Andrew moved forward, his scrawny arms piled with pale, grayish white linen and a single knife that glinted silver in the weak light. "I-I got the sheets from the laundry room. I didn't see any bandages specifically—"

"Good. Start ripping them in two-inch strips. But first, wash your hands in soap and water and then rinse in this carbolic acid. Don't let the sheets hit the floor. Put them on the bed." Ian surged to the door and stuck his head out, hollering into the dark hallway. "Soap! I need soap, damn it, and hurry."

Within seconds, Lara appeared in the open doorway, holding a rough bar of ash soap.

Ian snagged it from her pudgy fingers and started washing his hands, rinsing them in the stinging carbolic acid before he returned to the woman's bedside. Kneeling, he looked down at her. He heard the rapid, uneven tenor of his own breathing in the quiet of the room; it lent this moment a strange, almost surreal feeling, as if he were somehow detached from the drama, watching it. Behind him, he heard Andrew thrust the knife into taut linen, heard the methodic rip-hiss of the fabric being rent in strips. The bedside lamp flickered, the yellow-red flame spitting and writhing inside the smoky globe.

The woman lay as still as death.

He pressed forward on his knees and slipped his hand beneath her head. He tensed instinctively, waiting for the onslaught of images. But again there was nothing.

The touch was so damned *normal* that he wanted to cry.

His fingers moved gently along her scraped flesh, through her blood-and-seaweed-matted hair, to the hairline crack at the base of her skull. He tested, probed, cataloged her injuries the way he'd done so often at New York Hospital, talking quietly to himself. "Left occipital cerebral contusion. Enlarged right front cerebral contusion. Basilar skull fracture, just above spinal column." He drew back, shaking his head. "Jesus, she was lucky. . . ."

Footsteps thundered up the staircase and burst into the bedchamber. Ian turned slightly as Edith slid into the room, her arms loaded with sheets and fabric and bottles. "I'm here, Doctor," she wheezed. "What c'n I do?"

"Get Maeve and Victoria up here with the ice. We're going to have to pack her in it. We've got to keep her head cold."

"But the poor wee thing'll catch pneumonia—"

"Don't question me, Edith."

"Sorry, Doctor." Edith swallowed hard and raced from the room.

Ian turned back to his patient, blotting the blood from her nostrils. He was so engrossed in the task that he barely heard Andrew come up behind him. "The bandages are done, Doctor. Are you going to operate?"

He wanted to. Sweet Jesus, he wanted to hold a scalpel as he'd done so many times, wanted to feel the energy pulse through him, the confidence, the unbelievable arrogance that came from his skill. He wanted—once more—to be God. But he couldn't, not this time.

"I can't, Andrew. The surgery is too advanced; besides, she'd die of infection. This damned carbolic acid isn't perfect. All I can do is try to relieve the pressure on her brain—hopefully she'll keep bleeding from her nose and ears. That, and keep her cold. She's going to have to win this battle on her own."

For the next hour, Ian worked like a demon to save her life. He shaved, cut, bandaged, and wrapped until his fingers were shaking from fatigue and slick with her blood.

Finally, he'd done all that he could do. Throwing everyone but Maeve out of the room, he slumped forward on the stool beside her bed, cradling his face in bloody hands. The woman lay stretched out before him, her arms pressed close to her body, her head layered in bandages. Blood was everywhere; on his hands, his clothes, the floor, the bed.

A three-inch layer of crushed ice covered her whole body, caught the lamplight and gave her the shimmering look of an illusion. More ice was her pillow, the clear peaks stained pink with her blood. Half of her face was covered in bloody bandages; the other half was a bloated, indistinguishable mound of purple bruising, her one eye stretched beyond recognition.

He'd shaved a triangular section at the back of her

head and brought the rest of her hair forward, tying it in two twisted, matted tails that trailed along her arms. He should have shaved her whole head, but he hadn't had the time, and it probably wouldn't matter anyway. She was so damned weak. Her pulse was sporadic and shallow, her breathing almost nonexistent. Her teeth weren't even chattering, for God's sake, though she lay in a bed of broken ice.

"Don't die," he whispered, hearing the scratchy desperation of his plea and not caring at all. He knew he was being selfish in his wish to save her—he'd always been selfish in his need to perform miracles. But he needed her, this broken patient whom he could touch and heal, needed her as he'd never imagined needing anyone. She could save him, give him back his profession, his reason for living. She could be his first true patient in years.

"Will she live?"

Maeve's quietly spoken question invaded his thoughts. With a tired sigh, he looked at his patient through his objective clinician's eyes. The horrible swelling on her brain had abated a little, helped by the stream of blood that even now trickled from her left nostril. He'd bathed her head in carbolic acid and covered it in a layer of waterproof silk, then added precisely eight layers of carbolized linen bandages and finished with two layers of soaked gutta-percha. The whole stinking mass had been coated in liquid resin and paraffin and encased in two more layers of waxed taffeta. Her swollen, bruised head looked like a cracked gray croquet ball shoved atop a rag doll's body.

He'd followed Joseph Lister's technique to the letter, but still there was precious little hope that she would recover.

"I've done all I can, Mother."

Maeve kneeled beside him, her hands coiled in her lap, her red hair tied in a loose cluster of curls at the base of her neck. Her body moved in a ceaseless back-

and-forth motion, her fingers gripping a small, tattered scrap of old satin. The ribbon she hadn't released in fifteen years. A tawdry scrap of her wedding veil. Her eyes lacked the clarity they'd held earlier. He recognized the signs; his mother was slipping back into her delusional state of mania.

He sighed again, ran a hand through his hair. "Go get Edith, Mother. Tell her to bring up the man."

Maeve stopped rocking for a second and stared blankly at him. "What man?"

"The lobsterman who brought the woman here."

"Oh, him. I gave the poor old man a cup of coffee and sent him on his way."

Ian was so stunned, it took him a moment to respond. Slowly, steeling himself not to explode, he pushed the words out. "You got his name, I assume?"

She heard the anger in his voice and started rocking again, faster, not looking at him. "Of course I did."

"What is it?"

"What's what?"

"His name, Mother. What's the man's name?"

"Who?"

Ian controlled an explosion by sheer force of will. "The man who brought her here."

"Oh, that. I can't remember now."

"Jesus . . ."

She frowned in concentration. "No, I would remember if he'd been called Jesus. . . . I believe it started with a *B*. Or perhaps an *R*."

"Oh, Mother." He leaned forward and closed his eyes, rubbing his temples.

"Why?" She didn't look at him, stared at the ribbon she worked so madly in her hands.

"Who the hell is she? And where did she come from? And how did she get injured?"

She stopped suddenly, looked at him. "Oh." Her voice was a whisper, throaty with the same shame he saw in her hazel eyes. "He said something about a boating accident."

Disgusted, he turned away, stared dully at his patient. Jesus, they might never know who this woman is. Or was.

"How will she live?" Maeve asked in a timid voice.

He didn't even try to understand the question. "What do you mean?"

"Will she be ... normal?"

There was a holy reverence in his mother's voice when she said the word *normal*. It was so important to her, being normal, and he supposed he understood why. She'd never been normal a day in her life. He sighed, feeling suddenly drained. "I don't know. It's unlikely."

Maeve squeezed her eyes shut, rocking faster, turning the ribbon through her fingers. "I hope she's normal ... in the head. She would want to be normal."

He turned away, unable to look at her, unable to see her pain and know it mirrored his own, and know that neither one of them could change it. "Yes, Mother. Wouldn't we all?"

Ian studied the woman's maimed face, searching for some hint of the person beneath the bandages and the bruises. She smelled of wax and acid and blood; it was a smell he knew well, one that lingered in the halls of New York Hospital, clung stubbornly to the operating rooms. No amount of soap and water could remove it—and not nearly enough was spent in the effort.

The smell of death. He dumped another bucketful of ice beside her head, tucking the freezing chunks close to her bandaged skull.

Then he set the empty bucket on the floor. It hit the hardwood with a tinny clank that he barely heard. Backing away from the bed, he turned to the open window and stared out.

The storm had long since passed. Fog had rolled in,

impenetrable and moody; the thick haze lay huddled along the shoreline. Somewhere the sun was rising, casting uncertain light through the gray-white shroud, but from this window, there was nothing but the stifling gloom.

Will she be normal?

He couldn't forget the question. Once, he might have cared only that she survived. But if nothing else, the past few years had taught him that there was life— breathing, heart-pumping animation—and there was *life*. He understood the pain of abnormality now, the agony of isolation. Of being wrenchingly different from your fellow man. No longer could he tell himself that life at any cost was a triumph.

He squeezed his eyes shut and bowed his head against the cold, damp glass of the window. *Don't give her half a life, God. Make it all or nothing.*

"All or nothing," he whispered aloud, a small, bitter smile curving his lips. His breath clouded the clear pane.

It was the prayer he should have offered six years ago. Instead, all he'd said was *let me live*.

When he turned back around, he saw the faces peering at him through the open doorway.

"Come on in," he said wearily, too tired to fight them any longer. They wanted to see the woman, and he couldn't blame them. She was the most interesting thing to happen at Lethe House in years.

The inmates shuffled in slowly, silently. One by one, they pulled up chairs and formed a ring around the bed, scooting in like some macabre quilting bee for damned souls. The hushed murmur of their voices filled the quiet room, and suddenly he was glad for their arrival. Maybe they would somehow reach the woman beneath the bandages, maybe the sound of their voices would draw her from the coma.

It wasn't much of a hope, but it was all they had.

* * *

Pain. Immeasurable, inexpressible, it wrapped around her, invaded her bones and ate at her flesh with tiny, piercing teeth. Slicing, burning, aching, freezing . . .

She wanted desperately to cry out, but all she could manage was a bleating whimper, a hesitant sound like that animal—puffy, white, four legs. *Mackinaw . . . rubber.* Words came at her, drifted by in a hazy kaleidoscope that had no meaning whatsoever. She thought of the animal again, pictured it, saw it moving in a herd, but no name came to her.

She moved restlessly, felt the stinging cold wrapped like an icy blanket around her body. Her teeth chattered, her fingers trembled.

"SweetLord . . . shemadea sound. . . ."

It was a voice. Out there, beyond the freezing darkness . . .

She tried to speak, say something, shriek for help, but nothing made it past her chapped lips, her aching chest. Another shiver wrenched through her. She gasped at the intensity of it, clawing the wet fabric beneath her fingertips.

Lamb. The word for the animal burst into her mind. She pushed it aside, not caring anymore. The pounding in her head was excruciating. Blinding blows, a thrumming torment. Her heart pumped hard, drowned out every sound except the evidence of her own life.

Where am I?

She had the one coherent thought before another volcanic blast of pain slammed through her head. She squeezed her eyes shut, breathing hard. *Oh, God, it hurts it hurts it hurts.* She couldn't take it anymore. She screamed—or thought she did, wished she did—and then it was over.

She was drifting again, moving back into the comforting black waters of oblivion.

Back to the place where there was no pain.

Chapter Three

~~∞∞~~

Ian glanced at the bottle of scotch on the green bed-side table. He ached for a comforting drink, but it was a pleasure he'd forcibly denied himself for the last four days. He wanted to be sober when she awoke.

If she awoke.

"Please wake up." He said the words softly, hearing the throaty catch in his voice and not caring. He was tired, so tired. He'd been sitting by her bed for days. One hour blurred into the next and the next and the next. He stared at her in morbid fascination, watching every struggling breath she took, wishing with everything in his soul that he could breathe for her.

In the past days, she'd become more than his patient. She'd become his world. He'd tried at first to remain detached and professional, but such distance was beyond him now. The coldness he'd once worn like a frock coat was now impossible to find. He wanted her to live so badly that sometimes he couldn't breathe. Every time he looked at her, he got an aching pain in his chest, and he knew what caused it.

She would probably die without ever once waking up.

"Just open your eyes," he whispered. "Please . . ."

He sat perched on the small, straw-seated mahogany chair, his long legs folded tightly against the painted green bed frame. Moonlight fell through the open windows, puddling on the pale woman in the bed. Diamond chips of ice lay melting all around her. Yet, even so, her fever climbed higher and higher, and there wasn't a damned thing he could do to stop it.

Her bruising was so much worse now; there was no hint whatsoever of her face. But not all of the news was bad, and Ian clung to the good news like a lifeline. She'd accepted the feeding tube well, and the third set of bandages around her head was finally beginning to stay white. The bleeding had eased off and the swelling on her brain had abated. She might actually have a chance . . . if the pneumonia didn't kill her.

She wanted to live as much as he wanted her to. He could see it in every laboring breath she took.

He leaned forward and took one of her hands in his. It lay limp and unresponsive in his grasp. He stroked her hot, damp fingers, noticing the soft pliancy of her flesh, the whispery hairs at her wrist, the hard calluses at each fingertip.

She was making him a little mad, and even though he knew it, he couldn't stop it. Didn't really even care, because for the first time in years, he felt truly alive.

Sometimes, when it was late at night and he was alone with her, he could close his eyes and imagine her waking up, smiling, laughing, beckoning to him.

Madness . . .

Madness to care about her, to even pray for a complete recovery, but he couldn't seem to stop himself. He needed her to awaken, needed to save just one more person in his sorry life. Needed to be a doctor again.

He smiled down at her, his patient. He couldn't see her face at all because of the bruising, but it didn't matter. She was beautiful to him, the most beautiful woman he'd ever seen. His goddess, his mystery, his chance to practice medicine again.

That's what he would call her. A name that reflected the magic and mystery of the moon.

"Selena . . ." He brushed a matted, bloodied streak of hair from her cheek. "Fight the fever, Selena. . . ."

In the next instant, a Gatling-gun burst of whispers shot through the silence.

Ian spun in his seat and glared at the people huddled along the wall. Lord, he should have thrown the crazy lot of them out yesterday. They had no business here. "Shut up or leave."

Johann strolled forward. Flinging his angular hip to one side, he planted a thin hand on it and sighed with his usual drama. "Apparently, Herr Doctor, there's some dissension about your right to name the human sausage."

Ian's brows pulled together in a low, forbidding frown intended to silence the fool. He stood and strode toward the group. "Now, look here—"

"Where?" Maeve interrupted.

Ian glanced at his mother. Her eyes were clouded and vague, and she clutched one of his father's old hunting trophies against her chest. Today it was a badger, frozen forever in a defensive snarl, its padded body stiff and rock-hard. She was certain that Herbert's soul resided in one of the animals—she simply wasn't sure which one.

He looked away, disgusted, sweeping the rest of the misfits with cold eyes. Before he could speak, they started talking again, arguing among themselves like magpies.

"I found her—" someone said.

"I opened the door—" Edith argued.

"I believe *I* carried her to the sofa," Johann drawled. "Without me, she'd still be a bloody spot on the carpet."

"I'm the queen; I shall bestow a name on my poor, unknown subject."

"I-I believe we should vote," Andrew said softly, looking to Ian for confidence. The boy raised a cautious, shaking hand. "I vote for Selena."

"Weakling," Johann hissed. "I vote for Violet . . . in deference to her skin color. What's your vote, Maeve?"

Maeve whispered to the stuffed badger in her arms,

then gave Johann a serious look. "Ian's father votes for Colleen."

"Aagh! Guard! Off to the Tower with all of them," Queen Victoria said, puffing her mammoth chest out, rapping the floor with her pinewood scepter. "My subject shall be called Alberta."

"Enough." Ian yelled the word so loudly that everyone gasped. "Her name is irrelevant. When she wakes—if she wakes—she will tell us her given name. Until then, I shall call her Selena. You may each do as you wish."

"No!" Dotty hissed. "You must never use real names. It's too dangerous. Call her the seabird."

Johann rolled his eyes. "Someone has got to convince oatmeal-head here that the War Between the States is over. However, I do believe that we must choose one name. Otherwise she'll be confused."

"Who will?" Maeve asked, stroking the badger.

Ian forced himself to take a deep breath. He needed that scotch now more than ever. His mother's dementia was hard enough to handle without the whole damned circus. "I believe he's speaking of our patient, Mother."

"Oh."

"We *must* follow Dr. Carrick's lead," Andrew pleaded, looking at his housemates.

"All right then," Johann conceded. "Selena it is."

"Then we are agreed," Ian said, thoroughly disgusted by the entire affair.

"On what?" Maeve asked, frowning.

"The patient, Mother. We shall call her Selena."

Maeve's frown deepened. "Oh. I thought you'd decided that hours ago."

"Her fever's gone."

Ian heard Edith's words through a fog of exhaustion. It took a moment to register.

Fever . . . gone.

He snapped up so quickly, the chair wobbled beneath

him. Suddenly he was wide-awake. He ran a hand through his dirty hair and surged to his feet. "Are you certain?"

"Aye, Doctor. I am." She handed him the long, narrow thermometer designed by Hicks.

He took the prismatic strip of glass and looked down at it.

His knees almost buckled in relief. He realized in that instant the magnitude of his obsession with her. As desperately as he wanted her to live, he hadn't thought it would happen. Not really. Not with his view of the Almighty.

He reached out for the back of the chair and clutched it for support. "Jesus, it *is* almost normal."

"You said if her fever went away, the poor wee thing might have a chance."

He gave Edith a grin. "It's a start, anyway, Edith. Hurry up now, let's get this ice off of her and close the windows. Get her a warm flannel nightdress and drawers, and new sheets and blankets."

"Aye, Doctor," Edith answered with a smile, and bustled from the room, leaving him—for once—alone with his patient.

Ian pulled his chair back to Selena's bedside and sank onto the familiar straw seat, leaning toward her. He felt an overwhelming surge of emotion for the woman who lay motionless before him.

"You did it." His voice broke. "You did it." He took one of her hands in his, reveling in the warm, dry, healthy temperature of her skin. "That's it, Selena. You're doing my work for me."

She lay there as always, limp and unresponsive, the slack opening of her mouth invaded by tubing. The rough, rattling determination of her breathing was the most beautiful sound he'd ever heard. It was the fight for life, and she hadn't once given up.

"I never tried as hard as you're trying right now," he whispered, surprised by his own confession and the truth of it. All his life, he'd taken the easy road and run away from anything that frightened or confused him. Normally he didn't think about his cowardice or his failures, but now, sitting here all alone with his goddess, he couldn't avoid thinking about them, his lost and broken dreams. He remembered a dozen moments, memories he'd thought had seeped away.

Times Maeve had taken him in her arms and read him stories and stroked his hair and kissed his brow; times she'd stared at him, unable to remember his name; times she'd screeched at him in front of his boyhood friends, railing at him about some imagined slight. And then there were the dark days, after his father's death, when she'd strolled through the manse like a lost spirit, moaning, crying, unrecognizing of everything and everyone. For almost two years, she hadn't spoken a word to anyone except those damned stuffed animals she kept in her room. He remembered so many nights, standing at her open door, his slim, adolescent body pressed into the shadows, watching her talk to those animals. They both needed consolation in those days, but she'd never come to him, never even looked him in the eyes.

So many failures. So many lost chances . . .

He leaned back, sighing heavily. "Christ, Selena, why can't I forget? What's wrong with me?"

He looked down at his silent patient, realizing he'd just said more to her than he'd ever said to another person.

It was a little frightening. In the endless hours he'd sat at Selena's bedside, he'd somehow given her a personality, a past and a future. Even worse, even more warped, he'd begun to fall in love with the fiction he'd created. A woman who didn't really exist.

God help him.

She was floating. The wind around her was warm finally. It buffeted her on soothing currents, rocked her as gently as a ... thing, small, green, stuck on a branch. ...

She frowned, trying to come up with the word, but the effort was paralyzingly difficult. The thought drifted away from her, left her with no more than a niggling sense that something was wrong. And then even that was gone.

"Howare youtoday ... goddess?" A low, rumbling bass noise from somewhere in the darkness.

She tried to open her eyes. She felt them begin to open, slowly, like the reluctant movement of a door that had been rusted shut for ages.

She saw something ... circle ... out of focus. No, not a circle ... round. Round, yes. Face. A face fringed by pale golden light. A halo.

Angel.

"Wellhellothere." It was the same voice, soft and caressing and intimate. She realized now that she recognized it, that she'd heard it before today. It was the voice that had always been with her in the great, cold darkness, the voice beckoning for her to *fightselena.* She didn't know what it meant, what he wanted of her, but it was comforting somehow.

"Areyoucold?"

Gibberish. Her head started to ache. The raw fire in her throat came back.

"... knowwho ... youare?"

She could feel his expectation, his need, and she wanted to do what he wanted, but she didn't understand. Frustration welled up inside her.

She knew he was talking to her. She should be able to speak back to him, but she couldn't remember any of the words, or how to form them, or what to say.

She started to utter a low, growling sound of irritation, but the noise aborted itself, cut off by the harsh, unrelenting fire in her throat.

"Wouldyoulikesome ... water?"

Water. The word surprised her. She understood it.

Yes, water. She had need of it in her throat. How did she tell him so?

The angel leaned closer. He pulled the thing from her throat. The pain was exquisite. She trembled, whimpered.

Then the thing was gone, and the pain in her throat lessened.

"Hereyougo." Something warm and strong curled around her neck, brought her slowly upward. At the movement, her head started pounding. Hammering pain. She made a small, moaning sound and almost passed back into the darkness.

"Shhhh . . . s'okay . . ."

The angel's face swam before her eyes, wavery and out of focus still. Something cool and smooth touched her mouth. Water beaded on her lips. She could smell it, remember it. Her mouth watered, she became dizzy with the need to taste it, but she couldn't remember what to do.

A hot ache pulsed behind her eyes, left a film of stinging moisture.

"Don'tcry. . . . s'okay . . . here." He pressed the cool surface—glass!—between her lips. His touch was soft and sure and calmed her immediately. The strange moisture in her eyes dried. The clear vessel tilted, sent a tepid flood of water into her mouth.

She sputtered, coughed, then accidentally . . .

Swallowed. That was it. That's what she'd been supposed to do. She drank greedily, feeling the warm, slick water slide down her throat. Finally, exhausted, she sank back into the softness and closed her eyes.

The familiar darkness curled around her, and for a second, she was afraid. Afraid she would never awaken again, never see her angel's face again, never hear his gentle voice. Her heart beat faster.

He talked to her. The low, soothing strains of his voice wrapped around her, comforted her immediately. Very slowly, she opened her eyes again.

This time she saw him in complete focus, and he was so handsome that for a second she couldn't breathe. His hair looked like a gold coin glinting in the sunlight, and his eyes, they were the color of ... shoe? leaf? She didn't know, couldn't remember the word to describe his eyes, but she knew it didn't matter. She was looking at an angel, fallen from the heavens. Or God Himself.

Yes, she thought sleepily. She'd been saved by God Himself.

It was her last, pleasant thought as she slipped back into the darkness.

She had opened her eyes.

Even now, hours later, Ian clung to that glorious heartbeat of time, living and reliving it, shaping and reshaping it in his mind until it was bigger, better. She hadn't said anything, but that meant nothing. Less than nothing.

She had opened her eyes. It was a miracle.

Grinning, he raced down the overgrown granite path from the house and surged into the dark night. Overhead, the moon was a brilliant opalescent ball, wreathed in a glowing halo of light.

It was silent except for the methodic crunching of his heels on the timeworn stone. The sea was a distant thrum of waves on rock. He pushed his hands deeper in his pockets and laughed aloud.

Christ, he felt good.

Over and over, he saw the image of Selena when she'd finally wakened. Finally, he'd seen the dark, mysterious brown of her eyes.

Just thinking about it sent exhilaration, blistering and liquid, coursing through his blood. He realized in that instant that he hadn't believed she'd wake up, not really. He thought she'd lie there in that too narrow bed and simply fade away.

For years, he'd pictured the Almighty as a cruel jokester, sitting on His gilded throne, playing with humans as if they were meaningless pieces on a great chessboard. That image, he could understand, could hate with equanimity; it allowed him to sit in the dark and nurse his animosity, allowed him to hide his curse from himself and an uncaring world.

But no more. God had finally answered one of Ian's prayers.

He turned in to his mother's sanctuary, the small garden she tended so zealously. Elegant wrought-iron fencing closed him in, created a small envelope in the darkness that was subtler, soothing. Every flower his mother planted was white, designed to catch the light of the moon. A great arching gazebo, grayed by time, stood in the center of the garden, its posts swaddled in thick brown wisteria vines. Inside, the gazebo sat a forlorn granite bench, its lion's-claw feet set amidst a blanket of silvery new narcissus blossoms.

He closed the gate behind him and went to the bench, taking a seat on the cold, hard stone. Closing his eyes, he let the moonlight wash his face. Usually he stayed away from the yard when the moon was full; it somehow increased his psychic powers. Sometimes, on nights like tonight, he could "read" people's thoughts from far away, could know things about them by simply bringing their faces to his mind. But tonight he didn't care. He felt too good, too hopeful, to be afraid of anything—including his curse.

I can heal her, save her.

Touch her.

Mesmerizing possibilities drifted through his mind, images beckoned and challenged him. A dream took shape, bursting full force in his mind. She would be his greatest challenge yet. He would set the medical world on its ear with his brilliance. When he was finished with her, she'd be as healthy as she'd ever been, and doctors would come from miles around to see her, touch her, study her. And they would know that Ian Carrick was still the best physician in the world.

He closed his eyes and imagined his glory in full, vibrant color. He saw the amphitheater at Harvard full of his colleagues, sitting forward on their seats, watching with greedy eyes as he led Selena onstage. His miraculous creation, smiling, walking, talking, after a vicious brain injury. He could almost hear the thunderous applause, almost see the standing ovation.

Soon, he thought. _Wake up tomorrow and we can begin. . . ._

Ah, he'd give his soul to see her wake up again, smiling and full of life. To hear the sound of her voice and the content of her thoughts.

He looked up at the sky and laughed heartily. _Is that what You want? My soul?_

"Fine," he said softly, "take it." Useless, unnecessary thing anyway.

What did he need with a soul, when the world lay open to him again, glittering, forgiving, accepting?

His for the asking.

Chapter Four

❧❧❧

She felt herself floating toward the light. It beckoned and drew her forward. Very slowly, she opened her eyes. The light hurt. She blinked hard and tried to see the world around her, but everything was gray and dismal and hazy. Blurry and out of focus. Nothing familiar.

"Ohmygod . . . get doctorcarrick."

People swarmed around her, their voices a great cacophony of frightening sound. She shrank into the comforting familiarity of the bed, clutching the lacy hem of the quilt.

The blurry strangers moved closer, so close that she could hear the muffled pattern of their breathing. Heels clicked on the floor, a knee banged the bed frame. They stared down at her, making noises, their mouths opening and closing, their fingers pointing down at her. Meaningless noise. Gibberish. She closed her eyes and tried to find the darkness again, but this time it was deep, deep inside her. And the light felt so good on her skin.

"Isshe stillawake?"

"He'shere." There was a burst of sound, a shuffling movement of the small crowd.

She writhed fitfully, afraid and hurting. Everywhere, pain. Her throat was on fire, and her head pounded. She squeezed her eyes shut, wishing they would be quiet, wishing they would leave her alone, wishing—

"Wellhellothere Selena. You'reback."

A great, soothing sense of calm moved through her at the sound of that voice. The tension in her taut body eased, her fingers unfurled slowly, shaking from the effort it had taken to keep them clenched. *God. The angel who'd saved her.*

She opened her eyes slowly. This time she could almost focus. The people were staring at her with worried looks on their faces, but they were farther back now, giving her room to breathe. Strangers, she thought. Strangers . . .

God was in the center of them all. He moved toward her, his breathlessly handsome face cast in an easy, reassuring smile. Very gently, he sat beside her on the bed. She felt the mattress dip heavily beneath his weight, heard the planks beneath it groan quietly.

"You gaveus quite ascare."

She didn't understand the sounds he was making, but the tone of his voice, so soft and caring and familiar, made her shiver in response. She felt an overwhelming surge of emotion for this golden man, this god who'd talked her through the darkness and touched her with such kindness. That hot, stinging moisture came back to her eyes.

"Don'tcry Selena. Don'tcry." His finger brushed the wetness away.

The words were lovely, as lyrical as a melody. She wanted to lean forward, to press her hands against his chest and feel the warmth of his skin, the rhythm of his heart. Behind him, the strangers moved in closer.

God turned to them. "Do you mind?"

In the single heartbeat that he turned away from her, she felt colder, lonelier. The sense of fear returned, became a low pounding in her blood.

Don't leave me. The words blossomed in her mind, full-blown and understood. She tried desperately to say them, to plead with him to crawl beneath the bedclothes with her and never turn away again, but somewhere between her brain and her mouth, the words mangled, became a croaking mush of hoarse sound.

He turned back to her, smiled, and became even more exquisite. "It'sokay. Youneedn't speak."

Speak. Something about the sounds, *speak,* seemed familiar. It was a word. The sudden perception stunned her. A word, she thought, trying to fit the pieces together and failing miserably. A word that had some meaning.

She frowned. It was important that she remember, but she couldn't.

He brushed the hair from her eyes, and it felt so good. She didn't want to think about words that meant nothing. She closed her eyes to savor his touch, and realized only after he'd withdrawn it that something was wrong. Her hair felt . . . matted. For the first time, she wondered how she looked. Was she worthy of this god's attention? Did she look like a fallen angel herself, sheathed in the pale ivory of the bed linens, her hair splayed out along her arms?

She couldn't imagine what she looked like, couldn't draw a single image of herself, not eye color or skin color or anything. But it didn't matter. She saw herself reflected in God's blue, blue eyes and knew that she pleased him.

"You didit doctorcarrick. You saved her."

Saved. It was another word she almost understood. The meaning taunted her, teased her consciousness with strange, unconnected images—a bank building, a cookie jar, a cross with a half-naked man nailed to it. Saved. Saved.

Understanding came like dawn, slow and creeping and with a shivering warmth. This god had saved her life. Kept her alive. But how? And from what? How did he know her?

She tried to ask a question, but her throat caught fire again and pain spilled down into her stomach.

"Justaminute." He eased the long, clear thing from

her throat, and when it was gone, she breathed a sigh of relief. The pain abated.

She forced herself to try again. "Where ..." She frowned, her train of thought lost. What had she been going to say? *Where* ... She tried to remember what the word meant. It had come naturally to her, as if she had once understood and used it easily. Now it was gone, drifting away like an image from a dream, unremembered upon waking. All that remained was a vague, illusory memory.

"Maine." God answered her forgotten question with another meaningless word. Once again, his deep, melodious voice washed through her, soothing even the pain in her throat. "You're at Lethe House onthe coastof Maine. I've been caringfor you."

She had no idea what he'd said, but she could tell that he was waiting for her to respond. Images tumbled through her mind. Each new thought, each new image for which she had no word, added to a growing sense of unease. Tension tightened the muscles along her neck and shoulders. She wanted this god to stay beside her, talking to her in that wonderful voice, brushing the hair from her face. Without him, she would slip back into the darkness—she knew it somehow, knew he was the light through which she'd come back—and she couldn't face the nothingness again.

Words teased her, fuzzy and meaningless. She tried to latch on to one, to find some way to communicate, but nothing pushed through the quagmire of her mind. She swallowed, blinking slowly up at God, making certain he didn't look away.

He didn't. His blue gaze held hers in a velvet, reassuring grip. His smile was so bright, it felt like sunlight on her face, heating her, warming her. "I amIan," he said softly. "Who are you?"

She concentrated very hard, watching his mouth move, and she thought she discerned three word patterns in the gibberish he spoke. Very slowly, she tried to repeat it. "I . . . am . . . Ian."

A tiny frown flinched in his thick eyebrows. The brightness of his smile dimmed a fraction. "Say, Ian."

She'd done something wrong, had somehow disappointed him. She stared up at him, her mouth trembling, trying to divine the answer in his eyes. But nothing came to her. She was trying so hard to please him, but it felt as if she were wrapped in clouds, layers and layers of fuzzy gray softness.

Say. What did that mean . . . say? She frowned in concentration, staring into his blue eyes as if they held the answers to the universe.

And it came to her. She knew suddenly, simply knew. Say meant speak. Talk. *Say Ian.* He wanted her to repeat what he'd said.

She opened her mouth to answer him and forgot what she'd been going to say. She made a small, moaning sound of frustration.

"It'sokay," he said finally. "Whoareyou?"

Whoareyou? She tried hopelessly to decipher the code, to find the secret meaning of his words. Whoareyou?

He released a small sigh. "It'sokay . . . okay . . . enoughfor today. We've been calling you Selena. That will have to do for now." He turned slightly, and she felt his weight shift off of the bed. He was leaving her.

"No!" She reached for him, clinging to his arm. *Don't leave me.* The words exploded in her head. She fought to release them, to make him understand what she was feeling, what she wanted. To explain how, even now, the horror of the darkness sat curled in the shadows of the room, waiting . . . waiting . . .

The moisture in her eyes burned, cascaded down her cheeks. Her whole body shook with frustration. She couldn't find the words. Somewhere between her brain and her mouth, the plea was lost forever. She stared at him, ashamed and afraid. *Please* . . . The single word flitted through her mind, too elusive to catch or fully understand.

"You want me to stay?"

Stay. The word was like a gift from God, perfect. She understood.

"Tree," she said in a rush. At his frown, she knew that she'd done something wrong again. The wrong word had slipped from her mouth. He didn't understand. He was pulling away again.

She tightened her hold, feeling the hard muscles of his arm beneath the soft fabric of his sleeve. "Basket." She winced. *No. Not right again.*

The smile he gave her this time was a little sad. "You'll be allright," he murmured, stroking the matted hair from her forehead, wiping the moisture from her cheeks. "Youneedn't cry."

Cry. The moisture in her eyes. She remembered suddenly that the water was called tears when it came from the eyes. She'd been crying tears.

"You'llbefine . . . need sleep." He sighed again, and like the smile before it, the gesture was strangely sad.

She offered him a smile, though it hurt to do so. She wanted so much to express what was in her heart, to tell her golden god that she already was fine, that she was everything he wanted her to be. She couldn't remember anything, couldn't find the words to unlock her emotions or tell him how she felt, but still she knew. In some hidden, primeval pocket of her soul, the knowledge existed. She loved him.

"I am . . . Ian," she whispered, placing her hand over his, feeling the comforting warmth of his flesh against hers. Of course she was fine. God was with her.

Still smiling, she fell asleep.

Ian stared down at Selena. She was sleeping peacefully now; there was no evidence that she'd slipped back into the coma.

She had spoken to him, touched him. Even now,

he could feel the warm imprint of her hand on his arm, could feel the warm moisture of her tears on his fingertips.

She had been confused and aphasic, but that was normal, that was to be expected. According to the dozens of books he'd read, no one knew precisely how damage to the brain could affect behavior. Every case was different. But some level of aphasia was to be expected. It was completely normal that Selena would have difficulty retrieving words and speaking and remembering the morphology and syntax of the English language.

Normal.

He sighed, feeling suddenly old.

He'd forgotten what it was truly like to be a doctor. In the past six years, he'd idealized it, had cultivated a glistening, perfect memory of his halcyon days in medicine. He'd remembered the successes, the parties, the flamboyance.

Somewhere along the way, he'd forgotten the terrifying uncertainties, the agonizing fear. The constant dread that a patient would die.

Or be brain-damaged.

Jesus, how had he forgotten all that? How could he have forgotten the times he sat up all night, standing in the shadows of a patient's room, just watching the person breathe? Praying that each breath would be followed by another, and another, and another?

How had he lived through it back then?

It came to him all at once.

Confidence.

That was how he'd manipulated his world and made it from day to day, brushing off the failures and relishing the successes. He'd been supremely, arrogantly selfconfident. He'd *believed* in himself, in his hands, in his power to heal.

He needed that confidence again.

Aphasia was normal. Her recovery was proceeding

nicely. He repeated the words over and over again until he believed them.

It was too early to think that something was wrong. He'd keep working, keep believing in her and in himself. Together they could slay the medical dragons, together they would triumph. Dr. Carrick and his most challenging patient, changing the face of medical science.

"Together, Selena," he whispered, taking her hand in his. "Together, we'll get through this. You'll be fine."

He closed his eyes and imagined Harvard again, his triumphant return to medicine.

It would happen because he demanded it. She would awaken and she would be injured—of course, she'd be terribly injured—but not irreparably damaged. He would work with her, test her, devote his life to her. Anything to heal her.

And if he had to, he'd create her.

Pushing back in his chair, he got to his feet. "I'll be right back, Selena. I promised the rabble I'd give them a report."

They were all in the drawing room.

He paused at the door, hating the thought of opening it. In the six years since his return, he'd kept himself as removed from these people as possible. They were only here to assuage his guilt, anyway. He'd wanted Maeve to be less lonely, and he'd willfully misinterpreted her requests for companionship. She'd wanted Ian with her. In answer to her need, he'd turned Lethe House into a private asylum and opened their home to people like his mother, pretending that that was good enough. He'd tried to give her a family instead of being her family. They didn't need a doctor, this group of misfits and lunatics that society had washed from their collective conscience. Oh, occasionally Ian prescribed a headache powder or directed Edith to dress a wound or stitch a cut, but nothing more taxing than that. He was their keeper, nothing more, and it was more than enough for the families of these poor unfortunates. For Lethe House provided what the families wanted, what proper Victorian society demanded: pretense. And that's what everyone—including Ian—did so easily. Shut these people away and pretend they didn't exist.

He went inside and immediately regretted it. The room made him think of his father, the memories wafting back into his subconscious as subtly as the fragrance of the old man's cigar. As a young boy, he'd come into this room often, slipping into the darkness and curling onto the crushed velvet of the settee, to wait for his father to come home.

She didn't know who I was at supper tonight. Why is she like that, Papa . . . why?

Neither this room nor his father had ever held an answer to Ian's questions. And now he was here again, seeking answers to questions he couldn't even name, waiting once more.

It was a studiously powerful room. A huge mahogany fireplace dominated the burgundy and black chamber. On its carved mantel, a trio of silver candleholders housed bloodred candles, their flames reflected in the immense seventeenth-century mirror that hung above it. Ornately framed paintings covered every square inch of the claret-painted walls, red and black Aubusson rugs covered most of the planked flooring.

The chamber was dark and somehow bloody, just as his father had intended it to be. A man's room in a man's house, full of hunting trophies and pictures of dying soldiers. Even the knickknack tables were thick and heavy and held ashtrays instead of vases.

No woman had ever had a hand in decorating this house, and it showed in every room.

"How is she, Doctor?"

Ian heard Andrew's question and he ignored it as he poured himself a Madeira.

"Why, I would say she's damned poor, Andrew,"

Johann drawled. "Unless, of course, you think 'basket' was what she meant to answer. And there *is* the possibility that she's named, most coincidentally, Ian."

"Shut up, Johann," Ian said, not taking his gaze from the red and gold highlights in his glass.

"Ah, Dr. Carrick," Johann said with a dramatic sigh, "once again you comfort me. I can only imagine the help you'll be when the syphilis actually kills me."

Finally, Ian looked up and saw Johann in the rippling, silvered glass. "You've been 'dying' for years. I think you enjoy the drama of it."

A flash of honest emotion—maybe anger, maybe pain—flashed through Johann's eyes. "I promised someone I would keep breathing. Even if I didn't want to." He paused for a second, drew in a deep, shaking breath, then forced a smile. "Of course, that's not something the mighty Carrick could ever understand."

"Dr. Carrick?" Andrew said.

Ian knew that he had to answer them. If he didn't, Andrew would just keep asking and asking. It was either turn and run, or turn and answer. And he was too damned tired to run.

He turned around slowly, faced the group of people clustered in the eastern corner of the room. Andrew stood stiff and at attention, his arms pressed close along his sides. Johann leaned against the wall, his shoulder insolently pressed into the painting of a battle. Dotty was hiding amidst the velvet curtains that separated this room from the parlor—apparently the broom closet was full tonight. Queen Victoria was sitting on the dainty settee, her threadbare skirts splayed out around her. Lara lurked in the shadowy background alongside Maeve.

He sighed at the sight of his mother. She sat in a rocking chair, clutching a stuffed squirrel, laughing quietly to herself, twirling that damned scrap of fabric through her fingers.

Ian drained the last of his Madeira and put the glass on the mantel. "The truth is, I don't know how she is."

"Certainly you don't. You're a doctor," Johann said.

Ian ignored him. "She just came out of a coma that lasted nearly twenty-one days. Anyone would be ... disoriented. But she showed some signs of understanding. That, at least, was encouraging, I should think."

"Very encouraging," Andrew said solemnly.

"Oh, for God's sake, why don't you fling yourself at him and be done with it?" Johann snapped, shoving Andrew toward Ian.

"Enough," Ian hissed. "Jesus, why do I bother with you people?" He grabbed his empty glass and strode for the door.

Johann's sarcastic voice followed him out. "That's easy, Herr Doctor. You're one of us. And so, apparently, is your precious Selena."

Chapter Five

They were all in her room again, God and the strangers. She felt their eyes on her, felt their combined expectations like a consistent, crushing weight on her chest. She wanted to please God, wanted it desperately. But he was easily disappointed, and she was so sleepy. The pain in her head was agonizing.

He moved toward the bed and sat down on his chair. She heard the wooden legs skid across the floor as he scooted close. "Selena." His warm, honeyed voice melted across her skin like a caress. "How about a few tests?"

She groaned. A vague memory taunted her mind, some dim recollection of a movement that signaled her refusal. She concentrated, willed it to the surface ... something about her head, moving it in some way ... side to side ... up and down. It wouldn't come. She looked up at him, pleading with her eyes for understanding.

"Please?"

The softness of his voice tugged at her heart. She saw the disappointment in his gaze and felt ashamed. This was the man who had *saved* her. She struggled to rise to her elbows. At the movement, the pounding in her head intensified. Nausea settled heavily in her stomach.

His strong arm curled around her waist, drew her close. Sliding the coverlet back, he gently tilted her upright. Her bare legs swung over the bed and dangled above the floor. He moved out of the chair and sat beside her on the bed. She let out a little sigh and leaned against him, pressing her cheek into the solid ball of his shoulder.

"Are you okay on your own now?"

She stared at his mouth, trying to unravel the secret of his words, but it was hard to concentrate. Her head was on fire.

He started talking again, too fast, always too fast. Asking questions and more questions, looking at her, staring at her. Waiting.

Frustration magnified the pounding in her skull. She opened her mouth to speak, but no sound came out except a gasping, guttural groan, and then, finally, a wheezing ". . . now . . ." that seemed to take forever.

"Take your time, Selena. Concentrate."

She couldn't understand him. Nothing. Her frustration spilled into anger. She should know how to speak, should be able to understand and answer his questions. Then, all at once, the anger was gone, and all she had left was the pain. She curled forward and cradled her hammering head in sweaty hands. *Make it stop . . . make it stop.*

He slipped his arms around her and drew her close. "It's okay, Selena. Don't worry. It's okay."

She melted into his arms. The urgent sense of despair faded away. As always, the sound of his voice eased her frustration and fear.

"Here, come with me." He tightened his hold on her shoulder and helped her stand.

The floorboards were delightfully cold on her bare feet. He maneuvered her across the room, past the strangers, to the small glass box in the wall. With one finger, he flicked back the lacy white curtain and offered her the world.

It was so beautiful, so unexpectedly magnificent, that for a second, she forgot her headache. The large lawn, wearing the lush green coat of spring, rolled out from the house into a thick glade of towering evergreen trees. Dozens of pale new buds sparkled on still bare tree limbs. Beyond, the sea was an endless, hammered sheet of silver, rolling gently into the rocky shoreline. A single bird circled above the water, crying out its keening wail as it dove, wings tucked, into the icy blue.

She reached for the bird. Her knuckles cracked into something cold and brittle and invisible. She drew back, confused. "Want . . ." was all she could manage to say.

He touched her wrist, gently drew her hand toward him. "Let's do another test, okay?"

She tried to tell him that she wanted to go outside, wanted to see the world that lay beyond this dark, too quiet room. Her mouth opened, closed. Nothing came out. She could think the thoughts, but she couldn't translate them into speech. The headache started again.

He led her back to the bed and gave her a small board. She sat down and stared down at the thing he'd placed in her lap. It was a small wooden oval, dotted with holes.

He handed her a square peg. "Now, put that in the square hole."

Square hole. Neither of the words meant anything to her. She had no idea what he was asking her to do. She stared at the little wooden spike in her hand, trying to ignore the pounding in her head.

"Go ahead."

Frustration exploded inside her, made her feel sick and shaky and utterly alone. What about her head?

"Selena—"

She threw the spike across the room and lurched to her feet. Unsteady, shaking, she started walking toward the strangers. She wasn't sure where she was going, or why, but suddenly she needed to move.

The people parted wordlessly. Behind them, she saw a small table, draped in lacy white fabric. A thick black tube sat on a pewter holder. Above the tube, a golden-purple light throbbed magically.

The beautiful, flickering light mesmerized her. She turned to God, tried to tell him how lovely it was, but again the words were lost between her brain and tongue.

He stared at her in silence, watching her through assessing, narrowed eyes. For the first time, she felt a coldness in his gaze, as if he'd given up on her.

Her stomach clenched. She looked away, moved toward the table.

He said something—meaningless mush of sound. Too fast. He was talking too fast, and she didn't want to listen anyway. She just wanted to see the sparkling color up close. She reached for it.

"No!"

She heard the shouted warning a second after she touched the wondrous light. Pain ignited on her fingertips. She gasped and yanked her hand back, staring down at the bright pink spots forming on her flesh.

"Jesus Christ." God pushed the strangers aside and grabbed her by the wrist, pulling her toward the commode. There, he splashed water from the pitcher into the porcelain basin and plunged her hand into it.

The pain vanished in liquid.

Confused, she glanced back at the tube. The bright color was gone; in its place, a skinny black string floated upward.

"Fire," Ian said, pointing to the tube. "Fire. Jesus Christ . . ."

The minute he said "fire," she remembered. The tube was a candle, and the beautiful red-gold spot was a flame. She looked up at Ian, tried to tell him that she understood. It took forever for her to say the single word. "Bench."

That disappointed look darkened his eyes again, and she felt a crushing sense of shame.

"Poor thing, she's a bloomin' idiot," one of the strangers whispered.

"You should know," another answered before God shouted for silence.

She didn't understand the words, but she knew they were all disappointed in her. She'd done something wrong again.

"Go back to bed, Selena. We'll try again tomorrow." He looked at her. When she didn't move, he sighed and rolled his eyes. "Do you understand? Go back to bed now."

She swallowed the thick lump in her throat. She understood. He was disgusted with her. She was bad. Stupid.

He turned away. "Edith, take care of her."

". . . God . . ." She wanted to know what she'd done wrong. How to make him smile at her again.

He gave her a weary look. "Tomorrow you'll be fine," he said, but she could see that he didn't believe it.

And neither did she.

Ian walked through his silent forest cathedral at the break of day. Pinprick streams of sunlight spilled down through the evergreen ceiling, danced in golden patches on the brown-needled forest floor. It was quiet here, as it always was at dawn, the only sound the low, even breathing of the sea.

He closed his eyes and exhaled slowly, feeling the sting of the wind against his eyelids as he came to the water's edge. The smooth wool of his black cape whipped out behind him, flapped softly in the salty air. Overhead, a gull wheeled and cawed.

He sat down on a hulking square of granite and pulled out his journal. Flipping to a blank page, he put on his spectacles and began to write.

Twenty-first, April, 1882.

Ran visual, auditory, and touch tests today on patient. Consistent failure on patient's part to recognize

familiar items, to name such items, and to exhibit any
understanding of function. Patient had no realization
that glass was solid or that fire was hot. Exhibits almost
childlike innocence of everything around her.

On the question of mental impairment—

He stopped midsentence, unable for a second to write
the next words. Images hurled themselves at him.
Selena, unable to put the square peg in the square hole,
mouthing an endless string of nonsensical words. Crying, pleading wordlessly, touching fire . . .

The tests had gone on and on, failure building upon
failure. And the hell of it was, though she couldn't pass
a single one, she seemed to understand her ineptitude.
She wanted to succeed, wanted it as badly as he wanted
it for her. It was like Maeve all over again, wanting the
moon and getting nothing.

Except that he'd stopped wanting anything from
Maeve years ago.

Selena was different. He needed to believe in her future. If she had no future, *he* had no future. It was as
simple, as devastating, as that. Without her as a patient,
he would be nothing again. A forgotten man in a forgotten place.

No. He refused to consider failure.

She was damaged, yes. More so than he'd thought.
But he was Ian Carrick, the great *Doctor* Carrick to
whom lesser surgeons had genuflected for years.

He could cure her, and when he re-created a whole
human being from the fragments of her broken brain, he
would be more revered than ever. She would be his
greatest triumph.

He closed his eyes, drawing forth the dream, wrapping himself in its seductive warmth. The watchful eyes
of his colleagues as he leads her onstage. The astonish-
ment as he reveals her scar. The hushed murmurs of
awe as he recites her case history . . .

When he didn't need it anymore, he let the fantasy
fade and brought his pencil back to the paper. *On the*

*question of mental impairment, there can as yet be no
determination. It would be precipitous to infer mental
deterioration from a mere inability to form words.*

Yes, he thought. Yes.

It was still early in her recovery. All she needed was
time, time with people and time alone. Time without
pressure.

Perhaps then her memory would float gently to the
surface. As difficult as it would be for him to keep his
distance, he'd give Selena some time to acclimate herself to the strange world in which she'd awakened. It
would be difficult, but he wouldn't test her again for a
while, wouldn't invite her to fail so repeatedly.

He'd sit back and study her, watch and record her every move until the time was right. Then, slowly, patiently, confidently, he would begin to work with her,
heal her mind as he'd healed her body.

It would work.

She hadn't seen God in a lifetime, and she missed
him. Every time the door opened, she turned, hoping—
praying—to see her god, but he hadn't been back in
days. Not since she'd been so bad. So stupid.

She felt better today than she had yesterday, and yesterday had been better than the day before. The tube
was gone now from her throat, and the fiery pain had
gone with it. Even the headaches were less frequent.
She finally felt ready to try the horrid tests again.

She turned slightly and stared up at the square glass
box above her bed, trying to remember what it was
called.

Window. The word came suddenly, and she smiled.
Golden light streamed through the glass and brushed
her face, as soft and warm as God's touch. She reveled
in the feel of it, the smell of it. Tiny green leaves fluttered against the glass, tapping when the breeze was just
right. She wondered what the leaves smelled like, what
they felt like, how they hung against the glass without

falling down. Her gaze slipped downward. She stared, mesmerized, at the millions of motes of dust that danced in the thick sunlight, wishing she could reach out and touch them, taste them.

Everything she saw amazed her, sparked a dozen unvoiced questions. There was only that thin sheet of glass separating her from some glorious world out there, a place where leaves hung suspended as if by magic, where great puffy white shapes drifted through a blue, blue sky, where tiny winged creatures sang and chattered. A magical world lay just beyond her reach, just through the closed oak slab of her bedroom door.

She was sure of it, and soon—maybe even today— God would take her by the arm and show her the marvels of this place.

Be good. Be . . . smart.

She closed her eyes and tried to remember words, any words, anything that would impress her golden god and make him smile down at her. Before, she'd failed him. Today she was determined to do better. The answers were inside her mind, locked up somewhere in a vault she couldn't quite open. But they were there. She knew it.

Leaves . . . window. Every minute, she was improving.

Suddenly the door swung open. "Well hello there, Selena," God said, strolling into her bedroom. The strangers shuffled in behind him, lined up against the wall.

Her heart lurched at the sound of his voice. Today, she told herself. Today she would be smart enough.

She turned to look at him. Click, click, click went his bootheels on the floor. Tap, tap, tap, his pen on the silver metal bookcase—no, tray—in his hands.

She did her best to beam up at him, though her face was still so swollen, it was difficult, and it hurt to move her jaw.

He set the tray down with a clank on the green table

beside her bed and sat down beside her. "Good morning, Selena."

She began to hear the rhythm in his voice, the way he breathed between certain patterns of sound. Two words. Good . . . morning.

Good . . . morning . . . It was a greeting. She looked up at him, wanting so badly to impress him. She concentrated very keenly, thinking the word over and over again. "M . . . morning." She finally managed the single word, and disappointment washed through her. He'd said two words to her, two, and she couldn't remember the other one now, couldn't return the greeting.

He gave her a disappointed look, and she realized that he thought she'd simply repeated his word. How could she let him know that she'd understood? She frowned, searching for the words she needed and finding none.

"Today we're going to take the bandages off, Selena. Did Edith tell you that?"

He was speaking too quickly. Helplessly she stared up at him.

"It's okay, don't worry. It's okay to be confused. Normal. I'm not going to give you any more tests yet."

Confused. The word registered. "Yes. Con . . . fused," she croaked.

She saw the pleasant surprise in his eyes and was proud. He had understood her.

He picked up a pair of pants—no, something else, something silver and sharp—from the tray and very gently began to cut away her bandages. Snip, snip, snip. The layers and layers of linen fell away, became a blurry heap beside his feet.

He touched her chin, gently turned her face to the side. "The fracture is healing nicely, as is the bruising on your face. Soon we'll know what you look like. Yes, very nice . . ."

Nice. She understood nice. He liked her. "Thank

you." The phrase popped out of her mouth almost before she understood it.

"You seem well enough for a bath today, Selena. Edith will give you one soon."

She didn't remember what a bath was, but she wanted him to give it to her. She tried to tell him, tried to find the words. "No . . . you."

He laughed, a low, throaty sound that struck her as magic. "Even a rake like me knows that's not proper. I don't think so, Selena."

Rake. Gardening. She frowned, trying to understand. "Confused," she whispered.

"Shhh, it's okay." He touched her swollen jaw, his finger lingering for far too short a time. "Soon, Selena," he whispered, stroking her puffy, discolored cheek. "Soon you'll be able to tell us what you want and who you are."

But she knew what she wanted. She'd known it from the moment she first heard his voice in the darkness. She wanted Ian beside her, forever and always. She tried to tell him. "Want . . . God . . . need . . ." She lost her train of thought completely. "No . . . Aagh!"

"Don't worry, Selena. We'll get you fed and bathed and then we'll try again. It'll all come back. I promise."

She worked so hard to understand what he was saying. She recognized one word pattern; over and over he said it to her. It was part of the first word she remembered, *fightselena*. She concentrated with all her effort to force the single word up her throat. "S . . . Selena?"

"We've been calling you Selena. Until you tell us your name, we have no other."

She was hopelessly confused. He was talking so fast. . . .

He touched his chest. "Ian." Then he touched her, a breezing caress beneath her chin. "Selena."

She understood. He wanted to be called Ian. And she was Selena.

"Selena." This time the word rolled off her tongue

like a song. It was beautiful, this name, and Ian-God had given it to her. "Selena. Nice." She started to say something else, but she couldn't remember what it was.

Chapter Six

❦

"Is her bath ready, Edith?"

"Aye, Doctor."

Selena didn't understand the words. Ian-God was talking to one of the strangers—a fat, gray-haired lady with a wrinkly face.

Ian-God moved toward her and sat on the edge of the bed. "Would you like to walk?"

She gazed up at him, mesmerized by the incredible hue of his eyes. She remembered suddenly that they were the exact color of a blue jay's wing. A giddy happiness bubbled up in her, and a sound slipped from her mouth. It wasn't laughter, not quite. Something else, something softer, but she couldn't give it a name. It felt good, though. Wonderful. She was so happy that even the pain in her head seemed insignificant. God was here, beside her, smiling at her and asking her something.

Asking her something. She'd forgotten. She blinked up at him, trying to remember how to ask him to repeat what he'd said and to do it more . . .

"Slow," she said, suddenly remembering.

"Certainly," he answered, easing back the coverlet that hid her body. "Would . . . you . . . like . . . to . . . walk?"

She forgot to listen to him again. She was enthralled by the sound of his voice and the sight of her own body.

He peeled the quilt back slowly, so slowly, revealing a thin, bruised body sheathed in clinging ivory lace. The nightdress bunched around her middle and twisted across her thighs. Pale legs stuck out from beneath the lacy hem.

He touched her calf. She felt the warm dampness of each finger on her skin. "Would you like to walk—like before?"

She looked up at him. Some part of her mind wanted to answer, but she couldn't remember what to say. Then she couldn't remember what he'd asked.

He threaded his fingers through hers, provided her with the anchor of his presence and gently pulled her forward. Her back arched, and her heavy, heavy head fell back. At the movement, pain shot into her skull.

She moaned softly, squeezing her eyes shut.

He was beside her instantly, holding her, stroking the swollen side of her face, his arm curled comfortingly around her shoulders. "It's okay. Breathe deeply, relax."

The words spun through her pain-ridden head, merging, elongating. Meaningless.

But it sounded so nice. She let his voice wrap around her, soothe her. She concentrated on that, only that, until the pain melted into a dull, throbbing ache. That, she could live with.

Letting out a sigh of relief, she opened her eyes, and found herself in his arms.

"All better? Nod if you're better."

She frowned. What was nod?

He touched her chin, held it in a soft grip, and forced her head up slowly, then down. "Nod," he said, repeating the gesture until she understood.

"Now, do you feel better?"

Hesitantly, staring up at him for approval, she nodded.

He gave her a bright smile. "Good." Carefully he eased his arm beneath her knees and helped her to stand. Holding her close, he guided her to a slow, unsteady walk.

The strangers parted in a separating wave. She caught sight of a thin, yellow-haired girl sucking her finger and a frail, red-haired woman. She wanted to say something to one of them, but before she could think of a concrete word, he had moved her past the crowd.

In a sweeping gesture that made her laugh, he picked her up. Her bare legs crooked over his powerful arms, swung in the cool, cool air. He carried her to the end of the darkened hallway and stopped at a small wooden door that made a lovely creaking sound when he pushed it open. He went inside the room and put her down.

"This is the bathing chamber."

It was lovely, so different from the plain, white-walled room that was all she'd ever seen. There were tiny pink flowers and green leaves everywhere. It looked just like the world beyond the window, glowing and vibrant and alive.

She walked toward the walls and put her hands out to touch the beautiful flowers.

Flat. Frowning, she pressed closer, sniffed the small pink buds. No smell, either.

She looked back at Ian God, trying to find words to express her confusion.

"Wallpaper," he said, coming up beside her. "Painted flowers." He drew a single flower from the vase on the mantel and presented it to her. "Real."

She had never seen anything so beautiful. So exquisite. She wanted to feel it, taste it. A perfume-sweet fragrance wafted to her nostrils, teased her with a treasured, unexpected memory. She grabbed the flower from him.

A dozen spikes drove into the tender flesh of her palm. With a startled cry, she drew her hand back. Dots of red oozed from her skin.

"Damn it." He yanked the flower back and stomped it beneath his heel.

"No!" But she was too late. The beautiful pink petals were crushed, the flower broken. She looked up at him, confused.

"Thorns. Don't touch it again." At her puzzled look, he grabbed her hand, pulled the bloody palm up toward him. "See? Pain. Thorn. Oh, Christ . . ."

She didn't understand. Had she done something wrong?

He stared at her for a long time, saying nothing. Then he touched her cheek and sighed. "Who are you, my goddess," he whispered softly, "that you don't remember about thorns?"

He was talking too fast again. She didn't understand the words, but she heard a wistful sadness in his voice. Somehow, she'd failed him again.

"Good-bye, Selena. Be a good girl for Edith."

She stared up at him, afraid he'd hear the tears in her voice if she spoke. Slowly she nodded.

And then he was gone.

Selena stood in the center of the room, alone. Fear welled up inside her, made her want to cry. She bit down on her lower lip, wishing she knew what she'd done wrong.

Edith bustled in from the open doorway. She withdrew a single flower from the vase on the table and wrapped a towel around the thorny stem. Keeping her gaze locked on Selena's, the old woman moved forward, the blossom outstretched. "Here you go, lassie. 'Tis a rose."

Rose. The flower was called a rose, and she remembered all at once that it came in many colors.

"I'll put some scent of roses in your bathwater, eh, child?"

Selena didn't understand. The woman—*Edith*—was speaking too quickly, and there was a strange foreignness to her words. She didn't sound like Ian. Still, it was better to simply nod and pretend. Better that than speak and disappoint.

She nodded.

Edith moved toward her and began unbuttoning the small circles on Selena's nightdress. Selena watched in fascination. The woman's pudgy pink fingers took hold of a pearly drop—button, she remembered suddenly—and pushed it through the hole. One, two, three, four, five.

"Arms up," Edith said.

Selena nodded.

Edith took hold of her wrists. "Arms," she said with a little squeeze for emphasis.

Selena understood.

"Arms up," Edith repeated, and this time Selena knew what the old woman was asking for.

Slowly she pushed her hands up into the air.

"Good girl." She eased the nightdress over Selena's head and draped the lacy garment over the back of a burgundy velvet chair.

Selena stared in utter fascination at her naked body. Slowly she ran her hands over her breasts, feeling the pink tips pucker and tighten. At the touch, a shiver passed through her belly.

Edith laughed nervously. "Come along now, none of that." She took hold of Selena's hand and led her to the small, white stool along the wall. Long brass tubes ran from the back of the stool, disappearing into an ornately scrolled white box just beneath the ceiling. A chain dangled from the box.

"Toilet," Edith said, pointing at the stool. "Do you remember how to use one?"

Selena moved slowly toward the toilet and stared down at it for a long time, waiting for some hint of an image to surface in her mind.

"Sit down on it, lassie. Maybe that'll remind you."

Selena straddled the thing and sat down. It felt cool and slick on the inside of her thighs. She stared at the brass pipe, marveling at the color.

Edith touched her arm. "Turn around." When Selena

failed to understand, Edith helped her move her position.

It felt instantly familiar, sitting on the circular opening, and she remembered what she was supposed to do. A second later, she felt a rush of moisture and the tinkling sound of water dripping on water.

"Good girl," Edith said, handing her some wadded-up paper.

Selena used the paper and stood up.

"Now, over here," Edith said, taking her by the arm. "Bathtub."

Selena stared at the white thing full of water and understood. "Bathtub." She walked toward it, noticing the heated, cloudy haze that clung to the surface of the water. She could smell the humid scent of it, almost remember the slick, hot feel of it against her flesh. She clutched the sleek white edge and started to climb in, but before her toe touched the water, she saw something that surprised her.

Behind the bathtub was a pink stone fireplace, with a small fire blazing in the grate. Above the mantel hung a huge mirror. Inside the glass, another naked woman was getting into another bathtub.

Selena stopped, staring at the glass. A swollen, purple face stared back at her.

She frowned. The woman in the glass frowned.

She turned to Edith, trying to ask the question. All she could manage was the word, "Who—"

Edith's laughter was low and rolling. "Why, 'tis you, lassie. Selena." She took Selena by the hand and led her to the glass.

"That's Selena in the mirror. You."

She stared at the face. Dark brown eyes stared back at her from a puffy, cut, discolored oval. Her face was purplish black, with seeping yellowish patches along her jaw. The skin was so swollen and bloated, there were no features left at all.

She remembered the word for what she saw. "Ugly,"

she whispered. Tears caught in her eyes, blurred the image, and she was glad for them, glad for the soft veil they created. "Ugly."

"No, lassie, not ugly. Hurt." Edith touched Selena's cheek. "The ugly will pass when the hurt is gone."

Selena didn't need to understand the words. She could see the answer in the mirror. And finally she understood why Ian-God had left her.

Minutes crawled by on weak legs. Ian pulled his pocket watch out—again—and checked the time: 11:15.

What was taking them so blasted long?

"Apparently bathing the princess is a protracted procedure," Johann said. "No doubt she keeps drinking the water."

"Shut up, Johann," Andrew said, shooting a quick look at Ian.

Ian did his best to ignore them all. The crazies were in the drawing room with him, sprawled in corners and sitting on chairs and lounging in doorways. He felt their collective stare like a slow, suffocating weight on his throat.

He stared at the small, square board in his lap.

Square peg in a square hole. A child can do it, for God's sake. Even Maeve could do it.

"You're holding that damn game as if it were a sword," Johann drawled, strolling toward the fireplace. "She won't pass, you know. The poor incompetent still thinks her name is Ian."

Ian leveled a cool, contemptuous glance at the younger man. "She'll pass."

Johann's thin lips slid into a strained smile. "Ah, a dreamer. How quaint."

Maeve looked up from the stuffed owl in her lap. "I dreamed I went to Paris last night. It was beautiful."

Queen Victoria grunted. "I spit on France."

Ian rolled his eyes. Lord, would it never end? He looked at the closed door. He should push through it and go back to the quiet darkness of his room, but strangely enough, he found some comfort in being with other people right now. They were all here, drawn by the mystery of Selena, each in his or her own twisted way hoping that she would pass the upcoming tests.

Even Johann. The younger man was afraid to believe in Selena. He'd worked so hard at creating his hatred for everything and everyone in the world, he couldn't admit that he cared about their sleeping beauty.

But Johann cared. Ian saw it in his eyes, in the way he lurked in the shadows outside her room. Johann was no different from the rest of them. Selena had become a symbol of something to him. For Ian, she symbolized the redemption of his career. For Johann and the others—who knew?

Footsteps thudded down the stairs.

A quietly indrawn breath moved through the drawing room. Almost everyone straightened, leaned infinitesimally forward.

The crystal doorknob turned. Edith walked into the room, her fleshy cheeks rosy, her hair a kinky mass of curls. "She's done . . . sort of."

Ian frowned, came to his feet. "What do you mean, sort of?"

"I couldn't wash her hair. I tried to twist it up some, but she wouldn't let me pin it up." Edith shrugged. "She screamed. I guess that meant it hurt."

"Oh. Well, that's fine."

"Certainly," Johann piped up. "What's a little lice among friends?"

Edith puffed up. "That poor wee thing doesn't have lice."

"Ignore the syphilitic bastard," Ian said, reaching for the pile of pictures he'd set on the table beside him.

Johann plastered a skinny hand to his chest and sighed dramatically. "Ah, Dr. Carrick, you're such a comfort to me in my time of need."

Tucking some pictures beneath his multicolored vest,

Ian strode from the drawing room. When he reached the foyer, he paused unaccountably at the bottom stair. The stairwell loomed before him, dark and uncertain.

All of a sudden, he had a staggering sense that he should turn back. Johann was right. She wouldn't pass, wouldn't even come close to passing. It wasn't just aphasia, wasn't just that she could think the words but couldn't form them, couldn't speak. It was something else ... something he couldn't fix.

Permanent brain damage.

It was the thought he'd kept at bay by sheer force of will. He couldn't think of it, for if he did ...

He pushed the words away and climbed the stairs. He heard the crazies behind him, a dull thudding of feet. They moved in a hushed, respectful silence, afraid of angering him by shadowing him, more afraid of being farther than ten feet away from their moody master.

Finally he made it to the top of the stairs and turned toward her room. The door was open a crack. He gave it a push. It whined on tired hinges and swung wide.

The room was empty.

Ian raced inside, his gaze sweeping the small chamber in an instant. The window was closed, the bed made. The chair was empty.

His heart started hammering in his chest. Jesus, where was she?

He started to turn away when a glimmer of white caught his eye. Frowning, he eased into the room and bent down.

She was lying on the floor beneath the bed, talking in some nonsensical way. Words that made no sense, strung together as if they were a sentence.

"Peach ... chair ... mouse."

"Selena?" He couldn't keep the dread out of his voice.

She made a sharp, grunting sound and crawled back toward him, her pantalooned fanny high in the air.

He saw the back of her head first, her long, tangled

locks separated to reveal the triangular swatch of shaved skin, covered now in a peachy fuzz. Her healing scar was a blistering red trail through the new growth.

She turned suddenly and thrust her hand out at him. There was a dead mouse in her palm. She stroked the soft gray fur and smiled up at him.

"Jesus!" He surged down and batted the thing out of her hand. It plopped on the floor and skidded back under the bed.

Her smile slowly fell. "I am . . . Ian?"

Christ, he didn't know if she was talking to him or the mouse. He sighed heavily and ran a hand through his hair, trying to hold on to his temper, trying harder to hold on to his hope.

"Come here, Selena." He reached down and grasped her hand, leading her to the bed. She sat on the soft mattress, her bare feet swinging above the floor, her hands clasped together in her lap. Turning, she gave him a look of such pure, childlike confusion that he wanted to cry.

"Can you understand my words?"

She stared at his mouth a long time, and he could see her struggle, see her trying to understand and answer. It took her about three minutes, but finally she nodded. "Bowl." Her mouth twisted in what had to be a smile.

"Good. Let's try a few questions again, shall we? I think we'll st—"

She touched his arm. "Slow."

"I'm sorry. Questions . . . tests. Yes?"

Two minutes later, she nodded. "Yes."

"Do you know me?"

Slowly she nodded. "Ian-God."

He couldn't help himself, he laughed. "Ian. Only Ian."

"Ian," she repeated, staring at his mouth.

"Where are you?"

He could see her surprise at the question and knew

that she understood. He watched her frown deepen. Finally she shook her head. "Cup."

He thought she was trying to say no. "You don't know where you are?"

"Don't . . . know." Her face scrunched up in a frown. A few moments later, she managed to say, "Should . . . know?"

He shook his head. "No, you shouldn't." It was true. There was no reason for her to know where she was. He told himself it didn't matter that she didn't ask. "Who are you?"

"Selena."

"No. Before Selena. Who were you before Selena?"

It took her at least a minute to answer, but this time when the words finally came out, they were stronger and clearer. "Don't . . . know . . . who."

He waited for her to ask a question, battling disappointment and anger. She looked up at him, through her dark, mysterious eyes, and he felt as if he were being strangled. Time stretched between them as he waited for her to ask the all too obvious question. He noticed a dozen tiny things in that moment, the maple-syrup hue of her eyes, the quiet sound she made when she breathed, the pale triangle of milky skin at the collar of her nightdress. With every second, every breath he drew, he felt his hope that she could ever be normal fade.

She wasn't going to ask if *he* knew who she was. It seemed completely unimportant to her. "Can't answer or don't know?"

"Don't know."

He spoke very slowly—too slowly—trying to keep the rising frustration from his voice. "Do you want to know?"

"Why?"

The question stunned him. Jesus, how could she not care? She woke up in a strange bed, tended by strangers, and she didn't have the least interest in her past, her history? "Family," he said, clutching at straws. "You might have a family out there who loves you, who's looking for you." He knew he was speaking too fast, but he didn't care anymore.

"Ian." She frowned, touched his cheek.

He pulled back and stood up. The game slipped through his nerveless fingers and thudded to the floor, forgotten and unimportant now. What did it matter if she could fit a square peg in a square hole? She had no mind left. She was a blank slate, a childlike adult who didn't remember that fire was hot or glass was solid . . . or that dead mice weren't family pets.

Irreparable damage to the brain.

She couldn't be his miracle. She could get better—might even one day be able to formulate a complete sentence, but no more. His dreams of redemption were just that. Dreams. As unattainable as the stars.

And if his life looked bleak, hers was unimaginable.

She looked up at him. He saw the first sheen of tears in her eyes. "Ian . . . test—"

It hurt to look at her. He glanced at the ceiling and gave a bitter laugh. The puppet master had won again.

God had given Ian the only patient whom he could touch, and she was damaged beyond repair.

Ah, the irony. The only person who was immune to his powers . . . and she had no mind. No mystery to unlock, no secrets to reveal. He could never be Pygmalion to her Galatea. He was closer to Mary Shelley's famous Dr. Frankenstein, pining to be a god, wanting to create articulate, intelligent life from a lump of animated flesh.

Madness . . .

"Test," she whispered in a small, stricken voice.

"No." He backed away. "No more tests today. I've seen enough." He turned and headed for the door. As he reached for the knob, he couldn't help himself. He turned back to her.

She sat slumped on the bed, her matted, dirty hair streaming down her back. Tears spilled from her eyes and splashed on the white lawn of her nightdress. He knew she didn't have an idea in the world why he was leaving, or what she'd done wrong. All she knew was that Ian-God was disappointed in her . . . and she was alone.

"I'm sorry, Selena." His voice cracked. "Jesus, I'm so sorry."

Then he ran from the room and slammed the door shut behind him.

The lunatics were in the hallway, waiting for him. The small crowd pressed in on him from all sides, talking, whispering, gesturing.

"Quiet!" Johann hissed. "What is it, Ian?"

He lifted his head slowly, stared at the faces around him. Surprisingly, it was Johann alone who looked as if he understood.

"When I got into the room," Ian said in a tired voice, "she was playing with a dead mouse."

Maeve looked up. "Really?" She reached for the doorknob.

Ian started to grab her wrist, then realized what he'd been about to do and yanked his hand back. "You can't have the mouse, Mother." He looked at Edith. "Take care of it, will you?"

The older woman bobbed her head. "Certainly, Doctor. And I'll feed the poor girl in there."

Ian sagged back against the door. He'd never felt so old and beaten and alone. "Yes, please do."

"What are you going to do, Dr. Carrick?" Andrew asked timidly.

"I'm in over my head, Andrew," Ian admitted, his voice trailing off. It humiliated him to even say the next words. "Maybe an alienist could help. . . ."

"You'll have to speak to one, then," Maeve said. "One with orange hair."

"There's Dr. Wellsby at the asylum in Pollusk," Johann said in a quiet voice.

Ian flinched. Yes, he knew there was Dr. Wellsby.

"Wellsby." Maeve said the name in a quiet, shaking voice, her eyes brimming suddenly with tears. "He doesn't have orange hair."

Ian sighed and closed his eyes. He didn't want to go see Wellsby—the thought of going back to that hellhole scared Ian to death. But he couldn't just forget about Selena, just pretend she'd never existed. Maybe there was something he'd overlooked, some radical treatment to the brain Ian didn't know about.

Wellsby would have the answers Ian needed.

If only he had a friend or family member to accompany him, but of course, his years of isolation had robbed him of any support he'd once had.

Johann stepped forward. "I could go with you."

Ian swallowed hard, his eyes opened slowly. He wanted to make some smart, cryptic comeback that would put Johann back in his place, but he couldn't.

He didn't have to go to that hellish place alone. He could at least sit in the darkened carriage with another human being. . . .

He nodded curtly and looked away, hoping Johann hadn't seen the naked gratitude in his eyes. "We'll leave in the morning."

Chapter Seven

Selena couldn't seem to stop crying.

She'd done something horribly wrong, and she had no idea what it was. She wiped the moisture from her slick, swollen face and flopped back on the bed. At the contact, pain exploded in her head.

She stared up at the cracked white ceiling, feeling the tears slide down her cheeks.

Ian had given up on her. She had seen the disappointment in his eyes when he looked at her, the burgeoning disgust when she touched him. She saw it, understood it, but there was nothing she could do about it, no way for her to tell him how sorry she was . . . how much she missed his smile and his voice in the darkness.

He wanted her to care who she was, but she didn't. Those feelings just weren't inside her. Everything before waking up in this bed was gone, like that candle flame when she touched it. Gone.

She'd tried. For Ian, she'd tried to find some answers in the garbled mush that was her mind. But there was nothing inside her except for a great gaping hole where the memories should be.

She was bad. *Stupid.*

And she wanted another chance. "Please . . ." Please what? She didn't even know what to pray for, what to hope for.

She rolled onto her stomach, burying her ugly face in the soft quilting.

A quiet rat-ta-ta-tat roused her.

Blinking, bleary-eyed, she crawled to a sit and looked around, trying to find the source of the noise. "Ian?" She said his name and felt a surge of hope.

The doorknob turned, the door opened.

The fat woman—*Edith*—stood in the doorway, holding a silver tray filled with steaming bowls. There were a few of the strangers behind her. The fragile-looking woman with rust-colored hair and the thin girl who sucked her finger. *Thumb*. The girl who sucked her thumb.

Edith made a quiet tsking sound. "Poor thing. 'Tisn't your fault you're feebleminded."

Selena sniffed and wiped her runny nose on her sleeve. She got to her feet and moved toward Edith. Words floated through her dazed mind, formed themselves into blurry sentences, questions. "Why?" was the only word that made it past her lips.

The rosy color seeped out of Edith's fleshy cheeks. She paused, her kind eyes fixed on Selena. "I can't answer that for ye, lassie. 'Tis God's way to make some people sick."

The red-haired woman walked toward her. "Selena?" Her voice was lovely and lyrical, more song than spoken.

Selena tried to ask the woman's name. "Bottle ... answer." She groaned in frustration. She couldn't do it, couldn't find the right words to express her thoughts.

"Maeve." The woman answered the question Selena had meant to ask. When Maeve reached Selena, she slipped her small, cold hand into hers and gave a reassuring squeeze. The touch was soothing. "I understand."

Selena looked down into Maeve's sad hazel eyes and believed her. Somehow, this woman *did* understand Selena's pain and fear. The realization was so powerful that Selena's knees buckled. For the first time since Ian left, she felt less alone. *Thank you.* The words blossomed in her mind, full-blown and understood. "Sea . . ." She squeezed her eyes shut, ashamed that she couldn't even express the simple acknowledgment.

"Don't worry, child. You'll get better. And if you don't—" Maeve shrugged her slim shoulders. "You don't. Believe me, you can get used to anything."

"Come on now, Maeve," Edith scolded. "Don't depress the lassie. She might not know she's . . . you know . . ." Her voice fell to a stage whisper. "Brain-damaged."

Maeve gave the housekeeper an arch look. "She does now."

Edith blanched, then bustled forward and set the tray down on the bedside table. A foreign aroma wafted to Selena's nostrils, and she had a vague recollection.

"Food," she said suddenly, remembering what it was, but not what to do with it.

"Aye, lassie. Food. We have a lovely fish stew for you."

Selena didn't understand the words, but the scent brought back a deep-seated instinctual need. A strange rumbling moved through her stomach. She moved toward the tray, dragging Maeve along behind her.

Selena hiked up her nightdress and sat down on the straw-seated chair, scooting in close to the table. Maeve sat down beside her, and the thumb-sucking child stood behind Selena, hovering and silent.

Edith dished a bowl full of the steaming red and white stew and set it down in front of Selena. "There ye go, lassie. Dig in."

Selena frowned. Dig? She pictured a shovel and mound of dirt, a headstone.

"Eat," Maeve whispered.

Selena wasn't sure what *eat* meant, but her stomach rumbled again and she reached for a floating chunk of whitefish. The broth scalded her fingertips. With a yelp of pain, she drew back and plunged her burnt fingers into her glass. Milk sloshed over the sides and spilled across the table. The relief was instantaneous and she was proud of herself for remembering the remedy. She smiled.

Maeve gently eased Selena's hand from the glass and gave her a flat metal strip with a round end. A spoon, Selena remembered suddenly.

Maeve kept her fingers coiled around Selena's and showed her how to dip the spoon into the soup, pick out a chunk of fish, and bring it to her lips.

Selena recalled what "eat" was. She breathed in the thyme-sweet scent of the stew and smiled. She opened her mouth, then recalled the burn on her fingers. "Hot," she said, pulling back.

"Good," Maeve said. Then she blew on the broth in the spoon.

Selena watched in fascination as the clear, reddish liquid swirled and rippled in the silver hollow.

"Not hot," Maeve said. "Eat."

Selena could barely contain her excitement. This felt so normal, so *right,* as if she'd done it a million times in her life. She could almost bring those pictures to mind, almost remember eating before.

She leaned forward and tasted the soup.

Nothing. There was no taste at all. She frowned. Something was wrong. She turned to Maeve, trying to find the words to ask the question and failing. "Taste," was the only word she could manage.

Maeve smiled brightly. "I know. It's good. Now, eat up, child; you need some strength."

Selena shook her head. "No . . ."

Maeve looked her directly in the eyes. Her smile faded slowly. "Eat."

Selena felt a sharp stab of fear. She didn't want this beautiful lady to turn away from her, too. Then she'd be utterly alone. What difference did it make if the food had no taste, if something about that seemed wrong? She gazed into Maeve's hazel eyes and nodded slowly.

I'll be good, she thought. *Don't leave me.* Leaning forward, like a good girl, she took another sip of the flavorless stew.

Maeve's smile returned, filling Selena with immediate relief. She brought a cold hand to Selena's face, pressed it to her cheek. "And don't worry, child. I won't leave you if you're bad." Maeve looked away suddenly. Her pale lips trembled slightly. "I know how much that hurts."

Later, long after the tasteless food had been eaten, long after she'd watched Ian's carriage disappear into the darkness of the night, Selena lay in bed with the covers drawn to her neck. The room was dark, so dark. She wished they'd left her a candle, a lantern, anything that would cut through the blackness and make her feel less alone.

But they hadn't trusted her. She'd understood enough of their too fast conversation to know that. Edith had been afraid she'd *burn herself* again, or *torch the bloody house*.

She twisted slightly and stared up at the window. The glass sheet seemed to hang suspended in the darkness, lit for a glorious second by a trembling wash of moonlight.

The light was gone almost before it came, and the blackness swallowed her again. For a strange, elongated moment, it seemed as if she'd disappeared altogether, or perhaps had never existed at all. She lay there, breathing hard, trying not to cry, waiting for another shimmer of light.

None came. A brief wind grazed the window, made the glass shudder. The night seemed suddenly filled with noise, when only moments before it had been too quiet. She heard footsteps shuffling back and forth behind her locked bedroom door, heard a dull ebb and flow of voices. Frightened, she huddled beneath the protective coverlet.

Nameless, faceless people, just outside her door. They were out there, talking, walking, laughing, whispering. It made her feel even more isolated, more ugly and stupid and alone.

"Help . . . me," she murmured to the strangers, but her voice was weak and reedy, even to her own ears. "Please . . ."

But there was no answer, not even a break in the murmur of their voices. She listened to the restless shuffling of their feet and wanted so badly to join them, but she didn't belong with them and she had nothing to say. All she had was this empty room with its one window to the world.

She eased the heavy quilt back and got to her feet, feeling her way along the bumpy painted walls to the window. Just then a cloud broke free of its moorings and drifted across the distant half-moon. Pale, bluish light slid through the pane and cast an eerie glow in the darkness.

A tree shivered outside, the branches creaked. Tiny black leaves studded the stark limbs, reminding her suddenly that it was *spring*, the time of year when life began anew. But not hers. She was different, somehow, shut off from the world. So alone in the dark room.

If only he'd come back. If only he hadn't left.

Didn't he understand? Didn't he care that he was all she had? That without him, the world was a frighteningly strange place, cold and lonely and empty?

As she'd lain in her bed all those weeks, nestled in the bowels of some unimaginable darkness, her head pounding, her throat on fire, she'd known that Ian was there. She heard his voice, felt his touch. He'd coaxed her back from the pain-riddled void. It was for him that she'd finally opened her eyes.

Outside, the night beckoned in a thousand twisting, moving shadows. She wanted to be out there where Ian was, wanted it so badly she felt desperate.

She needed to experience life beyond the glass, to

smell the unknown scent of the rain and feel the forgotten kiss of the wind. To be a part of something.

The glass was so deceptively thin. So easily broken. So easily ...

Break the glass ... touch the world ... The outside beckoned in a sly, seductive voice.

She drew her hand back and made a fist.

No. Somewhere in the back of her mind, she knew that it was dangerous to break glass. She would *be hurt.*

What she needed was to open the window.

She smiled, remembering suddenly how to do it. She twisted the little metal paddle and pushed the lower half of the window up. It creaked loudly, scraping as if it hadn't been moved in ages. An icy blast of wind hurled through the opening and slapped her cheeks.

She laughed in triumph. The world smelled so wonderful, so fresh and clean. Rain splattered her face in big droplets. She closed her eyes and let herself experience the moment—the taste, the smells, the sensations: sweet, sweet rain, cool, inviting wind that smelled like salt and wet earth. The trees whistled, waves smacked against hulking, black rocks.

She planted her hands on the wooden sill and stuck her head outside, breathing deeply. The secret, sensual world embraced her, filled her with a heady sense of possibility. It was all out there. Everything she'd ever wanted, ever would want.

Waiting for her ...

She climbed onto the sill. Her white lawn nightdress stretched taut from her collar to her knees. The wind picked up, whipped through her tangled hair and stung her cheeks. The tight fabric of her gown fluttered in a quiet, thumping beat. For the first time since waking up, she felt alive. She licked the cold raindrops from her lower lip and shook her head.

Behind her, the bedroom lock clicked, the door squeaked open. "Sweet Mary!" someone cried out.

Footsteps thundered toward Selena. Light split the darkness. "Don't jump—you'll kill yourself."

Kill yourself. Selena felt a sharp, sudden chill at the words. She looked down. The lawn was a small, black patch two floors below. She knew suddenly that she could fall, could *be hurt,* but she hadn't thought of that before.

A hand curled around her wrist, steadied her. "You're okay, Selena." The man's voice was squeaky and weak. As if she wasn't okay at all.

Slowly, afraid now to fall, she turned around, and found herself staring into a concerned pair of pale gray eyes.

"I'm Andrew," he said quietly. "Do you remember me?"

She didn't remember him. Not him, and not any of the shadowy people clustered just beyond the door, but that didn't matter. What mattered was the warm, solid feel of his fingers around her wrist. What mattered was that someone had finally come for her, had touched her and seemed to care if she was *okay* or not.

She tried to answer him, but nothing came. It was as if some part of her brain had simply gone to sleep. Frustrated, she leaned toward him. *Help me,* she thought, *please . . . help me. . . .* The silent plea filled her heart. Her chest ached with the need to speak, and still the words were beyond her.

The boy, Andrew, touched her damp cheek and gave her a sad, understanding smile. "It can be very lonely here."

He curled an arm around her shoulders and drew her off the ledge. Closing the window with one hand, he helped her back to the bed. When he'd retrieved the lamp and placed it on the bedside table, he turned to the open doorway and said, "Come on in, everyone. She's fine."

Gray-clad people moved into the room in a slow, shuffling procession. Selena recognized the red-haired woman—*Maeve*—and the thumb-sucking girl. Behind them was a fat, wrinkly-faced woman who wore a tarnished crown on her graying hair. The three women formed a semicircle at the foot of the bed.

Andrew knelt before her. A lock of dark blond hair fell across one eye, and he brushed it back impatiently. "We know how lonely it can be here . . . how frightening your first days can be. But we wanted you to know that you aren't alone." He got to his feet and backed up. "Go ahead, ladies."

The crowned woman stepped forward and thrust a small, perfectly rounded gray rock in Selena's hand. "That's a worry rock, subject. When you're scared or lonely or worried, you rub it between your thumb and forefinger." She yanked it back and demonstrated. "Like this." Then she tossed the rock into Selena's lap and scuttled out of the way.

Selena stared down at the rock, too surprised for a moment to respond. The word she needed came effortlessly this time. This strange woman had given Selena *a gift.*

It was a thing that friends did. That family did.

"Go ahead, Lara," Andrew said.

The girl—*Lara*—came to the bed next and drew a tattered rag doll from behind her back. The fabric was slashed along the doll's gingham-sheathed chest, revealing a swatch of quilting, and one black button eye was missing. A few fuzzy strands of red yarn remained on the back of its head.

The girl withdrew her thumb and stared steadily down at Selena. "Sarah," she said in a slurred voice, and popped her thumb back in her mouth.

Selena took *Sarah* carefully. The ragged toy was soft and comforting. Instinctively she brought it to her chest and rocked it gently against her breast. Lara gave her a wide, gap-toothed grin, and Selena knew she'd done the right thing.

Maeve cocked her head toward a heap of rust-colored

silk. "I brought you a gown. Edith will alter it to fit you."

Finally, Andrew returned to the bed and knelt once again in front of her. The women shuffled in close behind him. He withdrew a small, rectangular thing from the waistband of his pants. "This is a children's book. I thought perhaps you would enjoy looking at the drawings."

Selena took the thing reverently, smoothed her hand across the tooled leather surface. For long seconds, she just stared down at it in awe. It was a most exquisite gift. Then Andrew gently eased it open. Immediately words popped out at her: *Cat. Dog. Me. And. Home.*

Once, she'd known how to read. The knowledge stunned her, filled her with an almost giddy sense of discovery.

She swallowed hard, looked down at Andrew. The honest concern in his eyes gave her a new strength. This man wouldn't laugh at her, wouldn't get disgusted with her inability to speak and her lack of knowledge about the world. He was a gentle soul, this one, and he knew what it meant to be lonely and afraid.

Maybe he could help her, teach her to be smart enough to bring Ian back.

She wet her lips, trying to dredge up the words to ask for help. "Fancy . . . goods." The words slipped out; she had no idea what they meant, but she knew that they were wrong. She frowned, concentrating as hard as she could, so hard the headache started to pulse at the back of her skull. She felt the quiet stares of the people around the bed, but there was no disgust, no judgments being made. They were simply waiting for her to speak.

"Red," she blurted. *No. Not right, but close.* "Read." She pointed down at Andrew. "You . . . me . . . read."

"Y-You want me to read to you?"

"No," she managed, shaking her head, unable to say more. *I want you to help me to read.* The sentence turned through her mind in a ceaseless, frustrating rhythm. She tried hopelessly to bring the words forth, to form the simple request, but it was impossible.

Mute and frustrated, she stared down at Andrew. He stared up at her, a helpless, pathetic frown on his face. "I don't understand. You want me to read to you?"

"Of course she wants you to read to her, Andrew," Maeve declared at last. "We all do."

Lara nodded wildly and clambered up on the bed beside Selena. Within moments, all five of them were settled in the comforting softness of the bed.

The young man—already Selena had forgotten his name—started to read. The quiet, sweet-sounding words washed through Selena, and each one sparked an image, a memory of meaning. *Rabbit. Wagon. Sun. Family.*

Then, very softly, Maeve slipped her fingers through Selena's. The touch was gentle and soothing and comforting.

Selena glanced around her, at the faces drawn so close to hers, and felt an incredible tenderness swell in her heart. These people, whose names she couldn't remember for more than a few moments, had given her more than their unexpected gifts. They made her feel safe and cared for.

"Selena . . ." she said, searching for the other words she needed.

Andrew paused in his reading and looked at her. She felt all their eyes on her.

"Selena's . . . family," she managed finally.

The thumb-sucking girl—Lara—gasped. She slowly withdrew her thumb from her mouth and gazed at Selena, her gray eyes glistening with sudden tears. Selena remembered the word for that look.

Longing. Selena understood longing. It was what she felt for Ian.

Andrew laughed. "Yes, I rather suppose we are your family."

Selena tried to draw her gaze away from Lara's, but she couldn't. She saw such pain and fear and hope in the child's eyes. For the first time, she understood that here, in this great and lonely house by the sea, she was not the only lost soul.

Chapter Eight

❦

Evening fell in silken folds of lavender across the sky. In the distance, a tall, white church spire caught the last rays of the setting sun. Newly blossoming trees clung to the sides of the narrow gravel road, their leaf-studded limbs fanned out, wooden fingers tapping on the carriage's roof.

Ian sat deep in the squabbed burgundy velvet seat, his knees tucked carefully against the door. A cloudy pane of glass was his window to the outside world, and through tired eyes, he watched the scenery crawl past. The town was an endless stream of small, well-tended white clapboard houses on squares of spring grass, their flanks guarded by a battalion of evergreen trees. In the center of it all sat a glassy blue lake, the type of lake that cried out for ice-skaters in winter and picnics in the hot days of summer.

The carriage hit a pothole and quaked to the right. Ian slammed into the wall, and Johann's knees rammed into his in an electric touch.

The images hit Ian before he had recovered his balance. *A pine coffin, bare and unadorned . . . a pale, dark-haired woman strapped to a dirty-sheeted bed, writhing, whimpering Johann's name through her tears . . . a door slamming shut, a lock turning with a click.*

And this time there was more than just the concrete mental pictures. There was a feeling, an emotion so all-consuming and powerful that Ian felt jolted back in his seat.

Sadness. Grief that could swallow a man, turn his soul inside out.

Ian's head snapped up. He found Johann staring at him. As usual, the younger man wore a sardonic half-smile. "Going to read my future, Herr Doctor?"

Ian searched Johann's thin, angular face, stared into his watery green eyes. His heart was pumping so fast, he could hear it, and the familiar headache was a dull thudding behind his eyes.

Johann's sarcastic smile faded. He pulled back, swung his legs farther away from Ian's. "You *did* read my thoughts. I was thinking of my wife."

Ian knew he shouldn't say anything, should retreat into the icy silence that had been his world for so long. But he couldn't manage it. He was too shaken by what he had seen and felt. "I had no idea . . ."

Johann's whole face seemed to soften. For once, there was no cynicism in his eyes, no bitter curve to his lips. "Like everyone else, you heard it was a scandal." He shook his head. "It was a crime."

Silence slipped between them, less comfortable than before. "You know." Johann said the words so quietly, Ian wondered if the man had meant to speak at all. "I fell in love with Marie the first moment I saw her."

Ian didn't know what to say. "She must have been everything you'd imagined her to be."

"No." Johann turned, stared out the cloudy window. His shoulders rounded forward, his head banged tiredly against the cushioned wall. "She was different, my little Marie. People called her a whore—of course, she was one. But to see the truth of her, I had to look deeper. Past the heavy cosmetics and obscene costumes and practiced responses." He turned back to Ian, and there was no mistaking the tears in his eyes. "I had to see her with my heart and tell the world to go to hell. When she got sick with the syphilis, I stayed with her, nursed her to the end."

"And look what it's cost you."

"My death?" Johann laughed quietly, a surprisingly unaffected and honest sound. "If that's all you felt when you touched me, Ian. Touch again. The good memories far outweigh the bad, and loving her was worth any price. I died the moment she did. . . . My body simply doesn't know it."

Ian remembered the pain he'd felt at the simple touch and knew Johann was telling the truth. He looked away, gave Johann what little privacy he could in the intimate confines of the carriage. He stared out the window, saw the last white house disappear from view as the coach hurtled into the shadowy, forbidding woods. The gravelly road twisted through groves of maple and pine, trees so thick in places that a man could lose himself in the darkness. They were going deep into the Maine woods now, into a place uncharted and wild, where night fell early and the sweet smells of moss and mud and mystery were common. A place hidden from "nice" society.

The hospital at Pollusk was like all state-run lunatic asylums. Cold, distant, ignored. The seat of fear in a sleepy community, something wanted by all Maine residents, but not in their hometowns, not near their precious children. He knew without asking that stories surrounded this place, ghost tales told and retold at family gatherings, threats offered by exhausted parents to keep rambunctious children quelled. The stories would be about ax murderers and child killers, and they would have some limited basis in fact—enough to keep the good townspeople frightened. Enough to keep this place isolated and forgotten.

He'd seen it all before. In the early years, when he'd first returned to Lethe House, Ian had occasionally gone into town. Everywhere he went, he heard the whispers, felt the stares. Old ladies made the sign of the cross as he walked past them. One had even fallen into a dead faint when he looked at her.

Yes, he knew what it felt like to be feared and ignored. And these good Mainers were probably no different from the ones at home. They hated what they feared, and they feared anyone different.

Unfortunately, this asylum, like all of them, wasn't filled with murderers. Instead, it warehoused society's lost souls. People suffering from melancholia, dementia, mania, monomania, and idiocy. Sad, lonely people like his mother, more likely to hurt themselves than any hapless passerby.

But of course, the good people of Pollusk would never believe that.

The carriage lurched to a stop.

Neither man moved. Finally Johann spoke. "I hate this godforsaken place." He shivered, reached for his cloak. "I was here, you know. When I first fell in love with Marie, I told my father that I wanted to marry her. The great Frederick Strassborg beat me within an inch of my life and informed me that no son of his would marry a whore." He gave a soft, bitter laugh. "But I never was much good at listening. Marie and I ran off to be wed, and my father found us. He dragged me away from the church and brought me here. The law's a bit slack on family commitments, as you know. I was institutionalized for three years—it took that long to extract an apology from me and a promise never to see Marie again."

Ian didn't want to be drawn into another personal conversation with Johann, but he couldn't seem to stop himself from asking the question. "What happened then?"

He grinned. "I was never too good at keeping promises, either."

The carriage door handle clicked hard, and the velveted door swung open. The elderly driver stood in the opening. Behind him, the hospital sat amidst the trees like a huge granite bird of prey, silent and watchful. "We're here, Doctor."

For a split second, Ian's fear was so great, he couldn't move, could barely breathe.

"You need the answers, Ian," Johann said quietly.

Ian knew he was right, but it didn't end the fear. He reached for his cloak and slipped it on, suddenly cold. "Don't let anyone touch me, Johann."

Johann gave him a sad, knowing smile. "Isn't that what this little sojourn is about, Herr Doctor?"

Ian pretended not to understand. Without answering, he got out of the carriage and began the long walk to the asylum.

It lay sprawled before him, waiting. A great wooden door, protected by Gothic-scrolled granite walls and an elegant green hedge, scrupulously trimmed, flanked the walkway and hemmed the giant building in. Trees stood guard, swaying quietly in the nightfall's breeze, whispering among themselves of the things they'd seen in this place, the screams they'd heard.

Johann came up beside him. "Ready?"

Ian hadn't realized that he'd stopped walking. He stood on the threshold, staring at the closed door. Hell no, he wasn't ready, not to enter this place again.

He was a fool to have come here, to have put himself in the lion's path for a woman who couldn't improve.

Ian had a crazy urge to run—back to the carriage, back to the isolated house in the woods where memories lurked but didn't intrude. Even crazier, he wanted to confide in Johann, spill out the whole sordid story of what had once happened in this place, of Ian's singular betrayal.

Time paused, drew a quiet breath.

The moment of weakness passed. "I'm fine." Ian started to reach for the door, then paused and looked suddenly at Johann. "Can you go in?"

Johann smiled. "A most un-Ian-like question." His smile faded. "Yes, I can."

Ian nodded and knocked on the door.

Moments later, it swung open. A scowling, swarthy man with beefy arms towered in the opening. "Bug-heads get dropped off durin' the day." He gripped the door and started to slam it shut.

Ian shoved the door open so hard, the guard staggered backward. In concerted motion, he and Johann slipped inside.

The stench of unwashed bodies hit him in the face. Ian almost staggered at the force of it. For a terrifying moment, he thought he was going to be sick. He swallowed hard, squeezing his eyes shut. Voices echoed in the shadowy hallway. A droning, maddening buzz.

The guard surged forward. "Now, wait a damn minute—"

Johann stuck out a booted foot and tripped the man, who fell flat on his face. "Oh. Did I do that?" Johann plastered a hand to his throat and clicked his tongue. "So sorry."

The guard clambered to his knees. "You ain't sorry yet, you two-bit bugger, but you will be."

Johann held out a hand. "I should introduce my . . . employer. This is Dr. Ian Carrick."

The guard froze in his tracks. Slowly he turned to Ian. His face tightened into a squinty frown. "You're Dr. Carrick?"

Ian had seen that look a thousand times in the old days, a dawning realization that the object of so many rumors had appeared in the flesh. A curiosity, then a slow-building fear.

The guard took a step backward—also a standard response. "Dr. Wellsby said you was comin'. I din't believe it."

"No doubt it was intellect that secured you this job," Johann drawled, making a great show of crossing his arms. "Now, take us to your superintendent."

The guard rushed past them and slammed the door shut, then almost fell over himself in his haste to leave.

He spun around. "Third door on the right. You can follow me. I'll . . . hurry ahead and tell Dr. Wellsby you're here." He was gone before the echo of his words had faded. The rapid thudding of his footsteps disappeared in the shadowy corridor.

"Do people always treat you like that?" Johann asked.

Ian felt inexpressibly old and tired. "This is a mistake."

"Then follow my lead, Ian. I make them all the time." Turning, Johann began walking down the hallway.

Ian stood there, in the sprawling, shadowy darkness, feeling utterly alone. Sounds battered his ears: the echoing vibrations of a woman's scream, the dull shuffle of feet going in circles, the magpie chatter of nonsensical conversation.

It was so like before, so sickeningly the same. The same smell, the same incredible roar of voices in pain. For a second, Ian couldn't move. He stood rooted to the spot.

It smells here, Ian. I'm afraid.

He shivered, drew his cape more tightly across his body. The air was fetid and motionless, thick with the smells of death and dying and disuse.

I'm sorry, Ian. Whatever I did . . . I'm sorry. Please don't leave me here. Oh, God . . . please, Ian . . .

Somewhere, a door slammed shut, and the noise drew Ian from the morass of his memories. Up ahead, Johann stopped, turned back to face him.

"This place releases all the demons, doesn't it?" Johann's voice was shaky.

Ian didn't respond. He forced himself to keep walking, through the darkness, into a different hallway where the shadows were invaded by gaslight sconces on the uppermost rim of the wall.

They turned a corner and suddenly there were people everywhere, clustered around the puddles of light. Desperate fireflies hurling themselves against the golden warmth. They spoke to one another and themselves in low, droning voices devoid of emotion.

Ian kept moving, past a man hitting his head on the plaster wall, past a weary-faced woman who sat curled in a shadowy corner, slowly pulling her hair out by the roots, past a man in a straitjacket who chewed his tongue so vigorously that blood eased down his stubble-coated chin and splashed on the dirty gray linen of his pants.

Don't leave me here, Ian. Please . . .

"Jesus . . ." Johann croaked.

Somewhere, a door smacked open. "Ian!" boomed a male voice.

People scattered at the sound. As one, they jerked to their feet and scurried into the hidden corners from which they'd come, like insects sneaking back under cold rocks.

Superintendent Giles Wellsby strode down the hallway, his hand outstretched. "Ian, old boy, what a surprise. Damn fine to see you. After all the Christmas party invitations you'd declined, I thought you'd died."

Ian stared at the man's hand in rising horror. He tried like hell to suppress the childish emotion, but the more he tried to rein it in, the more it consumed him. It was a simple greeting, he told himself, nothing more. Just a goddamn way to say hello.

Giles came to a stop. "Ian?" The superintendent's slim, colorless face tightened into a disapproving frown.

Ian knew he had to respond, had to respond *now*. If he didn't, this whole journey would be for nothing. Giles would treat Ian as a pariah instead of a colleague. Taking a deep breath, he steeled himself for the onslaught of images and thrust his gloved hand toward the superintendent. "Giles," he said stiffly. "How have you been?"

Their hands locked. Giles's thoughts slammed into Ian's mind in a jumble of pictures and words and feelings. *What happened to him? Rumors . . . psychic . . . lost his mind . . . looks bad . . .*

"Good to see you, Ian. You look wonderful," Giles said with a toothy smile. He was too much the old-world gentleman to ask the questions that filled his mind, and Ian was glad of it. "The missus was asking about you just the other month."

Ian slid his hand free of Giles's grip. Immediately the images subsided and the headache began. He tried to remember what the superintendent had just asked him, but he couldn't. He looked down at the man, knowing his eyes were as blank as a lunatic's and unable to change it.

"Ian?" Giles prompted.

Johann stepped forward, his hand outstretched. "I'm Johann Strassborg."

Giles seemed startled by the interruption. He turned slowly and shook Johann's hand. A frown creased his forehead. "Strassborg? I seem to recall a patient . . ." His head snapped up. The color leeched out of his fleshy face.

"I see you remember me," Johann said.

The color returned to Giles's sallow cheeks with a vengeance. He cleared his throat and turned to Ian. "So what brings you to my little corner of the woods after all these years?"

Ian shot Johann a grateful look, then turned to the superintendent. "The last time I was here, you had just taken in a woman who'd fallen from her horse. Hit her head on a rock."

Giles nodded. "Elizabeth."

"I have a similar patient myself. A woman was brought in unconscious. A coma. When she finally came around, she exhibited profound speech problems and . . . other things."

Giles pulled at his pointy chin. "Aphasic?"

"Yes, but it seems to be more than that. Certainly the expected syntax, morphological, and semantic problems are in evidence. Beyond that, however, she exhibits a significant mental deficiency. Probably brain damage, but I suppose it could be an unusual form of amnesia."

"Meaning?"

"It's not merely a temporary inability to recall the experiences of her past. It's . . . global. Not only does she have no idea of her name, or where she came from, or who she is; she also has no memory of the rudimentary knowledge that she *must* have learned at one time. She's . . . childlike. Infantlike, for Christ's sake. She doesn't know that fire is hot, or that glass is solid, or that a dead mouse is not a toy. She talks to leaves and expects them to answer."

Giles frowned. "A complete loss of all previously learned knowledge as well as a loss of identity. Most unusual. Did you want to send her here for observation? I could certainly—"

"No!"

Giles stiffened and drew back, obviously offended. "Ah, well, then. So what can I do for you?"

"I'm sorry, Giles. It isn't you, of course. I'm here because you're the best alienist I know. It's simply this place. The memories . . ." He let his sentence trail off.

Giles's face softened. "I understand. And how is the lovely Maeve?"

"The same, I'm afraid."

Giles nodded slowly.

A pause enveloped the trio, then Giles cleared his throat. "So, back to the point at hand. You've come to see Elizabeth and how she's faring, I take it."

Ian's heart seemed to stop for a second. "Is she still alive?"

"Yes," Giles answered in a voice so soft, Ian could scarcely hear it. "She's still alive, and still here."

Still here. That was not a good sign.

Ian dreaded the next question with everything in him. "Any improvement?"

"I think you'd best see Elizabeth for yourself, Ian. Then we can discuss the particulars."

Chapter Nine

❧❦

The shadowy corridor was filled with the same gray-clad people, milling aimlessly to and fro. Ian walked stiffly forward, with Johann on his right side and Giles at his left.

An old, gray-haired woman hurled herself at Giles, her withered fingers clawing at him. She shrieked, spraying spittle, yanking at her clothing. "I need to leave, Superintendent Wellsby—"

Giles kept moving, and the woman fell in a sobbing heap at his feet.

People, everywhere people. Crying out, reaching, yelling and screaming to be heard. Their pleas jumbled together, merged into a great, keening cry.

". . . a terrible mistake—"

"My husband, Superintendent Wellsby, have you seen my husband yet today—"

"I'm drowning, drowning—"

Ian tried to shut the voices out, to hear nothing except for the repetitive click of their bootheels on the marble floor or the hushed jangle of Giles's keys, but it was impossible. The noise was deafening.

They turned a corner, and almost as if on cue, the rabble dispersed, leaving in their wake a hallway that was lonely and dark. Closed doors lined the walls, windowless, locked. Low, moaning voices slid beneath the cracks and wafted through the dank air.

"This is the catatonic ward," Giles said. "Even the inmates are afraid to wander down this hallway." He stopped at the last closed door. Reaching down to the heavy chatelaine on his belt, he pulled up the clanking mass and extracted a single key.

He fit it in the rusted lock and clicked it open. Before he pushed the door open, he turned to Ian. Giles seemed, in the pale gaslight, to have aged ten years during the short span of their walk. His cheeks were waxen, his face a map of tiny, downward wrinkles. "Once in," he said quietly, "they never come out."

The door opened with a whining creak, revealing a room of surprising size and comfort. Square ivory walls, dotted with ornately framed pictures, surrounded a large, four-postered bed, its surface heaped with a snowy coverlet.

An old woman sat in a wooden rocking chair, her head turned to the barred window at her left. Long strands of curly gray hair sheathed her face, fell in wispy folds to her lap. Ian heard the soft, muttering murmur of her voice, but he couldn't make out any words, just a jumble of confused, halting speech. In her lap, her hands lay curled like fishhooks. A silver and diamond ring glittered on the third finger of her left hand.

"Elizabeth?" Giles said her name in a hushed tone.

She didn't move, didn't look up.

Giles motioned the men to follow him as he walked slowly up to her chair and kneeled at her feet. "Elizabeth, honey, I've brought some people to see you."

For a long, breathless moment, she was unresponsive, then, very slowly, as if the movement hurt, she turned away from the window. Pale moonlight slid through the clear glass and iron bars, slashed across her small face.

She was much younger than he'd expected, and even in the paltry light, he could see the breathtaking beauty that she had once been. Thick black lashes fringed eyes the color of whiskey; eyes that were now vacant and glassy. A silver line of saliva seeped down from the corner of her slack, pink lips, hung in a cobweb-thin line to a wet spot on the bosom of her blue gown.

Giles pulled a pristine white handkerchief from his coat pocket and wiped the drool from her lips. She blinked down at him, apparently trying to focus.

"The . . . paper," she said in a scratchy voice. "Sliding or spring." She forced her chin up, gave the room a cursory, glassy-eyed glance. "Wine the drink grass." She turned away and stared out the window again. Her rocker started moving, back and forth, back and forth, in a rhythmic, scratchy thumping.

Giles's head bowed forward. "Believe it or not," he said to no one in particular, "this is a good day for her."

Ian wanted to distinguish Elizabeth from Selena. He tried to ignore the similarity of the cases—the nonsensical sentences, the injury itself—and searched for a disparity, some small thing that separated Selena's prognosis.

Giles hadn't tried enough. Yes, that could account for a difference. Maybe Giles had given up too early and there was still hope. . . .

He clung to the notion. "What treatments have you tried?"

"Everything. Shock treatments, sheet treatments, ice baths. Every half-baked psychological theory to come along—even that crazy Freud's psychoanalysis. Nothing worked. She's not crazy, Ian. She's brain-damaged. Pure and simple." He shrugged. "Her brain just doesn't work anymore. She can parrot a few words, she can feed herself and walk if she really wants to, but that's about it. Every once in a while she surprises me with a sentence that makes sense, but not often, and she never gets any better."

"Perhaps if you tried—"

Giles turned to Ian. A tear slid down his cheek and he made no effort to hide it. "She's my daughter."

For a second, Ian couldn't even respond. Shame crushed in on him. "Oh, Jesus, Giles. I'm sorry."

Ian wanted right then to walk out of this hellhole and never look back. But he couldn't relinquish his hold on the tender strand of hope that remained. He needed to touch Elizabeth, delve into her psyche and see what was in her head. He had to know. . . .

"Leave me alone with her for a moment." The words were out before he could stop them.

Giles's head snapped up. Watery eyes focused hard on Ian. "Why?"

"I need to touch her hand. That's all. It won't take a moment."

"It's true, then? The rumors that with a touch you can read a person's mind."

"Sometimes," Ian answered, then amended his half-truth. "Usually."

Giles stood up and faced Ian. "What if I don't want to know what she's feeling?"

Ian's gaze was steady. "Welcome to my nightmare, Giles."

Giles turned slightly, stared dully at the window. "If it's pain . . . if she's inside there somewhere, hurt and lonely and lost . . . don't tell me. Jesus, don't tell me."

Without another word, Giles turned and walked out of the room. Johann followed him, and closed the door quietly.

Ian kneeled before the young woman. She didn't seem to notice him. She kept rocking, back and forth, humming quietly to herself. Another stream of spittle slid down her chin.

"Elizabeth?" He said her name softly, wanting her to respond.

She kept rocking, kept humming. A quiet giggle slipped from her mouth.

He pulled off one glove and reached for Elizabeth's hand. Her fingers were icy cold, curled as tight as steel.

The first touch brought nothing. No sensation or image or thought at all, and he had a brief thought that maybe he couldn't "read" such broken minds.

Ian slid his hand into hers, locked his warm fingers around her cool flesh and squeezed. Heat flared in his fingertips, throbbing, burning.

An image crept into his mind, almost coyly at first, dancing at the edges of his consciousness. He had to make an effort to clasp it, had to concentrate as he'd never done before.

Green fields dotted with flowers . . . raindrops splashing from one autumn red leaf to another . . . a dapple gray pony cantering along a twisting silver river.

She stopped rocking and turned to look down at him. Her apathetic eyes fixed on him.

"Elizabeth?"

She almost smiled, or so it seemed. "Elizabeth," she repeated.

A young black-haired girl picking flowers . . .

Ian withdrew his hand slowly. She wasn't in pain, of that he was certain. She wasn't *in* anything. She was a blank slate, a feeble, childlike adult who would never get better, never be the self she was before, a vegetable in a woman's body, granted the rudiments of speech but no ability to understand or empathize or experience.

For a second, he couldn't breathe for the pain in his chest. The last bit of his hope died hard.

He'd been wrong. He'd thought that caring for Selena was like caring for Maeve. But it was much, much worse. At least Maeve knew her name and had a few good days. Even Elizabeth, brain-damaged beyond repair, had thoughts inside that beautiful head of hers. Selena had nothing. That's why his psychic powers didn't extend to her. Her mind was gone, empty. There was nothing to see, no images to pick up.

She wasn't his chance for professional salvation.

The fisherman had been right to bring her to Lethe House. It was where she belonged, among the other half-wits and crazies who never improved. At the realization, he felt a stinging sense of shame, then a burning loss. Shame because, as usual, he'd thought only of himself, his needs, and loss because the fantasy he'd created shattered in a million broken bits. He could never heal Selena, never re-create a vibrant human being from the pathetic shell-like woman sitting before him. He could be Selena's keeper, but she had no need for a physician. She was nothing to him; they were simply two people who shared a roof, coexisted in a place where lost, lonely people came together but never quite connected.

It was as good a definition of hell as he'd ever heard.

Selena. Elizabeth. SelenaElizabeth. The images of the two women blurred in his mind, merged until they were indistinguishable.

There was no future for his mysterious goddess, just a lifetime of perpetual care, years spent sitting in chairs and stroking dead animals and mumbling nonsense.

And through her, there was no future for Ian. Just the same dark, lonely present stretching out before him like a prison sentence in solitary confinement.

With a tired sigh, he rose and walked out of the room.

Outside, in the darkened hallway, Giles and Johann stood side by side. Giles looked up at Ian, a pathetic question in his watery eyes.

Ian closed the door shut behind him, trying to ignore the headache that had begun at the base of his skull. "She's not in any pain, Giles. She's . . . in the past. Her childhood, I expect. I've never felt such happy, peaceful thoughts from a person before."

Giles's face crumpled. "Oh, thank God . . ."

For the first time, Ian experienced a certain joy in his curse. "I'm glad I could tell you that, Giles."

Giles swiped at his eyes and looked up. "Now let me tell you something, Ian. I know the trials you've had with Maeve, and believe me, they're nothing compared to the hell of brain damage. I'd trade my soul for one moment a year when Elizabeth knew who I was."

Ian nodded. He knew that Giles expected more, but he couldn't find a voice, nor words to speak.

"Don't expect anything from your patient. Send her to Bloomingdale or Danvers. Forget about her, and don't get emotionally involved. This kind of thing . . ." Giles's voice vibrated with emotion. "It can break your heart."

Ian couldn't answer. Nodding, he turned and headed down the shadowy walk. He could hear Giles and Johann behind him, but he didn't care, didn't pay attention. He just wanted to get the hell out of this place.

The carriage hurtled through the countryside, down one jet black dirt road after another. Wind slashed at the sides of the coach, rain thumped on the roof. Light wobbled through the dark interior from a small lantern bolted to the wall.

Ian pulled his cloak tighter to his throat. He was cold, colder than he could ever remember being, but there was no warmth to be found in his cape.

He needed a decanter of whiskey. Maybe with its help, he could crawl into some dark, cold place and drink until he was blind and deaf and dumb, until nothing that happened on this earth could affect him.

"You got exactly what you expected, I imagine." Johann broke the silence at last, and Ian sensed that he'd been biding his time. "We all do, after all."

It took a great effort for Ian to lift his head. He tilted his chin just enough to slant a shuttered look at the man in the seat opposite him. "Cryptic and philosophical. I see you're back to your old self, Johann."

"That makes two of us, then."

"Meaning?"

"The brief flirtation with humanity has ended."

"Keep talking, Johann. You'll have me in a coma in no time."

Anger flashed in Johann's eyes. "You're the blindest,

most selfish, self-obsessed person I've ever had the displeasure of knowing. You make me sick."

"Oh, stop. You're breaking my heart."

Johann leaned forward. "You fool. You have been birthmarked by the gods, destined for greatness, and yet you walk away from your potential like a spoiled child."

Ian sighed heavily. He looked at Johann's serious face, and felt suddenly old—too old for a thirty-five-year-old man.

"Selena is not Elizabeth," Johann said into the lengthening silence.

The words surprised Ian, and they hurt. Jesus, just hearing her name, soft and rounded and redolent with the mysteries of the goddess, hurt. He used bitterness to keep the ache at bay. "Selena is not Selena, either."

"It's too late, you know."

Ian wanted to ignore Johann's enigmatic statement, but he couldn't feign disinterest, not this time, not about Selena. And God help him, Johann was one of the few people who could actually understand Ian, who saw through the bitterness to the pain. Their lives were so similar; two affluent, educated men trapped in a hell-hole of abnormality, thrust into the bowels of madness by physical conditions they couldn't control and a world they couldn't fit in to.

He looked up, met Johann's gaze. *Tell me something that will save me.* The thought came to him out of nowhere, humiliating him in its intensity. He forced his voice into a casual drawl. "Too late for what?"

"Dr. Wellsby's advice was very scholarly, probably even well thought out and accurate, but that's the problem with you doctors. You think that healing is a science. It's not, never was. Never will be. Healing is a spiritual art. It requires the heart and soul to save the body."

"Ah, medical advice. What a good choice, Johann."

"Wellsby is an idiot. If there's a chance to save

Selena, it lies not in your books or your medicines or your knives; it resides in your soul and heart. You *must* get emotionally involved—as you already are. Your willingness to save her may be all that she needs."

Ian snorted derisively. He'd been down that road before, and there was nothing good at the end of it. "What should I do then, Johann, spend the rest of my life wiping the drool from her chin?"

"If that's all there is, then that's what you do. And you pray for more. Every day, every moment, you pray."

Ian closed his eyes, wishing he could forget the prayers he'd offered, the thousands of childhood nights he'd spent kneeling beside his bed, praying that his mother would get better. "And those prayers will be answered," he said bitterly. "Just as yours were."

"I forgot to pray," Johann said softly.

Hearing those words, quiet and honest and suffused with pain, Ian felt himself weaken. The thin, disguising veneer of bitterness fell away, left him with a painful nothingness inside. "I've tried that route before. It's a damn universe of pain. It sucks you in and strangles you, and . . ." He sighed. "You, of all people, should understand. Sitting there, helpless, watching someone you care about sink deeper and deeper into oblivion." He shook his head, ran a hand through his hair. "Christ, to do it again . . ."

He tried not to think of Maeve, but he couldn't help himself. He remembered the night, so many years ago, when he'd tried to extricate himself from the horror of her madness. An eighteen-year-old boy with nowhere to turn and no one to lean on. He could still remember the night, taste it, feel the cold kiss of the snowflakes on his face and hair.

She'd tried to kill herself—again—and Ian had found her, naked and shivering and bleeding in the big copper washbasin in the kitchen, her pale arms drawn protectively across her chest. She hadn't wanted Ian to have had to clean up the blood. . . .

She hadn't minded that he'd find her body, or that he'd know how little she valued their family, or that he'd be utterly alone without her. All she cared about was the mess, and so she lay curled tight in the tub, the only thing out of place in the gleaming kitchen except for the still-dripping butcher knife she'd used to slit her wrists.

Ian had snapped, unable suddenly to take it anymore. After he'd stopped the bleeding, he bundled her up and carried her into the carriage. They hadn't stopped until they reached the hospital. He'd deposited her in Dr. Wellsby's arms and walked away, his shirt and hands still smeared with his mother's blood.

Ian, don't leave me here. I'm sorry. Please . . .

It was a crystallizing moment in his life; he knew that now. The fact that he could leave her in that place, sobbing and alone, had defined the greatest weakness in his character.

Oh, he might tell Johann he would help Selena, might even try to, but it would be a halfhearted attempt, an easily forgotten vow. In the end, mental illness terrified him, ripped out what little goodness lurked in his dark soul. It didn't matter that three months—and two suicide attempts—later, he'd returned for Maeve, rescued her. There was no redemption from the selfish cowardice of his true nature. But there was honesty. There was truth.

"I can't do it, Johann." He sighed and bowed his head, sickened by his own character, repulsed by his own weakness.

"She needs you to care about her."

"There is no *her*, Johann."

"The amnesia—"

"Didn't you learn anything from Wellsby? It's not amnesia, Johann. It's brain damage. She's not going to get her memory back. She'll never be normal. That's why I can't read her thoughts. There's nothing there to read. No past, no present, no future."

Johann stared at him for a long time, so long that Ian started to become uncomfortable. Finally Johann reached into his breast pocket and pulled out a small glass vial.

Ian frowned. "What have you got there?"

"Cachou lozenges." Slowly he opened the vial and poured out the tiny white pills. Then he threw the empty bottle to the ground and cracked his heel down on top of it.

"What are you doing?"

"Making a point." Johann bent down and retrieved a small, nickel-sized piece of glass. Light caught the jagged edges and set them afire in sparkling prisms of blue and red and yellow.

Johann's voice fell to a seductive whisper, so soft that Ian involuntarily leaned forward to catch the words. "Why do you demand such wretched commonness from those you would care about?"

Ian slammed back in his seat and crossed his arms. He was disgusted with himself for having leaned forward at all. "Jesus, Johann, don't be so dramatic. I simply don't find mental illness or brain damage appealing. It's hardly grounds for execution."

"You saw the bottle, yes?"

"I'm not blind."

"It was pretty and fulfilled perfectly the function it was designed for."

"Yes. So?"

"Now, see the bit of glass." Johann extended his hand, until the sharp edges of the glass were almost magical in their colored illumination. Slowly he turned the piece, letting light play across the surface in a shifting fan of yellow and purple and red and gold. "It's broken."

"Yes."

"But it has its own beauty now, its own value; if only

one looks past expectations, past 'normality,' there is an almost magical effervescence here. Something seen that wasn't anticipated. A gift." Johann met Ian's frowning gaze, gave him a slow, soft smile.

Ian stared at the jagged bit of glass so long, it blurred like a teardrop in the half-light. He couldn't blame Johann—the younger man couldn't know that Ian had thought the same thing a thousand times in his life. He'd tried to see the beauty in Maeve, tried so damn hard. As a young boy, he tried every day to expect nothing of his mother, to simply love her as his father had. But every time she didn't recognize him, every time she slapped him or walked past him without a word, it hurt.

Johann's theory didn't work; not for Ian, anyway. He looked at life head-on, without blinders or rose-colored glasses. Maeve would always be sick and undependable. Selena would always be brain-damaged. He'd wasted enough time already on hopeless dreams—most of his life, it seemed—and he was tired of it, exhausted by the disappointments.

"You won't try again, will you? Won't even hope that Selena can be cured."

"Oh, I'll hope, Johann." Ian couldn't keep the bitterness out of his voice, and he didn't really try. It comforted him, gave him an emotion that didn't hurt so badly. "What I won't do is care."

"Will you help her when we get home?"

"When *you* get home. I'm not returning to Lethe House right now."

"But—"

Ian raised a hand for silence. "Don't bother, Johann. And for God's sake, don't break any more bottles to prove your point. I'm heading for all the train stations and postal offices between here and New York. I'm going to post notices about a nameless, faceless woman in my care and beg for information about her. Maybe that damned lobsterman will read a notice and come forward."

"You're hoping someone will come and claim her."

"You're damn right I am. Let her break someone else's heart."

Chapter Ten

❦

The quiet gurgle of running water.

The rhythmic thunk-splash of wet cloth on a wash-board.

Women talking in low, muted voices, too softly for any single word to be heard.

They were talking about something important, something just out of reach. Selena felt terribly alone, disconnected from the sights and sounds and movements around her. A stranger in the darkness, waiting, watching.

Random images floated through her mind, taunted her with wisps of remembrance.

A wicker laundry basket, a metal pie tin, a small, perfectly round wooden box.

She had no words to label the items, no memories to match them. Simply a vague realization of things ...

"Sshh, hush, little one. Sshh ..."

Selena heard these words more distinctly. They were spoken in a quiet, lilting voice that was familiar. She realized suddenly that she was asleep, that she had been *dreaming*. The memory of what that word meant and the experience it implied slipped into her mind.

"Sshhh, little one. I am never so far away as you think."

A hand caressed her cheek, and even though there

was a lingering remnant of pain in her jaw, it felt good, that touch, so good.

She came awake slowly, and the strange dream drifted out of reach, forgotten almost immediately. The room was steeped in darkness, with only a sliver of moonlight through the glass windowpane to relieve the shadows. Night stained her coverlet a deep, charcoal gray.

"Sshhh, little man. Don't cry now."

Selena turned toward the voice, and noticed for the first time the woman sitting beside her bed, drawn close, her rail-thin shoulders draped in a lace shawl so delicate, it looked to be made of cobwebs. Reddish blond hair lay twisted and piled on her head. She was moving slightly, rocking back and forth, though the chair wasn't moving. Something satiny—a timepiece . . . no . . . lantern . . . no.

Selena couldn't name the thin strip of silvery white that twined through the woman's thin fingers.

Maeve. The name came almost effortlessly this time, and her ability to recall it filled Selena with joy. She tried to remember what to say now, the proper greeting of woman to woman. "Maeve," she whispered, "hello . . . there."

Maeve didn't glance at her, seemed not to notice she'd spoken at all, and Selena wondered if she'd said the wrong thing again. "Maeve?"

"I heard your weeping," Maeve said finally. "You mustn't worry. He'll be back. Your father always comes back."

Anxiety rustled the hairs at the back of Selena's neck. She frowned and pushed up to her elbows. "Maeve?"

Once again, there was no sign of recognition, no glance or touch or sound that indicated a response. Her face was downcast, but even so, Selena could see Maeve's moist hazel eyes. A glistening droplet clung to her pale lashes and stubbornly refused to fall.

Selena glanced down, saw the patch of moistness on

Maeve's gown, a seeping darker patch on the white lawn of her nightdress. The place where tears fell.

Maeve reached out, stroked Selena's cheek again. Her touch was soft and comforting, her skin papery and dry. Slowly, in a trembling voice, she started to sing quietly, "Hush little baby, don't say a word. Mama . . ." Her voice cracked. Tears filled her eyes and slipped down her hollow cheeks, dropped on her hands. She drew her hand back, let it fall in her lap. "Mama . . . can't do anything, can she? No . . ."

Selena heard an incredible pain in her friend's voice, a sadness that seemed to parch the woman's spirit. Last night Maeve had been laughing and happy; tonight, somehow, she'd fallen into darkness.

Selena knew how that felt, to fall inside yourself and be trapped. "You will . . ." She searched for the words. *Find a way* "Out."

Maeve brought a pale finger to her lips. "Sshh, little boy." She shook her head. The single tear streaked down to her lap, melted into the wet patch of lawn.

Selena did the only thing she could think of, the thing that she would want someone to do for her. She shifted sideways in the bed and flipped the coverlet back in invitation. ". . . Maeve . . . sleep."

Maeve looked up. For a split second, the confusion in her gaze dissipated, and Selena saw the raw need that lay beneath.

"Sleep." Maeve sighed and shook her head.

Selena patted the mattress beside her, wishing desperately that she could find the words to ease Maeve's pain. But she couldn't find them, if such words even existed. Instead, she said the only word that came to her, made the only offer she could think of. "Sleep."

Maeve pushed to her feet. The wooden stool crashed to the floor beside her, but she seemed not to notice. The vague, glassy look returned to her eyes. She stared through Selena as if she were invisible.

"Your father should be home now." She leaned forward and pressed a warm, moist kiss to Selena's forehead. "Sleep well, my child."

"Good . . . night, Maeve."

Maeve stiffened and drew back. "No good ones," she whispered, tears springing to her eyes once more. Wrapping the silver strand more tightly through her fingers, she walked away and closed the door behind her.

Selena stared at the door for a long, long time, unable to fall asleep again. She remembered the black place she'd been in when she couldn't wake up, the swirling mists of pain and fear that clung like a shroud to her body. She'd heard Ian's voice then, and that had been enough, a lifeline between the world of darkness and the light that lay beyond. Knowing that he was out there, that he cared, had pulled her through. It pulled her through even now, kept her reaching forward.

She wondered if Maeve had a voice in the dark silence.

Strangely, Selena thought that the old woman did not, that perhaps she was even more alone than Selena. Else why would Maeve be here in the middle of the night, alone, her nightdress stained with silvery tears?

Maybe only Selena knew what the darkness felt like, knew how cold and lonely it felt to be lost inside yourself. If that was true, then only she could help Maeve.

Selena felt the first tug of a smile.

She could help Maeve the way Ian had helped her.

And maybe then they'd both feel less alone.

Whack. Whack. Whack.

Selena came awake slowly. At first she thought the strange, pounding beat was in her head, some remnant from another unremembered dream, but gradually she realized that the noise was real.

She pressed up to her elbows and scanned the room quickly, noticing the chair and commode were in their rightful places. The limp white curtains shimmied against the plaster wall.

Selena pushed back the heavy coverlet and went to the window, shoving the curtains out of the way.

A florid-faced older man peered at her through the window. Surprise widened his black eyes at the sight of her. "Holy hell!" he wheezed, spitting nails from his thick lips.

She frowned. He was standing on something . . . a ladder. She tried to ask him what he was doing, floating out there in front of her window, but the only words she could form were, "Sky blue . . . standing."

He shook his head and reached into his pocket for another nail. "Poor thing. Ye're crazy as a bedbug, jest as the missus said."

Selena watched as he withdrew a thick iron bar from a bucket hanging from the ladder's uppermost rung. He pressed the bar in front of her window and began hammering it in place.

That's when she noticed the other two bars on the left side of the glass. A dim sense of panic started. They were locking her in, taking away her only picture of the world outside. She scrambled for the bottom of the sash window and shoved the glass up. It hit the housing with a crack.

His head snapped up. "What in the hell . . ."

She stared at him, her mouth gaped open, her heart thudding in her chest. She didn't want to be locked in, didn't want to be an animal in a dark box, all alone. She had so much to do, so much to see *out there*.

"What . . ." Nothing else would come out. She heard the query in her mind, circling endlessly, increasing her panic, but she couldn't release it. *What are you doing? Why are you locking me in?*

"Puttin' bars on the window, miss. Ye'll still be able to see out. Ye jest can't get out."

Selena shook her head, searching frantically for the words she needed. "No. Thank you . . . please."

"Doctor's orders, miss. I was supposed to do it days

ago, but I forgot. Last night the missus got on me but good. Seems ye thought about jumpin'."

She frowned. "Bottle . . . But . . ."

"It's to keep ye safe. Doctor always bars the windows."

Selena didn't understand each word, but she understood the old man's point. Doctor. *Ian* had ordered the bars to be put on the windows to protect Selena. Not to keep her in, but to keep her safe.

It made her suddenly sad. Ian didn't understand her any more than she understood him most of the time. He was afraid she'd jump out of the window and *kill herself*. But she'd already learned that lesson. She understood that she could *be hurt*, that she could *fall and break her bloody neck*.

Last night she hadn't been able to communicate her understanding, though, and they'd all thought she didn't see the peril. They thought she was *crazy* and *stupid*.

And *brain-damaged*. She remembered when she'd first heard those words from Ian. There had been such hopelessness in his voice, such regret. She understood that, too, now. He didn't want her to be damaged. He wanted her to be whole and pretty.

She swallowed hard. They were the two things she would never be. She knew she was ugly; she'd almost accepted that. But she didn't want to be so broken that she had to live here forever, locked in a room with bars on the windows. Alone.

She turned away from the window, let the curtain flutter back into place. Hugging herself, she paced around the small room, finally slumping onto her bed. A small, nagging pain pinched her chest.

She was used to that pain. She'd carried it around with her from the moment Ian turned away from her.

All he saw was the outside, the ugliness and the failure and the frustration. He didn't see her at all.

She sighed. She was so tired of feeling lost and alone, afraid. And she sensed she'd lived this way for a very long time. Whenever she tried to remember life before Ian, all she felt was a lingering sorrow. As if she'd been sad for two lifetimes.

No more. The words slipped into her mind, gathering force. At first she didn't really understand what they meant; they were simply words. Then, all at once, she knew. Her heart was speaking to her, loudly, with a clarity she hadn't known before. Her heart and soul were tired of the sadness, the sorrow, the tears.

And she was tired of this room, of breathing but not really living, of waiting for other people to give her opportunities. It was time to make herself happy.

She had to do things for herself, had to learn about the world on her own. She had already figured out everything this room had to teach her—commode, bed, quilt, window, pitcher, water, basin.

Now she needed to get out and explore the world.

What first?

Dress.

She smiled at the ease with which she retrieved the information. Leaning forward, she grabbed the gown off the chair beside her bed. The slippery rust-colored fabric felt soft and wonderful against her rough-skinned hands.

Silk. She was thrilled at how quickly the word came to her. The moment she touched the fabric, she knew what it was called. Silk. She focused all of her mind on trying to say the single word. "Tree." She frowned. No. Not correct. She refused to give up, she tried again and again. Minutes ticked by, slowly, irritatingly.

"Broom. Clock. Silk."

She grinned. It had taken time—but what was time? She wasn't stupid. She *wasn't.*

All she needed was help. Just a little. But who could help her? Maeve was lost and Ian was gone.

The answer came to her so suddenly, she wondered why she hadn't seen it before.

She leapt off the bed and ran for the door, pounding

on the hard wood. She wanted to yell for Andrew, but the words wouldn't come.

She stopped when she heard footsteps outside her door. "Selena, is that you?" came a soft, male voice.

"Andrew?" *Unlock the door. I need your help.* She tried to force out the words. "Help . . . Selena."

The doorknob turned. Selena stumbled back just as the door swung open. Outside, in the shadowy hallway, stood a cluster of people. Edith, Maeve, the queen. And Andrew was in the middle.

"What is it, lassie?" Edith said, breathing heavily, wiping her fleshy hands on the floury front of her apron.

Selena knew what she meant to ask for, but she couldn't find the words. The minutes ticked by, slowly, thickened by the breathing of the crowd. Selena closed her eyes and stamped her foot in frustration. "Help," she managed.

"It's all right, Selena," Andrew said. "Take your time."

Selena clasped her hands together and stared at him, trying to draw strength from his quiet acceptance. "Basket." She shook her head. "No. Not . . . Selena . . . stupid. Sick."

Edith clucked. "Poor wee thing. Her brains are scrambled."

Maeve looked up, her eyes glassy. "Eggs would be nice, Edith. Thank you. Be sure and ask the master if he's hungry."

"Do hush, you two," Andrew said harshly. "Can't you see that she's trying to tell us something?" He moved closer, encouraging her with a nod. "Go on."

Selena pointed to her head, then to her mouth. "Broken." At Andrew's blank look, she repeated the gesture and tried a different word. "Hard."

Maeve nodded. "It's hard for all of us to speak our minds sometimes. Isn't it, Herbert?" she said to the stuffed owl in her arms.

Andrew made a quiet, gulping sound of excitement. "Is that what you're trying to say, Selena?"

Selena nodded, grinning. "Yes. Think ... good. No ... talk. Help ... Selena?"

Andrew's smile fell. "We can't help you, Selena. We're crazy."

The queen rapped him sharply on the back of the head. "Speak for yourself, young man. Royalty is overbred, not crazy. I've got plenty of things I could teach the chit."

Selena tried to follow the queen's speech, but couldn't. Instead, she reached for the children's book and pressed it to her chest. "Read. Learn." She pointed to the window. "Outside ... see. Learn words."

Andrew gazed at her, frowning. "You don't care if we're crazy?"

She gave him a smile and reached forward, touching his fuzzy chin with her hand. "Not crazy."

Andrew smiled unsteadily. Tears glistened in his eyes.

The queen shook her head. "Oh, Jesus, the pup's gonna start bawling."

He wiped his eyes. "I'll help you, Selena." He turned back to the gray-clad people behind him. "What do you say, lunatics? We can teach Selena everything about life. It'll give Dr. Carrick a mighty surprise when he returns."

"Dr. Carrick don't seem particularly fond o' surprises," Edith said with a frown.

The crowned lady snorted and placed her fat hands on her hips. "And just who gives a shit about that?"

Andrew struggled with a smile. "Then it's decided. We'll teach Selena everything she needs to know about life."

Edith rolled her eyes. "Oh, Lord. Don't the poor child have problems enough?"

Chapter Eleven

❦

"I think she should get dressed first." Queen Victoria peered at Selena from behind a cracked, dusty monocle. "Clothes are the window to the soul."

Edith frowned. "They are? I thought—"

"Please don't," the queen interrupted. "You're giving me a frightful head."

Selena watched Edith and the queen talk back and forth. Every now and then she understood a word or two—dressed, window, head. She couldn't quite put it all together, but she could feel herself getting closer. The words were coming with less effort; she was understanding more. Ian had been gone for two sunrises—she was sure of that—and with each new day, she felt herself getting stronger.

She could remember their names effortlessly now. There was Lara, the child-woman who sucked her thumb and wanted a family; Andrew, the earnest young man with the shaking hands and hopeful eyes; Queen Victoria, who spoke in a strange voice that vibrated with self-confidence; Edith, the housekeeper, who almost always seemed angry with the others. Sometimes the quiet one, Dotty, flitted through her room before disappearing into a closet or armoire.

"Where is Maeve?" Selena said suddenly.

A stunned silence fell over the jumble of conversation.

"Sweet Mary," Edith said, pressing her pudgy hand to her gaping mouth.

It took Selena a moment to realize what had taken place. She'd spoken her thoughts in a clear, understandable way—and she'd done it without a moment's hesitation.

Hope accelerated her heartbeat. Maybe that was the key. Maybe she'd been concentrating so hard and trying so valiantly, she'd made it impossible for herself. Perhaps that was her mistake. Ian had made her tense and nervous, desperate to perform well. Here, in the midst of her new friends, she felt no such pressure.

Smiling, she tried again. "Maeve came ..." *to my room last* "... night."

Her smile fell. Defeat rounded her shoulders. Staring at Andrew, she gave him a futile little shrug. "Not so better."

He stepped toward her. "You're much better, Selena. Naturally you have trouble speaking. I expect it's normal after such a bash to the noggin."

Selena understood the most important word: normal. It sifted through her heart and made her smile again. She reached out, took Andrew's hand in hers.

He blinked and tried to draw back. "What ... what are you doing?"

"Thank ... you. Andrew."

The queen sighed. " 'E gods, they're going to kiss."

Andrew's face flamed. He jerked his hand back and spun around to face Edith, the queen, and Lara. "All right, ladies, as of now, we're Miss Selena's teachers."

"I say she gets dressed first," the queen said. "Clothes are the window of the soul."

Edith shook her head. "Really, Your Highness, we've had this discussion. 'Tis the *eyes* that are the windows to the soul."

"Clothes."

"Eyes."

Something about the argument seemed absurdly

funny to Selena. She couldn't help herself. She started
to laugh.

Beside her, Lara giggled.

"How could eyes be made of glass? Everyone knows
that windows are glass," the queen said earnestly.

Andrew shot Selena a funny look. His eyes crinkled
in the corners, his mouth twitched.

Edith frowned and glanced at the faces around her.
"They're laughin' at us, Your Highness."

The queen's eyes rounded. Then a quick smile
quirked one side of her mouth. A deep, breathy chuckle
slipped out.

There was a moment of stunned silence, and then everyone was laughing. The booming sound filled the tiny
room.

Selena had never experienced such exhilaration. She
felt wonderfully, joyously alive.

"I . . . love . . . to laugh," Lara said with a gap-
toothed grin.

Finally the laughter melted away, leaving a silence
that was warm and welcoming.

The queen wiped the tears from her cheeks and
turned to Selena. "Thank you, child. It's been a long
time. . . ."

"You're welcome," Selena answered automatically.

The queen rapped her on the nose with her open fan.
"You're welcome, *Your Highness*. That's me. You may
address me as Queen Victoria or Your Highness."

Selena watched her mouth form the words. "Your . . .
Highness."

The queen beamed. "She will come to me for lessons
first, of course."

"What will you teach her?" Andrew asked.

"The essentials. How to walk with books on her
head. How to wave and curtsy. An overview of the
peerage." Her fleshy face scrunched in a thoughtful
frown. "Tea etiquette is crucial."

"*That* should help her in the real world," Andrew said.

The queen looked up sharply. "Do you think she'll ever see the real world?"

"Why not? She's not crazy."

"Neither am I," snorted the queen. "If it weren't for my evil twin sister, Vicky the sneak, I'd be on the throne right now." The queen turned and began pacing the room, fanning herself, muttering.

Selena went to the queen. "Help me."

The queen paused, turned. "You accept that I am the real and true inheritor of the throne of England?"

Selena had no idea what she'd just been asked. So she nodded.

The queen smiled. "Today we shall begin with my realm of expertise."

Edith rolled her eyes. "This is all nonsense. But I shall teach her how to do housework. Assuming she doesn't burn the bloody house down, that should give her a way to earn a decent livin'. Ye needn't speak to be a good housekeeper."

"Don't need much of a brain, neither," the queen added.

Andrew seemed to think for a minute, then he grinned. "I don't have many necessary skills, but I can improve her vocabulary. I'll start by marking the items in the house and yard."

"But who's going to teach her to think?" Edith asked.

They all looked at each other blankly, from one to the other. Then, slowly, Lara raised her hand. "I will."

The queen heaved a sigh. "Phew. So it's all settled. Now, what shall she wear for teatime?" She glanced around the room and spied the bronze silk gown Maeve had left. "Ah, perfect." She picked up the dress and turned to Selena. "This shall do for today."

Selena stroked the soft fabric. "Silk."

"So it is."

Edith came forward, touched the buttons on Selena's

lawn nightdress. "Remember buttons . . . how to un-hook them?"

Selena understood. She unbuttoned her gown and whipped it over her head.

Naked, she grinned at the faces around her.

Andrew swallowed. His face turned scarlet. "Oh, Lord," he said in a thick, reedy voice.

"Get out, Andrew!" Edith screeched, motioning for the door.

He spun and scrambled out of the room, slamming the door shut behind him.

Selena knew she'd done something wrong again, but she didn't know what it could possibly be. She'd unbut-toned her gown and undressed just as Edith had taught her. She looked at Edith. "Wrong?"

Edith nodded. "Don't get undressed in front of peo-ple. It isn't proper."

Selena looked at the faces around her. She thought that people meant more than one person, but obviously she was wrong. "People?"

"Andrew," Edith clarified. "Don't get undressed around Andrew."

"Oh," Selena said. There was something special about Andrew. "I understand."

"Good. Now, let's get you dressed."

Edith showed Selena how to tie her lace-edged knee-length drawers and slip into the flimsy chemise. Selena concentrated very carefully, making sure that the queen wrote down every motion required, so that Selena could read and reread it.

There were more clothes than she could have imag-ined. Selena repeated every word she heard at least twice, until she understood and remembered that the small brown items were *boots* and that the silken leg coverings were *stockings*.

"Next is the corset." Edith held up an hourglass-shaped white satin bodice with pink ribbons at the clo-sure. It looked very stiff.

"Corset," Selena repeated, standing still as Edith fitted the garment over her breasts and beneath her arms.

"Hold on to the bed frame," Edith said, "and suck in a breath."

Selena did as she was told.

Edith yanked the corset tight.

Selena gasped for air. Blinking white lights danced in front of her eyes. Her fingers released their grip on the wooden post, and she wrenched sideways.

"It ain't tight enough. Come back—" Edith ran after her.

Selena stood her ground, arms akimbo, her breath coming in great, wheezing gasps. "No. No corset."

"But *ladies*—"

"No."

"But 'tis proper. Dr. Carrick—"

The queen hushed Edith with a wave. "He isn't here. Besides, the muddle-headed doctor will hide in the dark like he always does. What does he care if Selena here wears a corset?"

Edith shrugged. "I give up. Fine, Selena, no corset for you."

Selena smiled. "Hurts."

The queen laughed. "See, Edith? Even a woman with half a brain knows that damned thing ain't right."

Edith sighed. "You're the queen. Change the fashion."

"I will—just as soon as my evil twin dies. Then ... then I'll let women wear pants."

Edith cracked a smile. "No wonder they locked you up."

Selena looked up. "Pants ... like Andrew?"

Edith shook her head. "No, Selena. Absolutely not."

The narrow main street of Alabaster, Maine, glowed like its namesake in the rising sun. White clapboard houses, placed neatly on brown patches of dead grass and hemmed by white picket fences, told in wordless prose the tale of ordinary family life. Although it was quiet now in the last moments before dawn, the streets devoid of sound or motion, Ian could imagine this place on a summer's day. Crowded sidewalks and teeming streets; the warm, humid air thick with the sounds of a small town—children's laughter, adults talking, the steady clip-clop of horses' hooves on the stone pavement.

The carriage hurtled down the street without stopping or slowing, which was just as well, for Ian had no reason to do either. He had been through a hundred towns like this in his life. They dotted the New England countryside like pearls tossed across an immense emerald canvas.

Ever since childhood, Ian had secretly dreamed of living in a place like this, a place where neighbors knew each other and shared Sunday suppers, where mothers wore aprons and smiles and never spoke to their dead husbands aloud.

"I hate towns like this," Johann said dully. "Pretty on the outside and rotting within."

Ian felt a flash of anger. "Now who's the cynical bastard?"

Ian glanced out the window again. The brilliant orange sun had just crested the thick, black blanket of trees, throwing light on the still-darkened houses.

"Ah," Johann said, crossing one leg gracefully over the other. "I bet you wish you'd grown up here. Scratch the surface of a scientist and you'll find a dreamer."

Ian refused to be drawn into this conversation. "We'll be at the local law office any second. After that, I'll expect you to return to Lethe House and make my apologies."

"Not a chance."

"What?"

"If you must desert our fair moon-goddess, then do so. But you and you alone will tell her what you've done. I will tell them simply that you've gone to the city for brain surgery and a soul replacement. It certainly *should* be true."

"Fine."

An awkward silence fell into the carriage. Ian stared out the window, seeing little beyond the jostling blur of white and green.

Finally the carriage jerked to a stop. There was a scrambling overhead, then a thump, and the door creaked open. Ian's driver, Fergus, stood in the opening, his breath coming in great plumed feathers. He hooked a thumb at the building behind him. "There's the office, sir."

"Good. Unload my things, Fergus, and engage me another carriage. I shall be going on to New York City posthaste."

"And Mr. Strassborg?"

Ian's gaze remained steady. "Mr. Strassborg will be taking my carriage back to Lethe House immediately ... where he belongs."

"Ah, Ian." Johann's voice rang with derision. "You wound me to the quick."

Ian ignored the soft cadence of Johann's laughter as he jumped out of the carriage and strode up the dirt path to the squat, single-storied clapboard building that housed Alabaster's jail, courthouse, and post office.

At the door, he paused, then drew a deep breath and pushed through.

The room was large and airy, lit by several lanterns that hung suspended from rough-hewn beams across the ceiling. In the corner, a thin, stoop-shouldered old man sat behind a rickety wooden desk, a heap of rusty keys by his hand.

The old man looked up, an expectant light in his pale eyes. "Hello." He planted his hands on the desk and pushed to his feet. Stepping around the desk, he shuffled toward Ian, his hand outstretched in greeting. "Jed Larkham. What can I do for you, young man?"

Ian stared at the big-knuckled, gnarled hand. Instinctively he drew back and shoved his hands in the huge pockets of his cloak. "I'm Dr. Ian Carrick."

Jed jerked to a dead stop and yanked his hand back. Recognition widened his rheumy eyes and leeched the color from his cheeks. "Dr. Carrick." He whispered the name, glanced at the exit door behind him. "What a surprise. We'd heard—" He realized apparently that to speak was to err and snapped his mouth shut.

Ian's lips shifted in an amused sneer. "I'm sure you have."

Jed swallowed hard and hurried back to the safety of his desk, sitting down with an audible sigh. Only after long moments had passed in awkward silence did he look up. "Why are you in Alabaster?"

Ian walked across the room and sat down in the chair opposite the old man. "I've found a girl . . . woman . . ." He paused, trying to find the right words.

Jed strummed his finger nervously on the desk. "A l-local girl?"

Ian's chin snapped up. He stared at the man through narrowed eyes. "This is not a matter of the heart, Mr. Larkham. The woman has come into my care in a medical matter. I simply want to return her to her family."

"Oh." The man's relief was palpable. "If you'll give me her name, I can tell you—"

"That's the problem," he answered. "She's suffered an injury to her brain from some manner of fall or collision. She doesn't recall her name . . . or much else, for that matter. But someone out there must know an adult woman who is missing."

"You offering a reward?"

"And draw every crackpot for a thousand miles? No, thanks. I want someone—hopefully her family—to claim *her,* not just a pile of money."

Jed pulled his drawer open and extracted a sheet of paper and a pen. "What does she look like?"

"That's a problem, as well. She's bruised extensively. So much so that I cannot accurately describe her features. However, she has very long, reddish brown hair and brown eyes. I suppose she's about five foot seven inches tall." He thought a bit, trying to come up with anything else that would help her family identify her. "She has all her teeth and came to us without jewelry. Her age is probably somewhere between eighteen and fifty."

Jed set his pen down and plopped his chin in the palm of his hand. "This doesn't help much."

"I am aware of that. Is anyone missing in town?"

Jed shook his head. "Nope. But I'll post this for you and keep my eyes and ears open."

"Thank you, Mr. Larkham." He pushed the chair back and got to his feet. Turning, he headed for the door.

"Uh ... Dr. Carrick?"

Ian stopped but didn't bother to turn around. He knew what was coming now. It was what always followed. "Yes, Mr. Larkham?"

"I ... uh, that is, we all heard about your accident."

"It was no accident, Mr. Larkham."

"Yes, well, anyway, we heard that you'd been ... changed by the ... event."

Ian released a bitter laugh.

"The mayor of Alabaster—that's old Thomas Markette—he lost his twelve-year-old daughter recently. All we found was a bit of lace from her gown. I thought maybe if you could touch it ..."

Ian clenched his jaw and closed his eyes. It was always the same. People were afraid of him and didn't really believe in the rumors of his psychic abilities, but they weren't sure. They wanted him to prove it to them, help them answer the inexplicable and find the utterly lost, and then they would believe—for a second. But they would still be afraid, still shun him the second after he helped them, and God save him from their wrath when he failed.

Jed pulled a dirty, ripped bit of lace from a desk

drawer. It looked small and frail in the man's gnarled fingers.

Ian stared at the lace, felt the familiar sense of panic, of uselessness, descend. He wanted to turn away, to tell the old man to forget it, that he was no real psychic. But he couldn't. As always, the lure was there, the hope that this time it would be different.

Slowly he reached out, took the scrap of fabric, scratchy, limp, and fragile.

Of course, he got no images, no information. Just the same sickening thought anyone would have—that a girl, a child, was out there somewhere, alone and lost. And there wasn't a damn thing Ian could do to save her.

He released the piece of lace as if it were suddenly on fire. It drifted to the desk, a blot of white against the burnished wood. "You have obviously been misinformed, Mr. Larkham. My gift—" the word dripped sarcasm "—does not extend to fondling bits of lace. Good day."

Ian strode down the gravel path, his head held high. He knew he was being absurd, but he felt unseen eyes on him, heard the whisper of gossip on the wind, felt it nipping at his heels.

He ought to be used to Larkham's reaction. It was common enough, but it had been so long since he'd been out in the world, he'd almost forgotten. Or the memory had become blurred, faded by too many bottles of scotch and too many nights alone. In some ways, he'd forgotten how frightening and compelling his curse was to everyone. People viewed him as something more than a man, and something less—a terrifying incarnation that was part Gabriel and part Satan. Except for the dreadful few who followed him like lapdogs, begging for the parlor trick of his touch.

He saw Fergus and the rented carriage awaiting him. Without a sideways glance, he climbed into the coach and thumped his fist on the ceiling. The carriage lurched forward, the door slammed shut. They were off to the next town.

The next town. The next pair of frightened eyes watching him warily, waiting for the infamous doctor to dissolve into hysteria, the next outstretched hand . . .

He sighed. Perhaps he should give up.

What was Selena to him? He could continue to feed and support her for the rest of her life without a thought to the cost. She could remain under his roof for years, a nameless, faceless presence in the darkened hallways, saying nothing, thinking less. What was one more broken soul in the house of insanity?

Even as he had the thought, he knew the answer.

Selena would never be just another lunatic at Lethe House. She would haunt him with her presence, with her very existence, every day, every night, for the remainder of his sorry life. With every movement she took, he'd find himself reaching out to help her; with every stumbling word she uttered, he'd find himself praying for more. He remembered her as she'd been the other morning—sitting on the floor, her hair and face a horrible mess, a dead mouse dangling from her fingertips. Then he remembered Elizabeth, sitting by the window, a silvery trail of drool rolling down her cheek, plopping on her lap. The two images merged in his mind and caused a sickening sense of loss and shame. If only he were a stronger, better man. A man who could care for her as she was—brain-damaged and imperfect. A man who needed less and therefore saw more.

But he wasn't such a man. For him, nothing could be worse than seeing Selena slowly disintegrate into Elizabeth. Nothing. It would kill him, just as it killed Giles. Bit by bit, day by day, Ian would lose what little hold he had on his own sanity. It was that simple. He had to get rid of her to save his own soul.

It was childish and selfish . . . and true. He wasn't one to glamorize his failings or pretend they didn't exist. He was a selfish man and always had been. But never had it been as disgustingly apparent as it was right now.

He'd stay away as long as he could, meet as many strangers as he had to. And he'd pray that someone would come for his broken goddess.

Chapter Twelve

Selena lay in bed with the thick folds of her coverlet drawn close. For a few precious seconds, before she came fully awake, the promise of a new dawn filled her consciousness. It was still dark outside, but soon, soon the dawn would come.

Today they'd promised to take her outside.

She eased her eyelids open and stared at the window. Even the shadowed streaks of the iron bars couldn't daunt her enthusiasm today. She stretched languidly and pushed the coverlet back. Sitting up, she glanced around the room, trying to remember the morning sequence she'd been taught by Lara.

Wash your face. Sit on the toilet.

Selena smiled at the ease with which she retrieved the memory. She swung her stockinged feet onto the cold wooden floor and walked to the commode. It felt strangely inappropriate to walk. On such a special day, she should move in a flowing, magical way.

She poured tepid water into the porcelain bowl and washed her face. Reaching for the towel beside the basin, she caught sight of her reflection in the oval mirror and paused, her hand frozen in midair.

She leaned closer to the mirror, able to see the shape of her face at last. Her eyes were no longer swallowed by swollen layers of bruised flesh. She could see them clearly now, and in looking into her own eyes, she felt as if she were finally seeing some portion of herself.

Mesmerized, she touched her own cheek and marveled at the soft pliancy of her flesh. The ugly purple and black bruising had softened to a sick greenish yellow with tinges of brown.

Selena thought it was the most beautiful color she'd ever seen. It was the color of change, the color of *healing*.

She touched the cool, slick surface of the mirror. "Who are you?" she whispered, watching in fascination as her pale pink lips formed the words.

Dark, mysterious brown eyes stared back at her.

She tried to care about the answer, genuinely tried. It was what they all expected of her, what Ian expected.

But she couldn't manufacture concern where none existed. She didn't care about the past; what she wanted was the future. She ached to begin, to cross the threshold of this room and this house and explore this new world, to experience sensations and thoughts and feelings that she couldn't even imagine.

Today she'd take her first step. Yesterday she'd spent all day in the house. Edith had taught her to pluck the feathers from a dead, clammy bird (which she refused on principle to eat; it was horrid, really, to think of eating a once-living animal). After the plucking fiasco, Edith had moved her from the kitchen to the parlor and taught her to wipe the furniture with a thick, waxy substance that smelled heavenly.

So heavenly that Selena had eaten it.

That's when Edith moved her into the bedroom. Selena still didn't entirely understand the teachings of that day, couldn't pinpoint exactly what she'd done so wrong, but she'd learned one lesson clearly: She could eat dead animals, but not the cleaning supplies.

It was a strange world with inexplicable rules.

In the bedroom, she'd had a wee bit of trouble. She'd started out well enough with making the bed. Lara showed her how to beat the quilt and pillow into shape, and Selena had learned that lesson well.

She'd been doing fine until a beautiful white feather burped out of the pillow and floated on a draft of air from the open window.

Selena had never seen anything so lovely in all her life. A million motes of dust filtered the cold, sun-drenched air. The curtains fluttered softly against the pane. And that exquisite feather just floated and floated, then fell to the floor.

Suddenly the pillow became a magical storehouse of hidden treasures. Selena ripped it wide open and plunged her hands in, tossing the down feathers all around. She and Lara laughed and played, mesmerized by the beauty and feel of the feather-storm.

Edith had not been mesmerized. All she'd seen was a *mess,* and when Selena tried to show her the elegance of a single feather in its dancing spiral to the floor, Edith was unimpressed.

In fact, the housekeeper had said *quit this bloody nonsense.*

Neither Selena nor Lara understood the word "nonsense," but Edith had shown them what "quit" was. The housekeeper had thrown her hands up in the air and stomped out of the room. She had not returned.

Selena understood then that she was no longer learning to be a housekeeper. It disappointed her, that unexpected failure, but she had tried not to be unhappy about it. She tried instead to focus on each new lesson.

She'd failed as a housekeeper, but she'd done well as a *subject of the Crown.* The queen had expressed great pleasure over Selena's successes. Even now, Selena recalled how to drop into the strange motion called a curtsy. She remembered, too, that she was to curtsy to everyone in the house except Edith, who was *the help,* and Lara, who was *feebleminded,* and Edith's husband, who was a *hopeless drunk and stupid besides.*

Everyone else, declared the queen, was Selena's social superior and, as such, required a curtsy. Especially the king.

Selena had curtsied so much, she felt dizzy every time someone new walked into the room. But she'd done it, followed the odd custom and mastered a new skill. She could also pour and sip the tasteless, tongue-scalding liquid called *T,* and do it with her pinky finger pointing to the ceiling. And the queen pronounced Selena's royal wave *second to none.*

Selena turned away from the mirror at last and reached for the bronze gown, which lay heaped over the back of her chair. She winced at the thought of putting it on again and involuntarily drew her hand back.

Everything they'd taught her about being a *lady* was either uncomfortable or senseless. She wanted to refuse, wanted to wear pants like Andrew's and a big silk shirt that hung loose to her knees. She wanted big, bold colors, too, colors that reminded her of words like sky, sea, dandelion, iris, grass. Somehow, the colors brought back more images and memories than anything else. A white nightdress made her think of snow and frost and starlight, of a steaming stream of milk from a cow's pink teat, of a daisy's velvet petals. Sometimes she had the words to match the images, sometimes she simply received a mental picture and the word would inexplicably pop into her head an hour later. It didn't matter; all that mattered were the so-called memories, the bits and pieces that hinted at a beautiful world out there, a universe of sight and sound and vibrant color. A mysterious world that beckoned her with seductive possibilities.

And today she would see it for the first time. She picked up the dress, which reminded her suddenly that green leaves turn brown in the autumn, and slipped it over her head. Smoothing the folds of ecru lace at the throat, she buttoned the tight bodice and skirt and went to the bed to wait.

Freedom was moments away.

* * *

The knock came. Selena lurched out of bed and heard the wrenching hiss of torn fabric. Wincing, she glanced down, and saw that her bodice had ripped open, revealing a wide swath of her white chemise. Her breasts swelled over the lacy neckline.

The knock sounded again. "Selena?" Andrew said through the closed door. "Are you decent?"

Selena frowned. *Decent*. She must have misunderstood the word—she thought it meant moral, and moral meant nice. Why would Andrew ask if she was nice? "Yes."

"Good." The door opened wide and Andrew walked through. He grinned down at her. Then suddenly he froze. His gaze widened, fixed on her chemise. "Y-Your gown."

"Tight."

Color crept up his neck and fanned across his face. "Y-Yes, but . . ." He glanced back at the door, as if he was going to run away.

She pitched forward. "No go." She grabbed his arm and anchored herself to him. "We go . . . outside. Learn. See."

Andrew licked his lips and looked everywhere except at her breasts. Before he could answer, Edith and Maeve walked into the room.

Edith took one look at Selena's gown and rolled her eyes. "Jesus, Mary, and Joseph. I never had so much trouble keepin' a lunatic dressed."

Maeve gave Selena a slow, sleepy smile.

Selena felt a tightening in her chest. She didn't realize until that moment how much she'd missed Maeve, how afraid Selena had been that her friend had somehow vanished. "Maeve. Missed you."

Still smiling, Maeve turned slightly and started hitting her forehead against the wall.

"Stop that," Edith growled. "You're giving *me* a headache."

Selena rushed to Maeve's side and touched her shoulder. "Maeve," she whispered.

Maeve kept striking her head.

Every *thump-thump-thump* of Maeve's head against the wall hit her like a blow. She turned to Edith. "Why?"

"Don't bother askin', lassie," Edith said quietly. "She's mad as a loon some days. Ye never know when."

"Mad?" Selena repeated the word, then frowned. She grabbed Maeve by the shoulders and drew her away from the wall. Maeve turned, looked up at Selena through dull, watery eyes. A puffy discoloration marked her forehead already.

Maeve didn't look angry; she looked sad. "No," Selena said quietly, brushing a straggly, dirty lock of hair from Maeve's eyes. "Not mad. Hurt."

Maeve blinked slowly and a smile tugged at one corner of her mouth. Selena knew that Maeve was going to recognize her finally, going to speak to her. She smiled in encouragement.

Maeve gave her a full-fledged grin. "My husband's home. I can hear the carriage." She yanked up her heavy skirts and raced for the door, disappearing in less than a second.

"I'm goin' mad at last, myself," Edith said, shaking her head. "I can hear a carriage, too."

Andrew hurried to the window and wrenched the curtains aside. The still-dark sky filled the glass. "Someone's here."

Selena's heart seemed to stop. The moment spilled out, breathless with anticipation. A single word burned through her mind, filled her. "Ian," she whispered.

"It's Johann," Andrew said after a few moments. "He's alone."

Selena sagged in disappointment. Before she could muster the enthusiasm to speak, Andrew was beside her, clasping her hand, pulling her into the hallway.

"Come along, Selena, hurry. We need to speak to Johann."

They hastened down the steep stairway and rushed through the darkened foyer. At the door, Andrew paused. He jerked his outstretched hand back, plunged it in his pocket, as if the doorknob frightened him.

Selena reached past him and pulled the door open. Cool air swept into the house, brought with it a swirl of bright green leaves.

She stopped, awed by the feel of the breeze against her face, the smell of it. Her skirt fluttered against her ankles, hair whispered against her forehead.

The night-stained lawn pushed away from her, melted into the shadowy stand of trees. Bloodred streamers of dawn wafted across the distant horizon, a blurry cascade of fire in the darkness.

Johann slammed the coach door shut and walked up the path, his bootheels making a marvelous crunching sound with every step. "Better hurry back inside, Andrew. It'll be morning soon."

Andrew cocked his head toward Selena. His eyes bulged in silent communication.

"I see. You've found a companion at last." Johann laughed at his own wit. "Sort of brings Mary Shelley to mind, don't you think?"

"It's not what you think, Johann," Andrew said in a breathless voice.

Johann paused, cocked his hip, and stared at Selena. His gaze started at her small, bare toes sticking out from beneath her gown, traveling up her body slowly to the place where her bodice was ripped.

Selena felt an odd heat begin in her stomach.

Johann loosed a slow smile. One eyebrow cocked upward. "Her face is much improved, Andrew. And she looks to have an impressive set of tits."

Selena didn't understand everything he said, but she knew he'd said something about her face. No doubt he'd noticed how much better she looked.

"Shh," Andrew hissed. "She can understand you."

Johann languidly lifted one arm and started straightening the lace at his sleeve. "Of course she does, Andrew, and I'm King George."

Selena immediately fell into a curtsy. Straightening slowly, she extended her right arm, wrist dipped, in greeting. She lowered her lashes in deference, as she'd been taught. "Your Highness."

Johann froze. The color faded from his cheeks and he shot a quick look at Andrew. "Holy shit."

Selena frowned. That wasn't the correct response. She must have done something incorrectly. She curtsied again and extended her arm. "Greetings, Your Highness."

Johann took her hand and kissed it. "Greetings, goddess," he said softly, looking at her over the ridge of her fingers. "Can you say something to me?"

Something about the way he looked at her made Selena uncomfortable. Her cheeks felt hot.

"She can read," Andrew remarked.

"She *what*?" Johann turned and went back to the carriage, reaching inside. Pulling a book out, he opened it to a random page. "Read this, goddess."

Selena focused on the words he'd pointed to, forcing herself to breathe deeply. " 'Keeps his pale court in beauty and decay. He came. Lost angel of . . .' " She frowned, unable to read the last word. " 'Par . . .' "

"Paradise," Johann said quietly.

She looked up and saw the genuine smile on Johann's gaunt face. "Paradise," she repeated.

"Sweet Jesus," he murmured, touching her chin, tilting her face up. "Our esteemed leader was wrong."

Selena ignored the confusing jumble of his words. "You help me learn?"

"Of course I will, goddess. Andrew and I shall teach you all the words you've forgotten." He turned to Andrew. "It should be quite a moment when Ian returns."

Selena's heartbeat sped up. "Ian?"

Johann turned back to her, a sad, understanding look in his eyes. "He's gone, goddess. I don't know when he'll return."

Selena understood *gone*. When you pinched the candlewick, the fire changed into smoke and was gone. She looked up at Johann, tried to force the words out. "Here is home."

Very slowly, Johann smiled. "Yes, this is home for Ian. And sooner or later, people always come home. Even idiots like Dr. Carrick."

One month to the day after he'd left, Ian returned.

He stood outside the closed wrought-iron gates of Lethe House, staring through the intricately formed black bars, listening to the fading sounds of his rented carriage as it disappeared back down the road. Night curled around him, comforting in its anonymity; he wished fleetingly that he hadn't wired ahead with notice of his return.

Overhead, the moon was a bright, pearlescent plate wreathed in glowing gray clouds. Wind whispered through the pine needles, brushed the hair at the back of his neck. He drew his cloak tighter around his body. It was an instinctive move. Though he knew it was cold out, bitingly cold in this midnight hour, he couldn't really feel it.

He felt detached from his body, his feelings as removed as the stars hidden behind the hazy veil, as distant as tomorrow's pale sunlight. With each passing day in New York, he'd felt himself sinking deeper into a darkness from which there was no escape.

He'd thought to find peace in the city, some respite from the guilt and desperation he'd felt in Alabaster. And for the first few days, things had been quiet enough. The staff had waited on him hand and foot, careful never to touch or speak to their infamous employer; no one said a word when he staggered through the house at night, blind drunk.

But somehow, word of his arrival had leaked out, bits and pieces of gossip sliding through the sewer system, tinkling in glasses of expensive champagne. The gawkers had been the first to come, hovering outside his front door, waiting breathlessly for a sighting of the notorious doctor. Next had come his fellow physicians, wanting advice from their peerless peer; all the while watching him from beneath hooded eyelids, smiling when he refused to shake their hands.

Surprisingly, he'd been less upset by them than before. He could handle the sickly curious. It was the others, the last to arrive, who had sent him scurrying back to the safety of Lethe House like the night crawler he'd become.

They invariably came dressed in black, their heads down, clutching a photograph, a bit of lace, an old daguerreotype. He knew the moment one of them arrived, could see the stark ravages of fear and despair in their eyes. The desperate.

Help us, Dr. Carrick ... we've lost our precious daughter.... My baby boy is suffering from a strange illness; touch him, Dr. Carrick, and tell me if he will live.... I'm dying, Dr. Carrick. Use your gift and save me.

Save me ... save me ... save me ...

Their words were always the same, always futile, hopeless pleas that filled him with shame and horror and disgust. He'd tried to run from it, but there was no relief, either inside the house or out. They reached out for him, clawed at him every time he left the house, fell to their knees when he passed them on the street. The soft aftermath of their sobs followed him wherever he went.

Liquor had only made things worse. With every swallow of fire, he'd become drowsier and more morose. Images of Selena besieged him, hovered at his bedside like a mournful ghost, taunting, teasing, beckoning. At first the images of Elizabeth had been ever-present, a weight on his shoulder that kept him reaching for the bottle, but as time went on, he had more and more trouble bringing forth the pictures. Instead, he imagined Selena. Not as she was, of course, but as he wanted her to be. Beautiful, normal, talking to him in a soft, husky voice that formed real sentences and spoke about real things.

For days, before the pathetic entourage began arriving, he sat in his study, steeped in the familiar bosom of scotch, trying to eradicate all thoughts of her. But the more he pushed her away, the more his obsession rooted itself in his soul. As always, he was incapable of doing anything halfway. Instead of hoping in a quiet, scientific fashion that she would survive, he'd imbued her with all his hopes and dreams and prayers. He'd thought she could somehow redeem him.

Such a fool. He'd known better. Deep inside himself, beneath the sick obsession, he'd known the truth from the beginning. There was no hope for Selena. Not one of the books he'd read promised even a ray of promise for a recovery. She was brain-damaged, and she always would be.

He stood there, swaying softly in the cold night air. Ahead, the house stood in the midst of the shadowy yard, alone and indomitable and in need of repair. Glass windows blinked in the inconsequential light, the white trim appeared dull and gray.

There were no lights on, and he'd expected none, and yet he knew that someone was awake in there, someone was watching him. He searched the windows, his gaze moving from one barred square to the next, trying to make out a shadow within a shadow, a whisper of movement when all else was motionless and still.

He's home.

The thought slammed into his head. He winced and staggered back at the force of the sudden knowledge.

He should have known better than to return on the night of a full moon.

Ian forced himself to walk down the path slowly, then he went up the creaking steps and into the darkened foyer.

"Come on out. I know you're here," he whispered into the still, black room.

No one answered.

He moved into the study and whipped off his cloak, tossing it over a chair. Lighting a lamp, he poured himself a stiff drink and headed up the stairs.

His mother stood on the landing, her unbound hair splayed out across her shoulders, her hands at her waist, her fingers furiously working the ribbon.

His breath released in a tired sigh. "Mother, go back to bed."

"Were you going to see Selena?"

"No."

"Many things have changed in your absence."

He sighed, saying nothing.

Maeve stepped toward him. He saw her fear in tiny, familiar movements—the way her fingers tightened around the strip of satin, the way she bit down on her lower lip. It sickened and shamed him as it always did—the proof that his own mother feared him.

She stopped directly in front of him and looked up. He didn't need to read her mind to know her thoughts. He needed only to look into her anxious eyes. She was afraid he'd laugh at her and turn away before she spoke. But still she was here, standing in front of him, blocking his path.

It was unusual, her sudden temerity, and it intrigued him. He leaned against the cold wall and crossed his arms, waiting.

"W-We've had a . . . meeting," she said in a breathy rush.

"We?"

"The residents of the house."

"Oh, really? Busting out, are you?"

"We've been helping Selena."

He stiffened, pulled infinitesimally away from the wall. "Helping her do what?"

Nervously Maeve wet her lips. Some emotion that looked like pride filled her eyes. She squared her shoulders. "I taught her to eat like a lady. The queen taught her to curtsy."

A horrifying image of Selena dropping into a mechanical, jerking curtsy flashed through Ian's mind. He closed his eyes and tried to banish it. "How nice. Good night, Mother." He started to turn away.

"I didn't give you permission to leave."

The authority in her voice caught Ian off guard. Surprised, he turned back to her. "Excuse me?"

"No, I do not." She licked her lips again and blinked up at him. He could see how much that order had cost her, how it frightened her to say it.

Something was out of the ordinary. She stood tall and straight, her flyaway hair a halo around her pale, oval face. Hazel eyes stared up at him, clear and lucid.

He felt a spark of pride at her composure. "What is it, Mother?"

"Selena is not like the rest of us, Ian."

"No, Mother. You're crazy. She's brain-damaged."

"No. She's almost normal."

Almost. The simple words caused a pain deep in his chest. He thought fleetingly of Elizabeth, hunched over in her chair by the window, watching a world she was no longer a part of. No doubt Maeve would think that Elizabeth was "almost normal" as well. "Because she can eat and curtsy? What was I thinking? No doubt she's ready to attend the opera."

"I want your word that you will teach her about the world."

"Fine."

"Tomorrow."

He frowned. "Sooner or later—"

"Tomorrow."

"Fine, Mother. I'll sit at her bedside and wipe the

drool from her mouth and tell her about this godfor-saken world we live in. Maybe she'll even understand something after I say hello."

Maeve seemed unable to stop a quick smile. "We shall see who learns what."

Ian rolled his eyes. "Good night."

"Good night, Ian. Selena and I shall meet you on the beach tomorrow morning."

"Of course you will, Mother. No doubt you'll be an-alyzing Plato."

He saw her reaction, knew instantly that he'd hurt her. He wished he could take the bitterness in his voice back, wished he'd simply walked away without uttering that last, telling sentence.

She expected something of him tonight, something that hadn't been a part of their relationship in years, in a lifetime. Honesty, perhaps. Understanding. He didn't know. But he could see now, in her sad, sad eyes, that he had failed her. Again.

"Oh, Ian . . ." She moved toward him, raising a pale, slim hand. At the last moment, when she was so close that he could see the sheen of tears in her eyes, and the network of lines around her mouth, she stopped. Her hand fell to her side again.

Strangely, he found himself missing the touch that had never been. "What is it, Mother?"

She stared up at him, unblinking, her face impossibly pale in the darkness. "I would change it all if I could."

Ian felt as if he'd been punched in the stomach. His breath released in a harsh sigh. He gazed down at her, trying to find the right words. But there were none, and both of them knew it. "I . . . know you're sorry. . . ."

Tears glittered in her eyes. "But you don't care." Be-fore he could respond, Maeve ducked her head and scurried away from him. She slipped back into her bed-room and shut the door behind her.

Ian leaned back against the wall and closed his eyes. Why couldn't he reach out to his mother? Why couldn't he be *human* around her instead of always acting like such an angry, petulant child?

With a sigh, he drew back.

She wanted what she'd always wanted from him—absolution; he was unable to truly forgive her. He wished he were different, wished he could smile and shrug and tell her it didn't matter.

But it would be a lie, more hurtful to both of them than a flat truth could ever be.

"I care, Mother," he said softly, his voice lost in the dark shadows of the hallway. Words felt so deeply, he couldn't say them any louder, couldn't say them to her face. He cared. He'd always cared.

He just didn't know what difference it made.

Chapter Thirteen

❦

The next morning, Ian walked down the path to the beach. The sound of feminine laughter filtered through the trees, intruding on the shadowy silence. For a split second, Ian's step faltered.

The alien sound came again, throaty and mesmerizing, drawing Ian through the trees to the shoreline. He paused in the shadow of the forest and gazed out to the beach, seeking the source of the laughter.

Maeve and Lara were directly in front of him, sitting on a high, lichen-covered granite ledge. Beside them stood a rickety easel, complete with multicolored canvas and a haphazardly stationed row of paint jars. A big paintbrush, its black tip stained a bright sunrise yellow, lay on the rock beside it, apparently forgotten. The painting was a whimsical rendering of the beach, with scarlet rocks and radiant blue waves and a rainbow of a morning sky above it all.

Maeve sat on the craggy lip of rock, her hands in her lap, her hair loose and flowing about her shoulders. She saw him instantly, and when she did, a small, mysterious smile curved her lips. Her gaze moved away from him, turned pointedly to the tide pools below.

Even before he turned, Ian knew what he would find, whom he would see. He knew it, felt it, and yet he couldn't believe it. Very slowly, he followed Maeve's gaze.

She was on the beach below, squatted down on a barnacle-covered rock, her face hidden by a thick mass of damp, stringy hair. She was wearing an oversized man's shirt and baggy pants that completely concealed her shape.

"Selena." He whispered her name in awe. She was out of bed, walking, moving.

Almost normal. His mother's words came back to him, stunning him with their seductive power.

Selena pressed a drinking glass over her right eye and tilted forward, plunging her face in the icy water. Her hair splayed out around her, floated on the surface of the water, then slowly sank.

Ian turned to his mother. "Jesus! She's going to drown."

Maeve peered over the ledge. "I don't think so. It's only a few inches of water."

Selena came up, flipping her soggy hair away from her face like some ancient mermaid. For a split second, he saw her profile, then the curtain of her hair descended again. Sparkling droplets flew behind her in a shimmering, sunlight-brightened veil.

She collected an armful of trinkets and shells, then looped a thick, slimy strand of kelp around her neck and turned toward the beach.

She splashed through the ice-cold Atlantic water as if it were the sun-drenched Caribbean Sea. With one hand, she shoved the tangled brown hair from her face.

For the first time in his life, Ian's knees went weak at the sight of a woman. She was exquisitely, unexpectedly beautiful. Long, mahogany-hued hair cascaded over her arms, dripping plump, silvery tears down the white lawn of her shirt. Her face was a pale oval, dominated by the largest, most liquid brown eyes Ian had ever seen. Her full lips looked ready to smile at any second.

She moved like the goddess he'd named her for, in flowing, graceful steps that seemed in rhythm with the movement of the tides. Her hips swayed in a gentle, feminine motion that mesmerized him.

When she reached the beach, she hitched up the baggy pants and skipped barefooted across the cold outcropping of stone to the spot where her stockings and half boots lay discarded. Setting down her treasures, she bent to put on her shoes.

Ian's heart was pounding so fast, he was certain she could hear it. He thought suddenly—irrationally—that God had answered his prayers, given him a seductive, beautiful woman steeped in mystery.

But it wasn't possible. She had to be damaged inside, she *had* to be. No brain could come through such a trauma unscathed. There was no hope that she could be normal. No real hope.

He thought of Elizabeth, sitting in the chair by the window, still beautiful . . . still broken and childlike and damaged.

Look at her, his mind taunted him with insidious, killing hope. *Believe what you see.*

But too many years of despair made such belief impossible. He couldn't believe in something without proof that it was real.

Regathering her shells and seaweed, she turned toward Maeve and Lara. She took one step, then stopped.

The rock was empty except for the easel. Maeve and Lara were gone. He saw the panic move across her face, fill her eyes. She bit down on her lower lip in a childlike expression of fear.

"Maeve?" Her full, throaty voice vibrated. "Maeve? Lara?"

He stared at her, a dozen questions circling through his mind. He tried not to care, tried not to have any expectations at all.

He stepped forward. "I'm here, Selena."

She spun toward him. The shells and pebbles she'd collected fell to the rocks with a clatter.

"Ian?" She said his name on a whisper, as if she weren't sure he was there at all.

"Hello there, Selena."

Her face split in a wide grin and she ran for him. Just in front of him, she skidded to a stop and fell into a deep curtsy. Rising slowly, her gaze fastened on his, she extended her hand.

He felt a moment's hesitation to touch her, then cautiously reached out. Their fingers brushed, twined. Her hand felt small and soft in his. No visions came to him, no images slammed through his mind. As before, there was nothing in her mind for him to see.

"I suppose the queen taught you to curtsy."

She positively beamed at him. "Yes."

"You do it very well."

"Thank you."

"You're welcome."

He couldn't take his eyes off her face, the way her full pink lips quirked in a smile, the brightness in her gaze. She was gloriously alive, so vibrantly animated.

It was a miracle.

No, not a miracle. A scientific phenomenon.

The old excitement moved through him. He understood all at once the implications of her recovery and what it meant to him. Just standing here, smiling at him in defiance of the odds, of science, she gave him everything. The fantasy came rushing back.

He could study her, begin to understand what no doctors before him had ever truly understood.

He could be a god again.

He grinned, letting the questions wash through him, exhilarate him. How was her mind? How far had she recovered? Could she think, understand, reason? Her mind was impaired—it had to be—but how much? What lobes were damaged and what behavior did the damage impact?

Jesus, he couldn't wait to study her.

"You are pleased with my face," she said.

He touched her cheek, felt the silkiness of her skin against his roughened fingertip. "You're beautiful."

"I see in the miner that it is much butter. *Better*. Now you will stay with me?"

"I don't understand."

"Now I am not so ugly."

His smile slowly faded. He considered the selfishness of his departure and was ashamed. "I did not leave because you were ugly, Selena. I left because *I* was ugly."

She stepped closer, turned her face up to him. A slow, stunning smile crept across her face. "You are beautiful, Ian."

It was surprising, the warmth her naive words caused. "Women are beautiful, Selena. Men are handsome."

She frowned briefly. "Oh." Then her smile came back full force. "You will test me again?"

He nodded. "If you'll let me."

She laughed. It was a low, throaty purr that didn't match her angelic face at all. A whore's laugh, whiskey-soft and seductive. "I shall let you do anything you wish to me, Ian. I have been waiting for you."

Such simplicity, such innocence. She clearly had no idea of the sexual innuendo of her words. He wondered what level her mind operated at—was she like Lara, a child in a woman's body, or was she still amnesiac?

"And I have been waiting for you, Selena," he said softly, realizing how true the words were. For six long years he'd been waiting for a patient, someone who needed him, someone who could give him back the promise of his past. And she was here, at Lethe House, smiling up at him with the guileless joy of a child. Understanding her would change medical history.

"I am pleased at the thought of more tests. I shall pass this time most certainly."

He smiled and offered her his arm. Together they strolled through the forest back toward the house.

For the first time in years, he couldn't wait for the next minute to take place, the next moment.

The medical mystery was inside her, waiting for him to discover. Him and him alone.

Selena sat on the edge of the overstuffed settee, her small feet pressed tightly together, her hands in her lap. She clamped her fingers together in a damp, sweaty ball to keep from fidgeting. Fidgeting was not ladylike, and she wanted desperately to be a lady for Ian. Rules circled through her head in an endless, mushy litany. *Sit still . . . don't speak until spoken to . . . don't fidget . . . crying is for babies and ye're no baby, Selena . . . eat like a bird . . .*

Selena tried to remember the rest, but Edith's words drifted in and out of her mind. Sometimes she remembered and sometimes she didn't. Sometimes she couldn't even remember what she was trying to remember.

"Would you like something to drink?"

Selena's head snapped up, her heart raced. He'd said something to her, asked a question, perhaps. She wasn't sure, couldn't remember. She tried to recall the appropriate word to express her confusion, but nothing came to mind. She gazed up at him, her mind an utter blank.

Tears burned behind her eyes. *Stupid. Stupid. Stupid.* She wanted to impress him. She'd been practicing for weeks now, every day, pushing herself to the very limit to improve. And for what? So that she could blink up at her god like a dead fish and breathe too quickly?

He motioned to the china teapot on the ornate silver tray. "Would you like a drink, Selena?"

Drink. Tea. He was offering her something to drink. She grinned in relief. "I am most thirsty. Yes, thank you, I would enjoy to drink tea."

He gazed at her a second longer than she expected, his eyes narrowed and assessing. "Good." Turning, he poured her a cup of steaming tea and offered it to her.

She smiled. "Hot," she said, proving to him once again that she was smart.

"Yes, it is hot. Do you take cream or sugar?"

"Where?"

"What?"

"Do I take them where?"

He laughed, a quiet, happy sound that made her feel like floating. "In your tea."

His laughter was contagious. "Oh," she giggled. "It does not matter to me, such things as cream and sugar and salt and pepper. I have no taste."

His smile died. Very slowly, he placed his teacup on the frilly piecrust table beside the settee and reached inside his coat pocket for a small book. Pulling the thin, leather-bound volume from his pocket, he slipped his spectacles on. "What do you mean you have no taste?"

She tried to marshal the words necessary to make her point. Finally she saw the salt shaker on the tray beside the watercress sandwiches. Grabbing it, she tilted her head back and poured a huge amount of the granules on her tongue. Then she swallowed and smiled at him. "No taste."

His eyes lit up. "You can't taste anything?"

"Nothing."

"How did you first notice this?"

"When I ate."

He smiled. "Let me rephrase that. How did you come to understand that you were different than other people?"

"Johann caught me drinking seawater."

He wrote furiously for several moments, then looked up again, an expectant light in his eyes. "And what about memories? Have you gotten any of them back?"

"No."

He frowned. His gaze burned into her with an intensity that made her vaguely uncomfortable. Then he started writing again. The quiet scratching of his pen on the paper seemed suddenly too loud. She started to shift her weight on the cushion, then froze. *Don't fidget.*

"You don't remember your name?"

"No, but I do not think—"

"Where you're from?"

She blinked in confusion at the sudden change of topic. He was going too quickly. Her mind could not keep up. "I do not know where I was from. Could you perhaps—"

"Family?"

"I do not know of them. It would help if—"

"How about opinions? Do you have any?"

"Edith puts them in her stew."

He frowned. "What?"

Opinions. Not onions. She tried to smile, but it was difficult. He was staring at her so intently, she felt sick inside, nervous and uncertain. "Opinions. You mean beliefs."

"Yes." His pen lowered again to the page, waiting.

"I believe . . ." Her words trailed off. Frantic to impress him, she tried to remember something—anything—that Johann had said, or Edith, or Maeve. Anything that might be an opinion. Ian expected her to have some; she could see the expectation in his gaze, feel it in the ebb and tide of his breathing. "I believe . . ." Her shoulders sagged, her voice fell to a thick whisper. "I believe I have no opinions."

"Really?" He drew the word out, as if savoring it, as if he were glad that she was so empty in the head.

She scooted closer to him, though it wasn't ladylike, and tilted her face up. He was so close, she could see the dark flecks in his blue, blue eyes, so close, she could feel his breath against her face. "I believe in you, Ian."

He laughed, only this time it was a harsh sound that made her feel stupid and small. "No opinions *and* no intelligence," he said, making a quick note in his journal.

"I am not stupid," she said in a quiet voice.

He looked surprised by her statement. "I never said you were."

"But you just said—"

"Oh, that." He cut her off with a wave of his pen. "That's simply sarcasm. I was saying that anyone who believes in me has no intelligence. You see, it's a joke at my expense, not yours."

She nodded, pretending to understand. But she didn't understand at all. Why would someone make a remark designed to inflict pain?

"I . . . I knew you would come back to me," she said, gazing up at him, waiting for him to reach out and touch her, to see her as something more than a patient to question.

"I wish I had sooner. This damned journal would be so much more complete if I'd documented every step of the recovery process." He got suddenly to his feet and went to the bookcase behind him. "Now, let's try some coordination and dexterity tests, shall we?"

Selena watched him. He turned, carried back an armful of board games and pictures.

Something was terribly wrong, and she had no idea what it was. She felt useless and stupid.

And she'd tried so very hard. . . .

He sat down next to her. Close, but not too close. Then he picked up the pen and poised it above the paper. "Let's see if you can put the square peg in the square opening this time."

For no reason at all, she felt like crying. She didn't understand her own reaction. She ought to be happy now, ought to be grinning at the prospect of this examination. She'd practiced it several times, so many that she could perform it in her sleep. For weeks, she'd looked forward to impressing him with her mastery of this very test.

But now, somehow, things were different. It felt as if passing wouldn't matter to him, wouldn't make him put down that pen and truly look at her.

She realized suddenly what the matter was. It came to her in a swift, breathless jab of pain.

He didn't care about her.

Oh, he wanted to understand her, wanted to take her apart and test her and see how she'd survived whatever it was she'd survived. He wanted to write down her thoughts and feelings and reactions, wanted to understand why she couldn't remember her name and why she had no opinions, but he didn't want to know *her*.

He didn't believe there was a her inside all that missing information. Inside that broken brain.

"I am a patient to you, am I not?"

"Of course you are."

"You think you will repair me?"

He wrote very quickly, as if afraid of missing a single word. "I don't know precisely what's wrong with you yet. Except, of course, that you're brain-damaged." He gave her a brief, heartless smile, then resumed writing.

Selena bit down on her lower lip and looked away. The dreams she'd spun so easily in the last weeks began unraveling, separating like strands of old silk. He was backward, but she couldn't tell him so. How could someone like her—broken and inexperienced—tell a great man of science that he needed to search for what was right with her, not what was wrong?

She picked up the small wooden spike and put it in the square hole.

He drew in a sharp breath and grinned at her. "Good." Back to the writing.

She felt none of the triumph she'd prepared herself to feel, none of the exhilaration. Instead, she felt vaguely sick and lonely.

He reached for the stack of pictures beside him and picked one up. "Can you name this item?"

"Moon," she said dully.

"And this one? Do you know what it is?"

Selena looked at the stylized painting of a heart. "Yes," she said in a soft voice. "I know what it is. Do you, Ian?"

He looked up, startled. "Of course *I* know what it is."

"And do you have one?"

"No body can function without it, Selena. Now, what is it?"

"A heart."

He didn't look up from his journal, just kept writing. "Its function?"

"It is the storehouse of a person's emotions and dreams and desires. Johann says your heart is the dwelling of the soul."

"Don't listen to Johann. The heart is simply an organ, like your kidneys or your liver. It pumps blood throughout your body. Emotions stem from certain places in the brain."

"I am proof that you are wrong."

Ian looked up. "What do you mean?"

"I have forgotten my name, my place of birth, everything about the life I once lived. This is caused by the damage to my brain."

He wrote furiously. "Uh-huh."

"But I remember my feelings. I can laugh and cry and love. And I can be hurt."

He frowned at her. "So you're saying that your emotions *do* reside in the heart. Empirically, not figuratively." He tapped the pen against his lips and stared past her. "Interesting. Very sophisticated logic, too, I might add. Though you probably don't know what I mean."

She tried to smile. Her eyes met his, pled silently for understanding. He had missed the point entirely. "I mean I can be hurt, Ian."

He stared at her for a long time, saying nothing, not writing. Anticipation tingled in her blood. He was seeing her this time, she was certain of it. He wasn't analyzing or cataloging or diagramming her. She'd said something that touched him. A smile tugged at one corner of her mouth. She leaned toward him, a little out of breath.

Very slowly, he brought his pen back to the paper. "Everyone can be hurt, Selena."

She felt him fade away from her again, felt the moment of possibility disappear.

Lethe House was curiously alive. Ian stood in his study, sipping a warm glass of port, listening to the incredible din of voices in the hallway. There was laughter, for God's sake. He couldn't remember the last time he'd heard such genuine camaraderie among the residents of this place.

Selena had obviously worked her magic on all of them. From the moment she'd first appeared here, battered and bloodied and nameless, she'd struck at the very heart of every person under this roof. He could *feel* the enchantment in the air, hear it in the muted strains of laughter. She was drawing the inmates together, making a family out of strangers, turning a collection of lost and lonely souls into friends.

Yesterday he mightn't have noticed.

Today he was a doctor again. A doctor who wanted to understand every facet of his patient. She'd shown a remarkable retention today, an ability to reason that surprised him. He had so many more questions to ask her. As soon as she'd eaten her supper, he wanted to test her again.

Someone knocked on the door.

"Come In."

The door swung open and Edith bustled in, her fleshy cheeks high with sweaty color. She wiped her hands on her flour-streaked apron and cocked a thumb toward the door. "Supper is ready, sir."

He drained the last of his drink and set the empty glass down on the mantel. "Good."

Edith didn't move. Nervously she pushed a straggly strand of hair back into her white cap. "Selena wanted you to join us."

"Us?"

A slow, sheepish grin pushed through the wrinkles. "She's a force to be reckoned with, that she is, sir. Why, from the moment she began speakin', I haven't found a wee moment's peace. She wants to change every rule and custom to fit her curious brand o' logic. Said she'd run round naked if we didn't let her wear pants." She grinned. *"Pants."*

"What in God's name are you babbling about, Edith?"

"Selena, sir. She refused to eat unless we made an event out of it. Starved herself for two days, she did, until we agreed to serve supper in the dining room."

"The residents eat *together*?"

" 'Tisn't half-bad, I must admit. There's a wee bit of food tossin' sometimes, but other than that . . ."

Maeve floated into the study, her long white skirts trailing behind her. "What's taking so long, Edith?" She stopped beside Ian and cocked her head up. "Are you coming?"

He stared at his mother. "Are you suggesting I eat with the inmates?"

Maeve frowned and picked at the pale pink ribbon at her throat. "I'm . . . demanding it."

Ian looked down at her in shock. "Excuse me?"

"This is my house, I believe?"

"Yes . . ."

Maeve grinned, as if she'd just answered a most confusing query. "Yes, I thought so. As owner and Edith's employer, I shall make a new rule. No eating in bedrooms."

"Mother, you cannot—"

"I have. Now, Edith, serve supper. My son and I shall be along shortly."

Edith bobbed her head in a quick show of deference, then hustled out of the room, leaving the door open behind her.

Maeve moved closer to Ian. "I will not let you hurt her, Ian."

"What do you mean?"

"Selena has been practicing her table manners for weeks. She would be heartbroken if you didn't show up at supper."

Ian stifled a quick urge to smile. This was an opportunity he hadn't even considered. To watch Selena's dexterity at complicated tasks, see how her impaired brain function impacted her motor skills. "Lead on, Mother."

She frowned at him, then slowly turned and walked out of the parlor. He followed her down the hall and into the dining room.

The scene that greeted them stopped Ian in his tracks. The room was full of people. Lara, Andrew, Johann, Dotty, Queen Victoria, Edith, and Fergus were all seated around the oval mahogany table. A dozen candles dotted the table, casting quivering pockets of light atop the burgundy tablecloth. A large silver tray held a still sizzling roasted turkey ringed in baked carrots and onions. Beside the bird, two pewter bowls held mashed potatoes and turnips. Scattered randomly in between the serving dishes were apples, nuts, pieces of hard candy, and pickles.

"Rather odd assortment of food," Ian murmured.

"To feed a rather odd assortment of people," Maeve responded. She clapped her hands for attention. "Ian has consented to sup with us."

A roar of approval went up in the room. Ian's gaze cut to Johann, who sat sprawled in a chair, one leg drawn up, his arm draped across the knee. A half-empty glass of wine dangled from his long fingers. Johann gave him a slow, sarcastic smile and tilted his glass in a mock toast. "Why, Doctor, how nice of you to join us. I'm so sorry I missed your reunion today with the goddess." His smile graduated into a grin. "Such a staggering misdiagnosis. . . ."

Ian ignored Johann and turned back to the table. For the first time, he noticed the room's decorations. Bright gold cords were draped from the chandelier, their valleys deepened by small, hanging Christmas ornaments. There was a scrap of paper pinned to the base of the light fixture, upon which were written the words *chandelier—for light*.

Ian glanced around, suddenly noticing the dozens of other notes affixed to every item in the room. He went from one to the other, reading. *Sideboard—to hold hot food; table—to sit at for meals; rug; window—to see through; drapery—to keep light out.*

He felt Selena beside him without even hearing her come up. All at once, he simply knew that she was there. He turned to her. She stood tall and straight, her hair loosened around her face. She wore a baggy blue gingham dress with bits of lace at the collar and cuffs. A goddess in a gunnysack.

Her face lit in a smile. "Andrew wrote those, to help me learn words."

For a second, he was so lost in looking at her face that he didn't know what she was talking about. Then he realized it was the notes. "Did it work?"

"Yes. The moment I see the word, I seem to recall its meaning. I am relearning my old life."

"Good idea, Andrew," he said to the young man, who blushed furiously at the sudden attention. "I'd like to speak with you after supper. Perhaps you—and the others—can fill me in on Selena's recovery process."

"I would think Selena's current state would tell you all you need to know," Johann said. "Just look at her, for God's sake."

Ian frowned. "It's not her looks that interest me, Johann. It's her brain. How damaged is it? How difficult was the recovery process?"

Johann's eyes turned cold. "You would see only the imperfections, Ian."

"You will sit by me?" Selena asked quietly.

The question surprised Ian.

"Of course he will," Maeve responded.

Slowly Ian followed Selena to a seat at the table, watching her intently as the meal began.

She sat very stiff and erect, her napkin spread across her lap. She carefully placed an apple, a pickle, and two pieces of hard candy on her plate. Taking up her fork, she cut the apple in small pieces and began to eat.

Her actions were jerky and uncoordinated.

He put on his spectacles and pulled his journal and pen out of his pocket. *Patient eats with awkward, almost spasmodic motions. Appears to eat based on texture to substitute for lack of taste.*

Conversation buzzed around the table in stops and starts, people talking all at once, laughing uncontrollably and at inappropriate times. Beside him, Selena was talking earnestly—something about King George—in a voice so soft that he could barely hear her above the din.

He couldn't handle the noise. A dull, thudding headache started at the base of his skull and radiated outward.

He put his pen down suddenly, harder than he'd intended.

When he glanced up, he found Selena staring at him. She looked . . . uncomfortable. Like his mother when she was trying to separate fantasy from fact. Lost. A little despondent.

He leaned toward her and picked up the pen again. "Are you feeling well?"

The look in her eyes was familiar; it reminded him of the desperate souls who sought psychic answers from the infamous Dr. Carrick.

"You want to know what I feel?"

"No. I asked *how* you feel. Do you have a headache? Nausea?"

"Oh, for God's sake, Ian. Let her eat in peace," Johann said before she could answer.

"I hate to agree with Herr Strassborg—he *is* German, after all," the queen said in a huff, "but Dr. Carrick is being remarkably rude."

Maeve glanced up from her plate. "It's how he used to study insects when he was a boy."

"Just before he pulled their little wings off, no doubt," Johann remarked, taking a quick sip of his wine.

Ian rolled his eyes. He should have known better than to try to observe his patient in this crowd. Johann was his usual surly, antagonistic self, except that he'd developed a sudden paternalistic streak for their damaged goddess. Maeve and the queen were predictably incomprehensible, and Selena . . .

He sighed. She was somehow not what he expected. There was a sadness in her eyes that begged to be noticed.

He leaned toward her and pressed a hand to her forehead, feeling for a fever.

She gave him a quick smile that banished the sorrow from her eyes.

He drew his hand back, and she immediately frowned. As if she'd wanted something from him. "I'll get you some headache powders. We can resume our testing tomorrow."

"By all means, Ian, treat the body and ignore the soul," Johann said.

Ian slammed his journal down on the table and got to his feet. The fine Sevres china rattled. "Edith, send a meal to my room. Selena, I'll see you in the morning."

Selena stared up at him, a pathetic eagerness in her doe eyes. "Will you, Ian? Really?"

He didn't understand her question. "Eight-thirty in the parlor." He turned to leave.

She stopped him with a touch. Surprised, he turned back to her. "On the beach," she said in an unexpectedly firm voice. "I like the sunlight."

It made no sense to him, but what did a place matter? He could study her anywhere. "Fine."

Without another word, he walked out of the room.

Chapter Fourteen

❦

Selena sat on the bottom step, her knees drawn tightly to her chest, her arms looped around her ankles. Around her, the old house was quiet and dark. Supper had been over for hours, though the scent of turkey and cinnamon clung stubbornly in the air.

Something was wrong between her and Ian, and she had no idea what it was. All she wanted, all she could ever remember wanting, was his smile. When she first woke up, he was there, always, sitting beside her, gifting her with a glorious, loving smile, touching her brow with his strong, caring fingers. She remembered how it had felt to bask in the warmth of his smile. Peaceful. Safe. As if nothing bad could follow or find her when Ian was there.

But it had all been an illusion, a creation of her battered mind. She wondered now if she'd imagined it all, if Ian had ever looked at her with the loving gaze of her memories, or if it was all a lie. . . .

How could she know? She was *brain-damaged*. Ian had said it often enough, as had Edith, and now Selena was well enough to understand what it meant. She accepted it as truth that her brain—the part of her that contained her thoughts and knowledge—was irreparably damaged. Her friends wouldn't lie to her about such a serious sickness.

So she was damaged, broken. But what did that

mean? None of them could answer that. And now she was beginning to wonder, to question everything she knew and thought she knew. She *thought* Ian had once touched her with caring. But how could she know for sure?

The soft, tentative patter of footsteps broke through Selena's thoughts. She straightened. Hope filled her heart, sharp and painful. "Who is there?"

"It's me. Maeve."

Hope died. Selena slid closer to the wall. Maeve came down to the last step and sat down beside Selena, setting a candle on the floor in front of them.

Selena glanced sideways at Maeve, studying the older woman's profile. She'd learned in the last weeks that there were two Maeves in the same body. One was a bright, vivacious woman with a ready laugh and generous nature; the other was morose and withdrawn and self-destructive, a woman prone to talking to invisible people and kissing stuffed animals. Selena was trying to learn how to tell the difference.

"I thought you might still be up," Maeve said.

The soft tones of Maeve's voice filled Selena with relief. It was the healthy Maeve, the woman in control. Trying to smile, Selena rested her head on her friend's shoulder.

"Supper was very bad," Selena said dully. So different from what she'd imagined. In her daydreams of Ian's return, he always picked her up, swung her around, and held her closely. She'd never imagined the tension she felt in his presence or the objective coldness in his eyes. When he looked at her, all he saw was a damaged brain.

Maeve nodded. "Yes."

"I was . . . bad. Stupid. I wanted . . ." She couldn't find the word she wanted and she was too tired to try.

"Of course you wanted to impress him. It's only natural."

Selena looked at her friend in wonder. "Maeve, how is it you always understand me?"

Maeve gave her a small smile. "You're easy, child. It's the rest of the world that confuses me."

Selena was silent for a long time, then finally she turned to Maeve. "How do I make Ian love me?"

Maeve squeezed her eyes shut for a long moment. When she reopened them, her hazel eyes glittered with tears. "I don't know." Her voice cracked, thickened. "But I know how much it hurts to try."

Selena sagged forward. "I am doing much wrong with him."

"He will keep you at arm's length now," Maeve said quietly.

"Why?"

It was a long moment before Maeve answered. "Because you are broken."

Selena didn't need the words; it was what she'd already felt in her heart, and yet still they hurt. "Then there is no hope. I shall always be broken."

"I have never found hope with Ian. He despises me because I am crazy."

Selena heard the pain in her friend's voice and understood it, felt it. She slipped her arm around Maeve's slim shoulders and drew her close. "I feel love for you."

Maeve released a shaky breath. "I love you, too, Selena."

They sat that way a long time, silently, taking comfort in each other's presence. "He will see me someday," Selena said at last.

"Maybe," Maeve whispered. "Maybe."

The next morning, Selena dressed quickly in her oversized blue gingham gown and tied her hair back with a strip of pink satin, then grabbed the book Ian had left on her bed last night and headed outside.

She had lain awake last night for hours, huddled next to the meager light of a candle, trying to read the small, leather-bound book entitled *Either/Or: A Fragment of Life*. If she read slowly enough, she could comprehend the words, but making sense of them was another thing entirely. The story seemed pointless and silly.

Obviously she was not smart enough to understand the text. The realization saddened her, for she knew what it meant. Ian would listen to her feeble attempt at what he called *retention* and look disappointed by her failure. Then he'd write something in that book of his. Something that captured and memorized her imperfection.

She forced a smile. She would not think of that now. Today would be different from yesterday. She would *make* Ian see her, make him take her seriously. She didn't know how she would do that, but she believed in herself, in the possibility, and she would make it work.

She raced to the edge of the lawn, her skirts held high. She meant to keep running, through the forest to the shoreline beyond. Meant to.

But the towering old trees enthralled her, captivated her senses. She stopped and looked up. Green leaves and needles splayed out above her in a lacelike pattern that filtered the sunlight. A gentle breeze danced through, sent leaves spiraling to the lichen-covered floor.

She dropped to her knees and crawled over the damp earth to a singular white blossom that huddled amidst the ferns. She gently took hold of it, studying the satiny green leaves and milky white petals. It smelled so nice. . . .

"Selena?" Ian's voice, slightly impatient, boomed into the clearing.

She snapped back, breaking the flower in her surprise. "Oh, no . . . I am so sorry. . . ."

"Selena!"

She hitched up her now-dirty skirts and got slowly to her feet. With a last backward glance at the broken flower, she trudged through the forest and emerged onto the gray rock beach.

Ian was standing there, as tall and straight as the ancient trees beside him. He held a pocket watch in his hand. "Selena!"

She stepped into the sunlight. "I am here."

The watch snapped shut. He spun to face her. "Good. Then we can begin."

She tried to give him a smile, but her lips were trembly and wouldn't cooperate. She felt like the flower. Without thinking, she moved toward him. Her skirts dragged over the damp rocks.

He frowned, drew a step back. "What is it, Selena? Do you have a headache again?"

She kept moving. "No."

His frown deepened. "Why are you looking at me that way?"

"Why you are looking at me that way?"

"Don't repeat me. Answer me."

"I did."

"Stop." He said it so loudly, with such force, that she responded in spite of herself. She didn't know why she'd been moving toward him anyway, what she wanted of him except that he *see* her.

He whipped open his journal and pen and sat down on a hulking gray stone. He directed his analytical gaze on her, narrowed and probing. "Did you try to read the Kierkegaard?" At her obvious confusion, he clarified himself. "The book. Did you read any of Kierkegaard's book?"

She fought a rising sense of panic. Very carefully, she picked up her dragging skirts and moved toward him, kneeling on the hard, cold stones at his feet. "I stayed up early last night reading. I . . . concentrated very hard. I tried to understand—" She looked up at him. *For you, I tried so hard.* "But . . . I did not understand the words."

He scratched something in his book, then gave her a

smile that for a heartbreakingly perfect moment transformed his face into the angel of her dreams. Then it was gone. "Did you comprehend anything? Random words, sentences, ideas. Anything?"

She sagged back onto her heels. "The man in the story thought that life was hopeless and without meaning and ugly. And that only by believing in the very worst could God be found. It was . . . silly."

Ian stared at her. "That's exceptional, Selena."

She didn't understand the word *exceptional,* but she knew she'd disappointed him. Again. "I am sorry. I am too . . . brain-damaged to understand the otter's words."

"Author," he corrected her in a soft voice. Slowly he edged off the rock and kneeled beside her.

She couldn't look at him.

He touched her chin, gently forced her to meet his gaze. When she looked at him, her heart caught. There was a softness in his blue eyes that stole her breath.

He brushed a straggly lock of hair from her eyes. "You just described the theory of existentialism."

"I did?"

"You understood it."

The surprise in his voice made her want to cry. He expected so little of her.

She leaned closer and tilted her face to his. "Look at me, Ian. What do you see?"

He frowned, drew back a little. "What do you mean?"

She pulled the book from his hands and flipped it open to a random page.

Patient exhibits expressive and cognitive aphasia. Basilar skull fracture. Prognosis: unknown. Receptive and expressive aphasia appears to be impermanent, but future uncertain. Can speak somewhat, answer questions, and retain limited understanding. But can she reason? The last sentence was underlined.

She looked up at him through a blur of hot tears. "I

don't know if I reason, but I feel, Ian. Perhaps that is what saved my life."

He looked away. A deep breath filled his chest and then released in a hissing sigh. He was quiet for so long that she thought perhaps she'd reached him, thought maybe she'd forced him to think about *her,* instead of her injury.

He got slowly to his feet. "That's enough for this morning, Selena." Stepping away from the rock, he eased away from her.

"You know, Ian," she said without looking at him. "I may be brain-damaged, but I am smart enough to know something that you do not."

Reluctantly he turned to her. "What's that?"

She met his gaze head-on. "You need to be saved more than I do."

Ian stood at the window, gazing out at the front lawn. The glass of wine felt warm and familiar in his hand. Absently he twirled the delicate crystal stem.

He couldn't stop thinking about what Selena had said to him this morning. There was a core of truth in her observation. He'd always been better with facts and figures and challenges than with people. Whenever he had to deal with people he didn't understand, especially mentally deficient people, he drew back, cloaked himself in detachment. It was something he'd learned long ago, a survival skill Maeve had taught him.

He'd always seen mental illness in stark, black-and-white definition. A person was normal or abnormal. Period.

When had he stopped searching for the truth? Stopped seeing anything beyond the label?

But he knew, of course. He'd stopped a long, long time ago—with every slight from Maeve, every moment of irrationality. He'd been afraid to think of his mother as anything but irreparably broken, because if he saw her as a human—worse yet, a human in pain—he'd have to change. And change would hurt, just as expectations hurt, just as disappointment hurt.

Somewhere along the way, he'd become ugly in his selfishness. As Johann said, he'd demanded a wretched commonness from those around him. Healthy or sick— that's how he saw people, how he treated them. The world according to Ian Carrick.

He sighed, depressed by the realization.

He regretted that he'd hurt her, regretted even more that he'd been such a poor physician. He *knew* a good physician treated the mind as well as the body; unfortunately, he'd always had a wretched bedside manner.

Normally it didn't matter. Most of his patients didn't care about his personality at all. All they cared about was his skill, and that was unparalleled.

But nothing about Selena was normal. He owed her an apology.

Behind him, the door creaked open, then clicked shut.

"Contemplating your monumental errors, I hope," said a drawling male voice.

Ian flinched. *Johann. Christ.* "Go away."

Crystal clinked, liquid splashed. "I thought I'd join you for a drink."

Slowly Ian turned around. Johann stood next to the mahogany sideboard, wineglass in hand. Johann tipped the glass in a mock salute.

"Well, you've done it—what none of us was able to do in the month you were gone."

"What are you talking about?"

Johann set down the glass with a clunk on the table and peered up at him. "You stole Selena's smile."

Ian went to the chair across from Johann and sat down. "Did I?" He tried to make the words sound cold and disinterested, but he didn't quite manage.

"I know you're not a bad man—though I believe you're more than half stupid and certainly blind." Johann leaned forward. "She's an innocent, Ian. Doesn't that mean something to you?"

"Her brain—"

"Screw her brain." He leaned back and plucked his glass from the table, gazing moodily into the crimson liquid. "You think about things more when you're dying. I think about the way I've lived my life, the way I've treated people, and more than half the time, I'm ashamed. But then . . ." He shook his head, smiling just a little. "Then I think of Marie and the way I loved her, and I feel . . . redeemed."

The words hit dangerously close to home. "What makes you think I need to be redeemed?"

"Ten minutes in your company."

Ian laughed derisively. "Touché."

"Go to her, Ian. *See* her. There's a purity in her soul such as I've never seen before. She could change you."

Ian winced at the softly spoken words. For no reason that he could name, they caused a rush of emotion. Fear, maybe. Perhaps a little stab of hope. He pushed suddenly to his feet and turned away, striding from the room.

"Run along, little Ian, and hide your head in the sand. Or in your precious journal."

He ignored Johann's comments and kept walking, past the lawn, through the trees, toward the sea. He needed to think, to get away from this loathsome house full of damaged souls.

Selena was on the beach. She was wearing an old lawn shirt of his and those baggy pants, hitched at the waist with a fist-thick leather belt. Her long hair whipped out behind her, fluttered in the breeze. The pungent, clammy smell of low tide seeped up from the sand and rocks.

In front of her stood an easel. A pale cream-colored gown was pinned to the easel, and she was painting a huge yellow flower on the bodice.

She hadn't seen him, and he almost turned around, but something stopped him, something deep and elemental. He owed her something, words, a touch. An apology.

Quietly he came up beside her. "Hello, Selena."

She jumped at the sound of his voice and dropped the paintbrush, spinning around. "Ian," she mouthed.

Nervously he shifted his weight. The words he ought to say, needed to say, wedged in his throat, as thick and unwieldy as sand. "I . . . I'm sorry, Selena."

Her face broke into a dazzlingly bright smile. "You are?"

"I never meant to hurt you."

"Of course you did not." A low, throaty laugh slipped from her mouth, vibrated on the cool, crisp air. "And of course I forget you."

Her laughter was infectious. He couldn't help smiling. She made it so easy to be wrong. "You mean you forgive me."

She laughed again. Easily. So easily. "You are right. I do not forget you, Ian."

Before he could respond, she threaded her fingers through his. "Come with me," she said.

She pulled him away from the beach, drew him into the cold, primeval darkness of the forest. Laughing, she raced over the fallen logs, across the lichen-covered ground to a small, round clearing in the center of a canyon of spruce and balsam trees. Spears of sunlight stabbed through the trees in wavery, dusty streams.

Smiling, out of breath, her cheeks a high, pure pink, she let go of his hand and spun around. "This is my place," she said proudly. "Look." She let go of his hand and dropped to her knees, burrowing through a cavity in a rotted stump. One by one, she pulled out her treasures—a perfectly rounded white stone, a pink hermit crab shell, a dried strand of yellowish green kelp, a sand dollar, a broken bit of blue glass.

Ian stood back and watched her. Strange, unfamiliar feelings and sensations spilled through his body, making him feel almost light-headed. There was an other-worldly quality to this moment, this woman. She was not . . . normal; and yet, perhaps she was what normal should be, what it was once.

She plopped to a sit and drew her riches into her lap, motioning him over.

She was like no other person he'd ever known, an impossible mixture of ethereal beauty and earthy strength. And when she looked up at him, he saw in her eyes an eager innocence that couldn't exist in this tired, unjust world.

"Ian?" A small frown tugged at her thick, arched eyebrows, reminded him that he'd remained silent too long. "I . . . saved these . . . for you."

He couldn't take his eyes off of her. She sat there, her treasures in her lap, gazing up at him as if he hung the moon with his bare hands. For one blindly painful moment, he wished he were worthy of that look.

The sum of his life, his soul, passed before his eyes in that instant and he felt a crushing sense of shame. From the moment he'd met her, he'd thought only of himself, his needs, his desires, and when he thought she couldn't fulfill them, he'd abandoned her. Left her to rot quietly behind the closed doors of her room.

And still she looked at him as if he were the god he so wanted to be.

But now, this instant, he didn't want to be a god anymore. He didn't want to take her to Harvard and show her off like some macabre Frankenstein's creature or miracle of modern science.

He wanted to fall to his knees beside her and be a man again. Just that. A man.

He wanted his soul back. . . .

"Ian? Come here. . . ."

Reluctantly he went and sat down beside her. He didn't know what else to do.

Her smile came back, bright as a summer sun. She reached down and picked up the bit of broken glass. It glowed a brilliant blue in the filtered sunlight. "This one is special," she said quietly.

"Why is it so special?"

She opened her hand and offered it to him. Without the light, it was only a cold, dark spot of glass on her pink palm. "The color of your eyes. Blue."

Ian felt something inside him give way, soften. "You remembered the color of my eyes?"

She dropped the glass in her lap and leaned toward him, tilting her face up. "I remember everything about you, Ian. Johann says I am a manacle."

"A what?"

She laughed suddenly, a low, throaty sound that filled the clearing. "I am always doing that. Please to forgive me. Johann says I am a *miracle*."

Ian swallowed hard. "And so you are," he said in a thick voice.

She looked away for a second, her face scrunched in thought, then she turned back to him. "I . . . I know you want me to remember my life before. For you, I have tried, but there are no memories inside me. My head is empty, except . . ." Her voice trailed off. She bit down on her lower lip and glanced away.

"Except for what?"

"You will think I am stupid."

Ian remembered the times he'd mentioned brain damage in front of her and winced. *Such a heartless bastard.* He'd spent days studying her as if she were an insect under glass and yet he'd never seen her. Not until this very moment, and what he saw filled him with awe. "No, Selena, I would never think that."

"I have no memories, but I have a . . . filling. A feeling. Sometimes, when I am asleep or just waking up, I am so sad, without a reason." She looked up at him, a confusion in her eyes. "I believe my soul has been sad for a very long time. But now it is happy. I am with you and my family."

"You don't belong here, Selena. You're not crazy."

Strangely, the words caused an aching sense of loss, and not because he wouldn't be a world-renowned physician for saving her life, but because she would leave him. "You will improve daily. One day you'll be almost normal. Your memories may even return, though I doubt it."

She drew back, looked at him quizzically. "I am also crazy. We are all crazy. Except for Johann," she amended. "He is a genius."

Ian burst out laughing. "So says Johann, I presume."

She nodded solemnly.

Ian's laughter faded. He looked down at her earnest, innocent face and suddenly it wasn't funny anymore. None of this was funny. She was an accident waiting to happen; an utterly naive, completely gullible woman with no life experience, no memories of pain or hurt or betrayal. She was like a child, expecting the world to be a happy, just, honest place.

The pain she could experience was staggering.

"Ah, Selena. You're too trusting. Johann is not a genius simply because he says he is."

"You will teach me to be not so trusting?"

He laughed. "Certainly no one is more qualified to destroy your illusions and show you the dark side of life than I."

She looked disappointed. "Oh."

"What's the matter?"

"I was hoping you would teach me to play croquet."

Ian stared down at her. "Croquet?"

She regathered her treasures. "It is a game with balls and mullets where you hit the ball through a spigot. The queen says it is most entertaining, but Edith said she would not teach me such a game until hell freezes over."

Ian had to bite back a sudden bark of laughter. "Why not?"

"Edith said she would not put a mullet into that lunatic's hands. But now that you're back ..." She looked up at him hopefully.

Ian didn't have the heart to say no. "Okay, Selena, I will teach you to play croquet."

She gifted him with a radiant smile. "I can learn the dark side of life tomorrow."

Such innocence ...

"Very well. Now, let's go back into the house. It's cold out here. I'd like to see you read. You did so well with existentialism, I think we'll try something else."

"Something happy please."

He stood up and, without thinking, put a hand out to her. She stuffed her treasures back into the mealy tree stump, then took hold of his hand and got to her feet. Together, hand in hand, they walked back toward the house.

Halfway there, she stopped dead and yanked her hand back. "Wait!"

"What is it?"

"I wanted to show you something wonderful that Lara taught me."

"Lara?"

"The tall child who sucks her thumb."

"I know who Lara is. I simply wondered what she could teach anyone."

"Oh, she knows a great many wonderful things. Like this." Selena lowered herself into a crouch and pressed her hands into the soft carpet of needles. A quick cock of her head ensured her that Ian was watching, then she rolled forward into a somersault. She whacked into a pine tree and plopped to the side, her booted feet flailing for a second before she righted herself.

Twisting around, she grinned up at him, her hair full of pine needles and dead leaves. She looked like a fairy princess come to life from the forest floor. "Isn't that grand?"

Jesus. The world was going to kill her. He sighed. "Just grand, Selena."

"You try it."

"Me?"

She nodded eagerly, patted the soft earth. "It does not hurt one bit."

"I know that, Selena, I've done them. Years ago." He walked toward her and plucked the foliage from her hair, then offered her his hand. "Come along, now. I wish to see you read."

She sighed and took his hand, standing beside him. A leaf clung to her throat, but she seemed not to notice. "I think that is most unwise, Ian. You look like you need a somersault."

"What I need," he replied, "is a drink."

"Ah, yes. Johann promised you would teach me of the drink."

"*You* will not drink, Selena. Ever."

"Why not?"

"Men drink. Ladies do not."

She appeared to think about that. "The breasts make it impossible?"

He couldn't have heard her correctly. "What?"

"Johann explained to me that there was a difference between men and women. Women have breasts and unmentionables and men have—"

"Yes, I know what men have, and the anatomical differences are unimportant when it comes to drinking."

"Then why can I not drink?"

He rolled his eyes. "Because I said so."

"Johann always gives me reasons for everything. He said that that is how I learn."

"Johann is an idiot."

"Oh, no. He is a genius."

Ian took Selena's hand and led her out of the forest. He said nothing more about drinking, or Johann, or reasons for anything. It was safer that way.

Chapter Fifteen

Somewhere, a wildcat screamed. The guttural, violent cry vibrated in the air, distant and muted by the closed windows.

In the parlor, Ian poured himself another drink, stiffer than the last. Absently he twirled the heavy crystal glass, watching the amber and red highlights of the scotch. The sweet, smoothing scent of the alcohol wafted up to his nostrils.

He turned from the sideboard and walked across the room, the sound of his footsteps lost in the thick Aubusson carpet. He couldn't stop thinking about today, about Selena. He felt . . . changed by what had happened today, by how he'd felt when he looked into her eyes and heard her throaty laugh. He'd always been so damned frightened of imperfection, but she defied all definition of normal. Suddenly, compared to her, normal seemed boring, common.

He'd understood at last Johann's bit with the broken glass.

He heard the ferocious yowl of the wildcat again and walked to the window, peering out. The yard was sheathed in darkness. Towering black trees clustered around the blue-gray lawn. High overhead lurked a silvery comma of moonlight.

Something caught his eye. A whisper of movement

where there should be no movement, a flash of white in the darkness.

Frowning, he leaned closer.

It was a woman in a nightdress. He saw her for a split second, then she disappeared in the darkness of the trees.

The wildcat screamed.

"Jesus Christ!" Ian dropped the half-empty glass of scotch and raced outside, running down the steps and across the thick carpet of grass.

He skidded to a stop at the edge of the woods, trying desperately to see into the shadowy darkness. But it was black, so black.

"Hello, sweet thing," said a throaty, feminine voice. "You can come out."

Overhead, a cloud skudded past the slivered moon.

He saw Selena. She stood about twenty feet in front of him, sideways on the narrow dirt trail, her hand outstretched. Her white lawn nightdress fluttered against her breasts and ankles. With her wavy hair rippling down her back, her profile bathed in moonlight, her nightdress aglow, she looked like Aphrodite come to life.

The bushes in front of her rustled. He heard the low, even breathing of the cat.

For a split second, Ian was so terrified, he couldn't breathe. His heart hammered in his chest, sweat broke out on his forehead.

"Selena." He whispered her name, unable to hear his own voice above the pounding of his heart.

She turned, straightened, and gave him a bright smile. "Ian! How—"

"Shhh." He surged forward. "Don't move."

A frown creased her brow. "I do not u—"

"Hush," he said sharply. Slowly, achingly aware of every step, he moved toward her. The twenty feet seemed to stretch into a mile, then two.

Finally he reached her, took hold of her hand.

"Your hand is wet—"

He clamped a hand over her mouth and yanked her close, slipping an arm around her waist.

The bushes rustled again. Then came a low, warning growl.

Step by cautious, breathless step, they backed out of the forest. The cat followed them, the leaves rustling with every step.

Ian saw a flash of gold eyes. Branches snapped. Leaves parted with a rustling hiss.

He backed up another step, felt the soft cushion of the lawn beneath his heel. Swallowing hard, he kept moving backward, his eyes trained on the movement in the bushes.

The grass ended at last. He felt the crunching of small stones beneath his feet. They were on the path. It was now or never.

He swept Selena into his arms and turned, racing up the steps. The tired old boards squeaked and banged under his feet.

The cat screamed.

Ian didn't look back. He ran up the steps and into the house, slamming the door shut behind him. Selena slid out of his arms.

He spun to face her, so angry he was shaking. "What in the *hell* were you thinking?"

She stood still, her cheeks stained a bright pink, her untamed hair a wavy reddish brown halo around her face. The last lingering trace of a smile clung to her lips. "Thinking?"

The anger left him in a rush.

She hadn't thought at all. That was the problem. She'd heard or seen something that captured her attention, and she'd followed it, a curious Alice in Wonderland.

She had no more idea of the risk she'd faced than a five-year-old would.

Her smile trembled. "Maeve said cats are nice to pet. Soft."

Ian released a heavy sigh. It was pointless to be angry, and he wasn't really angry anymore. She'd scared him. He'd watched her there, in the forest, a wraithlike ray of moonlight against the darkness, with her pale, slim hand offered in greeting to a wild animal, and something inside him had snapped.

He walked toward her, took her small hand in his and led her to the settee. They sat down, and she gave him a look of such eager innocence that he couldn't help smiling. She was so pathetically anxious to please him. How could he make her understand?

"Selena, the world can be a very dangerous place."

She frowned. "But the kitty—"

"It wasn't a kitty. It was full-grown wildcat, and it could have killed you. Do you understand?"

She glanced back at the window. Realization dawned slowly. Her eyes widened. "The cat would hurt me . . . just for a pet to it?"

He hated to disillusion and frighten her, but he had no choice. She had to learn to protect herself. "You can't go outside in the dark alone, Selena. No more."

She pulled her gaze away from the window and frowned up at him. "I always go out at night. I do not need the sleep that others do."

"Not anymore."

She considered that. Finally she shook her head. "This is not a rule I shall follow."

Ian was stunned. He straightened, looked down at her sternly. "You will not go out at night."

She wet her lips. "Yes I shall."

Ian stared at her. Now what did he do? He'd given her a direct order, in his most authoritarian voice, and this slip of a woman who thought he'd hung the moon had said no. Quietly. Simply.

No.

"Selena, this is for your own good."

She nodded. "Oh, I am most sure of that. But I believe I must seek my own good, also. Too."

Ian didn't know what to do or say, how to enforce a rule that any normal adult would simply accept. *Everyone* followed his orders.

Except Selena.

"Fine," he said at last, "you may not go out alone."

She pondered this.

He found himself leaning forward, waiting.

"No. I cannot make this promise."

"No? Why not?"

She gave him a quick smile and raised her hands in a gesture of helplessness. "Sometimes the moon calls to me."

"What do you mean?"

"Have you ever seen it? Moonlight on the beach? It is glorious. The waves are silver and black and blue and alive. Sometimes I open the window at night and smell the salty air and I am ... powerlust not to follow the moon."

He saw the wonder in her eyes, heard it in the throaty catch of her voice, and he was lost. He could not be the one to take wonderland from his innocent Alice. All he could do was be beside her, watch her, protect her.

She'd won.

He sighed. "Well, you've had a big night. Time to get back to bed."

She gave him a bright smile. "It was a grand adventure. Thank you for rescue me from the killing wildcat."

He fought a smile. "You're welcome."

Grinning, she jumped to her feet and headed for the door. As she reached for the brass handle, she stopped and turned around. "I am attaining a party tomorrow with Maeve. You would like to join us?"

"Party?"

"Tea and biscuits. It shall be at three o'clock in my secret place in the forest."

He couldn't deny her. "Fine, Selena. I'll be there."

She gave him another dazzling smile and skipped from the room, leaving the door wide open behind her.

He listened to the quiet patter of her bare feet on the wooden stairs and smiled. Then he laughed softly.

Damned if little miss innocent didn't have an iron will.

Ian stood at the edge of the forest, listening. Muted strains of conversation floated through the emerald thicket. Every now and again, a woman laughed.

He felt like a fool for standing here, motionless, and yet he couldn't quite force himself to take another step.

Tea with his mother. What a nightmare this could be.

Steeling himself, he forged ahead, following the twisting, leaf- and needle-strewn path through the tall, moss-furred trees. Finally he veered to the right and stepped over the fallen logs and mushrooms and ferns to reach Selena's hideout.

What he saw stopped him dead again.

Selena and Maeve were seated at a small, oval table. A bright patchwork quilt covered the table and draped to the dirty ground, puddling in folds of vibrant color. Several of his father's hunting trophies sat clustered on rocks and stumps between the two women. An eerily wide-eyed white owl leaned against a badger, his face frozen in a vicious snarl, his waxen paws poised in mid-air. Several stuffed peacocks huddled on a flat slab of granite, their blinkless glass eyes focused on the lop-sided cake in the center of the table. Red apples and cut flowers were scattered around the purple cake.

Purple.

Selena smiled at Ian and clapped her hands. "He came, Maeve. Look, it is Ian."

Maeve's head turned slowly toward him. She gave him a blank look that made his stomach tighten. Then, wordlessly, she turned back to the stuffed coyote in her lap and pretended to feed him cake.

Ian groaned. *Oh, Jesus . . .*

Selena patted the stump next to her. "I saved you a seat. Come."

Reluctantly he sat down beside her.

Selena made a great show of pouring him a cup of tea and cutting him a slice of cake.

He balanced the tiny, delicate china cup on his knees and stared at the cold amber liquid.

Maeve waved a hand in the air. "Oh, put it anywhere. My husband loves bread pudding."

Selena looked up. "Truly? I do not believe I have had bread pudding. Perhaps we shall try it sun. *Soon.*"

Ian rolled his eyes and took a sip of the weak, tasteless brew. "You shouldn't indulge her sick fantasies, you know."

Maeve's smile faded. She closed her mouth abruptly and hugged the animal to her chest, rocking it frantically.

Selena turned to him. "Whatever do you mean?"

"You're encouraging her to be mad. She should be alone in her room when she's like this."

"She would be in her room too much."

"So she would."

Selena stared at him. Slowly she put her cup down, but she didn't look away.

Ian shifted uncomfortably. "What are you looking at?"

"You made her stop smiling."

He snorted. "I often have that effect."

Selena frowned. "That is not something to be proud of."

"I didn't say I was proud of it. I said I often have that effect on my mother. It's the simple truth."

She bit down on her lower lip. "I do not think it is so simple."

He set the teacup down with a clatter. "I guess I should leave. I'm spoiling the party."

"How would it hurt you to pretend?"

He looked down at her, struck once again by the innocence in her gaze. She didn't understand him, didn't understand the world, or the history of pain that coiled around him and his mother. All she knew was that he had a choice—he could hurt his mother, or he could not hurt his mother. And she couldn't imagine why he would choose the former.

It made him feel small and petty and ugly, the innocence in her eyes. She worshipped him, had from the moment she'd first seen him, and now he was proving to her how unworthy he was of that honor.

Part of him was glad, relieved to be rid of the burden of her expectations. But part of him was unaccountably saddened. As if a great opportunity were slipping through his fingers, right now as he sat at this tiny table in the middle of the forest, an opportunity he'd never imagined, never dared to hope for. And all he had to do was reach out and take hold of it. . . .

"What do you want from me, Selena?"

"I want you to stay."

So simple an answer. Black and white. Good or bad. Stay or leave. There was no gray for Selena, no acceptable level of rudeness, no tolerable pain. There was only right and wrong.

He wished to hell he could find that innocence within himself again, that long-lost moral core.

"Just say yes," she whispered, encouraging him with a smile.

So easy . . .

With an awkward smile, he scooted closer into the table. His knees hit the wooden rim and rattled the china.

Maeve's head snapped up. "It is Ian." She looked around. "Nurse, his teeth are coming in. Soothe him."

"I shall get him, Maeve," Selena answered.

Maeve frowned, worked her lower lip nervously with her teeth, gripped the animal to her chest. "He cries when I touch him." Tears glazed her eyes. "Why does he cry?"

Selena gazed across the table at her. "Maybe he does not know it is you."

Maeve swiped at an invisible fly. "The bathwater is too hot. Bring the wine."

Ian closed his eyes and sagged forward, resting his elbows on the wobbly table.

Maeve jumped to her feet with a scream. Yanking up her skirt, she cast a quick backward glance, then surged toward Ian, reaching for him. Her gnarled fingers curled around his wrist and tugged hard. "I can't find my baby." She looked up at him through glassy, hazel green eyes. "Help me find my baby."

Images slammed through Ian's head. *My baby. Oh, God, my baby. Herbert will want to see his son.* The words catapulted into his brain, cycling through in an endless litany. Then came the images, the amorphous transference of thought.

Panic. Fear. Desperation.

His mother's emotions swirled around him, sucked him in. He could feel her anxiety; it caused his own heartbeat to speed up.

And then suddenly, through the red mist of frustration, he saw her. His mother, sitting at the cockeyed table in the middle of the forest. Deep, deep within the barking layers of dementia, she was there, watching him, hearing him, needing him.

The revelation stunned him. He'd never thought she was even marginally conscious of reality when she was in this state, but now he saw the truth. She was in there somewhere, fighting off the whispering voices of her imagination, the myriad fictional images that besieged her. She was there, small and frightened and alone.

"Mother?"

She blinked up at him. For a split second, he thought that she would see him, speak to him. Hope brought him to his feet beside her.

She swiped at another nonexistent fly and shook her head as if to clear it. "The rain is ruining the rhubarb."

He released his breath slowly and waited for the inevitable sense of disgust to settle in.

Amazingly, it didn't come. For once, all he felt when he looked at his mother was compassion.

Maeve wrenched away from him and hurried back to her seat at the table.

Ian stood there, still too stunned to move.

Selena rose beside him, touching his arm gently. "She will be herself again soon. Would you like some tea?"

Ian almost laughed. Slowly he turned and looked down at Selena. She stood beside him, tall and proud and beautiful, her hair in wild disarray around her face. Smiling. Always smiling.

He knew suddenly, as surely as he'd ever known anything in his life, that he could fall in love with this woman. Not the woman he'd created or saved or imagined, but this woman, with her quixotic smile and exuberant nature. This woman who in two days had turned his world upside down.

He drew back, frightened of her and himself and everything that this moment held. Things like this didn't happen in life; at least, if they did, they didn't happen to men like Ian. Good things happened to good people, and Ian was far, far from good.

"I am now to make apple and flower necklaces," she said. "You would like to help?"

He glanced down at the apples on the table and smiled.

Jesus, apple necklaces. It was a whole new world.

He nodded. "If you want me to."

"Oh, Ian," she said with a throaty laugh. "I always want you to stay with me. I feel love for you."

Ian almost crumpled at the simple, oddly worded sentence. It was the first time anyone had ever claimed to love him.

Chapter Sixteen

❧

Ian stood at his bedroom window, watching the commotion below like Zeus tracking the goings on of mortals. He wrenched the window upward. It squeaked and whined, reminding him that it had been a long time since he'd opened it.

Below him, they were having a party.

Johann and Lara were the leaders, strolling arm in arm down the gravel path. Dotty darted from sheltering tree to sheltering tree, gesturing wildly. Maeve cartwheeled past them. The high, clear sound of her laughter floated upward. The queen strode forward, waving at invisible subjects.

Selena somersaulted across the lawn, skirts flapping, then she shot to her feet and clapped, twirling and twirling until she fell in a laughing heap to the grass. The apple and tulip necklace hung at a cockeyed angle around her throat. A single petal fluttered to the grass, a brilliant white spot on the emerald green carpet.

Selena said something he couldn't quite make out, and then everyone lined up along the porch and began somersaulting across the lawn. The sun gazed lovingly down on them, glinting off their shining hair and multicolored clothing. The joyous sound of their laughter rang in the warm, sea-scented air.

Ian tried to manufacture a familiar feeling of disgust; after all, it was such an exceptional display of lunacy.

But surprisingly, he felt no such contempt. A smile, slow and tentative, crept across his face.

Which was more insane—tumbling across the grass on a beautiful spring day, or hiding in a lonely, darkened room, feeling an unnecessary sense of isolation?

All at once, Selena looked up at him. Across the distance, their eyes locked. He saw in her gaze all the welcome he could ever want. She waved him down. Then Johann started walking toward the beach and the little party followed him.

He knew instantly that he, too, would follow. He could try to do otherwise, could pretend indifference and force himself to remain alone, but he wasn't so dishonest. He wanted to be with her.

He stepped back from the window and eased it shut. Images of yesterday flashed through his mind, warming him, cajoling him.

Amazingly, Johann had been right. In an instant, a heartbeat, Selena had offered Ian a choice, and with nothing more potent, more life-altering, than a smile.

I feel love for you, Ian.

The words circled through his mind again. All through the long, lonely night in his solitary bed, he'd heard them. Over and over and over, gaining momentum, promising a magic he'd never dreamed of. A future he'd long ago given up on.

He grabbed a shirt from the chair and shrugged into it. With the eagerness of a kid, he hurried down the steps and outside, emerging into the bright sunlight.

Warmth splashed his cheeks. He raced across the lawn and plunged into the cold darkness of the woods, following the sound of laughter.

They were down on the beach in a scattered array. The sea was at low tide, a foamy hem along the gray and black stone. Sunlight glittered on the still bay, gave the water the appearance of polished steel.

Johann was sprawled out on a blue blanket, his arms wishboned behind his head. Lara was crouched over a tide pool, her bucket placed precariously on a barnacle-roughened rock. Maeve was staring out to sea, her hand tented across her eyes. No doubt she was waiting for her husband to come home again.

"Ah, the prodigal son returneth," Johann drawled, rising languidly to his elbows. He brushed the straggly hair from his eyes with a fluid stroke. Very slowly, he smiled. "Good to see you, Ian."

"Ian?" Selena swiveled around and looked at him. The second their eyes met, she gave him a devastatingly bright smile. "You are here."

The sound of her voice, hushed and seductive and intimate, washed through him, warmer than the sunlight.

"We were to have a picnic," Selena said, waving toward the basket. "You shall join us?"

Ian felt himself start to smile. "I'd love to."

Hours later, only Selena and Ian were left at the beach. The meal had long ago been eaten and cleaned up, the last remnants taken away.

They lay side by side on the blue blanket, gazing up at the clear, blue sky. Books were scattered around them.

"Tell me another story," Selena said in a drowsy voice.

Ian smiled. She was surprisingly adept at understanding concepts and ideas, and she brought an exhilaratingly fresh viewpoint to the telling of any story. He'd read parts of the Bible to her, some Greek mythology, and several fairy tales by the Grimm brothers. The romantic poets were her favorites, and always she wanted more.

"There is the story of Pandora—this parallels in some ways the biblical tale of Adam and Eve. Pandora was the first human woman made by the gods. The story is that Jupiter made her to punish Prometheus for stealing fire from Heaven."

"The first woman was made to punish man?"

He knew she would pick up on that. "She was made in Heaven. Every god contributed something to make her perfect. Then she was sent to earth, and Epimetheus accepted her—though he was warned to beware of Jupiter bearing gifts. Epimetheus had in his home a very special jar which held all the ills of the world—"

"He should have thrown this jar away."

Ian stifled a smile. "Pandora was curious." Ian looked at Selena. "Curious is what makes a woman follow the sound of a wild animal into the middle of the night. Anyway, Pandora snuck down one night and opened the jar, releasing all the evil into the world. She closed the lid quickly, but not quickly enough. Only hope was left inside."

Selena rolled onto her stomach and pressed up to her elbows, peering down at Ian with a frown. "She released all the evils onto the world and gave them no hope?"

"That's the myth."

She thought about that for a moment. "And they say *I* am damaged in the brain. I do not like this story."

"The other interpretation is that Pandora was sent in good faith by Jupiter, carrying a box in which each god had placed a blessing. Thoughtlessly she opened the box and all the blessings escaped. All except hope."

She smiled. "This is sensible. Who would put hope—it is so precious—in a box full of evil?" She nodded. "Yes, Pandora was made to help man, not to punish him."

He reached up, smoothed a tangled lock of hair from her eyes. At the touch, so simple, so like something he'd done to a million women in his life, she smiled brightly.

Little things, a touch, a smile, they meant so much to her.

She plopped back on her back. "Tell me another story."

He reached blindly for a book, and finding one,

pulled it onto his stomach. It was the story of Tristram and Isolde. For nearly an hour, he read to her, as the sun made its slow, elegant slide into the sea. He spun the tragic tale of a man trapped by honor into marrying the wrong woman, and of his wife—a good woman— consumed by jealousy for the other woman.

When he was finished, he turned slightly and saw that Selena was crying. Silvery tears slipped from the corners of her eyes and trailed down her pale temples.

"That is very sad," she said in a throaty voice. "Why would Tristram's wife lie to him?"

"She was jealous of Tristram's great love for Queen Isolde, and her jealousy cost Tristram his life. He died believing that his love had deserted him in his time of need."

"Why did Tristram not marry the woman he loved?"

"He was an honorable man, and honor demanded such a sacrifice."

Selena wiped the tears from her eyes and gazed up at Ian. Her hair hung in wavy strands along her damp cheeks. "This honorable. You have spoken of it before. I do not understand."

"It is more for men than women."

She frowned. "That is a bird."

He laughed.

"I have mistaken again. Sorry. I meant *absurd*. Is it important to be honorable?"

He felt a rush of bitterness at the naive question. "You are asking the wrong man, Selena. I have never been honorable in my life."

"Define honorable."

"Quite simply, honorable means moral, living your life so as not to willfully hurt people. To keep promises that you have made and never lie."

"And you are not honorable?"

He snorted derisively. "No. In my life, I have been inordinately dishonorable. I've done things *designed* to hurt people, and keeping promises was never my strongest trait."

Her voice fell to a whisper. "Why do you tell me such things?"

He leaned closer to her, so close he could lose himself in the mysterious darkness of her eyes. "As a warning, Selena. I don't want you to idolize me."

She laughed unexpectedly. It was vaguely irritating how funny she found his statement. "I do not idolize you, Ian. I feel love for you. I believe there is a most profound difference."

He felt like a fool, and damned if it didn't feel good. "Must you *always* say what's on your mind?"

She touched his cheek, a lingering caress. "I cannot speak what is on your mind."

"Ah, Selena." He sighed. She stared up at him, smiling, her face streaked with tears and sand, her hair clotted with leaves and pine needles. That absurd necklace around her throat. She had never looked more disarmingly beautiful. He realized in that second that he'd never understood beauty before, never revered it as he did in this moment. She was beautiful on the inside, in her soul. "You are . . . perfect," he whispered.

"No. I am damaged."

He could have kicked himself for what he had taught her. "You are all that a person strives to be, Selena. Good, kind, caring, loving, honest. Don't let the world—or me—steal that optimism from your heart."

She pressed toward him. "You think such things can be stolen. It is childish, Ian. Silly."

"But—"

"And you *are* honorable. You became a doctor to save people's lives. This must be honor. You touched me when you were afraid to, and this surely is honor." She pressed closer, close enough for a kiss. He felt the whisper-soft flutter of her breath against his lips, and it made him ache for more. "We are the same, you and I."

The moment mesmerized him. She mesmerized him. "What do you mean?"

"Perhaps I was a bad woman before my brain damage. But I do not care what I was, I care only what I will be. The future is more important than the past."

"The future." He whispered the awesome word. Ah, the hope, the need. For years he hadn't allowed himself to think of tomorrow, let alone whatever came after that. And now here was this exquisite woman, telling him to believe in a future, to reach for it and believe in it. To believe in himself.

"I will make a begin with you, Ian." She gave him a heartbreakingly earnest look and got to her knees, taking his hands in hers. "I shall be honest and honorable—always. Will you vow the same?"

He got to his knees beside her. "Being honest is easy. Being honorable is damned hard work."

Her gaze didn't waver. "I shall not fail."

Fear washed through him, then an exhilarating sense of hope. She was right; he knew it. He'd always known it. Honor, morality, optimism, they were all choices. Long ago, he'd made the wrong choices, taken the wrong road.

Did he have the strength to change his course?

"This is not so hard, Ian. Just a promise to try."

He knew he would fail; he always failed. But right now, in this magical moment, he couldn't deny her, couldn't deny himself. It was his last, best hope for his soul. "For you, Selena. I'll try."

"Psst."

The lisping sound seemed to come at Ian from a great distance away, floating in the darkness of his slumber. He turned slightly, pressed his face tighter into the feather pillow.

"Psst. Ian. You forgot to teach me to play croquet."

Ian blinked, came slowly awake. Grit burned across his eyes. "Wha . . ."

Selena was sitting on the bed beside him, hunched over so that her face was inches above his. Candlelight cast a golden net across her face. She was gazing down at him through those beautiful, liquid eyes, and her lips hinted at a smile that was seconds away.

"You promised to teach me to play croquet," she said again.

He frowned, rubbed his eyes. Some hazy part of his mind thought this was a dream, that he'd somehow willed her here beside him in the middle of a cold night. "Tomorrow."

"You said today. Soon it will be midnight, and Johann told me that at midnight the day is over."

"Johann the genius? What does he have to do with this?"

"He helped me to set up the game in the backyard."

Ian wedged up on his elbows and looked up at her. She sat blithely beside him, wearing nothing but a wisp of a lawn nightdress. "Go to bed, Selena." His voice was hoarse and thick.

She flipped back his coverlet and pushed her small, bare feet in beside him. "All right."

He felt her slip into bed beside him. For a moment, he couldn't breathe, couldn't move, he was so stunned. He felt the heat from her body, the firm length of her thigh along his. His heart started pounding, sweat prickled his brow. No one had ever told her that a maiden doesn't crawl into bed with a madman.

Honorable man, Ian.

A promise to try.

He jackknifed up and threw the coverlet back. "Fine. We'll play croquet."

She didn't move.

Reluctantly he glanced down at her. She lay still, her hair a tangled red-brown mass on the candlelit-gold pillow, her breasts a gentle curve of white lawn. There was a serenity in her eyes that stole his breath. "I knew you would keep your promise," she murmured, her voice husky and soft.

Sweet Jesus, he wanted to touch her. In the flickering candlelight, her skin looked petal-soft. A desperate groan caught in his throat. He staggered out of bed and stood there, breathing hard. Finally he forced himself to look away from her. He went to the window and stared through the tarnished glass until his breathing normalized.

He heard the quiet creak of the bed boards and the whispered pat of her bare feet hitting the hardwood floor. She came up behind him and stood there, waiting.

He tensed. *Don't touch me. Please* . . . The plea winged through his mind, took on the strength of a prayer.

She touched his shoulder. "Shall we go?"

God help him, for a second, he leaned into her hand, felt its heat on his skin. With a muffled curse, he ducked and spun away from her. Yanking his pants off the chair where he'd thrown them, he stabbed his bare feet into the black wool and buttoned them up. Then he grabbed his wrinkled woolen coat and shrugged into it. He was careful not to look at her. "You'll need a coat."

She laughed, a low, throaty sound that aroused him as much as any touch ever had. "I shall get a rope . . . a *wrap* and meet you in the yard."

Ian bolted from the room in front of her and hurled himself down the creaking steps. He burst onto the back porch and slammed the door behind him, drawing deeply of the fresh night air.

He buttoned his coat against the chilly night and walked down the sagging porch, onto the blackened new spring grass. He was so deep in thought, it took him a minute to notice what she'd done out here.

Squat, yellow candles dotted the squared perimeter of the lawn. There was no wind, and the burning pockets of light danced and pulsed against the velvet backdrop of the forest beyond. Overhead, the sky was thick with bright stars, and the moon was a scythe of blue-white light that reflected itself in the metallic wickets scattered across the lawn. The sea was a distant, humming murmur in the background.

It was a lovely, magical setting, created by a woman who believed in fairy tales and happy-ever-after endings.

For years and years he'd stood on this porch, beneath the shadowy, wisteria-festooned overhang, and looked out over this yard. All he'd ever seen was a cold, square patch of grass bordered by towering trees. It had never occurred to him that it could be anything else.

When had he stopped seeing such beauty in the ordinary world around him? And why had he let the ability to create magic slip away from him without a fight? Even as he asked himself the question, he knew the answer. He'd never let the ability slip away; he'd never possessed it in the first place. Even as a child, he'd seen the world in cold, rational terms. It was something he'd learned early on. Life wasn't fair or just or kind. He wouldn't—couldn't—have conceived of creating a place like this.

The door whined behind him, then cracked shut. "Are you ready to play with me?"

The velvety bourbon of her voice washed over him, reminded him that for all his experience with women, he was out of his league with her. Her quiet naïveté undid him, left him defenseless and vaguely out of control *Are you ready to play with me?*

He shivered at the subtle sexual innuendo, knowing that she had no idea what she'd asked. Or what his answer could be. He stepped back from the candles and turned to her.

She stood at the top of the steps, tall and straight. She'd twined her hair into a thick braid that lay curled over one shoulder. A pale yellow wrap as sheer as a wedding veil hung in shadowy folds over her nightdress. Big, muddy men's work boots stuck out from beneath the hem. Smiling, she reached down to the small leather case beside her and flicked the latch. The case fell open with a thump, revealing a row of mallets and multicolored balls.

She grabbed a handful of balls and two mallets and glided down the steps toward him.

He took a mallet and red ball and gave her a mallet and blue ball, then he tossed the remainders back onto the porch. Stepping back, he tried to keep some distance between them. "Now—"

She moved closer. "Now what?"

He stepped back. She stepped closer.

"Selena, I'd like to keep a little distance between us, if you don't mind."

She moved up next to him. "I do mind." She tilted her face up and gave him a radiant smile that shot straight to his heart.

Ian stiffened and forced a weak smile. He wished he'd never promised her a thing. "Fine. Let's get on with it." He gripped the mallet and bent over, showing her how to knock the ball through the first wicket.

Her gaze never left him as he slowly straightened. "Your turn," he said.

"Show me how to hold the mallet."

Reluctantly he went to her. She promptly turned her back on him and bent slightly forward.

He stared at her back. The pale skin at the base of her neck glowed in the meager light, reminded him suddenly that she was naked beneath the sheer wrap and gown. No corsets or chemises or drawers . . .

"Ian?"

He banished the erotic images and moved closer to her. Cautiously he eased his arms around her body and gently took hold of her hands, guiding them to the correct hold on the mallet. She released a shivery sigh at his touch.

"Concentrate," he said sharply. "And hit the ball through the wicket."

Suddenly she released the mallet and spun in his arms. Her smiling face filled his vision. Her puffy, kissable lips were a whisper away from his. He could feel the soft strains of her breathing against his chin.

"Why should I care whether the ball goes through the wacket?"

For a second, Ian couldn't breathe. She was so lovely, everything a woman could be. Earthy, sensual, innocent, seductive. How could he ever have thought her damaged? He tried to find a voice, and when he did it was throaty and harsh. "Those are the rules. You wanted to learn to play the game."

"Perhaps I would rather play something else with you, Ian."

The way she said his name sent shivers dancing along his spine. He gazed down at her, losing himself in the liquid chocolate of her eyes. Moonlight streamed through her gown and highlighted the shadowy body beneath. Without thinking, he touched the tip of her braid. The cinnamon-hued strands coiled around his finger, catching him in a soft, silken grip that he had no desire to break.

"We should go in," he said, knowing it was true. Knowing he'd rather die than give up this moment and return to the cold, black seclusion of his room.

"I do not want to go in. I want . . ." Her voice trailed off.

He felt breathless, a little light-headed with anticipation. "What do you want?"

"You." The last word was no more than a whisper.

One little word, spoken quietly and with such conviction. Ian sighed softly, unable to fight his own nature even a second longer He leaned toward her.

The kiss was nothing at first, a light touching of lips that was over almost before it began. He heard her sharply indrawn breath, saw her eyes widen in surprise.

Reluctantly he drew back, gave her time.

"What was that?" she asked.

He touched her cheek tenderly. "A kiss."

"Why did you do it?"

"I wanted to. I shouldn't have done it."

She frowned. "Why did you want to?"

"A man has . . . needs." He looked away, aching for her so badly in that moment, he felt weak in the knees. "I don't want to talk about it."

She smiled. "Me, too."

"Me too what?"

"Such needs are inside of me, also. I liked it very much."

He groaned at her honesty. "Ah, Selena. You're so trusting, so naive. I could crush you."

She gave him one of her blindingly bright smiles. "But you will not."

"You shouldn't believe in me so much," he said in a thick voice. "I'm not a good man."

She laughed. "It must be easy to become a doctor."

The topical change caught him off guard, though he ought to be used to her by now. "Why do you say that?"

"Because sometimes, Ian, you are very . . . brain-damaged."

He laughed in spite of himself. "Selena, don't be so damned charming right now. I'm trying like hell to be honorable. And it is not honorable to take advantage of a scantily clad virgin in the middle of the night."

"What is a virgin?"

"Someone who has never . . . slept in the same bed with a man."

Her face scrunched in thought. "But what if I have slept with a man before? Then I would not be a virgin and it would be honorable for you to—"

"What?"

She gave him a blank look. A cool breeze molded her nightdress to her shivering body. "What what?"

Ian felt as if he'd just been punched hard in the gut. He couldn't catch his breath. Jesus, how had he missed it? How had he so blindly accepted her as a lost soul, unconnected and alone like everyone else at Lethe House?

What if she was married? Oh, Christ, what if she had children out there?

He covered his face with one hand, trying desperately to hang on.

"Ian? You are to scare me. . . ."

He'd never been so frightened in his life. Someone could be out there, waiting to take her away from him.

He thought about the trip he'd taken a few weeks ago, the lawmen he'd spoken to, the descriptions he'd given, and he felt sick with fear. "Oh, Lord, Selena, what have I done?"

She pressed onto her toes and touched his cheek. So soft was her touch, so firm and gentle and loving, that he wanted to cry when she drew back. "Kiss me again."

He grabbed her by the shoulders and yanked her to him. He wanted to draw her inside him, to a place where only he could see her, only he could touch her. "You're mine," he breathed. "Mine."

"Ian—"

"I won't let you go."

She frowned. "I do not want you to let me go."

He wanted to lose himself in her innocence, but it was too late. He drew her into his arms and held her tightly, clinging to her, breathing in the sweet perfumed scent of her.

"You're mine," he whispered into her hair, knowing he'd said the words before, hearing the desperate whine in his voice, but unable to change it, unable to think of anything else to say.

She laughed, a bright, clear sound. "Oh, Ian." She hugged him, whispered against the sensitive flesh of his throat. "Of course I am yours."

God, he'd give his soul if it were true. But he'd lost his soul too long ago to bargain with it now.

"Can you hear the music?" she whispered.

He was so deep in thought, he barely heard her. "There's no music out here."

The breeze whispered through the trees, flapped the skirt of her nightdress. She slid out of his arms and looked up at him. In the distance, the sea was a droning murmur as it crashed against the rocks. "Listen more closely. Johann said music was a beautiful sound. I hear it all around me."

"Selena." He said her name in a throaty voice. Just that and nothing more.

She gazed up at him. "It is all so extraordinary, isn't it?"

He envied her her innocence, her ability to spin dreams. "There is no music out here, Selena. Just the wind and sea. Ordinary sounds."

She smiled. "You will hear it someday."

Chapter Seventeen

Selena stood at her bedroom window, staring down at the still-darkened yard below. Dawn was a distant blur of bloodred against the black horizon. She wakened, as always, refreshed and excited. Ready for the new day to begin.

Time didn't matter to her as it did to the others. She had relearned how to read the clock, and she knew that now it read 4:30. To Maeve, it was a completely unacceptable time to rise. It was a time for sleeping.

But Selena had slept enough in her life. Too much.

She leaned forward, pressed her forehead to the cold windowpane. Anticipation thrummed through her. The memory of last night wrapped her in warmth. Ian had kissed her, and it was the most wonderful sensation she'd ever imagined. She couldn't wait to feel it again.

Outside, the dark world beckoned her, called to her in a thousand subtle ways. She lifted the sash window, listening to the wonderful creak of the old wood as it reluctantly slid upward. A gentle breeze rolled through the bars, bringing inside the tangy scent of the tide flats. The leaves whispered and danced.

She shouldn't go outside. Ian had warned her not to. She should not be so *curious*; it had hurt the woman Pandora. But Selena couldn't care about that.

She simply had to be out there, feel the breeze on her

face, touch the dewy moisture on the grass. She put on her robe, then crept down the stairs and slipped outside.

Night clung to the velvet blue sky. In the distance, the sea and the forest were a giant, whispering black shadow.

"You should be in bed."

Selena jumped at the unexpected voice and spun around.

Andrew sat huddled in the shadowy corner of the porch, his legs drawn in close to his chest. His pale, thin face appeared disembodied above his black-clothed frame. Dark hollows accentuated his tired, bloodshot eyes.

She moved toward him, sat down. "What you are doing out here?"

He shrugged. "I don't like the daylight. You've probably never noticed. . . ."

Selena was ashamed for never having noticed something like that. "You do not leave the house except at night?"

"No."

Selena couldn't imagine such a thing. "When I feel the warmth of the sun on my cheeks, I think that God is touching me."

"Not me."

She heard pain in his quavering voice; it reached out to her, wrapped around her heart in a tight grip. She took his hand in hers and urged him to his feet. "Show me the night."

His eyes brightened. "Truly?"

"Yes."

A smile worked itself across his pale face. He tightened his grip on her hand and half dragged her down the steps and toward the trees. "We have to hurry. It will be dawn soon."

Hand in hand, they ran through the trees to a small clearing. All around them, jet black trees pushed up to the sky, enclosing them in a murky circle pierced by spears of moonlight.

She was struck by the primeval beauty. What she'd tried to create last night with candles and light, God had wrought with shadows and silence.

Andrew lay down and patted the cold, black earth beside him. Then he pulled out a long strip of flannel. "It is even more beautiful in my imagination," he said, blindfolding himself. "Close your eyes."

Eagerly Selena stretched out beside the young man. Once again, she threaded her fingers through his and held fast.

When she closed her eyes, her other senses burst to life. She smelled the sweet, heady scent of pine and the tangy smell of the sea. A cool night breeze kissed her lashes, made her nightgown flutter against her breasts and ankles. They lay there forever, holding each other, dreaming whatever dreams slid through their minds. Gradually the sun drifted upward, pushed shafts of pale light through the still dark trees.

"I wish I were blind," Andrew said quietly, gripping her hand in sweaty fingers. "I've seen things . . . bad things. . . ."

For a second, Selena couldn't breathe. She felt as if he'd just shoved her out onto a precipice; below was a painful, ruinous fall, and she didn't know how to keep her balance. She needed Ian or Johann right now, someone smart and learned. But there was no one here, and she was the person Andrew had confided in.

Very slowly, she rose to her elbows and turned to him. She brushed a damp lock of mousy hair from his blindfolded eyes. In the warm, early morning light he looked impossibly young and frail. "You are not crazy, are you, Andrew?"

"Wh-What do you mean? We're all crazy here, except you and Ian."

"No. Johann is a genius, but he's ill. I am hurt and

perhaps a little crazy. You . . ." She paused, searching carefully for the right words.

He shivered, drew slightly away from her. "You'd hate me if you knew what I've done. . . ."

"I cannot imagine anything—"

"No. You cannot." He cut her off. "I don't want to be here anymore." He sat up and ripped the blindfold off.

Sunlight splashed his face.

Selena had never witnessed such stark, all-consuming fear. Andrew's eyes widened, turned glassy and frighteningly bright. Slowly he shook his head from side to side and lifted his fists, as if to ward off a predator that only he could see.

"Andrew?"

He made a small, strangled sound and started to cry. Scrambling backward, he pushed through the damp earth and slammed into a tree trunk. Needles rained down on his moist cheeks and stuck; he seemed not to notice at all. Whimpering, he curled into a small, shaking ball. "Go away. . . ." His soggy voice caught, trembled. He started clawing at the red scars on his wrists, as if he wanted to reopen the flesh. "Please . . ."

Selena crawled toward him. "Andrew?"

His vacant eyes rolled back in his head and he started to scream.

Selena lurched to her feet. "I need help." She yanked up the hem of her nightdress and raced from the clearing. Breathing hard, she bounded up the porch steps and careened into the house, taking the stairs two at a time. Without a knock, she wrenched open Ian's door and hurled herself inside. "Ian?"

He was sitting up in bed, reading, his white nightshirt gaped across his naked chest. His face was drawn and too pale, as if he hadn't slept at all.

He turned to her. "What is it?"

"It is Andrew. I have done something wrong." The horror of it washed over her. She brought a cold, shaking hand to her mouth and started to cry. "He is outside. . . ."

Ian closed the book. "Andrew never goes outside in daylight."

"I . . . took him outside." The words tumbled out of her, forming themselves into a desperate, rambling apology. "It was still dark out. I didn't know . . ."

"Christ." Ian threw the covers back and got out of bed. He grabbed a frock coat from the chair by the window and shrugged into it. "Let's go."

Selena barely heard the command, and she was moving.

She heard the screams the moment she opened the front door. The shrill, undulant cries echoed through the still, silent air and lodged in her heart.

Without even realizing it, she skidded to a stop.

Ian touched her hand. "It's not your fault, Selena. He just does this sometimes. Every few months something sets him off and we . . . lose him for a while."

She shook her head, knowing it wasn't true, knowing she'd done something terrible to her friend.

He held her face in his hands and forced her watery gaze to meet his. "This is a place for lost and damaged souls, Selena. Andrew is sick. It's not your fault."

"Whose, then?"

Ian looked surprised by the question. "I don't know. How should I know what's bothering Andrew?"

She frowned. Obviously she had phrased her question poorly. "But you are his doctor."

Ian stiffened. "No. I'm his keeper. There's a difference." His hands slid away from her face. Without his touch, she felt colder, more alone. "Now, show me where he is."

Selena tried to sort through the rubble in her mind. There were so many questions she wanted to ask Ian, points she didn't understand. She thought a "keeper" took care of animals and a "doctor" took care of people. But she was wrong. Again.

The questions jumbled and scrambled in her head until she couldn't think at all. She reached for Ian, but he was already past her, moving down the gravel path.

She stumbled to catch up and led him into the woods. When they were halfway there, the screams stopped. One moment the world felt split by sound, and the next it was utterly, preternaturally silent.

Selena picked up her skirts and hurried, scrambling over fallen logs and rocks and patches of lichen to get to the secret place. Andrew was still there, curled in a tight, trembling ball, his face stained with dirty tears, his eyes vacant.

Selena came to a stumbling halt.

Ian moved toward Andrew and crouched down close beside him. Selena followed cautiously, kneeled on Andrew's other side.

"Andrew." Ian said the boy's name in a powerful, authoritative tone of voice. "Andrew. Can you hear me?"

Nothing.

"Andrew." Ian said the name again and again. With each repetition, Ian's voice became a little more strained, until finally it broke. He massaged his temple and looked away, sighing softly. "Oh, Jesus."

"You need to get him to look at you," Selena said. She was fighting panic with everything inside her, but the insidious emotion nibbled at her composure, made her want to cry again.

Ian drilled her with a desperate look. "How?"

"Get closer, talk more softly."

He flinched at every word, as if they were tiny darts flicked into his skin. He gritted his teeth and sidled closer, leaning down. "Andrew, can you hear me?"

Once again, there was no answer.

Selena inched closer. "Touch him the way you touched me earlier. Force him to look at you."

"Touch him?"

Selena heard the fear in Ian's voice and she understood. Maeve had told her of Ian's gift and the pain it caused him. "You must."

"I can't."

Selena's gaze didn't move from his face.

He swallowed and looked away from her. For a long, silent moment, he stared out at the trees and said nothing, then, finally, he turned back to Andrew. She noticed that his hands were shaking as he brought them to Andrew's face. Carefully he pressed his hands against Andrew's cheeks and tilted the boy's face up.

"Andr—" Ian didn't finish. With a cry, he yanked his hands away from Andrew's cheeks. He careened backward and fell to his knees, burying his face in his hands. He started to shake. "Holy Christ . . ."

Selena went to him. "Ian, what is it?"

Slowly he looked up. His hands plopped lifelessly in his lap. "I didn't know," he said, gazing at Andrew. "No one told me. Jesus, how could I not know?"

"What did you see?"

He bowed his head and rubbed his eyes, releasing a small sigh. "There are some things I hope you never learn, Selena."

"But Andrew—"

"Is too young to know that kind of pain." He shook his head again.

She moved closer, lifted her gaze to his. "You will help him." She'd meant to frame the words as a question, but somehow they ended up as a statement.

"He doesn't need medical care."

"You will help him," she repeated herself, softly.

He surged to his feet and backed away from her. "Enough of the hero worship, Selena. I'm not capable of helping people. Besides, what Andrew needs isn't possible. We can't change the past."

"Then change the future."

"Ah, Selena." Ian's whole body seemed to sag at her simple words. He turned and looked at Andrew. "This is a dangerous time for him. After a short period of catatonia, he usually tries to kill himself. Fortunately, he isn't very good at it. Last year—"

She gasped.

Ian glanced down at her. She could see that he had no idea how callous he had just sounded, how ugly his detachment was.

The insensitivity hurt her more than she could have imagined. It made her feel fragile, uncertain, as if she'd just discovered that the anchor in her world was wrought of spun glass. She touched his arm, curled her fingers around his wrist, tried to find the familiar strength and warmth in simply being beside him. But for once there was nothing strong or solid about him. Beneath her fingertips, he felt as ephemeral as a ghost.

She gazed up at him, knowing her eyes held the heartbreak in her soul. "He needs you."

He sighed heavily and shook his head. "Ah, Selena . . ."

"You will do what is right, Ian. I know you will."

She tried desperately to believe her own words, but fear was a cold, hard lump in her stomach.

She understood, finally, what a lie was.

Ian stood beside Andrew's bed. The boy lay motionless beneath the mound of gray-white bedding, his cheeks a pale chalky hue, his eyes open and unseeing.

Ian wished he'd been stronger with Selena, wished he'd turned and walked away from her pleading eyes. But he couldn't do it, couldn't destroy her so completely, even though he knew it was the safest, most honest course.

He pulled up a chair and sat down beside Andrew. The dark window shade that Andrew insisted upon covered the window, blocked the bright sunlight and kept the room shrouded in shadows. Beside the bed, a candle flickered.

Ian understood more than he wanted to now. So much more.

Andrew's frequent bouts of depression and habitual suicide attempts were no longer a tragic character flaw or symptoms of madness.

The boy had suffered horribly in his short life, the most degrading, painful, humiliating physical abuse imaginable. And Ian would bet money that the pain had come from a relative. Perhaps even Andrew's father.

Ian felt sick at the thought. He remembered his own father, his own childhood, and suddenly the pain he'd suffered because of his mother's illness seemed immature and misplaced. What Andrew had suffered was so much worse.

On the bed, Andrew moved.

Ian leaned forward. "Andrew?"

The boy whimpered softly. Tears squeezed from his closed eyes and streaked down his temples. "Go away . . . not again . . ."

Instinctively Ian reached out, brushed the hair from Andrew's eyes. One casual touch was enough. The sickening images slammed into his brain. He winced, fought the pictures, held the horror at bay by sheer force of will. After a few moments, they softened, turned dim and out of focus. He let out a harsh breath of relief.

He had to help this boy. But how? How could such memories be eradicated?

Common sense told him that it was impossible, that Andrew would carry these images like a stone on his heart until the day he died. Until one of his feeble suicide attempts succeeded.

So what could Ian do? Return to Selena and apologize, tell her that some heartbreaks were irreparable?

Such surrender was inconceivable. All of his life he'd accepted challenges that other men walked away from. He thrived on insurmountable odds, on beating the whims of fate.

He felt a stirring of ambition. The doctor he'd once been lifted his tired old head, peered through the dusty jacket of Ian's soul, and smiled. He was a trained physician—once he'd been the best of the best—and he'd sworn to help people in pain. And Andrew was in more pain than any patient he'd ever treated.

Ian went to his bedroom and pawed through his books, pulling down anything about diseases of the mind. When he had everything, he went back to Andrew's room and resumed his seat.

One by one, he read the books, kept reading until the sun began its lingering descent into the silver sea. He closed the last volume at seven o'clock that night.

He threw it across the room and stared dully at the pile of books and papers beneath the window. He'd never studied psychiatry before, certainly not with so specific an inquiry in mind, but he'd always thought of it as a fringe science, a loose collection of tricksters and misguided doctors trying to cure the incurable or watch the inevitable. Still, he'd thought they knew *something*, that they'd at least developed a theory for helping their patients.

But they were dangerous men, ugly and frightening in their narrow-minded view of the world in general, and women in particular. He stared at the paper at his feet. Thomas Hawkes Tanner's "On Excision of the Clitoris as a Cure for Hysteria."

Hysteria. That's what they called it when a woman said she'd been raped as a child.

"Hysteria." He shook his head, thinking of the articles and ideas he'd read. They left him feeling dirty and ashamed of his profession. Dr. Freud—supposedly one of the best alienists of the time—had been the only beam of hope in a dark, dirty, misogynistic profession. At first Freud had believed the women who reported that they'd been raped as children, and his theories excited Ian.

Then, for no apparent reason, Freud had stopped believing. Suddenly these same women who years before had been victims were now suffering from "hysterical fantasies."

Ian had no source in his library that even allowed for the possibility of what had happened to Andrew. The respected psychiatrists would clearly treat the boy as if he were hysterical—no doubt they'd use electrical shock treatments on his genitals to cure him of the unacceptable "fantasies" that lurked in his mind.

It was sickening.

Ian shoved a hand through his hair, wondering what to do. Unlike his "colleagues," Ian had access to the ultimate, unvarnished truth. He knew Andrew was neither hysterical nor fantasizing. The boy was a victim, pure and simple.

And so, it fell on Ian's shoulders to treat his patient.

Anticipation nibbled at his consciousness again. He'd owned an insane asylum for ten years, and managed it for six; and now, finally, he was going to treat his first patient.

Andrew released a quiet moan.

Ian leaned forward and forced himself to touch the boy's shoulder. "Andrew? Can you hear me? It's Dr. Carrick."

Andrew blinked groggily. Slowly his eyes opened.

Ian felt a rush of pure adrenaline. Just like the old days. "Andrew? I'm here."

Andrew turned his head. "Dr. Carrick?"

Ian stared down into the boy's pale gray eyes. "Hello there, Andrew. You gave us quite a scare."

"You touched me," Andrew said softly.

"Yes."

Tears glazed Andrew's eyes. His lip trembled. "You shouldn't have done that, Dr. Carrick. I was always so careful around you."

"I'd like to help you, Andrew."

He turned his face away. "No one can help me."

"Maybe if we just . . . talked . . ."

Andrew pressed his face tighter into the pillow. "He said he'd kill me if I told anyone."

"He'd have to kill me first."

Very slowly, Andrew turned back toward Ian. "You'd protect me?"

Ian nodded.

Andrew started to cry quietly. It was a long time before he could stop.

Ian said nothing, just sat there, waiting. Finally Andrew wiped his face and looked up at Ian through eyes that were pathetically hopeful. "I need help, Dr. Carrick."

A lump formed in Ian's throat. "We all do, Andrew. We all do."

Chapter Eighteen

❦

The moon was bright and full and ringed by clouds. It cast a bluish white aura of magic across the dark night.

Selena followed Ian from the house.

He slipped through the garden's wrought-iron gates and went to the gazebo, sitting on the granite bench inside, leaving the gate open behind him.

She followed slowly, careful not to step on a twig or branch or make any sound. At the gate she paused, allowing herself—just for an instant—to believe that he'd left it open on purpose. A silent invitation.

But she couldn't lose herself in the fantasy. This morning she'd glimpsed another, darker side of Ian, and it had frightened and confused her. He had been cold and needlessly cruel.

His selfishness made her feel frighteningly alone. As if some integral, necessary part of her soul had splintered. For hours she'd sat on the porch steps, trying to understand what had happened. There was no one she could ask. Johann would be sarcastic; she was certain of it. Edith wouldn't allow herself to speak of "the master" that way, and Maeve . . .

Selena sighed. Poor Maeve had spent the day in the kitchen, making her long-dead husband a cherry tart.

Selena had wandered through the silent house, time and again passing in front of Andrew's closed door. She waited patiently, and not so patiently, for Ian to leave the boy's room, but the door had stayed closed until a few moments ago.

In her need to understand Ian, she'd consulted book after book, but none of them answered her question. Until finally, when she'd almost given up, she'd opened a book of poetry that Ian had once read to her. Almost magically, it had fallen open, and she'd found the words she needed so desperately.

> If thoust must love me, let it be for naught
> Except for love's sake only. Do not say
> I love her for her smile—her look—her way
> Of speaking gently—for a trick of thought
> That falls in well with mine, and certes brought
> A sense of pleasant ease on such a day—
> For these things in themselves, Beloved, may
> Be changed, or change for thee—and love,
>   so wrought
> May be unwrought so.

It had taken her a long time to understand the poem's true message, but finally she saw that Miss Browning was explaining the very nature of love.

With the words, Selena began to understand the emotion she'd given so freely. Her first true memory was of Ian. It sounded trite and ridiculous, but for as long as she could remember, he'd been her sun, her moon, her world. Naively she'd thought she loved him; it was the only word that fit the enormity of her feeling. But now she saw her mistake. She'd been mesmerized by Ian, bewitched by his quicksilver moods, captivated by the most brilliant smile she'd ever seen.

It had been an illusion, though, a young girl's whimsy. If she was to cross the yawning channel between infatuation and true love, she would have to do it now, with her eyes wide open and her heart too vulnerable to bear. She would have to accept his imperfections, his vices, his fallibility; just as he would have to accept hers. And it would only be a beginning, nothing more.

She took a single step forward, her fingers resting lightly on the chilly iron bars of the gate. The sweet fragrance of hyacinths, jonquils, and blossoming snowdrops hung in the crisp air, their white faces peering through the shadowy lattice sides of the gazebo. Ian sat on the granite bench, his back turned to her. Moonlight caressed his hair, gave it the appearance of a golden halo against the stark, unrelieved black of his coat.

"Hello, Selena," he said without turning around.

She gasped softly. "How did you know it was me?"

"No one else would dare follow me here."

She clasped her hands and walked toward him on the small granite path that wound through the beds of white flowers. Her heart was beating too quickly, and a strange moisture dampened her palms.

This could be an end for them, right now, in the magical quiet of this garden. Ian could turn away from her, return her to the cold darkness of her life before his smile.

She released a shaky breath and twisted her damp hands together. For the first time, she spoke a thought that was not truly on her mind. "Did you help Andrew?"

He didn't turn to her. "Not yet."

At the answer, so quietly spoken, Selena felt a rush of affection for him. He probably didn't even know what the words meant, the effort they implied. She knelt before him and looked up. Their gazes met, and in his eyes she saw a quiet, resigned suffering.

"I disappointed you today," he said in a crisp, matter-of-fact voice.

"Yes."

He gave a laugh, soft and bitter in the darkness. "I told you I would."

She heard the finality in his voice and it angered her. "You yield too quickly."

He drew in a sharp breath and looked down at her. "I've always cut my losses fast."

"But love—"

"Love." He shot the word at her like a poison dart. "You know nothing of love and less of me."

"I know you as well as I know myself."

"So you do. Of course, you don't know your own name."

The caustic edge to his words saddened her. She didn't understand why he wanted so badly to believe the worst of himself. "Oh, Ian. You are so troubled with the unimportant. I know all I need to know of myself."

"And what's that? That you love me? Is that your defining characteristic?"

"No. I am like any other human. My opinions and emotions and beliefs define me—not some word I cannot recall."

He touched her then, and she saw the sadness in his eyes. "So you have found opinions at last. And what do you believe in, my goddess?"

For once, the words fell from her lips easily, forming themselves from the emotions in her heart. "Goodness. Honesty. Beauty. Second chances. The feel of a raindrop on my lips. Laughter and tears and the healing power of each." She eased up on her knees and tilted her face to his. "I believe in you, Ian."

"Selena—"

She touched his lips to still the protest. "Shh. Listen to me. I may be brain-damaged, but I am not stupid. I *watch* the world, Ian. Things that you long ago stopped seeing, stopped believing in, are still real for me. Who is more wrong—the child who believes in fairy tales or the adult who does not?"

He stared down at her. Brushing a knuckle along her jawline, he tilted her face just a little. "What in the hell do I do with you, Selena?"

Tears burned her eyes. She wished she had the intelligence to tell him what it was she felt, but she was no poet. "Just love me, Ian. Make a beginning with me."

He gazed down at her, his flame blue eyes almost luminescent in the pale moonlight. "What if it's wrong, Selena?" His voice broke. "What if you belong to someone else?"

This question that bothered him so much meant nothing to her. All she cared about was the look in his eyes and the way he made her feel when he touched her. "How could it be wrong?"

He gave her a smile that was heartbreakingly sad and touched her face. "Ah, Selena . . ."

She leaned forward, pressed her cheek into the heat of his hand and closed her eyes.

He made a soft, groaning sound and pulled her into his arms, holding her so fiercely she couldn't breathe.

Ian poured himself another huge glass of whiskey and tossed it down, tasting nothing, feeling only the false warmth in his gut.

Wobbling, laughing quietly to himself, he made his reeling way to his desk and sat down with a thud. The papers strewn across the mahogany surface blurred before his eyes.

For a split second, he saw the letters he'd filed at every post office between here and New York City. He'd told hundreds of people about the mysterious woman in his care. Hell, he'd *begged* her family to come forward.

He crashed his fist to the desk and swept the offending whiteness away. Papers scattered to the floor.

What was he going to do? Sweet Jesus, what was he going to do?

It was the question that haunted him, drove him to his knees and kept him reaching for the booze. Every moment, every second, every breath, reminded him that Selena might someday be taken away from him, that he—ignorant, selfish bastard that he was—had alerted the world to her presence. Every time the wind tapped on the windowpane, he jumped; every time Fergus drove into town for the mail, Ian stood at his window, sweating, obsessing, waiting for a letter to arrive.

To whom it may concern: I'm coming to claim my wife.

My wife, my wife, my wife. The mother of my children . . .

He grabbed the fragile lamp from the corner of his desk and threw it in frustration. It hit the paneled wall with a thwack and crashed to the floor in a spray of broken glass. Flames shot up from the pool of fuel on the wooden floor, licked the dark cherry paneling. The acrid scent of smoke wafted through the air.

He stared at the flames. In the reddish gold swirls, he saw her eyes, the color of maple syrup, eyes a man could lose himself in. And her hair, the wavy, untamed sweep of burnished brown. So soft and sweet-smelling; it slipped through his fingers like silk.

He squeezed his eyes shut, wishing he'd touched it more, wishing he'd kissed her more deeply, more often, wishing he'd peeled away her cheap gingham dress and stroked the petal softness of her skin. Wishing, ah Jesus, wishing . . .

The door to his study slammed open. "Good God, Ian," Johann barked. "What in the hell?" He raced over to the broken lamp and wrenched off his coat, using it to stomp out the flames.

Ian tried to focus on Johann, but the younger man was blurry, swaying. A semihysterical laugh slipped from Ian's mouth. "Drink, Johann?"

Johann yanked up his coat and turned to Ian. Charred bits of fabric fluttered to the pale carpet, smoke wafted up from the sleeves.

Ian laughed again. "Ah, look, a smoking jacket."

Johann rolled his eyes. "You're soused."

Ian waved him over. Anything was better than the loneliness, the sickening thoughts that sped unrelentingly through his mind. "Drink with me, Johann."

Johann poured himself a stiff drink and took a seat opposite Ian's desk. He dropped his burnt coat in a heap at his feet. "You don't look so good."

"I feel worse."

Johann frowned sharply. "My God, a human response. What is the world coming to?"

Ian rested an elbow on the hard wooden arm of his chair and rubbed his eyes, sighing softly. "What in the hell is wrong with me?"

Johann's face softened, a smile caressed his thin lips. "You don't know?"

"All I know is that I've finally gone over the edge. One word from Selena, a word, and my mind . . . snapped. I can't get it out of my brain."

Johann leaned forward. "What did she say?"

"Slept. As in, maybe she slept with a man before her injury."

"Holy mother of God." Johann slowly sank back into his chair. "She's so innocent. . . . I never considered that she could be married. What are you going to do?"

There was the question again, the one he couldn't outrun. "I'm going to kill anyone who comes for her."

Johann got slowly to his feet. "No wonder you've been locked up here for days."

It felt so good to talk about it with someone, to be less alone. "I'm afraid to see her, Johann. An honorable man would stay away."

Johann took a long sip before responding. "It was my understanding that you reveled in your dishonor."

Ian released a steady breath. "You said she would change me, and she has. I know I'm a selfish bastard, but I don't think I can change it. If I see her, I'll take her to my bed, and if I do that, I'll kill any man who comes for her."

"Frankly, that's the most sensible thing I've ever heard you say. So what's the problem? You're rich. The rich can murder anyone and get away with it."

He looked at Johann. "What if she has children, Johann?"

Johann's smile faded. "I don't know what to tell you."

He stared at Johann, wishing suddenly that the scotch could warm him. "Tell me this, then," he said softly. "Tell me how to have a normal life."

"You ask me?" Johann raised his hands in the air. "There is no normal life."

Ian leaned back in his chair and ran a hand through his dirty, disheveled hair. "I want to sleep, Johann. I want dreams instead of nightmares. I want . . ."

"Selena."

Ian squeezed his eyes shut, and knew it was a mistake the instant he did. She came full force into his mind, taunting, teasing, reminding. *I feel love for you, Ian. I believe in you. Kiss me again. What if I am not a virgin? What if—*

His eyes popped open. Despair coursed through him, made him ache for another drink. "What would you have done to keep Marie?" The question slipped out on a drunken slide, intimate and tinged in desperation. Ian tried not to look up, tried to keep his gaze focused on the desk, impersonal, cold.

The silence stretched out. Ian heard the soft, rhythmic pulse of Johann's breathing, and his control snapped. He looked up, staring at Johann through bloodshot eyes. "Answer me," he whispered, needing something from Johann in that minute that he couldn't fathom, didn't want to explore. Absolution, understanding; he didn't know what, but it made him feel weak and pathetic.

Slowly Johann lowered himself to his seat. His voice, when at last it came, was soft and uncertain. "I would have done anything."

Ian's tension released in a rush. He sagged forward, buried his face in his hands. He wanted to take comfort in Johann's words, to believe that he was normal in his reaction, but he wasn't yet so delusional. Ian had never done anything halfway in his life; there was no moderation in his soul. He had always been full speed, obsessive about everything. When he was a doctor, he was only that, nothing else. When he decided not to be a doctor, he hid away in the darkness, being nothing, substituting nothing. He'd lived either in the full light or in the full darkness, nowhere in between.

"I won't let her go," Ian said softly, not particularly to Johann. He simply said it, meant it.

Johann frowned. "But if she's married—"

"Enough." Ian barked the word, so loud his own voice rang in his ears. He couldn't stand it anymore, couldn't live this way. Once, maybe it had been fine, he'd been content to wallow in self-pity and hide away from the world. Once, the alcohol had been enough. Now nothing was left to him, nothing but Selena. She'd brought him out of his paralysis, shoved him into the full light of day, and he couldn't go back. Wouldn't go back.

He grabbed the crystal decanter and poured himself another drink, tossing it back without tasting it. "Get Edith and Fergus and everyone up here. Now."

Johann studied him. "What are you up to, Ian?"

He threw his empty glass at the fireplace, watching it shatter against the green marble. "I'm going to lock this place up tighter than a nun's drawers. No one will come in or go out. I'll send word to all of the towns I visited, telling them that the mysterious amnesiac has been claimed. I'll stay with Selena night and day, be beside her. No one will ever find her."

It was a long moment before Johann spoke. "You're describing a prison."

Ian gave him a steely look, wishing suddenly that he hadn't spoken to Johann at all. "Think of it as a sanctuary."

"Ian—"

"Don't," he said sharply, too sharply. He saw the concern in Johann's eyes and felt a flash of conscience.

He shouldn't do this. It was wrong. Dishonorable. The words shot through his mind like needles, trying to find purchase, seeking some remnant of the rational man he'd once been.

But there was nothing left in him except a driving, burning obsession to keep her beside him, to stay in the light. He couldn't just sit and wait for the end.

To whom it may concern . . . my wife . . .

"No," he screamed, surprised to hear the sound of his own voice. He couldn't give in so easily.

"Ian, you're—"

"Mad," he said with a shrill laugh. "Yes, I am. But no one will take her from me, Johann. *No one.*"

He heard the words for what they were.

A gauntlet thrown down to God.

Selena didn't understand what was happening. Last night Ian had been a stranger to her, frightening and distant. He stood in the center of the parlor, his eyes cold and narrowed, pacing the small room like a caged tiger, crashing into the walls, reeling with every step. He'd issued order after order in a voice she didn't recognize, slurred and ugly. No one was to leave the property for any reason. The doors were to be locked and kept locked. Only Ian would answer the door, only Ian would speak to strangers. No mail would leave the asylum, not even Lara's letters to her parents, and no mail would be received. Fergus had been sent on a mysterious mission; he'd left in the dark and not yet returned.

In an instant, everything at Lethe House had changed. The change had something to do with Selena, it was somehow her fault, but she couldn't understand what she'd done so wrong.

She'd tried to ask Ian, but he wouldn't look at her, wouldn't touch her. When their gazes happened to cross, he would look away quickly, but not before she noticed the pain in his eyes or the shaking in his hands.

He was out of control and it frightened her.

He talked about her all the time. Every sentence he uttered carried her name, only there was no softness in his tone, no love in his voice. When she took a step, or reached for the door, or looked out her window, he was there, screaming at her to *get back*, to *get inside*. It was as if the night in the garden were a dream, a twisted vision of intimacy created by her battered mind.

The glorious world beyond the doors was suddenly closed to her, closed to all of them.

Maeve and Lara and Andrew had immediately gone back to wearing gray, to whispering among themselves with downcast eyes and hushed, hurried voices.

Selena moved to her window, all that was left to her of the world, and stared out. Another night was falling, creeping along the horizon in lengthening shadows.

She had not been out all day. She felt restless and fidgety, bruised by her confinement. She didn't know what she had done to incur Ian's wrath, but she knew that she couldn't live this way.

Perhaps he could survive in the dark, like some low, marshy forest plant, dwelling forever in the shadow of the ferns and the trees, but she could not. She was like the flowers that bloomed in the wide-open spaces, the daffodils that splashed in a yellow cascade down the grassy hillsides. She needed the sunlight on her face. It wasn't enough to breathe the air in this house, she needed to feel it fluttering against her skirts, needed to soak in its salty scent.

Straightening her spine, she plucked up her long skirt and went to her door, opening it slowly. It creaked and whined in the unnatural silence. Her heart sped up, anticipation brought a smile to her lips.

She crept down the shadowy hallway, past the closed door to Maeve's chamber, past the stairway that led to Ian's room. Down each creaking step, pausing, then moving slowly downward. At the wide, open foyer, she stopped, breath held, listening.

A low, droning murmur of conversation wafted from the parlor. Ian and Johann were arguing again.

It was now or never. She wrenched open the front door and barreled outside, forcing herself not to laugh as she sped along the gravel path and through the night-time forest.

The beach welcomed her in a thousand little ways. Wispy purple clouds crawled across the twilight sky, casting a myriad of shifting, dancing shapes on the undulating sea. Tiny stones rattled in the breeze. The air smelled of seawater and pine and life.

She hugged herself and twirled around, reveling in the freedom, then she walked to the edge of the cliff, staring down at the swirling, turbulent white-tipped waves below. The sea breathed and pulsed, drew back, then hurled itself against the black rock ledge. Spray splashed her face. All around her, flowers shivered in the cold night air, tossing their multicolored faces in the breeze. A low hedge of phlox crept out from the shadow of the forest, as if seeking the magificent view for itself.

"Selena!" Ian's angry voice broke through the silence.

She stiffened and slowly turned around.

He stood at the edge of the forest, half-dressed. Black breeches hugged his long legs, and a white lawn shirt hung at an awkward angle over his naked chest. "What in the hell are you doing?" There was a cold evenness to his voice that chilled her to the bone.

"I needed to be outside."

He surged toward her, his booted feet striding across the uneven layer of gray rock. When he reached her, he grabbed her by the upper arm and yanked her away from the ledge. Holding her in an iron, unforgiving grip, he half dragged her through the forest and back toward the house.

At the lawn, he paused for a second, and she wrenched

free. Her breath came in great, wheezing gasps. "I misunderstand what you are doing."

"Get in the house."

Nervously she wet her lips. He stood there, tall and incredibly handsome, his gold hair glinting in the half-light, his eyes an almost incandescent blue. She longed to be what he wanted, to do what he asked, but she couldn't give up the sun. Not the sun. "No."

He closed his eyes for a heartbeat, but not before she'd seen a flash of raw pain. "Get inside."

Her instinct was to go to him, take his hand and kneel before him, drawing him down into the warm grass beside her. To touch his cheek and gaze into his eyes and ask him what he was scared of, but she dared not get so close to him.

She had seen something in him in the past day that frightened her. A desperation, an anger that was too close to the surface. He was like a wild animal, prepared to do anything, hurt anything, to be free.

And he looked at her differently as well. It broke her heart the way he looked at her, reminded her of the days when he'd seen nothing but a patient. Now he saw nothing but a possession, something to keep at all costs. Once again, he wasn't seeing her.

He lunged toward her, grabbed her by the shoulders and dragged her close. "I'm trying to keep you safe, you little idiot. Don't fight me."

She gazed up at him. "I cannot be you, Ian."

"What do you mean?"

"I will not live in darkness to be safe."

"It's the only way, Selena."

"Then let me go now."

A wild fury flashed through his eyes and he yanked her close again. So close, she could feel how he was shaking, smell the alcohol on his breath. "Never," he hissed. "You're mine."

Selena stared up at Ian; suddenly he was a man she'd never seen before.

He didn't want to love her. He wanted to own her.

The realization brought a wrenching sense of sadness and loss. "Do you remember that poem you read to me, 'The Lady of Shallot'?"

A little of the wildness left his gaze, and for a heart-breaking moment, he was her Ian again, seeing her, listening to her. "Yes."

"She was locked in a room, alone. She had but one rule to live by: She could not look down to Camelot. Then she saw Lancelot and she was powerlust not to look at him." Selena pressed up onto her toes, brushed the stubborn curtain of hair from his eyes. "I would have to look."

It was a long time before he answered. They stood there, touching and yet not touching, their gazes locked. In the depth of his blue eyes, she saw his uncertainty and his fear, and it called out to her, made her understand for the first time that life was unfair, and that love could hurt.

Lord, how it could hurt.

His hands slid down the length of her arms, and she shivered at the intimacy of the touch. "It killed her to look at him," he said softly.

"Yes," Selena said simply, knowing he saw the truth in her eyes. She, too, would die to see the world. Just once.

"Jesus, Selena ..." He looked away from her. His sharp, patrician profile looked to be hewn from granite, hard and unforgiving. But she saw the tremble in his jaw. Instinctively she reached out, pressed her cold hand to his warm, stubble-coated cheek.

She applied a gentle pressure, forced him to look down at her. "Do not be so afraid, Ian. I am not."

"You aren't afraid of anything."

"You are wrong. I am afraid of losing you. And I am afraid that you will look at me again as you have looked at me in the past few days."

"And how is that?"

"As a . . . possession."

He sank slowly to his knees, drawing her down with him onto the cold, damp grass. Night curled around them, warm and intimate and cleansing. It was as if there were no world beyond them, nothing that mattered except their two souls in the midst of a great, starlit darkness.

"I'm afraid, Selena." He said the words quietly. "And I don't know what in the hell to do about it."

She snuggled up to him. His arms slipped around her, drew her close. She tilted her face up to his. Behind them, Lethe House winked in windows of golden light; the stars smiled down.

"Kiss me," she whispered.

Very slowly, he brought his hands to her face, cupped her chin as if it were wrought of spun glass. Then he bent forward.

His lips claimed hers in a fierce, tender kiss that left her breathless. Instinctively she arched toward him, buried her fingers into the silky fringe of his hair, drawing him closer and closer to her. She couldn't get him close enough. She needed more, wanted him to be a part of her.

"Slow down, little one," he breathed.

The moist heat of his breath caressed her tingling lips. Drugged with newborn desire, she shook her head. "Don't stop."

He laughed shakily and drew back. "We'd better stop, goddess. Anyone in the house could be watching."

"I don't care."

He gave her a crooked smile. "Surprisingly, I do." He got slowly to his feet and offered her his hand.

A chill moved across her skin, brought a flurry of goose bumps. She looked up at him, feeling oddly off center. He stood tall and straight, his white shirt aglow in the moonlight. He acted as if nothing unusual had happened, and yet she felt as if the world had just slid off its axis.

Slowly she placed her hand in his, feeling the warm, moist heat of his flesh against hers, and she shivered again.

Suddenly she understood.

Locking her up, closing the doors. He'd been protecting her, keeping this moment possible. It wasn't about fear, although that was part of it; it was about stark, desperate need. About the essence of life.

Already she couldn't imagine a life without Ian. She needed this moment, this sensation, and a million moments like it in her future, needed it like the air she needed to breathe. And yet she knew that he was afraid it was a mirage, something that wouldn't last.

He thought there was someone *out there* who could take her away from him.

She launched herself forward, clinging to him, at last understanding his fear. For the first time, sharing it.

Please, God, she thought desperately. *Don't let me own a husband.*

Without Ian, she wouldn't want to live.

Chapter Nineteen

❦

The next morning, Selena woke early and went outside. She loved the twilight hours of dawn and dusk when the sun was a brilliant, colorful glow that obscured the horizon and painted the still-dark world in shades of purple and red and gold. As always, she wore only her nightgown. She cared little that the lacy hem got dirty and wet from her trek through the trees, that she came home with dark, freezing feet.

What mattered were the sensations, the thousands of tiny unexpected pleasures. A mushroom squishing between her toes, the chilly kiss of dewy grass against her ankle, the icy slickness of the beach stones beneath her feet.

She walked through the forest, touching everything, stroking a dozen leaves, noticing their different textures and scents. Birds twittered down at her from their invisible perches high in the spruce and pine trees.

Invigorated, she plucked up her soggy, dirty hem and strolled back to the house, trying to master the wonderful skill of *whistling*. When she reached the house, she expected it to be full of people, but unfortunately, everyone was still asleep.

With a sigh, she went to the parlor and retrieved her stitchery, snuggling into a comfortable leather chair to wait for the rest of her family to awaken.

Beside the chair was the ebony japanned notion box

that Maeve had given her. Lifting the lid, Selena marveled again at the colorful spools of thread and yarn. She chose a bright purple and began to work.

It took almost three minutes for her to lose interest—this was an improvement, and she was pleased. Yesterday she'd lost interest immediately. The small, white circle of fabric, drawn taut by a wooden hoop, taunted her, reminded her with every prick of the thumb that her fingers didn't work correctly. Normally it was not something she noticed except at mealtimes, but tasks like this were an unavoidable reminder. There was a curious tie between her brain and her hands, something Ian called motor skills, and hers were *impaired*.

She laughed at the thought. Who cared? She didn't want to make needlepoint, or eat, for that matter; she did both only to please Maeve. Selena herself saw no need for another pretty pillow in this house. What Lethe House needed was gardens, lots and lots of gardens, where the flowers bloomed year round, in a dozen brilliant colors. And paintings of sunny days and brilliant blue oceans. And laughter, always more laughter.

The study door creaked open. "Lord, Selena," Johann said, stumbling into the room. "Don't you ever sleep?"

She gave him a quick smile. "Not much."

He made a growling sound deep in his throat and took a long drink of the delicious-smelling brew called coffee. Forming his fingers around the delicate china cup, he glanced at the fallen needlepoint. "Having your usual success with fancywork, I see."

"Yes. It is most frustration." She looked at him sharply, seeing the dark circles that accentuated his watery eyes. "You do not look healthy."

He gave her a lackluster smile and sat down in the chair opposite her. "I'm dying, don't you know."

Something cold touched her heart at the words.

"Aren't you going to say something?" he quipped. "Some vapid remark about my future?"

She released a quiet sigh. "But you told me that you *are* dying. I cannot lie to you about that."

He gave her another smile, this one sad and honest. "I appreciate the honesty, Selena."

"What does it mean, exactly, that you are dying?"

He looked at her strangely, and she thought for a second that he wasn't going to answer, then, very slowly, he said, "That is a big question, one that has obsessed the philosophers for ages. Death is . . . like sleep, maybe, except that you never wake up. When your heart stops, the body cannot function anymore. You're dead. Then they bury your lifeless body in the ground." He shrugged. "And your life is over. Most people don't know when or how they will die, but I'm different. I know that the syphilis will kill me—years from now. By the time I go, I'll probably be mad as a hatter and won't care at all."

At his softly spoken words, Selena felt a sharp sting in her heart. A wave of emotion moved through her, unlike anything she'd felt before. The thought that Johann would one day be gone. "I know something of this sleep where there is nothing around you, nothing beyond you, from which you cannot awaken. It is frightening, the nothingness."

"Yes," he answered.

She leaned toward him, touched his hand. "You are so lucky, Johann."

"What do you mean?"

She smiled. This was one truth she understood. "Each day in the light is a gift."

He looked surprised. "Yes," he answered, and she saw the sheen of tears in his eyes.

She didn't want him to cry, so she said, "Tell me something that is not so sad. Tell me about Marie."

"How did you know," he said with a soft smile, "that I always want to talk about her? No one ever really asks." He leaned back in his chair. "She was the most incredible woman I'd ever met, and I was crazy in love with her. Before I met her, I was . . . selfish and rich and thoughtless. She made me question everything I thought I knew about right and wrong, and after I'd asked the questions, nothing was ever the same again. Death ..." He raised his palms in a casual gesture. "I would have died to spend a day with her, and God gave me years."

"How did you know you loved her?"

"How do you know it's raining out? Or that you're hungry or cold or tired? Darwin thought it was instinct at its sharpest—nature selecting a mate for survival of the species—and maybe he was right. But when it hits you, it doesn't feel like science. It feels like magic."

Selena remembered the first time she'd heard Ian's voice, the first time she'd looked in his blue eyes, the first time she'd felt his touch. Every memory with him, every moment, felt steeped in magic.

"The way you feel about Ian," he said quietly.

She laughed. She was unable to hide her thoughts the way healthy people could. Every thought, every emotion, felt larger than life to Selena; they filled her to bursting, made her laugh when no one laughed and cry when no one else cried. It was a simple fact. "Yes ..." She loved Ian, loved him with all her heart and soul. But was it enough? Lately, she wasn't so sure. At least, it didn't seem to be enough for Ian.

"Out with it, Selena. I can see your mind working."

"This word ... husband. It troubles Ian much."

One eyebrow winged upward. "That's an understatement."

Sarcasm; she ignored it. "What is a husband? Exactly."

He blew out his breath in a loud sigh that ended in another rattling cough. "Well, on the most superficial level, you know that a man and a woman can marry. Yes?"

"That was the next word I was going to seek a definition of. Marry."

He steepled his fingers and rested his chin on his fingertips, peering at her. "Marriage is a promise before God to stay together until 'death do you part.' "

"So if I have a husband, it means I have vowed to God to live with that man forever."

"In a nutshell."

She frowned. "We must live in a nutshell? I thought—"

He laughed. "In a nutshell means . . . exactly right."

"Oh. So Ian is right to be afraid of a husband of mine."

His smile faded. "Yes."

"How could I forget such a man?"

"I don't know—stranger things have happened. But I know that you weren't wearing a wedding ring when you came to us. All married women wear wedding rings to symbolize their vows."

Selena brightened. "Truly?"

"Truly." He smiled again. "It's something that women devised to wheedle money from their betrothed."

Selena smiled at him. "I am much relieved. This proves that I am not a wife to some husband."

"Well, it's an indication. Proof would require something more . . . physical."

"I misunderstand. Such as a marking of some kind?"

His lips twitched. "No, tattooing of spouses hasn't caught on yet. Men mark their territory in a more . . . romantic way."

"Ah. Kissing." She nodded. "Ian said that kissing me would be dishonorable."

"Kissing and . . . other things. Things that men and women do in bed together. And I will not tell you any more regardless of how prettily you ask."

Selena felt very smart at the moment. "In bed. Yes. You mean a virgin."

Johann took a quick sip of coffee, covering a smile. "A virgin is not a wife."

"Ian must find out if I am a virgin, then."

Johann spit up his coffee. It was a long moment before he spoke, and his mouth twitched suspiciously the whole time. "That would certainly answer the question of marriage once and for all."

She sighed and sank back in her chair, inordinately pleased with herself. Really, this thinking business was not so very difficult.

There was a buzz of magic in the air, of long-forgotten dreams resurrected and given life. Even nature felt it; the sea was a crashing wall of white, hurling itself against the shadowy barrier of distant stone. Overhead, the sky was endless and empty and black. A low blanket of fog caressed the ocean and slipped through the blackened forest. There was no reality anymore, no ground, no stars, no moon. Just an ethereal haze that curled around the house, lifted it above the earth like some magical Camelot in the woods.

Selena's heart was pounding so fast, she felt lightheaded. Anticipation was a thrumming, pulsing presence in her blood.

What should she do first? How did she go about this testing of her virginity?

She'd tried to find a glimmer of information about the night that lay ahead, the task she'd set for herself, but such information was impossible to find. She'd tried first the big book in Ian's study—the dictionary. It told her nothing at all, gave no hint or reference. Then she'd asked people, everyone she saw. Johann refused to answer her questions; Andrew's face had turned the color of geraniums and he'd bolted from the room; Lara hadn't understood the question any better than Selena herself; and Maeve had only smiled softly and told her to clean up her room.

She was on her own, that much was obvious.

She stared at her face in the mirror. She thought it was a pleasing face, in a pale, quiet kind of way. Idly she brought her hand up and began weaving the long mass of her hair into a braid, then tied it with a pink ribbon. A dozen flyaway strands curled along her forehead and cheeks, but she didn't waste time in trying to pin them back—they'd only pop free in a moment or two.

Slowly she walked to her armoire and flipped the heavy mahogany door open. Maeve had filled the closet with dozens of colorful gowns. Silks, satins, velvets.

Selena frowned. None of the dresses felt right. And all of them required that torture device of a corset. She drew back, thinking. If she didn't wear girl clothes, that left only two choices: the breeches she'd seized from Andrew or her nightdress.

She turned back. Her nightdress lay across her bed, a filmy concoction of white silk and French lace that buttoned from the throat to the hem.

It was the most comfortable gown she owned, and now, in the darkened room on the white, white bed, the color made her think of starlight and moonlight and magic.

Smiling, she slipped out of her chemise and drawers and slid into the nightdress. The soft folds of silk caressed her bare breasts and legs.

Then she twirled and went to the door, wrenching it open. The black hallway, quiet and still, lay before her. She hurried through the darkness and up the narrow stairway to Ian's room. There, she paused to catch her breath. It was too ragged and frayed to be blamed on the climb. Her heart was beating hard. So hard.

She knocked sharply on the door. The sound was a gunshot in the silence, *rap, rap*.

"Come in," Ian's voice slid through the door. He sounded tired and cranky.

She flung the door open and surged inside. The room curled around her, shadows stacked on shadows. The only light came from a half-opened window.

Smiling, she peered into the gloom and stepped forward. "Ian?"

"I'm here." His voice, rich and melodious, came from the shadows near the armoire. She heard a movement, then the *whoosh* of a match lighting. Blue-yellow light flared in the darkness, brought with it the acrid scent of sulfur. Candlelight haloed his sad face. He was sitting in a heavy black chair, pressed deep in the shadows, drinking his whiskey. A white lawn shirt gaped across his chest, slid down the ball of one shoulder.

She moved toward him.

He straightened, drew back in his chair. She heard the familiar tinkle of fine crystal against wood, and knew that he was drinking.

"I thought you had stopped drinking."

His answering laugh was short and sharp. "More of a pause, actually. Now, you should go."

"I have come to ask for your help."

Another laugh, softer, harsher. "And what do you need from me?"

She stood before him. The moment felt brushed with magic, rich with the intoxicating scent of possibility. She drew in a quiet, shaky breath and smiled down at him. "You have been much concerned about my husband."

He flinched. "Your *potential* husband."

She laughed nervously. "Please to forgive me. My possible husband is upsetting you."

"Yes."

A quietly spoken word, steeped in so much emotion. It tugged at her heart, filled her with love for this man who sat here in the dark, brooding, thinking so strongly that he was dishonorable, and yet he hadn't touched her. Not last night and not now, when she wanted him to touch her so badly, her flesh felt tingling and raw.

She knelt on the cold, hard floor before him, setting her candle on the floor. He stared down at her through eyes that were dark with pain. "I know you are in pain," she said softly, "and so am I. It is the uncertainty—that is the right word, I think—the uncertainty that pains us."

The glass slipped out of his hand, hit the floor with

a crash. The pungent scent of bourbon wafted upward. "That's what I feel like," he said in a rough, throaty voice.

She frowned. "I do not understand."

"I feel like a bit of spun glass in your hands, Selena. If you but close your hands, I would be crushed."

The words confused her. She tried to make sense of them, to find some strand of meaning that she could draw forth, but nothing came to her. He was speaking of being crushed by her, but he should be speaking of the husband. She gazed up at him, her look steady and true. "Then I shall not close my hand."

He released a ragged sigh. "Ah, Selena, everything is so simple for you. So easy."

She smiled. "We have had this speech before. And everything is so difficult for you."

"I made you a promise, damn it. I vowed to be honorable. For once in my miserable life, I'm trying to do the right thing, and here you are, in my bedroom in the middle of night, dressed for love. . . ." His voice thickened and broke off. "You should leave."

"What of him, Ian? What of this husband who may someday come for me?"

He flinched at her use of the word *husband,* and slowly turned his gaze down to hers. "I can't look at you without thinking of him."

"What if I am a virgin?"

A frown flicked across his brow. "Then you aren't married."

"See, Ian?" She breathed, smiling. "So simple."

He drew in a sharp breath, then appeared not to breathe at all. "What are you saying?"

"I want to know. This uncertainty is unacceptable to me."

He gave a laugh that sounded forced and looked away from her.

She leaned forward, slid between his bent legs and

gazed up at him. "You know how to answer this uncertainty, do you not?"

"You don't know what you're asking."

"No. But you do, and I trust you completely."

"You are asking me to love you," he said quietly, and she heard the wonder in his voice, the hope, and it filled her heart with a painful, aching emotion.

"I believe you already do."

His gaze slid away from her face. He stared for a long, silent moment at the bed, his eyes narrowed and unreadable. "What would you do," he said at last, "if he came for you?"

The question hit her like a slap. She bit down on her lower lip and stared up at him, understanding why he didn't look at her, why he stared, unseeing, at the bed behind her. It had never actually occurred to her, this question, so stark and ugly and terrifying, but she saw in an instant that it should have. It was the truth she'd failed to understand. *I feel like spun glass in your hands, Selena.*

Yes, she understood it now. Understood his devastating fear. It was not merely that a husband was out there, it was not even that he would come for Selena. It was the choice that she would have to make.

She wished that she could lie. Slowly, feeling sick and uncertain, she looked up at Ian. Leaning closer, she touched a hand to his cheek and forced his gaze down to hers. "If I understand this word *honor*, and the word *marriage*, I would be forced to return to this husband."

Pain glazed his eyes, gave his strong mouth a twist. "Yes."

"But I do not believe I have a husband out there, Ian. My heart is too certain of itself. God would not test me in so cruel and unjust a way."

Ian laughed harshly. "Ha. Such sacrifices are God's raison d'être."

"All right. Let us suppose I do own a husband, and he is searching for me even now."

"Yes." It was a whisper of an answer.

She leaned closer, her mouth a heartbeat from his. She was so close, she could smell the bourbon on his breath, could feel the whisper of his breathing against her lips. "Then we should love each other as best we can now."

He slipped his arms around her, drew her tightly against him. "If we go to that bed over there, Selena, it will hurt even more if your husband comes for you."

She laughed quietly. For once, he was the innocent, and she saw the truth. "Not more," she whispered.

He leaned down to her, kissing her lightly at first, then more deeply, claiming her with his tongue. One hand slid up from her waist, curled around her neck, anchored her to him. His kisses trailed away from her lips, rained across her cheek, to her ear, down the sensitive curve of her neck. There he paused, rested his lips against her throat. "I love you, Selena. No matter what happens . . . I love you."

She heard the thickness in his voice, the rusty tone of the words, and wondered if he'd ever said them before. She understood at last the power of language. How a simple trio of words could make you want to cry. "I love you, too, Ian," she whispered.

He stood up and swept her into his arms in a move so sudden, it left her breathless. A laugh slipped from her mouth, her head fell back. The crafted copper of the ceiling glowed like sunlight in the candle's glow.

He took her to the bed and laid her down. He was back in seconds with the candle, murmuring something about wanting to see her, but she wasn't sure, didn't care.

He unbuckled his belt and unbuttoned his pants and shirt. The garments slid away from his body, puddled on the floor at his feet. Impatiently he kicked them away, then strode toward her, his naked skin dark and glistening in the candlelight.

She felt a rustle of fear.

"Don't be afraid," he murmured, crawling into bed beside her, drawing her close. Lowering his head, he kissed her, a deep, passionate kiss that stole her breath and made her whole body tremble, then he rained kisses down her throat, kissed her breasts through the sheer silk of her nightgown.

Before she knew what was happening, her gown was unbuttoned. Cool air brushed her nipples. Then she felt the heat of his breath on her skin, the moist touch of his tongue.

She touched him, tentatively at first, suprised by the moist heat of his skin.

"Yes," he breathed encouragingly, "touch me. . . ."

Her hands slid down his body, exploring, feeling, caressing.

He bunched her nightdress in his hands and peeled it away. His hands swept down her body, touching her in a thousand unexpected ways, making her shiver with excitement and ache with need. Places she'd never touched herself exploded with sensation beneath his practiced fingers. It went on and on, his ardent exploration of her body, until she thought she couldn't possibly take another moment of such sweet, exquisite torture.

He rolled on top of her.

Their gazes locked. He lay above her, breathing hard, his hair a tangled curtain of gold against his unshaven cheek. She saw a desperation in his gaze she didn't understand, a fear that sliced through her budding desire like a cold breath. He was thinking of the husband and he was afraid.

"Ian—"

He silenced her with a kiss, and she was lost again. Gently his hand glided down her body, pulled one thigh to the side and slid between her legs. His intimate touch sparked a flood of hot, pulsing desire. A tiny gasp of pleasure fell from her mouth, her arms tightened around his slick, moist back.

He slipped inside her.

The pain was instantaneous. She cried out with it, tried instinctively to push him away. "No!"

He froze, staring down at her through wide, disbelieving eyes. His brow was dampened with sweat, moist strands of hair stuck to his temples.

He was so quiet, he scared her.

She'd done something wrong, something bad. "What?" she whispered.

He leaned down, kissed her forehead, then drew back and gazed down at her. Tears filled his eyes. "You're a virgin."

Before she could ask how he knew, he pulled her into a crushing embrace and buried his face in the crook of her neck. She felt him tremble, heard the throaty catch of his voice. Warm, damp tears slid along her throat, tangled in her hair.

At the feel of his tears against her skin, she began kissing him, softly at first and then with a fevered need. She kissed his cheek, his neck, his shoulder.

He groaned softly and slid his hands between her legs, touching her with a seductive intimacy, coaxing her body to life.

Very slowly, he slipped back inside her, stretching her, filling her. The pain was still there, still sharp, but her joy was so intense, she didn't care, barely noticed.

She clung to him, her hips moving instinctively against his, grinding, thrusting. Gentle and then not so gentle, sweeping her up in a tide of pure, electrifying sensations. She gave in to the emotions, the feelings. He knew the exact moment she couldn't stand it anymore. He knew what she needed more than she did, and he gave it to her, sinking deep, deep inside her.

Afterward, he clung to her, and wouldn't let her go, and that was what she wanted. He lay beside her, their hot, damp flesh pressed seamlessly together, sheets tangled between their legs. She could smell the sweet, new scent of their love.

He turned to her suddenly, rolled over and pressed her deeper into the warm bed.

She glanced up at him, surprised by the look on his face. He was smiling broadly, a crooked, lopsided grin that melted her heart. He had never looked so young, so carefree, so blindingly handsome. "There's no husband out there, Selena."

The words filled her with an indescribable happiness. This was her home now, truly. No one would come in the middle of the night and force her to make a heart-wrenching decision. "You are certain?"

"I'm sure."

"And you know this because of . . . what we just did?"

"Oh, yes."

"I do not know." She gazed up at him, surprised to realize that she wanted him again. A smile crept across her face. "Perhaps we should do it again. Simply to be certain."

He leaned down to kiss her, whispering against her still-swollen lips, "Ah, goddess, I couldn't agree more."

Chapter Twenty

◦◦◦◦◦

They didn't come out of the room for four days.

Ian lay sprawled in the bed, the covers tangled around his naked legs, the pillows piled behind his head. The candle beside him hissed and sent the acrid scent of smoke into the air. Beyond the bed lay shadows, heaps and heaps of shadows, with only the moonlight at the window to remind him that he was even in his house, in his own room.

He closed the book in his lap and gazed down at Selena, asleep beside him.

She lay snuggled beside him, naked, her hair glowing with red and gold highlights. He dragged a finger along the warm, velvety curl of her shoulder. She sighed and smiled in her sleep.

It was everything that Ian had ever been told that love could be, a universe of emotion in every look, every touch, every whispered word. Obsession, possession, conquest, defeat, joy, and pain. He felt them all, reveled in his ability to feel so deeply, to yearn so completely. *Magic.*

She made a quiet sound and rolled over. Her hand slipped through the hair on his chest and settled in the pit of his arm. He felt the warm heat of each finger against the sensitive flesh. Her leg crooked, slid over his in a smooth, erotic motion.

Jesus, she was beautiful, her cheeks flushed with

sleep, a veil of hair tangled around her throat. He knew she was awake when she pressed a slow, hot kiss on his left nipple.

"Have we waited long enough?" she whispered, teasing him to hardness again with the husky bourbon of her voice.

He groaned. She could arouse him with only her voice.

The need for her came back, as strong and sharp as before. And before. And before.

He slid an arm beneath her and dragged her up to him, slanting his mouth on hers, savoring the softness of her lips, the humid, salty taste of her.

She pulled away with a throaty giggle. "I am hungry again."

He touched her chin, tilted her face up to his. "And for what this time?"

She smiled. "What does it matter to me?"

His gaze flicked to the table beside the bed. It was heaped with empty dishes and glasses, piled with half-eaten fruit and bowls full of candy. "You're right. We ought to keep our strength up."

She reached blindly behind her and picked out a ripe peach. Bringing it between them, she took a big, moist bite, laughing as the pale juice slid down her chin and plopped on his chest. He leaned down, took a bite, then he kissed her deeply.

She flopped into the heap of pillows beside him. "I miss the sunlight on my face. Let us go for a walk."

Ian felt a stab of fear at the words. It came, hit him hard, then dissipated. He had nothing to be afraid of anymore. She'd been a virgin—her maidenhead and her pain and the blood on the sheets had been all the proof he needed. There was no phantom husband lurking behind the door or beyond the gates. Nothing to be afraid of anymore.

It was an incredible feeling, this lack of fear, this sudden, exhilarating hope for the future. He had lived so long without it, maybe always, and to have it now, at thirty-five, was the most precious gift he could imagine.

"I'm not afraid." He said the words softly, wincing when he heard them spoken aloud. They sounded so silly and puerile. How could she know what they meant?

"What will you do now, with this fearlessness?"

He frowned. It was not what he'd expected her to say, although such a thing shouldn't surprise him. She *never* said what he expected. He stroked the silky hair from her face and smiled down at her. "What do you mean?"

She scrunched her face in the familiar expression of deep thought, chewed on her lower lip for a second. "You have lived here as people's . . . keeper for many years now, yes?"

"Yes."

"This has been because of fear."

"Yes."

"Then you should change your life now."

"I have changed it."

"How?"

He drew her close. "I've spent four days in bed with a woman I love."

She gave him a broad smile. "That is not what I mean. The dictionary defines change as transformation, alteration."

"I don't—"

"What is your dream?"

"Dream?" Like an idiot, he parroted the word. He shrugged. "I don't know, loving you until I die?"

"Silly. That is not a dream, that is a . . . fact." She gazed up at him, very seriously. "I shall expect more of you."

"Oh, really?"

"Yes. I shall expect you to be more than a keeper here. You are a doctor. You could do much good in the world."

"But my hands—"

She waved airily. "Do not be so selfish. I am brain-damaged, Johann is dying of syphilis, Andrew is battling great demons of memory, and Maeve fights for a clear thought every day of her life. What are hands that know too much? You will learn to stop seeing the images."

"It's not that easy. The visions—"

"It is no different than ignoring Maeve when she is directly in front of you, and you have done that for years. It is no different than ignoring mealtime conversation to hear only one voice. It is a skill which you must teach yourself."

He started to argue, then stopped. What if it was possible? What if he could learn to tune out extraneous images as easily as he tuned out unwanted noise?

He could be a doctor again; if not a surgeon, then an alienist. As an alienist, he could use his curse to actually help people, so see the truth in their minds.

Good God, he could start over, could be a better man.

Selena stared up at him. A slow smile crept across her face, gave her eyes a sparkling light. "This is the change I was spouting of. *Speaking* of."

"I could be a doctor again."

"Now you speak with the voice of a dream. But your dream is too small."

He grinned. "*Nothing* on me is too small."

It took her a moment to understand his meaning. When she did, she smiled broadly. "I am not speaking of that—as you well know. I mean that there is more to your life than medicine. You need to be more than a doctor."

He breezed a finger down her naked belly. "I'm trying my damnedest to be a father. If you'd stop talking, we could try again."

She laughed. "Do not try to tell me that lie again about babies in bodies. I shall not believe it. Besides, you could practice to be a father right now."

"I think it's too late for me to be your father."

Her voice softened. "Lara needs a father most desperately."

He felt an unexpected pain at the words. "So did I. Life isn't always so fair, goddess."

She rolled onto her stomach and peered up at him. "Your voice is ugly and angry. Try again."

Looking down at her, into her beautiful, liquid eyes, he felt the bitterness fade. Love rushed in to take its place. "My father died when I was ten," he said softly.

"You must have missed him very much."

He said what was in his heart, the first time he could ever remember doing such a thing. "Every day of my life."

"Do you not think Lara feels this loss?"

He sighed. "I'm sure she does, but what—"

"Ease her pain."

"But—"

She pressed a finger to his lips. "Do not begin a sentence with this word. It is the beginning of no. I shall not accept a no."

He stared at her, lost himself in the dark pools of her eyes. As always, she was asking the best of him, the most honorable, most honest, course of action.

So simple, Ian.

Slowly he felt himself begin to smile. "I suppose I could try with the kid. . . ."

"Yes," she whispered.

At her quiet voice, so filled with love and certainty and honesty, he began to understand what it truly meant to love someone. *Magic,* he thought again, drawing her close for a kiss. "I love you," he murmured against her lips, tasting the sweet nectar of peaches.

She slipped on top of him and smiled down at him, her hair a reddish brown curtain that framed her face and tickled his arms. "Now I should like to have sex again," she said in a throaty whisper that sent a shiver rippling down his spine.

"Oh, really?" He ran a hand along the naked curve of her back and cupped her fanny. "I can see I'll have to teach you how to talk like a lady."

"I know this already, Ian." She fluttered her eyelashes and smiled. "Please may I have more sex?"

He laughed. God, it felt good to be here, with her, to lie in bed with the woman of his dreams, with shadows and candlelight stacked around them, the sweet smell of peaches and sex in the air, and to dream. So good to dream.

"Do ye think they're all right in there?" Edith hissed, cupping her mouth with a fleshy hand.

Johann laughed softly. "Probably a damn sight better than any of us are."

Andrew frowned, his wide-eyed gaze fixed on the closed door. "I don't think so. They haven't been out in days."

Lara started to cry. "I miss Selena."

The queen snorted. "That much screwin' couldn't be good for a body."

There was a moment of prolonged silence as they all stared at the door. This was the fourth time in as many days that they'd gathered outside Ian's bedroom door. They'd waited breathlessly for the first day, each one of them excited beyond measure to see what would be changed when Selena and Ian finally emerged from the room. On the second day, their excitement had lost its shiny glow. The first concern had been voiced. And now, by day four, only Johann remained calm.

Queen Victoria had voted three times to burn down the door.

Andrew wanted to knock.

Edith brought a glass to sharpen her eavesdropping.

And Maeve hadn't noticed until yesterday that either Selena or her son was missing.

But she noticed now, and she was determined to find out what had happened.

She pushed through the crowd and strode up to the door. "Enough is enough." Lifting a pale fist, she rapped hard on the door.

There was a shouted curse from inside, then a giggle, then a loud crash.

Maeve wrenched open the door and went inside. Everyone squeezed in behind her.

They found Ian stark naked, lying on the floor, laughing. Selena, also naked, was sprawled on top of him. Peaches and apples were scattered across the hardwood floor. A dozen candles had burned down to the nub. Hazy tails of smoke wafted along the ceiling, clung to the corners.

Selena snapped to sit up on Ian's lap and waved brightly. "Hello!"

Ian snatched up a wrinkled bit of sheet and plastered it to her breasts.

She giggled. "Oh, yes. I forgot that I should not show my breasts to Andrew. Please to forgive me."

There was absolute, utter silence.

Then, softly, Johann started to laugh. The queen was the first to join in, then Edith.

Maeve took a step forward. She was not laughing. "I presume we'll be having a wedding now."

Selena straightened. "Truly? How exciting." She frowned suddenly. "What is a wedding?"

Maeve's face was uncharacteristically hard. "It's what two people do *before* they get into bed together."

Selena laughed, a bright, clear sound that filled the room. "Then it is too late."

"Ian," Maeve said, "I'll expect to see you in the parlor in ten minutes." She snapped her chin up and sailed out of the bedroom, forcing the gawking crowd to follow.

The door slammed shut behind her.

And then, very quietly, Maeve started to laugh.

Ian couldn't believe what he was doing. He was dressed now—damn it, anyway—and heading down the dark, shadowy corridor to the parlor, where his mother waited for him, presumably to lecture him on morality. His *mother*.

He reached the bottom of the stairs and stepped into the bright, sunlit foyer. The light hurt his eyes, reminded him once again that he was emerging from his love nest and returning to the world.

The parlor door was closed. He knocked sharply, heard his mother's muffled "come in," and went inside.

Maeve stood alongside the fireplace. She stood tall and straight, her hair hastily bound into a topknot that hung precariously above her left ear, her hands plunged into the pockets of her pale green cashmere wrapper.

Something was different about her, though he couldn't name it.

One reddish eyebrow slowly rose. "So you can still walk. I would consider that a triumph."

He realized suddenly what was different about her. There was no fear in her gaze, no nervous stroking of her ribbon, no awkwardness in facing him. She looked lucid and sure of herself. In control.

He was proud of her. "You look good, Mother."

A tiny smile tugged one side of her mouth. "Really?" She patted her hair, felt the tumbledown chignon and frowned.

Without thinking, he went to her, eased the knot of hair back to the center of her head, and reanchored it with a few hairpins. Images swirled through his mind as he touched her ear, her temple. She was thinking of his father, and how he'd once fixed her hair in this very parlor. Before a ball, no, after a supper . . .

He tried to control the images, and found that if he concentrated, they blurred, became an inconsequential smear of color and sound. No more irritating than a mosquito droning by one's ear.

He drew his hands back and stared down at his mother. There was a strange look on her face, and he realized that she'd been stunned by the familiarity of his gesture. "Thank you," she said quietly.

"You're welcome."

"You have slept with Selena," Maeve said at last. "And I mean this in the ... romantic sense."

"I don't suppose you'd believe that we were waiting for our clothes to dry?"

A laugh slipped from Maeve's mouth before she could stop it. "Don't be impertinent. I'm trying to be ... motherly here."

His smile faded. He looked down at Maeve and wished suddenly that he could take it all back, all the times he'd hurt her and snubbed her and rejected her. "You always were," he said softly.

More, he thought, *say more.* But there were no words, just a thick lump of regret in his throat and a burning need for absolution.

Tears puddled in her eyes, her mouth trembled. "No," she whispered. A tear streaked down her face. "No."

Ian wanted to close the distance between them, maybe even wipe the tears from her eyes. But he couldn't move, couldn't really fathom that kind of intimacy. Too much had happened, too much water lay beneath the bridge, dark and ugly and swirling with lost moments, a lifetime of miscommunication.

They stood that way for what seemed like hours, and Ian knew that she was as paralyzed by regret as he was. On the mantel, the porcelain clock ticked slowly onward.

You can hurt your mother, or you can not hurt your mother. Simple decision. Simple.

The thought came to him, sharp and clear and cleansing. It was as if Selena were inside him, urging him to be strong, to take a risk.

Everything is easy for you, Selena.

And so difficult for you, Ian.

She was right. The world did hinge on choices, some as simple as this one. He could reach out right now, touch his mother with words. It might not be much, might not right every wrong that had punctured their relationship for years, but it could be something he'd never imagined, and yet never stopped aching for.

A beginning.

He gazed down at his mother, seeing the silvery trails that streaked her pale cheeks, and he wished to Christ he could hold her. Just that . . .

But he couldn't, of course. Not yet. All he could offer was an uncertain start. "Mother, I . . . I'm sorry. For everything."

It wasn't much, he realized. A pale imitation of the emotion that was needed.

She was surprised by the apology. Her eyes widened, and then a slow, trembling smile curved her lips. "I'm sorry, too, Ian." She reached out one hand, pale and slim in the sunlight.

He stared at it, feeling a rush of fear, then hope. Slowly he slipped his fingers through hers and squeezed.

Images hurled themselves at him, forced him to squeeze his eyes shut. It took him a second to realize that they were beautiful images and heart-wrenching words.

I love you, Ian.

He opened his eyes. Their gazes met, locked. He knew in that instant that she wouldn't say the words aloud, not yet, not to him. She'd been hurt by him too often to trust him so easily, and she wasn't sure that this moment was real. Deep down, she was afraid that she was lost in the abyss of her own mind, and that she was making it all up, that tomorrow he'd ignore her again.

"It's real," he said quietly.

She said nothing, just nodded. Another tear streaked down her face. Then she cleared her throat. "What are you going to do about Selena?"

"Do? Why, I'll marry her, of course."

"Have you asked her?"

"No. But that's just a formality."

Maeve laughed. "Nothing is just a formality with Selena."

Ian laughed with her, and it felt good. "That's certainly true. Marriage will have to make sense to her." His voiced trailed off. A frown pulled at his brows. "Holy hell . . ."

"Yes," Maeve said. "It could be a problem."

Everyone was in the study, waiting for Maeve and Ian to join them. There was a heavy silence, as if no one knew what to say. Selena looked at the faces around her and felt a rush of love for each of them. Her family.

She smiled. "You all look so worried. Except you, Johann." She crossed the room and went to him, her smile broadening with each step. "You knew, did you not?"

Johann's grin matched hers. "I knew. So?"

The queen slammed her hands on her meaty hips and gave a breathy harrumph. "So what? No one has secrets in *my* kingdom."

Selena couldn't help herself. She started to laugh. Memories twirled through her mind and brought a flush to her cheeks. "It was wonderful," she whispered to Johann.

"And were you a . . . you know?"

"God damn it," the queen hissed. "Was she a you-know-what?" She marched up to Johann and rapped him on the side of his head with her closed fan.

"It is no secret, Your Highness," Selena answered. "Johann wants to know if I was a virgin."

This time the queen smacked Johann with her open hand. "That's no question for a man to ask a lady." Then she turned to Selena. "Were you?"

"I was," Selena said with a huge grin. "But I am not anymore. And oh, Your Highness. It was grand."

The queen sighed mistily. "It certainly is. . . ."

"Selena!" Ian's voice boomed through the room, and

everyone spun to face him. He stood in the doorway. "What are you talking about?"

She just about melted at the sight of him standing there, so strong, so tall, so loving. She wanted to run to him and throw her arms around him and kiss him. Everywhere. "Sex," she answered.

"Ladies don't discuss such things."

She frowned. "You mean I can do it, but I can't talk about it?"

He looked a little sick. "Oh, no . . ."

"Why, that's positively ridiculous. If I can kiss your—"

"Enough!" he shouted. "Everyone out."

The queen bristled. "Not bloody likely, young sir. This is getting good."

For a second, Ian didn't respond, he just stood there, looking like he was going to scream, and then, very softly, he said, "I have a question to ask Selena."

A gasp rose from the crowd.

Selena glanced from one friend's face to another. They were staring at Ian in stunned disbelief, as if they all knew something that she did not. And they were grinning.

"Hurry!" the queen shouted. "A man's decision is a fragile thing."

"Aye," Edith agreed. "He could lose the bloody nerve."

Johann stared at Ian, a slow, hesitant smile on his face. "He won't lose his nerve. He's only just found it."

All at once, the residents surged to their feet and hurried to the door, moving like a great multiheaded centipede, feet shuffling, hands clapping.

The door closed silently behind them.

"Ian," Selena said, feeling the first tingle of apprehension. "I misunderstand. . . ."

He gave her a smile that seemed tense and strained, then fumbled for something in his pocket. Moving toward her, he brushed a wayward lock of hair from his forehead and kneeled at her feet.

"Selena . . ."

Behind him, through the sheer curtains, she saw the crowd gather. They were squished together on the porch so that everyone could see through the window. She could hear a faint rustle of voices from outside, then a loud "shut up" from the queen and they fell silent.

Ian wet his lips and looked up at her. Slowly he withdrew a beautiful ring from his pants pocket and held it out to her. "Selena, will you do me the honor of becoming my wife?"

Muted clapping seeped through the window.

Ian froze the crowd with a sharp look, then turned back to her.

Selena didn't know what to do or say, had no idea what was expected of her. Was the ring a gift? Or were the words the important thing? "I misunderstand. You seek to have us marry?"

His breath released in a sharp sigh. "Yes."

"Why?"

"Because I love you."

She gave him a smile. "I feel love for you, also. *Too.* But what has this to do with marry?"

He seemed to choose his words carefully. "Marriage is a promise to stay together forever."

"Of course we shall stay together. I promise it now, before God. There, we are married."

"No. Marriage is also a . . . legal commitment. We must offer our vows before a representative of the church or the state."

She frowned. "My word is not good enough?"

He shook his head. "No."

"But I do not need another to give my vow truth. I have promised. I have honor. This is enough."

He covered his face with his hand. "Hell. I knew this would be a problem. You don't understand. . . ."

"I am not too damaged to understand the words, Ian.

It is the concept which confuses me. You ask for my vow, I have given it. But it is not enough. You want more, and you think I do not understand the legal commitment which you seek, but you are wrong. Earlier, I looked up this word 'marriage' in the big book, and I read its meaning In marriage, a woman is a wife, and a wife is a chattel. And cows are chattel, Ian." She leaned toward him. *"Cattle."*

He cursed beneath his breath. "Yes."

"I shall not choose to be a cow."

A quick burst of laughter shot from his lips, then, slowly, he looked up at her, and the sharpness was gone from his eyes. In its place, she saw only love and understanding and respect. "As usual, you put everything in a very neat perspective." He set the ring down on the table and scooted toward her, slipping between her legs. "Marriage makes no sense from a woman's point of view, I'll grant you. The husband gives up nothing and gains everything the woman has. Or so it would seem by the dictionary definition."

"Yes," she said proudly. "This was my understanding."

"But there's more." His voice was low, a caress that sent a shiver dancing along her spine. "Forget the legal and social and moral reasons for getting married. I don't ask you for those reasons. I ask you to marry me because of something infinitely more simple and yet profoundly more complex." He leaned toward her, close enough to kiss. "You changed me, Selena. You taught me to see the world through different eyes, to make decisions based on right or wrong, and to trust in the old words—honor, love, commitment. It is for those reasons that I come to you now and offer you my mother's ring. Not because of the law of ownership or the blessing of the church. It is for simple selfishness. I love you. You are my world."

"Oh, Ian . . ."

"Marry me because I am weak and selfish and unenlightened," he said in a harsh whisper. "Marry me because I need you so much."

She touched his cheek. "You need me to be your wife?"

"Yes."

"When?"

He grinned. "How about next Tuesday?"

She smiled back at him. "Tuesday would be perfect."

Outside, the crowd went wild.

Chapter Twenty-one

❦

Ian felt like a damned fool.

Standing on the porch, he stared out across the bright green lawn at the young girl crouched amidst the ferns at the forest's dark edge. She was all alone, sitting with a rag doll clutched to her breast.

What now, Selena? he thought. What in the world was he supposed to do—just walk up to the kid and say *Hi, Lara. Selena wants me to play daddy for you?*

He wished he'd never promised this. Never even pretended to promise it.

He glanced back at the closed door behind him. But it wouldn't do any good to go inside. Selena would just be there, waiting for him, a disappointed look in her dark eyes.

He took a tentative step forward. The old wood creaked beneath his feet. Crossing his arms, he forced himself to keep moving, down the steps, across the crunching gravel, to the end of the lawn.

There he paused again, just for a second, and forced his hands to his sides. "Hello, Lara."

A quiet breeze rustled through the trees and caught his words.

Lara made a sharp, squealing sound and spun to face him, moving so quickly that she toppled onto her side. The doll rolled out of her grasp and lay cocked on a granite stone, staring up at him through one black button eye.

"D-Dr. Carrick," she whispered, scampering backward into a wary crouch.

He gave her the gentlest smile he could. "Don't be afraid." The words came with a surprising ease. He moved toward her. When he was a few feet away, he lowered himself to the ground and sat down.

She lurched to a wobbly stand and glanced back at the house. "D-Did I do somethin' wrong?"

He felt a rush of shame at her obvious fear. "No, Lara. I just wanted to ... spend some time with you."

Her eyes widened. "You did?" A whisper of sound.

"I thought you might be lonely out here."

Her lower lip quivered a little and she bit down on it. "I ... I'm lonely lots of times."

The admission, so quiet and soft, pulled at his heart, and suddenly he was glad he was here. He tried to think of how to begin, how to reach out to a child. But he had no idea what would work, all he had was understanding, and perhaps a scrap of truth. "I used to be lonely a lot when I was your age, too."

"You did?"

"Life is hard sometimes, don't you think? A little scary?"

She moved slowly toward him. Picking up her doll, she cradled it to her chest and sat down beside him. He waited for her to speak, but she didn't, just sat there, staring up at him through wide eyes.

He pulled a small book from the pocket of his coat. "Perhaps I could read you a story?"

A lightning-quick smile pulled at her lips.

He opened the book and began to read to her, his voice strong and sure as he told her the story of Cinderella.

Somewhere about the time Cinderella was going to the ball, Lara wiggled a little closer to him. He thought for a second that she was going to rest her head on his shoulder, but she didn't, and surprisingly, he wished that she had.

When the story was over, she looked up at him, her eyes shining. "That was really a pretty story."

He wanted to reach out to her, push the tangled hair from her face, but he didn't move. It felt awkward, wanting to comfort her and yet not knowing how. He started to say something—he wasn't sure what—when a trembling squawk sounded.

A tiny bird fell from a nest above them, landed in a small, broken heap in the needle-strewn ground. It lay there writhing, its yellow beak snapping open and shut, its broken wing bent at an awkward angle. He scooped the frail little thing in his hand. "Poor baby," he murmured.

She stared at the bird as if it were a miracle. "C'n I touch it?"

Ian rested his hand on her bent knee. "Go ahead."

She stared at him for a long minute, then slowly reached out. Her pink, pudgy fingers whispered across the bird's head. She looked up at him, grinning. "Oh, it's so soft. . . ."

She bent closer to the bird and stroked its head, just as she'd done to her rag doll. "You'd better fly on home, little bird," she murmured.

"I think its wing is broken," Ian said.

Lara gasped and looked up at him. "Is the birdie gonna die?" she asked in a shaky voice.

His first reaction was to answer clinically: *Yes. This bird would probably die.* But when he looked in Lara's big, hope-filled eyes, he felt something inside him soften, give way. He realized for the first time that his honesty had always been a shield—he'd wielded it like a sharp instrument, using it to cut off discussions he didn't want to have, and avoid emotions he didn't want to feel. He'd cloaked himself with blunt honesty; now, sitting here at the edge of the woods with a retarded girl and her broken-winged bird, he saw that he'd been wrong.

There was two truths—ones that held hope and ones that did not.

"Maybe if he got fed every day, he could grow strong."

"We could put it back in the nest. He would get better there."

"Its mother wouldn't care for it anymore."

"Because its wing is broke?"

He nodded.

She looked away for a second, and when she turned back to him, her eyes were filled with tears. "Mommies don't like broken babies, do they?"

"Ah, Lara," he whispered, wishing suddenly that he could make things all right for this child with the big eyes and the quiet voice and the pain that lived so deep in her soul. He knew she wasn't talking about birds right now, she was talking about her own mother. Ian remembered the woman who'd dropped Lara off here— years ago. Back when Lara was a little girl with a ready smile and a giggly laugh.

Jesus, how could he dredge that memory up from his scotch-soaked past? But it was there, shivering in the darkness, waiting to leap out at him.

And he'd said nothing to her back then, hadn't taken her hand or dried her tears or anything. He'd just taken the woman's money and her daughter and said nothing. Not a damned thing.

He swallowed hard. "I'm sorry, Lara."

She blinked at him. "Sorry about what?"

So much. This time he did touch her, a breezing caress that wiped the moisture from her full check. At the touch, he felt her raw, misunderstood pain, seen in his mind as a red swirling mist of anguish and confusion and loss.

It shamed him to the core. What could he say? How could he atone for the pain he'd so blindly ignored, even fostered?

There was nothing, no words.

"I'll be different," he said quietly.

She frowned. "Dr. Carrick?"

He knew she didn't understand, and it didn't matter. Selena was right; the past wasn't the important thing in life. The future was what counted, the choices that were made. He gave Lara a smile. "How about if we try to find a worm for that little guy? Maybe we could even make him a nest out of batting or something."

"Truly?"

"Truly." Smiling, he stood up. "Come on."

She grabbed her doll to her chest and got to her feet. She started to take a step toward the house, then stopped. Without looking up, she reached for his hand. He saw the contact coming, and for once in his life, accepted it, even welcomed it.

The vision, when it hit, was completely unexpected. The anguish, the pain, the confusion, were gone. Her mind was filled with childish excitement—*I hope I find the first worm. . . . Hold on, birdie, I'll take care of you. . . .*

He had done that, he realized suddenly. With nothing more than a fairy tale and a few moments of kindness, he had made this child smile, had given her a moment of hope.

He looked down at her small hand tucked into his larger one, and for a second his heart was achingly full.

Damned if he didn't *feel* like a father for the first time in his life.

Together, they went in search of worms.

Selena knocked on Maeve's door. Behind the barrier, she heard the rustling of feet, then a hurried "Come in."

She twisted the brass handle and pushed the door open, stepping into an unexpectedly sunny room. A huge tester bed dominated the chamber, its surface draped in yellow and white checked silk and piled with Battenberg lace pillows. Around it, the walls were a clean butter yellow, papered here and there with bright pink rosebuds. Painted wooden bookcases covered one whole wall, the shelves filled with books and knick-knacks and dead animals, stuffed and sewn to look real.

A yellow and orange sofa, overflowing with flowered pillows, sat huddled alongside the marble fireplace, warm and inviting. Above the fireplace hung a gilt-framed painting of a naked blond woman draped in the sheerest curtain of gold. The artist's name, *Jonas,* was a gigantic black scrawl along the lower edge of the painting.

Selena stared around her in awe. "Your bedroom is beautiful, Maeve," she said.

Maeve gave her a broad smile. "Thank you. And thank you for coming." She turned and rifled through her walnut armoire, finally pulling out a lovely aquamarine silk gown and a bunch of dried flowers. "Here," she said, smoothing the gown along the end of the bed. "This was my wedding gown. I want you to wear it."

Selena moved slowly toward the gown. It was the most exquisitely beautiful thing she'd ever seen. She picked up the hem, fingering the silken softness of the fabric, the heavy ecru lace that lined the daring neckline and fell in soft folds across the shoulders, the billowy half sleeves that ended in layer upon layer of more exquisite lace. "Oh, Maeve . . ."

"Try it on. The wedding is five days away. We may need to make alterations." Maeve hurried to the chiffonier, wrenching open one drawer after another, piling her arms with lacy undergarments.

Selena saw the torture device called a corset and winced. "I shall not wear that."

Maeve laughed. "Corsets and weddings go together. It's a rule."

"I do not follow rules. And I do not want to pass unconscious at the first curtsy."

"All women do. At my wedding, ladies dropped like flies on the dance floor."

"It makes no sense."

Maeve shrugged. "Most of life doesn't. But I can tell you this: You'll never get your body into that dress if you don't squeeze into this first."

Selena sighed and walked toward Maeve, plucking up the corset. It dangled, stiff as steel, from her thumb and forefinger. "Who designed this?"

"A man. Do you need more proof of their evil?" Maeve gave her a broad smile.

"Are ladies truly so witless? Someone should have laughed at the inventor."

"Too true. Now, put it on."

Selena sighed. "Maeve, I believe that sometimes I prefer it when you are mad."

Maeve laughed. "Wait ten minutes."

Selena stood at the end of the bed, allowing Maeve to dress—and dress, and dress—her. Chemise, drawers, stockings, bustle, petticoat after petticoat, gloves, and camisole. The amount of clothing was endless, but finally Maeve slipped the elegant pale turquoise gown over Selena's head. The shimmering fabric floated around her and swooshed to the floor.

She felt like the Cinderella from the fairly tale. She swirled around, watching herself in the full-length cheval mirror. "Oh, Maeve," she said softly. "I look lovely."

"Yes." Maeve's voice was loving and soft. "Your mother—wherever she is—would be proud."

Before Selena could respond, Maeve took her hand and led her to the ornate walnut dressing table, gesturing for Selena to sit. The oval mirror framed them both.

Maeve began to brush Selena's hair. "Most brides wore white in my day. Even then I was different," she said with a little sigh.

Selena stared at Maeve in the mirror, seeing the pain in her friend's eyes, hearing it in her tired voice. "Have you always been different?"

Maeve looked startled for a moment, as if surprised

that someone would ask so intimate a question. Then she smiled. "That's the saddest part: no. Oh, I always heard voices—I thought everybody did. But they didn't stop me when I was a child, they were just there, like friends in the background, whispering and laughing, urging me onward. I was sixteen when I fell in love with Herbert, and he was nearly thirty, but he loved me as much as I loved him. We married quickly, thoughtlessly, and for a while I was so happy that the voices almost completely disappeared, the depressions I'd always felt became a thing of the past. I thought . . ." She shrugged, stared at Selena's hair. "I was young and naive. I thought everything would always be perfect. I had Ian almost immediately."

Her voice fell to a whisper, her fingers paused on Selena's hair. "I still remember how the change started, how the end began. I was afraid to nurse my baby. Can you imagine that?" She looked up, staring at her own face in the mirror through a veil of tears. "I thought he was sucking the life out of me."

"Oh, Maeve . . ."

"I tried to hide my feelings from Herbert, but he noticed, he always noticed everything. The voices came back, only they were louder this time, screeching at me, telling me that Ian was evil and trying to kill me, that Herbert didn't love me anymore. I started talking to the voices and to people who weren't there. I tried everything to make them go away, even banged my head against a stone wall, but nothing worked. When it got bad enough, I just . . . slipped inside myself. I imagined myself in a warm, dark room, curled in a tight little ball. After a while, the voices would go away. But they always came back."

Selena had seen Maeve like that once. She had sat on the floor, rocking, humming to herself, hearing nothing, answering no one. She had to be carried to bed.

Maeve set the brush down on the marble tabletop and kneeled at Selena's feet. "But I did not ask you here to speak of such things. Or perhaps I did. I . . . I wanted to tell you how happy I am that you are marrying my son. To tell you I love you and I welcome you into our family. And . . ." Her voice broke off. She cleared her throat and looked at the hands curled in her own lap.

"Maeve?"

Slowly Maeve tilted her chin and looked at Selena. "I won't make the same mistakes again. I won't frighten your children, Selena, I swear I won't. I'll stay away, I'll watch them through the window and touch them in their sleep."

"Maeve, what are you talking about?"

"I never thought that I could ever look into Ian's beautiful blue eyes and feel anything but shame for my madness. But you have changed him, softened him, and he is beginning to come back to me." Tears slipped from her eyes. "I would never do *anything* to frighten his children—you must tell him that."

Selena touched Maeve's wet cheek. "Oh, Maeve. Our children will never be afraid of you. They will know from the beginning that Grandma has good days, and not so good days. And they will know that you love them. That will be enough."

"No." Maeve said the word softly, shaking her head.

"Yes," Selena answered firmly, believing it with all her heart. "It's what Herbert should have told Ian long, long ago."

Maeve sat back on her heels and hung her head. "I pray you're right."

"Don't pray, Maeve, believe."

Ian leaned back in his chair and crossed his arms. "Checkmate."

Johann stared at the board, empty but for a few key pieces. Like Ian's king and queen and Johann's rook. "Damn."

"That's two in a row for Dr. Carrick," Andrew said with a bright grin.

Johann smiled. "I'd think about changing to poker, but with Ian's degenerate background, I wouldn't have a chance. How about charades? You're far too stuffy to perform well."

Ian started to answer, but his words were cut off by the sound of a carriage approaching the house. At once, Andrew and Edith and the queen surged to their feet and thundered to the front door. They squished together and stared out the small side panel window.

"Who'd be out on a day like this?" Edith said. " 'Tis rainin' cats and dogs."

"It's an old man on an even older wagon," Andrew said.

The queen gasped and dropped into a knee-popping curtsy. "It's Albert. He's come for me at last."

Edith made a clucking sound. "If that's the royal carriage, things ain't goin' so well in the homeland."

Ian pushed back from the game table and got to his feet, strolling toward the door. Opening it, he stood in the entrance. The wagon came to a slow, groaning stop, then a man climbed down from the driver's seat and walked up the gravel path.

The stranger was a big man, with the broad shoulders and beefy arms of a farmer. A floppy-brimmed brown hat, splotched by the rain, covered his face and fell in folds above his ears. He wore a brown, rain-marked woolen suit and heavy black boots. At the bottom of the porch steps, he paused. Without looking up, he climbed the stairs slowly, one creaking step at a time.

Finally, on the porch, he looked up and pulled off his hat, crushing it beneath his arm.

Immediately Edith and the queen screamed and scrambled backward.

Half of the man's face was horribly scarred. An old scar, by the looks of it. Ugly, purplish ridges creased his cheekbone; the skin pulled his left eye down in the corner. One ear was a dark hole in the middle of raised, welted flesh. Short, close-cropped gray hair grew thick and full on the right side of his head, and in tufted patches on the left.

"Hello," Ian said. "I'm Dr. Carrick."

The stranger reciprocated with an uneven smile that pulled hard at the scar tissue. "I'm Elliot Brown."

"Come in," Ian said, backing into the foyer.

The inmates scattered like ants, scurrying into dark corners to watch the scarred man's entrance.

Elliot stepped over the threshold and paused on the small rug in front of the door. His huge, booted feet made the rug look like a postage stamp. He stared down at the floor for a long minute, then cleared his throat and looked up. "I'm sorry to bother you. . . ."

Ian smiled. "Don't worry about it."

Elliot reached into his big, damp pocket, pulling out a wrinkled, dirty piece of paper. "I've come about the woman you found. She's my wife."

"Oh, Lord," Johann said from the parlor. His chair squeaked as he rose, his heels clicked across the hardwood floor.

Ian stared at the old man in shock. *What?*

"Ian! Look!" Selena's high, excited voice cut into the silence. She stood at the top of the stairs, wearing his mother's wedding dress. Her long hair cascaded around her flushed face.

Smiling, she hurried down the steps. When she saw the stranger, she came to a sudden stop. Her mouth fell open for a split second, and then she was smiling again. "We have a guest." She glided over to Elliot. "Welcome to Lethe House, sir. May we steal your coat?"

"Hello, Agnes," Elliot said, taking a hulking step toward her. "Sheriff Monahan told me a woman was staying up at this place. He knew you were missing. I've come for you."

Ian could barely turn, barely move. This man, this scarred, shambling man, had come for Selena. *Come for her.* The words cycled through his brain until he couldn't think of anything else, could barely breathe.

"You better have some goddamn good proof," he hissed.

Elliot flinched. "I don't under—"

"Show it to me." Ian spat the words. "Show me your proof."

Selena gave Ian a look of such stark, agonizing fear that he felt as if she'd struck him. Then she fainted.

Ian and Elliot both lurched toward her. Ian got there first, wrapping his arms around Selena, drawing her close. "Don't you touch her," he snarled, shoving Elliot away.

He scooped her into his arms and carried her to the parlor, laying her out on the overstuffed settee, loosening her gown so she could breathe. He saw the white outline of the corset. In another time he would have laughed at her, would have teased her for breaking her commonsense rule and wearing a straitjacket.

But there was no laughter inside him now. He kneeled beside Selena, stroked her face with a hand that couldn't stop shaking. He wanted a drink. Sweet Jesus, he wanted a drink. "It's okay, goddess, just rest a minute. I'll take care of this."

"Dr. Carrick . . ." Elliot said in a quiet, respectful voice.

Ian jerked to his feet and spun around.

Elliot stood in the middle of the room. The residents clustered behind him like children, gawking, touching, pointing. Lara was crying softly, rocking the little bird in her cupped hands. Andrew looked stricken. Even Johann was pale. It fueled Ian's anger that they believed the old man, that they were afraid.

"Get out," he hissed to the crowd.

He didn't have to say it again. Andrew and Edith and the queen disappeared like smoke. One minute they were there; the next, they were gone. Johann was the only one who stayed. He leaned against the wall, his arms crossed. His pose was languid and relaxed; only the sharp narrowing of his eyes revealed his anxiety.

"Go." Ian had meant to say *away,* go away, but nothing else made it past his lips, just a growling fragment of a word.

"But—"

"Go."

Johann gave Ian a last, meaningful look, then walked out of the room, closing the door quietly behind him.

Ian turned to Elliot, and felt the anger again, rushing, cresting, burning. Jesus, he wanted to punch him, wanted to smash his scarred face into the floor. "You are *not* her husband, old man. Now, you've got ten seconds to get the hell out of my house."

On the settee, Selena stirred, released a quiet moan.

She sat up slowly. She saw Ian and smiled brightly, then she noticed Elliot and her smile faded.

Elliot dug through his pockets, finally pulling out a small, framed tintype. "Here." He shoved out his fleshy hand. "This is our wedding picture."

Selena threw Ian a sharp look, then walked toward Elliot. Ian came up beside her. He longed to touch her, slip his hand through hers and squeeze, but he couldn't. He was afraid he'd crush her fingers in his angry, punishing grip.

Selena touched the picture first, caressed the tiny, ornate frame and took the tintype in her hand.

A wedding picture; there was no mistaking it. Selena and Elliot.

Selena gasped quietly.

Ian's anger shriveled, and dank, sweaty fear rushed in to take its place. He wanted to be angry again—howlingly, irrationally angry—but he couldn't find that kind of heat. He was cold suddenly, so cold.

"I look so young," she whispered.

"Twelve," Elliot answered.

Ian's head snapped up. "You married her at twelve?"

Elliot nodded. It looked for a moment as if he were going to speak again, perhaps to explain, but he didn't.

Just stared at Ian with a flat, dull-eyed look. His fingers closed reflexively around the picture.

"But I do not remember you," Selena said in a small, stricken voice.

Elliot looked at Selena for a long moment, then turned to Ian. "What have you done to her?"

"I saved her. What did *you* do to her? She came here half-dead, her head bashed in."

The color slid from Elliot's face. "What happened to her?"

"You tell me," Ian snapped.

"I don't know. How . . . how did she survive?"

"I'm a brilliant surgeon," Ian said bitterly. He wanted to believe that Elliot had caused her injury, but there was no mistaking the old man's sudden horror. Elliot hadn't hurt her—Ian had no doubt about that. But he wished he did. Oh Christ, he wished he did. It would give him the excuse he wanted to kill the man.

"Is that why she doesn't recognize me? A head injury?"

Ian heard the hopefulness in the old man's voice, the pain that lurked beneath the simple question. "Yes."

Elliot blinked hard. Tears filled his eyes as he looked at Ian. "I . . .I don't know what I'd do without her. Thank you."

The words, the plain little expression of gratitude, hurt more than anything that had preceded it.

"I misunderstand." She looked from Elliot to Ian to Elliot again, her eyes brimming with tears. "I-I was a virgin."

Elliot's face drained of color. He turned to Ian.

Good, Ian thought. *Be mad. Challenge me to a duel. Something.* Anything that would bring back the anger, the heat of emotion. Anything to fill the yawning numbness that was slowly suffusing his insides.

But there was no hatred in the old man's eyes, no anger. Just a draining, inexpressible sorrow.

And suddenly Ian understood, and the understanding

almost killed him. This big man loved Selena, loved her the way Ian loved her. He had come all this way, searching with blind faith for his wife, his love, and he found that she'd slept with another man and had no memory of their life together.

And all he said was a quiet, shaking, "Was?"

"I misunderstand," Selena said again, her voice rising with fear. "How can a virgin be married?"

The hat slipped from Elliot's big fingers and fell to the floor with a muffled thump. He crossed his arms and stared at Selena. "I married you to save you, Agnes. You were all alone, a little girl picking pockets on the streets of New York. When I found you, you'd been beaten up and left for dead." A smile twisted his lips, squeezed his left eye almost shut. "But you had a lot of fight in you, even then. You said your pa'd beaten you up and that he'd be back for you. You wouldn't go anywhere with me unless I married you. You thought I'd sneak out on you if we weren't legally wed. So I agreed."

"But still, we must have . . . touched."

He was silent for a second, then he said quietly, "Look at me, Agnes."

She did. "Yes?"

She didn't understand, but Ian did. Elliot's face had repulsed Agnes and kept them from being intimate. Sweet God, it must have hurt. Loving a woman like her for all those years and never being able to touch her . . .

"What has your face to do with our marriage?" Selena asked.

Elliot released a long, low breath before he answered. "You said my face . . ." He swallowed hard, looked away. "You didn't want me that way."

"Oh, Elliot Brown." Selena breathed. "Why?"

"Why?" He frowned. "I would think that's obvious."

"I mean why would you love a woman like that?"

An uncomfortable silence descended again. Selena looked at Ian, then back at Elliot. "I am certain you are a good man, Elliot; I can see it in your eyes. But I cannot lie to you. I feel great love for Ian."

Elliot squeezed his eyes shut for a long moment, then slowly opened them. "You are still my wife."

"What do we do now?" she asked quietly.

"Do?" Elliot repeated. "Why, we go home."

One word. One little, four-letter word, and it obliterated everything.

Home.

For a split second, Ian didn't care about Elliot's pain or his face or his life. He wanted to rip the man's heart out and bury him in a cold, unmarked grave where no one would ever find the body, and pretend it had never happened.

He wanted . . . oh, Jesus, he wanted it to be yesterday again.

Chapter Twenty-two

Ian stood on the porch, arms crossed, eyes at half-mast. He didn't move, barely breathed. He felt stiff and fragile, as if a single touch could shatter him.

The stranger was Selena's husband. Word had spread in a heartbeat, growing louder and louder, punctuated by great, keening cries of sorrow. Even the inmates knew what it meant that Elliot had come.

He envied them their ability to grieve. Ian couldn't seem to do it. He felt numb, empty inside. He tried to find some remnant of the man he'd once been, and found that there was nothing left of that bitter, cynical loner, no more cold casing on his heart. Now he was the man Selena had turned him into, and he felt life so sharply, he couldn't hide from it anymore. The pain was a throbbing, burning ache in his chest.

Woodenly he'd ordered Edith to prepare a room for Elliot, then he'd watched the old man shuffle away. But not far enough, just down the hall. Behind the closed door, the stranger waited for the dawn.

Ian wished Elliot were young and handsome and wealthy; *that,* Ian could deal with, could beat to a bloody pulp and walk away from. Anything but a scarred old man who'd searched for his wife and said he didn't know how he'd live without her.

He stared out at the night. She was out there somewhere, in the rainy darkness. He'd watched her run from the house more than half an hour ago, and he told himself to let her be, that it would hurt too much to see her, but he'd known. Known he would go after her.

Ah, but what would he say?

Ian walked slowly down the creaking porch steps and into the night, across the gravelly path, toward the forest. Overhead, the sky was a rolling, pregnant gray belly, disgorging itself with a stinging shower of cold droplets. Rain pattered the trees, smacked the leaves and pelted his face. He went into the forest and felt his way along the path, touching the strong, rough trunks of the trees.

Stepping over the fallen log, he wound through the darkness and found her where he'd expected to, huddled in the wet ferns and mushrooms in her secret place.

For a moment, he didn't say anything, just drank in the sight of her, letting the moment crystallize into a memory. She sat kneeling amidst the shadowy foliage, soaking wet, her head bent, her hands full of trinkets. He knew what she held: a shell, worn smooth by the sea's endless kiss; a dried skein of kelp, twisted and blackened by the damp earth; the pale gray ball of her worry stone; and the bit of broken blue glass that reminded her of his eyes.

The grief came on him so hard, with such a cold, stinging slap, that for a moment he couldn't breathe.

"Selena." Her name fell from his lips, a whisper, a prayer.

She didn't answer, just closed her eyes and reached out her hand.

He surged forward and dropped to his knees beside her, taking hold of her hand, clinging to it.

At his touch, she made a small, choking sound of grief and shook her head. Then, slowly, she opened her eyes. Rain slid down her face in rivulets, dripped off the end of her nose and collected on her full lower lip. Her eyes were red and puffy.

There were so many things to say, and yet there was nothing at all. He felt a surge of bitterness. She'd come to him as an empty shell, a lump of clay, and begged to be molded by him, instructed and rounded. And he'd done it, he'd opened her mind to the universe of poetry and literature and romance. He'd searched within himself for the goodness, and once he'd found it, he defined it and offered it to her.

If only he hadn't found that goodness inside himself. If only he hadn't taught her so well.

He wanted to beg her not to leave him, wanted to crawl on his knees and beg her to have no honor.

She looked at him. "I have been thinking and thinking." She gave him a watery smile. "So much, my head aches and my eyes feel as if they are on fire. I keep wanting this to be a decision, and yet . . . there is no decision, is there?"

There it was, the truth that had beaten him, stripped away his soul and left him with nothing but broken dreams. She would see the decision as no decision at all; he'd known that immediately, and though he wanted to doubt it, he couldn't.

I will be honorable, Ian. Will you vow the same?

He clutched her shoulders and pulled her toward him. "Christ, Selena," he whispered, hearing the ragged tenor of his voice. He couldn't help it, couldn't pretend to be strong. Everything about this moment hurt.

We could run away together. The thought spun through his mind, made him dizzy with the need to say it.

She touched him, trailed her fingers across his cheek, down his throat, caressing, claiming. Finally she drew back, let her hand fall into her lap. "You were right to be afraid."

He stared at her, losing himself in the darkness of her eyes, needing her more in that moment than he'd ever needed anyone or anything. "What will I do without you?" he whispered.

She started to cry, silently at first, and then in great,

heaving spasms. He folded his arms around her, drew her onto his lap and held her fiercely, burying his face in the wet, cold crook of her neck.

He thought of all the times he'd touched her, all the kisses he'd trailed along her throat, across her breasts. All the words she'd mangled and the laughs she'd given him. About how yawningly empty his world would be without her. *Oh, Jesus* ...

The tears came at last, burning his eyes, blurring his vision. They clung to each other for a lifetime, the only warmth in the cold, rainy night.

Too soon, she pulled away. Sniffling, she wiped her eyes and touched his face. "You told me many times that the world was cold and cruel and unjust." She tried to laugh, tried and failed. "I am beginning to believe you."

"I'll wait for you, forever if I have to. Someday ..." His voice trailed off. The tears in his eyes crested, slipped down his cheeks. "Someday ..."

She shook her head. "No, Ian. This would break my heart. I must go—we both know that. But ... but I love you so. Do not nail your life to a cross for this love of ours. I could not stand it." She leaned toward him, cupped his face in her cold, shaking hands and stared into his red-rimmed eyes. "Honor what we have had by finding it again. Fall in love, marry, have children. This is what I want from you." Her voice broke, and it took a lifetime for her to go on. "Please ... be happy."

He squeezed his eyes shut for a long, long time, shaking his head. "No."

"Please." She pressed a quick kiss to his lips. "Please, Ian."

His arms came around her hard, crushing her to his chest. His mouth slanted over hers, claimed her, possessed and plundered her, until he was dizzy and breathless and aching with the need to be inside her.

"Ah, Selena," he whispered against her ear. "I love you so damned much."

"And I love you."

He clung to her, reveling in the rainwater-sweet smell of her hair, the soft feel of her lips against him. He tried to memorize everything about this moment, this tiny heartbeat of time; he would need it when she was gone. Already he tried to change it in his mind, so that when he looked back on it—when finally he could—he would remember the love, the passion, the commitment. Not her eyes brimming with tears, or his own wrenching pain. He would remember the taste of the rain, not the taste of their tears. "I will never love another as I have loved you."

He wanted to say more, but it was too late. The dawn had not yet come, and already the time was past for them. Instead, he said the only word that was left. "Good-bye, Selena."

Good-bye.

Selena stood at the top of the stairs, her fingers curled tightly around the polished wooden railing. Sunlight pooled on the warm, honeyed floorboards of the entryway.

It was the last time she'd stand here, the last time she'd feel the familiar smoothness of the wood beneath her fingers, the last time she'd hear the quiet creak of the third step. . . .

She forced the thoughts back, deep, deep inside her, to that darkened place where she couldn't see them anymore. She hurried downstairs and opened the parlor door.

They were everywhere, filling the room in silent, gray silhouettes. The only family she'd ever known.

She bit on her lower lip, making eye contact with no one.

No one spoke.

The silence felt thick and heavy; the antithesis of every moment she'd ever spent in this room, every memory she'd ever made with these people.

"No sadness," she said sternly, walking toward Andrew and Lara, who sat huddled together on the settee. In front of them, she kneeled and looked up.

They both seemed heartbreakingly young and sad.

"We'll miss you," Andrew said with a shudder.

Selena looked at Andrew for a moment longer than she should have. For a second, her throat was painfully full. "The sunlight on your face will be my touch, Andrew. Remember that.

"I will miss you both." She drew them into a long, fierce hug, then slowly pulled back. Rising, she went to Edith, hugged her, then turned to the queen and fell into a deep curtsy.

The queen gave her a sad smile. "You're the only true subject I ever had."

"Good-bye, Your Highness."

Then she went to Johann.

"Goddess," he whispered.

It surprised her how much that single word hurt. Hot tears stung her eyes, blurred her vision, but she didn't wipe them away. There was no point being strong for Johann; of all of them, he'd always seen the truth of her.

"You don't have to go," he said quietly.

She wished it were true, wished it with her heart and soul and mind. "You know that is a lie."

He tried to laugh. "What do you know of lying, goddess?"

"Just what you have taught me, Johann." The teasing words slipped out, lightening their moods for a heartbeat. "Thank you," she whispered, throwing her arms around him. "That is the memory I needed, Johann. Thank you."

His arms curled around her, drew her close. "Be well, Selena."

After a second—not nearly long enough—she turned away from him.

Maeve stood with her back to the bookshelves. "Selena," she whispered, her lower lip trembling, her fingers spasming around the ribbon.

Selena hurled herself at Maeve, wrapped her arms around the thin, frail woman and hugged her tightly. "Take care of him, Maeve," she whispered hoarsely.

"I'll try," Maeve answered.

The words hung between them, and afterward, silence.

Selena knew it was time to turn away, time to move on, but suddenly she couldn't move.

"Selena." He said her name on a whisper, and just hearing it made her want to cry. *Selena*. The name he'd given her, a name steeped in dreams and myths and lore. Goddess of the Moon. No matter what happened in her life, she would always have that. The gift of her name, the gift of his dreams.

She turned to Ian. Their gazes met across the room, and at the look, so intimate and familiar, her world tilted, right slid into wrong, honor into love, and left her with a desperate nothingness. Numb, aching, she moved toward him. She wanted to reach out for him, feel the comforting roughness of his skin against hers, but she didn't dare touch him now. Not now. All that was left them—all that honor allowed—was in their eyes.

She reached up, brushed the hair from his face, and gazed into his blue, blue eyes. "Oh, Ian." She breathed.

She raised her left hand and began to remove the ring he'd given her.

He grabbed her wrist. "Jesus, Selena," he said in a ragged voice. "Don't . . ."

She didn't look up, just stared at the ring until it blurred against her flesh. She tried to forget this moment even before it was over. Later, alone in the darkness, she'd come up with another ending, one filled with romance and laughter and love. One that didn't hurt so much.

She didn't look at him again, she couldn't. With a tiny nod, she stumbled backward and turned to Elliot.

He stood in the shadows, his scarred, wrinkled face hidden beneath the brim of his hat.

She held out her hand to her husband. "I am done, Elliot. You may take me home now."

"Let's go," he said, leading her toward the door.

Selena didn't turn back around. She couldn't. Instead, she tilted her chin up and followed Elliot from the house.

The big door slammed shut behind her, the porch steps creaked beneath her feet. She placed her small hand in Elliot's larger one, and climbed onto the splintery seat of the wagon.

She kept meaning to look back, as Elliot clicked his teeth and snapped the reins, as the wheels creaked forward and crunched through the gravel. As the drive gave way to the iron gates, and the gates gave way to the forest. As they turned away from her beloved shoreline and plunged into the thicket of evergreens.

Yes, she kept meaning to look back. But somehow she never did.

For a long time, Selena didn't say a word, and neither did Elliot. The horse plodded onward, the wheels bounced through the pockmarked road. Gradually they wended away from the comforting familiarity of the shoreline and plunged into the dark shadows of the forest. Night drizzled across the treetops and puddled along the tree trunks. An owl hooted as they passed.

Selena hugged herself tightly and rested her chin in the vee of her bent knees. With every creaking turn of the wheels, she cracked her chin on the bony hump of her right knee, but she didn't care, could barely feel it.

Her thoughts drifted back to Lethe House, to the faces of her family. And suddenly she was afraid that she would forget them, that their beloved smiles would melt away, be gone one day like all the other memories.

"Lara does the best somersaults," she said in a rush,

clinging to the memory. "And Maeve does the best cart-wheels."

Elliot said nothing, and it was just as well. She wasn't speaking to him, she was speaking to herself.

She tilted her head and closed her eyes, remembering. "One day I tried to be a housekeeper. I was very bad at it, but as a subject of the Crown, I was most satisfactory." Memories wove themselves into a shield and strengthened her. No, she would never forget. Never. Not if she lived to be a thousand.

"And the tea party . . ." Her voice trailed off, turned wistful. That had been the beginning for Maeve and Ian, and she'd been so proud of him. "Ian poured tea for Maeve that day and didn't say a word about her pets."

"It sounds like an interesting place," Elliot said in a quiet voice.

Surprised, she looked at him. He sat hunched over, his hat drawn low on his head. From this side, she couldn't see the scar at all.

"It was more than interesting," she said. "It was . . . magical. I . . . I will miss them."

He didn't answer, didn't say a word, and something about the silence drew Selena's attention. She turned to him again. "Elliot?"

Again he didn't speak, but she saw the single tear that clung to his eyelash. He wiped it away with an impatient hand. "Yes?"

Her throat swelled, shame stung her stomach. Of course it would hurt him, her chattering on about her family, when *he* was her family. "I am sorry."

He yanked his hat even lower on his brow. "Don't be sorry, Agnes. I never wanted you to be sorry."

"What do you want from me?"

A brittle smile crooked one corner of his mouth. "Not an easy question."

She stared at him and felt . . . something. "I almost remember you."

"I could never forget you."

The way he said it was so sad, so beaten, as if she'd once wanted him to forget her. Or as if he'd tried and failed. "Well," she said with a forced laugh. "You are all I have now. My only family."

Finally he turned and looked at her. "It's always been that way, Agnes."

They stared at each other for a long, long time, then slowly, Elliot turned away.

Selena stared out at the foreign, shadowy road stretched out in front of her and felt a sudden chill. "I am afraid," she whispered.

He drew both of the reins into his left hand and reached out to her, closing his big, gloved hand around hers. "I won't let no one hurt you."

She tried desperately to take strength from his quiet promise.

Chapter Twenty-three

Ian sat on the beach, his legs stretched out in front of him, his palms pressed into the gritty sand. Tongues of foamy water licked at his bare toes, tickled the sensitive underside of his feet.

It was a gorgeous summer evening. The kind of color-drenched night that would have drawn Selena from her bedchamber and brought her down here. A salty breeze caressed his hair and rippled the white lawn of his shirt. If he closed his eyes, he could imagine her here, beside him, her voice low and throaty, captured in the whisper of the wind, her laughter caught in the cawing of the distant gulls.

The wind could be her touch.

He sighed. Ah, if only he were a better dreamer . . .

He heard the unmistakable crunching of footsteps behind him, the smacking snap of branches being pushed aside and twigs being stepped on.

He didn't need to open his eyes or turn around to know who was coming. It was all of them, gray-clad bodies creeping behind him everywhere he went. They didn't know what to think or how to feel; all they knew was that life had changed, dramatically and badly, and they missed the way it had been. They thought, somehow, that being near Ian was like being near Selena, as if some invisible essence of her had lodged within him.

Even Dotty had come out of her broom closet last night and stood with the others in the parlor.

As always, Johann was the first to speak. "She would have loved this night."

There was a clatter of agreement, and then the horde fell silent again. Waiting, always waiting for Ian to say something, as if by words he could make the horror less painful, spin the reality into a grand, elaborate fiction.

He slowly opened his eyes and was struck again by the beauty of the night, struck again by loneliness. In the two days that she had been gone, he'd spent hours upon hours sitting alone, trying to find the root of his grief. He kept thinking that soon—any second—he would hit rock bottom and it would change his life. He would either come out on the other side or he would sink into the darkness and never emerge again.

But there was no end in sight. The more he looked, the deeper he fell. Until now, finally, unless he thought of Selena directly, he felt nothing at all. Even drinking didn't help this time, and he'd only tried the one time. A half bottle of scotch—a drop by his former standards—and he'd curled into a ball in the shadowy corner of his room and wept. Tears that cleansed nothing, eased nothing.

Maeve sat down beside him, knees creaking. Her hair brushed along his cheek, brought with it the scent of lavender. She pressed her chin into the vee between her bent knees and sighed audibly.

Johann plopped down on Ian's other side, while the queen and Lara and Andrew sat down behind them.

"She was only here for a few months," the queen said, and he could hear the strain in her voice. How hard she was looking for solace.

"Ah," Johann said, "but what a few months it was."

Was.

Such a simple little word, nothing really, and yet it struck Ian like a slap. Was. Loved. They were speaking of her as if she were dead, grieving for her as if she were dead. Two short days and already she was slipping into the lexicon of a memory.

"She made me think about life again," Johann said with a sad laugh. "And just when I was enjoying my impending death."

"She was never very practical," the queen said. "You *are* dying."

Lara tugged on Ian's sleeve and whispered, "She's not dead."

"She is to us," Andrew said.

Lara tugged harder. "No."

Ian turned to the child, surprised at the ferocity of her tone. "Lara?"

Lara swallowed. "This . . . now . . . We would make Miss Selena so sad, she would cry."

"Lara's right," Johann said softly. "Selena believed so much in all of us. It would kill her to know how we've fallen apart."

For a few minutes, no one said anything. Each of them stared out at the night.

And suddenly Ian discovered something, a gift that Selena had left behind. She was there, deep down inside, in the pit of his loneliness and his grief and his sorrow, she was there, sharing it with him, smiling up at him.

"We have to go on," Ian said quietly, and in his mind he heard her voice, echoing his, he felt the heat of her smile in the last rays of the setting sun. "As much as it hurts—and it's going to hurt for a long, long time—we have to go on. If we don't, we'll forget her. Day by day, one selfish word at a time, we'll go back to our own solitary lives, and one day we'll wake up and no one will remember Selena. There will be nothing in us to mark her time here. But if we listen to the part of her she's left in our hearts, she'll never be gone."

Maeve got to her feet and held out her hands. One by one, wordlessly, they joined in a circle. Ian was the last to stand, the last to reach out. He felt a split second's hesitation to touch them, but the fear was overshadowed by his greater fear of facing this loss alone, of facing every moment in his life alone from here on out.

He looked around, at the sad faces of his housemates, and felt a stunning gratitude for them. Maeve was right; they needed to touch each other now, to connect and share and admit the grief. He'd tried it alone, long ago when his father died, and he knew from experience that grief ignored could eat a man up from the inside and leave nothing behind.

Slowly, squeezing his eyes shut, he reached out his hands. Maeve took one; Lara took the other.

Images hit Ian hard, so hard he staggered back. For a second, he was caught up in the swirling pain of their emotions. A headache started at the base of his skull, radiated to his eyes.

You will teach yourself not to hear the voices. . . .

Selena's words came back to him. He concentrated on other things: the feel of the wind, the taste of the sea in the air, the quiet rustling of the leaves all around. Gradually the pounding images faded, the voices merged into a dull, droning murmur not unlike the sound of the ocean at low tide.

He could almost hear Selena's voice in the gentle ebb and flow of their breathing. *It is a beginning, Ian.*

Great, bloated gray clouds rolled across the sky, cast lengthening shadows across the wagon. The road up ahead, pockmarked by muddy puddles, twisted around a bank of shivering red maple trees and disappeared.

Selena sat with her elbows braced on her knees, and her cheek cradled in one damp palm. An open umbrella was cocked above her head. The sky was ominously low, so close she thought she could reach up and trace a finger along its swollen underbelly. Only moments ago the rainy drizzle had stopped. She could still hear the rhythmic plop-plop of water down the sides of the wagon. Rivulets slid down the star points of her black umbrella and splashed on her gingham skirt. The fabric stuck in huge, moist patches along her thighs.

She missed the air at the coast already, and it had only been three days since she left.

There, the air was sharp and diamond-clear and smelled of salt and earth and sea. Here, in the wild inlands of Maine, the air was humid and heavy, as colorless and bland as a glass of watered milk. No breeze whispered through the endless acres of trees, and sunlight only broke through in patches of dazzling gold. And even when it rained, it was hot.

They turned the corner, and for the first time in three days, they were out of the forest. Green pastures rolled out away from them in several directions. Trees existed only in carefully planned pockets amidst the grass.

She cast a sideways glance at Elliot. He sat hunched foreward, the reins slack through his big, hairy fingers, his wet hat drawn low on his forehead.

She wanted to say something to him, but as usual, could think of nothing worth saying. She couldn't be cruel enough to speak to him of Lethe House or her family there, and without that, she had nothing at all to talk about. She'd tried to talk to him about poetry and literature, but he'd stopped that with a curt declaration, *I don't know how to read.*

After that, she hadn't known what to say, so she said nothing, kept her feelings padlocked inside her. Just sat there, mile after mile, unsmiling, watching the scenery change.

"That there's our community," Elliot said.

Selena turned, followed the invisible line of his pointing finger. Far away, nestled deep amid the rolling fields of green and gold, lay a huddled group of clapboard buildings, barely distinguishable from the gray sky. They looked different somehow from the other towns they'd passed through.

All white, she realized suddenly. The buildings were all white. Not some, not most. All.

"Is that not odd?" she asked him. "All of the buildings are the same color. In the last town—"

He turned to her, looked at her for the first time in three days. "You really don't remember, do you?"

She wasn't certain how to answer. Perhaps she'd misunderstood. "I told you—"

"I know what you told me. I just thought . . ." His massive shoulders shrugged. He turned his gaze back to the road. "I thought you might be lying."

"Oh, no. I do not lie."

He nodded, but didn't look at her this time.

She stared at the town, watching with increasing curiosity as the houses got bigger and bigger. What kind of house would they live in? What kind of people would be their friends and neighbors? "The town is well taken care of."

He jerked his hat down on his head suddenly, in a nervous gesture. "It's not really a town, Agnes. Not in the ordinary sense."

She waited for him to say more, to explain, but he said nothing. Nerves jangled in the pit of her stomach, and for no reason that she could fathom, she started to talk. "I cannot imagine living with other people so closely. Lethe House is so isolated. I shall miss the beach. How far are our neighbors?"

It was a second before he answered, but in that second, she knew that something was wrong. "I haven't made myself clear, Agnes. We are members of a religious group known as the United Society of Believers in Christ's Second Appearing. Believers, for short. Although, in the world, they call us Shakers."

He was talking so quickly, using so many words she didn't know. "I misunderstand."

"Whoa, girl." He drew back on the reins and brought the wagon to a halt. Ahead, the sleepy little village awaited them, long rows of white buildings on either side of the road, the buildings perfectly alike, perfectly spaced. It was gray and cloudy, but even at this distance, Selena could see that there were no flowers growing along the fence lines, no gardens in front of the houses.

"There is much you will need to relearn about our ways, but I haven't time to teach you now." His gaze skittered to hers, then darted away. "I suppose I should have been teaching as we drove."

"You can tell me all of it once we get home."

"No. We aren't allowed to speak on such an intimate level. It's contrary to order."

She frowned. "I misunderstand. We are married, you and I, are we not?"

"Not to the Believers. There is no such thing as marriage here. There is only the community. We live as one big family, the men separated from the women. You and I came to the community married, but we don't live as man and wife here. We're just Brother Elliot and Sister Agnes."

Selena got a sick, sinking feeling in her stomach.

"You'd best get in the back of the wagon now," Elliot said, getting down and offering her his hand.

"In the back?"

"It isn't permitted for a woman and man to sit so closely. I . . . I'll tell them you rode in the back the whole way."

Selena gripped her umbrella in cold fingers and placed her other hand in Elliot's big, callused palm. Lifting her skirts, she climbed down the squeaky step and plopped onto the wet road. Her boots sank into the oozing mud.

She looked up at Elliot, trying to think of what to say now, what to do. But no words came.

Elliot squeezed her hand. "I'll always be here for you, Agnes. Always." He made the vow in a quiet, solemn voice, then led her back to the tail of the wagon and helped her climb in. She settled on the cold, wet planks and drew her legs in tight to her chest.

Elliot started to turn away.

She reached out for him, grabbed him by the wrist. "Elliot?"

"Yes?"

"Was . . . was I happy here?"

The question seemed to surprise him. For a second, he looked frightened, but of what, she couldn't imagine. He waited so long to answer that she thought he wasn't going to. Then he yanked down his hat again, shielding his eyes. "I reckon."

"What does that mean, 'I reckon'?"

His voice fell to a throaty whisper. "It means I hope you were, Agnes."

With that, he turned away from her and shambled back to the front of the wagon, climbing slowly aboard. He sat on the plank seat with a grunt and a thump. His massive shoulders rounded, his head tilted so far forward that she could see the untanned strip of neck beneath his cropped gray hair.

Without seeing his face, she knew what he would look like right now, defeated and alone and lonely, and she wondered why a return home would affect him so.

It means I hope you were, Agnes.

She didn't doubt his words, but she had enough brains to know that there was a hidden meaning to the sentence. It meant he didn't know if she'd been happy; it meant that perhaps she hadn't been, and perhaps he'd known it.

As she stared at his broad back and hunched shoulders, she thought about what he'd said about Shakers, about them.

We don't live as man and wife here.

Fear settled in the pit of her stomach, cold and hard and sharp. She realized suddenly that this man, Elliot, this husband whom she'd known for three days and spoken to for less than an hour, was the only face she'd recognize in this new world. And it was *contrary to order* for them to speak.

She was alone now, more alone than she could ever

imagine being. She knew one person in the whole wide world, and he wouldn't speak to her.

She reached for her only belonging, the doll named Sarah, and drew the pretend baby into her lap. She put her nose in the doll's hair and drew a deep breath, but all she smelled was yarn and wood and wet linen. There was no lingering scent of Lethe House or Lara in the doll. It was just an inanimate object with one button eye and threadbare lips.

Chapter Twenty-four

❧

They approached the village slowly. To their right, a fruit orchard fanned out from the road, defined on all sides by a pristine white picket fence. Apple, peach, pear, and cherry trees marched in precise lines through the undulating fields.

When they reached the center of the town, people began appearing, walking toward the wagon. Smiling, waving, murmuring greetings in quiet, controlled voices.

They were all dressed alike. Women in plain, ankle-length pleated dresses in dark, somber colors, with large shoulder capes that fastened at the throat, their upswept hair covered by starched, white net caps or bonnets. Men in dark pants, linen shirts that closed at the throat, and button-up vests.

Elliot brought the wagon to a stop and got out. The crowd enclosed him. He shook hands with several of the men, then walked back to Selena and offered her his hand.

She squeezed the doll tighter to her chest and stared down at this man, this husband, and felt wretchedly out of place. She shouldn't, she knew. She was supposed to be home. All around her, people were waving and smiling and offering her a welcome. But it didn't feel like home. Home was an isolated mansion on the edge of the sea with dark, primeval forests that hemmed you in. Home was louder than this place, wilder, more free.

Swallowing hard, she took Elliot's hand and climbed down from the wagon, dangling the doll in her other hand.

"Welcome home," he said in a voice so soft that only she could hear. "I missed you."

Then he swiftly withdrew his hand and plunged it back in his pocket.

The dark-clad crowd buzzed in around her, talking in subdued voices.

A tall, elderly woman pushed through the horde. When she saw Selena, her narrow, wrinkled face broke into a bright smile. "You are home."

Selena looked at Elliot quickly. She didn't know what to say, what to do. She saw the welcome in the old woman's eyes and knew it was a true welcome, but she couldn't feel it.

"Sister Agnes was injured, Eldress Beatrice," Elliot said. "She has no memory of us."

The crowd fell silent. Selena felt their eyes on her.

It was a moment before Beatrice spoke, and when she did, her voice was whispery and soft. "No wonder you were gone so long. Someone will show you around and get you reacquainted. You will want to change from your worldly clothes and cover your hair as a proper sister should. You may rest for the remainder of this day, then begin your rotation in the laundry tomorrow morning." She smiled at Selena and squeezed her shoulder reassuringly. "I'm sure it will come back to you in no time. You have lived with us for many, many years."

"Her injury is extensive," Elliot said. "She will perhaps need help from the women."

The eldress gave her another quick smile. "Our Sister Agnes always did need extra help." She turned. "Sister Lucinda. Show Sister Agnes to the dwelling house and get her settled in."

A small, birdlike woman with jet black hair and twin-

kling blue eyes slipped through the crowd. She was
dressed in the same fashion as the other women, but her
gown was a velvety shade of blue that matched her
eyes. "Hello, Sister Agnes," she said, offering Selena a
genuine smile. "I've missed you."

Another welcome that should have warmed Selena
and didn't. She did her best to smile. "Hello ... Sister
Lucinda."

The woman winked and slipped her arm through
Selena's, drawing her close. "Call me Lucy," she whispered, leading Selena through the crowd.

Selena passed Elliot, and he didn't say a word, didn't
reach out to touch her. She got a quick look at the taut,
controlled expression on his face, and wondered what
he was so angry about, but she didn't have a chance to
ask. Lucy maneuvered them at a rapid pace through the
people, through a white picket fence and up a well-
tended path toward a huge, white house.

The dwelling sat on a little knoll, hemmed in by old,
broad-leafed trees. Precisely spaced windows, framed
by dark green shutters, marched in two even rows
across the first and second floors. Two front doors, ac-
cessed by two separate sets of steps, were in the middle
of the building.

"The men use the east door," Lucy said brightly.
"And the women use the west."

Before Selena could remark on the oddity of this,
Lucy was pulling her up the west steps. Lucy twisted
the doorknob and opened the door to reveal a spacious,
wooden-floored foyer. The entryway led into two separate, side-by-side hallways that ran the length of the
house. At the end of the corridor an old grandfather
clock stood guard between two identical open doors.
Through the doors, Selena could see identical rooms,
filled with wooden benches.

"Women on the west," Lucy said again, leading
Selena through the left door, down the hallway, and up
the stairs—also divided by a spindly railing.

At the top of the stairs, the split hallway continued, leading to four equally spaced rooms, two on the right, two on the left. Lucy guided Selena toward the first of these doors and led her through.

It was a big, bright, airy room, with a wooden floor that reflected the sunlight. Selena liked it immediately. Warm, creamy walls framed the room, unadorned by pictures or paintings. A thin strip of wood ran in a straight line at eye level along each wall. The plank was set with wooden spikes, and from these evenly spaced spikes hung mops, brooms, and two elegantly simple ladder-back chairs. One whole wall was exquisite built-in drawers. In the center of the room sat a small cast-iron woodstove, its pipe running straight to the ceiling, then across the room in a perpendicular line. Narrow single beds occupied each corner. The only other piece of furniture in the room was a commode with a water pitcher and basin. Four neatly folded hand towels hung on hooks beside it.

Not a thing was out of place. Not a thing was unnecessary or ornamental, and yet the craftsmanship of the woodwork made it seem elaborate.

"This is our retiring room," Lucy said. "You and I share it with Sister Bertha and Sister Theresa."

Lucy glanced quickly back at the door, then darted over and closed it. "Is it true?" she whispered.

Selena turned to her, confused. "Is what true?"

"You don't remember any of us?"

"Why would I lie?"

Lucy smothered a sharp bark of laughter. Once again her gaze leapt to the closed door. "If you have to ask, you don't remember."

Outside, footsteps sounded up the stairs. Lucy edged away from Selena. "We'll talk later. You get settled in—that first bank of drawers is yours. Get dressed for supper."

Selena felt a rush of anxiety. She couldn't do it. Not yet, she couldn't go down with those strangers and have supper. It would bring back too many painful memories. She needed one more night, just one, she told herself, and then she'd throw herself into this strange new world.

But not yet. Now she needed a little more time alone, to remember. To forget.

"I . . . I am not hungry." At Lucy's frown, she fumbled to come up with a better excuse. "It was a long trip and I have the aching head."

"Oh, a headache." Lucy nodded. "You always get them."

Selena frowned. "I do?"

"At least, you used to."

An awkward silence drifted between them; Selena thought that Lucy wanted to say more, but the woman didn't speak, just stared at Selena through sad eyes.

"What is it, Lucy?" she whispered.

Lucy moved toward her, touched her in a quick, bird-like gesture. "I thought you got out," she said quietly. "All this time . . . since you left . . . I thought you were happy."

Behind them, the door opened and Eldress Beatrice appeared in the opening. "Come along, Sister Lucy. Give Sister Agnes some time to regather herself. Brother Elliot tells me she is still weak from her injury."

Selena lifted her hand to her head. "I have an aching head . . . Eldress. I shall go to bed now."

"Certainly. Tomorrow morning you'll feel much better."

In an instant, the two women were gone and Selena was alone.

She walked around the room, touching everything, letting her fingers trail over the rough linen of the hand towels, along the smooth surface of the perfectly crafted drawers, searching for *something* that would spark a memory, something to combat the growing sense of unfamiliarity.

There was nothing, nothing at all. Nothing but a rising, sharp-edged desperation, a sense of wrongness about this place, about everything.

She slipped her hand in her pocket, closing her fingers around the smooth-edged bit of blue glass.

Oh, Ian . . .

It felt so wrong. She didn't believe she'd been here before. She wanted to tell this to someone, to run to the door and wrench it open and scream that it had all been a horrible mistake, that Elliot had retrieved the wrong woman.

But he hadn't, and she knew that, too. When she looked in Elliot's eyes, she saw a terrible sadness, and now she knew where such emotions sprang from.

Love. Only love could cause such a devastating pain. She understood finally why the poets wrote of it, why the ballads were filled with tales of love found and love lost. Because with love, there was life, and without it, there was only this terrible emptiness.

She drifted toward the window, and immediately wished she hadn't. Just being there, standing there, she couldn't think of anything except that it was the wrong window, the wrong place.

"Find something," she whispered to herself, hearing the break in her voice that matched the tear in her soul. She clutched the talisman in her pocket and gazed out.

She would find contentment here, too, somewhere, with someone. She would get past this pain. A person couldn't go on living with such a gaping emptiness inside. Sooner or later, the gnawing hurt would fade, and the people whom she'd chosen to live among—these Shakers—would slip one by one into her heart, anchoring her to this place the way she'd once been anchored to Lethe House.

She leaned forward, pressed her forehead against the cold glass of the window and closed her eyes. Memories crept toward her, crooked an invisible finger, and pulled her into their warm, comforting embrace.

I love you, Selena. Someday . . .

She wished now, just for a second, that she'd let him finish the sentence, spin the dreams for her. Maybe if he'd said the words aloud, she could find strength in them, knit them into a shield against the loneliness. But she hadn't let him finish. She'd been trying so hard to be honorable and fair, to leave him with a future as she went alone into her past.

Somewhere, a bell rang.

Footsteps clattered up the stairs and down the hallway, unaccompanied by voices. The door behind her creaked open and Lucy slipped into the retiring room, followed by two women whom Selena hadn't seen before. One was tall and gray-haired and thin as a rail, the other short and heavy with bright pink cheeks. A stick and a biscuit, pressed side by side. Both wore bright, welcoming grins.

As one, they surged toward Selena and enfolded her in a fierce hug, then bounced back. "Welcome home, Sister Agnes," they said together.

"Hello," she said quietly.

The stick stepped forward. "I'm Sister Theresa. This here is Sister Bertha."

Before Selena could respond, another bell rang.

All three women hurried to the drawers and retrieved their plain, white nightdresses, undressing and redressing quickly. Then, one by one, they lined up at the commode and washed their faces and brushed their teeth. None of them said a word.

They turned around together and stared at Selena.

Lucy was the first to smile. "She's forgotten, Sisters."

Sister Bertha nodded. "You will remember the rules any day."

"Rules?" Selena whispered, clutching the bit of glass in her pocket.

Sister Theresa's head bobbed affirmatively. "The bells give us our direction. It is time to pray and prepare for bed. At the next bell, we'll blow out the lights and go to sleep. Remember?"

Selena's stomach lurched. They couldn't do this to her, couldn't dictate every moment of her day as if she were a child. She took a step backward, then another and another, until she hit the wall. "But ... but I want to take a walk. Outside."

Lucy walked toward her, and now there was no brightness in the woman's eyes, just a sad, tired resignation. "You always felt penned in by the rules, Agnes."

"But—"

"Tomorrow we work together in the ironing house. I'll answer any questions you have then."

Selena couldn't think of what to say, so she went to the drawers and got a nightdress.

Don't think about the lace one, about the night you put it on and went to Ian's bedroom. . . .

Biting down on her lower lip, she stepped out of her gingham dress and slipped the nightdress over her shift as the other women had done. Then she washed her face and brushed her teeth, and went to the only available bed, climbing in beneath the soft cotton sheeting.

Another bell rang.

"Good night," everyone said at once, and the lanterns were blown out.

Selena lay there a long, long time in the unfamiliar darkness, listening to the quiet tenor of the women's breathing. Sometime after midnight, it began to rain, a quiet *thump-thump-thump* on the gambrel roof.

She drew the doll to her chest and tried to go to sleep, but peace eluded her. Memories clamored for her attention; and she was weak, too weak to fight them off anymore, they came to her in the darkness, whispering soft nothings, seducing her.

I love you, Selena. Love you, love you, love you . . .

Tears stung her eyes, slipped down her temples, and disappeared in the flat linen pillowcase.

* * *

Elliot stood inside the brothers' retiring room, staring at the closed door. Behind him, he could hear the shuffling sounds of the brethren preparing for bed, the gurgling splash of water, the rolling creak of the bed wheels as a brother sank into bed. As always, there was no talking going on, just the hushed whisper of solitary prayers. The brethren were tired, as they always were at the close of a full summer day. They had probably been shearing the last of the sheep.

He strained to hear impossible sounds—the sisters' nightly routine, Agnes's voice lowered in prayer.

What was she doing now? What was she thinking?

"Brother Elliot," someone whispered. "The bell rang. I must blow out the light."

Elliot nodded without turning around. For the first time, the routine felt stifling. He didn't want to silently slip into his bedclothes and go to sleep. He wanted to cross the invisible boundary of the hallway and knock on the closed door, wanted to take his wife's hand and lead her into the darkness of the night and talk to her.

Lord, just *talk* to her.

He sighed tiredly and stepped back from the door. He quickly changed his clothes and slipped into bed, drawing the thin woolen blanket up to his chin.

The last lantern was extinguished, and the room fell quiet. Pale moonlight seeped through the windows.

He turned his head and stared at the inconsequential light. Thoughts and memories filled his mind, took on the sharp edge of regret, of shame.

He remembered the days when they'd first come to the village, the hulking scarred man and his thin, frightened child-wife. It had seemed like an oasis to both of them, a family that opened its arms and drew one in, welcoming the homeless with a warm fire and a hot plate of food.

It hadn't seemed like much of an exchange. He and Agnes signed a covenant of faith and donated their wordly goods—nothing—to the Believers, and magically, they had a home. A place where they belonged. It didn't matter that they didn't sleep in the same room; they never had. It didn't matter that they couldn't speak for more than fifteen minutes without permission from the elders; they'd never had much to say to each other. All Elliot had ever needed from Agnes was her presence, and all she'd ever needed from him was protection. The Believers had fulfilled them both.

He sighed quietly and crossed his arms behind his head, staring sightlessly up at the ceiling. He remembered the day he'd first seen Agnes. A scrappy, hungry young girl with a black eye and a broken wrist, searching through garbage pails for food.

He'd approached her cautiously, flipping her a dollar piece. She'd grabbed it and run away. But he'd come back, time and time again, until she began to wait for him, to stay and talk with him after he'd given her the money.

He still remembered how he'd felt around her. For the first time in his life—and he'd been thirty-four years old—he wasn't just a big, scarred man with one bad hand and a lifetime of pain. He'd looked in Agnes's brown eyes and saw himself as she saw him. A savior.

In the years since he'd asked her to marry him, he'd told himself that he did it for her, but now, alone and in the darkness of his room, he faced the bitter truth. He might have started down this long road for both of them, but somewhere he'd turned and started going alone. As the years went on, it became more and more about him and his needs.

She wasn't happy as a Believer.

He knew that. He'd probably known it for years, but he hadn't faced it until she left.

He should have let her be, should have gone quietly on with his life, taking strength and joy from the knowledge that she was free and happy. Somewhere.

But he hadn't been that strong. He missed her. Lord, he missed her like he missed the sunshine on a cloudy day. Each day of her absence had eaten at him, twisted his insides until he couldn't think or eat or sleep or pray without mouthing her name.

He told himself he only wanted to know if she was all right, if she was happy. But then, in the great, light-filled mansion on the sea, he'd seen the happiness in her eyes, shining through, reflected in a smile he hadn't seen in years, and he'd known the truth: He didn't care if she was happy; not really. All he cared about was himself.

He couldn't breathe without her beside him.

"Oh, God," he moaned, hating himself, cursing his weakness. He turned onto his side, burying the ugly half of his face in the soft folds of the pillow. What was he going to do now? What could he do?

A good man would release her. Kiss her on the cheek and smile and say a quiet good-bye.

The thought sliced through him, caused an ache so deep, so sharp, that for a second he thought he was having a heart attack. He welcomed the pain, almost wished for a swift, sudden death. For he had looked into his soul and seen the agonizing, ugly truth.

He wasn't a good man.

Chapter Twenty-five

The first morning bell rang at 4:30.

For a few seconds, before Selena was truly awake, the first pale glimmer of daylight was welcome on her face. She blinked sleepily and stretched her arms, thinking of the day to come.

Beside her, a bed creaked, then another and another, reminding her sharply that she wasn't home.

"Get up, old slug," Sister Bertha teased.

Selena pushed up to her elbows and glanced around, surprised to find that Lucy and Theresa and Bertha were already dressed in the same clothes as yesterday. They stood in a loose triangle, staring across the room at her.

Another bell rang.

All down the hallway, doors squeaked open. Feet shuffled almost silently past their room.

"You'd better hurry," Lucy said. "It's five minutes till the next bell—and by then we're supposed to be in the men's retiring rooms, picking up their laundry."

Bertha clucked reassuringly. "Lucy, you stay here and help Sister Agnes. Theresa and I can do the men's rooms today."

"Bertha—" Theresa said in a low, warning voice, her gaze darting to the closed door.

"No one needs to know." Bertha flashed Selena a quick smile, and pulled Theresa toward the door. Bertha peeked out, then they both scurried across the hallway and disappeared.

Selena pushed back her covers and swung out of the narrow bed. Lucy came up beside her and showed Selena in swift, spare movements how to draw back the blankets and fold them over the foot of the bed to air them out.

"Keeps the linens fresh," Lucy said with a wink before she scurried to the wall and pulled a broom from the hook.

Lucy swept the smooth pine floor, brushing the wood chips and ash from the place near the stove. Then she wiped down the woodwork and windowsills, and refilled the oil lamp from a big bottle beside the commode.

Selena stood there for a second, not knowing what to do, then she went to her drawer and pulled out the brown cotton and worsted gown. Dressing quickly, she washed up and went to the window.

Another bell rang.

Lucy replaced the broom and dustbox on their wall hooks and turned to Selena. "Time to start our chores."

Selena gave one last look to the doll who lay on her bed, then turned and followed Lucy from the room.

The hallway was filled with people. Men on the east side, walking silently, single file; women on the west. They nodded silently and greeted each other in subdued voices, barely making eye contact.

Except for Elliot. He stood alone in the doorway of his retiring room, his big hat crushed in his hands. Selena stared at him. Across the row of people, their eyes met.

There was such regret in his eyes. She frowned, wanting to reach out for him, to beg some answers, but the second passed too quickly.

He crammed the floppy-brimmed hat on his head, dropped his gaze to the floor, and merged into the male crowd, disappearing almost instantly down the stairs.

Lucy's hand slipped into Selena's and squeezed. "Come on," she whispered.

Selena clung to the woman's hand, a lifeline in the shifting strangeness of this segregated, silent house. Together they marched down the stairs and around the corner, past the kitchen that was just beginning to waken amid the sound of clanging pots and splashing water and feminine voices.

Women streamed through the west door like a neat herd of cattle, emerging into the still-darkened world, where they scattered in a dozen different directions. Lucy led Selena down the quiet, tree-lined street toward a small white house, as unadorned and plain as the others. Pushing through the door, they entered a big, square room filled with long wooden tables. In the center, sitting on a huge square of hammered steel, was a conical stove filled with irons. Baskets heaped with laundry lay along the wall, and wooden trees were laden with drying white sheets and aprons and caps. Wooden stocking forms hung from pegs on the wall. Through the windows on the opposite wall, Selena could see a dozen women, bent over huge, black cauldrons.

Lucy flicked open a panel in the conical stove and started a fire. Within moments, waves of heat pumped from the stove and filled the room.

Then Lucy yanked up a big basket and spilled the contents out on the trestle table. "As soon as the irons are hot, we can begin."

Selena went to the table and stood across from Lucy. "Tell me about this place."

Lucy gave her a weak smile. "You have seen enough already to know what it's like. It's a religious community."

"What is this religion that requires bells and separation and silence?"

"We practice celibacy."

"I do not know this word, celibacy."

"I wish I could forget it," Lucy said with a little laugh. "Sex. You know that word?"

Memories hurled themselves at Selena, sharp and sudden and sweet. "Yes. I know this word."

"Quite simply, we don't have sex."

"But the married people—"

"Marriage is 'contrary to order.' It is not considered proper for men and women to form such special relationships," Lucy said bitterly.

"I understand this emotion, bitterness. Why do you express it so?"

Lucy looked surprised for a second. Then she smiled. "I forget that you don't remember me. My husband, Blake—he lives in another dwelling house. And our son, Samuel, lives in a third."

"I misunderstand. You have a child and a husband, yet you do not live together?"

"You understand perfectly."

"But a child needs his mother."

"Not here." Lucy spread an apron out in front of her and sprinkled lavender water on it, then she reached for an iron and began pressing the linen. "Last year Sammy came down with the chicken pox. They wouldn't even let me see him until I threatened to burn the place down. Raising children is a 'community activity,' you see. It isn't proper for a mother to have a special bond with any one child."

Even Johann had never sounded so bitter. Selena copied Lucy's movements, drawing a wrinkled white apron from the basket at her feet and smoothing it across the table. Carefully she withdrew a hot iron from the stove and began pressing. "Why do you stay?"

Lucy sighed. "Where would I go? My husband made the decision to join without me. He donated all of our worldly belongings to the society and brought Sammy. He told me I could make my own choice, but I couldn't have our son on the outside. For the first few years, I tried to run away, but he always found us, always brought us back here. I'm a woman. I have no choices."

"But—"

"All I have is Sammy. I live for the moments when I see him across the yard." Tears gathered in her eyes, slipped down her cheeks. "Maybe when he's older . . ."

"Are all of the women trapped here?"

Lucy brushed a tear away. "Oh, no. For many of them it's a wonderful place to be. Bertha and Theresa think it's heaven. Most of the women do. There is no want here, no beatings, no hunger, and they are respected. Our founder, Mother Anna Lee, was a woman."

Selena ran the hot iron over her thumb. With a yelp, she dropped the iron and shoved her aching thumb in the lavender water. "Did . . . did I like it here?"

Lucy shook her head. "The rules always bothered you, but before you left, you'd started talking about babies. You wanted one so badly. You scared me with how badly you wanted it. You used to say that death was the only way out for you, but you didn't want to hurt Elliot. Otherwise, I think you might have killed yourself right in your room. And then you disappeared." A smile breezed across her face. "I was so proud of you, Agnes. I thought . . . I thought you were free."

"I was," she answered quietly. Bending, she retrieved the heavy iron and awkwardly lifted it back to the table, setting it down on the apron.

"Where did you go? What did you do?"

"I do not know. One day I simply woke up at a very special place up by the sea. I was hurt badly and my memory for almost all things was gone."

"How did you get hurt?"

Selena shrugged. "No one knows."

"What was it like up there?"

Pictures sprang to mind, all of them painful in their beauty. Her fingers curled tentatively around the iron's wooden handle. "There was a man. . . ." Her throat closed. She couldn't say any more.

"You loved him."

Selena looked away, unable even to nod.

"You shouldn't have come back."

"What choice did I have, Lucy? I was a married woman and my husband came back for me."

A silence fell between them, swollen and poignant.

In that moment, Selena understood that this was all there was for her. Friendship with a few women, perhaps, and a life of rigid control. No hunger, no beatings, no deprivation, but also no freedom. No real family, no laughter.

"Agnes?" Lucy stared at her. "Are you all right?"

"No," Selena said quietly. She definitely was not all right now that she'd glimpsed her future. Her life stretched out before her, long and lonely and governed by the ringing of the bells.

The breakfast bell rang at precisely 6:00, and by then Selena was tired and sweaty and her hands were creased with dozens of tiny burn marks. Her thumb throbbed with pain. She and Lucy finished with the shirts they were pressing and returned the irons to the stove.

Together, silently, they walked back to the dwelling house. People were everywhere, marching in orderly, noiseless lines up through their segregated doors, into their silent dining rooms.

Selena wanted to scream, to jump up and down and wave her hands and screech like a seagull. But she was too tired to do anything but follow the crowd.

It wasn't just the ironing that had exhausted her—although her motor skills were not good enough for such a complicated physical task. It was everything; every silence, every closed door, every rule that had to be followed. She wanted to pass by the kitchen and go to her room, such as it was; she wanted to crawl into her old worldly clothes and climb into bed, pull the covers up to her chin and sleep. Sleep and sleep and sleep and never wake up again. She could feel herself sinking into despair, and she couldn't find a way out, couldn't make herself smile. She looked around this sterile place and saw nothing of value, nothing to care about.

She knew that she was being unreasonable, that this place was filled with loving, caring people, but they weren't the right people. She didn't want to be welcomed or loved by them. She wanted her family back, the only family she'd ever known. She wanted forests instead of fields, shorelines instead of riverbeds. Ian instead of Elliot.

Oh, Ian . . .

Lucy slipped her hand in Selena's and squeezed. "Don't do it, Agnes," she whispered.

"Do what?" Selena asked, but she didn't care, not really.

"You're getting that desperate look again."

Selena bit back a sharp laugh. "Do not worry about me, Lucy. I am sure I shall be fine. I am simply tired. My head aches."

Another lie, she thought sadly. And it came so easily.

The brethren and sisters moved through the house in two quiet streams, entering the dining room through separate side-by-side doors. The men sat at tables on the east side of the room; women at tables on the west.

Lucy led Selena to a table. Across the room, Elliot stood at another table. Their gazes met. He glanced quickly from side to side, then mouthed *Are you well?*

She had no answer for him. He looked so concerned that she wanted simply to nod, but the action wouldn't come.

A bell rang, and the Believers all dropped to their knees, murmuring prayers.

Selena was just realizing that she should kneel when everyone stood up again. Lucy grabbed her around the waist and guided her to her seat. The stark wooden plank table groaned beneath the weight of the food. Boiled potatoes, fried sausage with onions and turnips, wheat bread with freshly turned butter and raspberry jam, stewed applesauce that smelled of cinnamon, and pitchers of creamy milk.

The family ate in silence, the only words spoken an occasional, whispered "thank you" as food was passed from one hand to another. Selena tried not to think of the meals she'd eaten with the family at Lethe House, of the laughter and the teasing and the camaraderie. Of food that had sometimes been thrown to make a point, or the silly little prayers they'd offered to a fun-loving God. *Over the gullet, past the tongue, look out stomach, here it comes.*

She would have smiled at the memory if it didn't hurt so much.

Selena had barely laden her plate with food when the bell rang again. All around her, forks clanged on the china as the plates were pushed to the center of the table. The men stood all at once, then dropped to their knees for silent prayers.

And then they were gone.

Selena took a last bite of tasteless, greasy sausage and pushed her plate away from her. She didn't bother to kneel and offer a silent prayer to a God whom she didn't understand, but no one seemed to notice. Lucy took her by the hand and led her back down the women's hallway, through the women's door and across the yard.

The ironing house was hot and humid.

Selena glanced around, saw the dozens of perfectly pressed shirts and aprons and sheets that she and Lucy had folded and piled. Then she saw the host of heaped baskets that remained to be done.

They would never be done; she understood that finally. This was not a job that ended, it was a job that went on. Day after day, month after month, year after year. It had never occurred to her before. At Lethe House her clothes seemed to magically appear, but now she realized that someone, somewhere, had washed and dried and ironed her clothes. And she and Lucy were expected to do all of the ironing for one hundred people. Just as the women outside did all of the washing, and the women in the kitchen did all of the cooking.

Hard, backbreaking work and it never ended.

"Is this my life?" The question slipped from her mouth, sounded pathetically weak.

Lucy looked up from the shirt she was ironing. Very slowly, she set down the iron. "Our tasks rotate. Next, you and I are baking pies—one hundred and sixty a week for supper alone. Then there's the fancywork. We sell it to people in the world."

Selena thought about how badly her hands worked, how poorly she did things like embroidery and baking and ironing. "I do not know if I can survive here, Lucy," Selena whispered. "I am afraid."

Lucy gave her a sad, tired look. "You always were, Agnes. And I was afraid for you."

Ian stood in his bedroom, sipping tepid water from a cut-crystal glass, staring through his window. Outside, a full moon hung in the velvet sky.

"Selena." He breathed her name, trying to feel her presence, trying to read her mind across the miles.

But nothing came to him.

He turned away from the window and walked from his room, down the darkened stairway, across the entryway and into the starlit night. For a second, he imagined he saw candles around the lawn, thought he smelled smoke. He closed his eyes and remembered it all. The clank of a mallet against a wooden ball, the throaty purr of her laugh, the silky feel of her skin as she touched his face.

Kiss me, Ian.

He sank to his knees and stared up at the starlit sky. He wondered if she was outside right now, staring up at the same full moon and remembering him.

Where was she? What was she doing now?

They were the first questions he asked himself every

morning when he woke up, and the last ones he asked before bed. He was sick with the need to know, to see her one more time. Constantly he thought of her, worried about her. Could she deal with loneliness? Had he taught her that?

He couldn't remember now if she'd ever been alone here. He'd taught her philosophy and religion and how to think, but had he taught her how to survive?

God, he wanted to go to her, follow her and sneak through the bushes like a criminal, watching her, just making sure that she still smiled. Still laughed. Still saw the sun behind every cloud.

But he couldn't go to her, he knew that, told himself the same thing every night and every morning. Honor demanded that he stay, just as it demanded that she go. And what would he say when he got there, anyway? Good-bye again? All he could give her now was the gift of his discipline. The gift of his absence.

I shall be honorable always. Always . . .

God, how he'd come to hate those words in the two months she'd been gone.

She had, as always, demanded the very best from him, the ultimate proof of his honor and his decency. Now he supposed he was as good a man as he'd ever been or ever would be. He'd done the things that would have made her happy—he'd begun building a true asylum on the property, one that would easily house fifteen patients. He'd contacted all of his old colleagues and told them that Lethe House was open for a very select group of disturbed patients; neither financial nor social considerations were relevant. He'd corresponded with Drs. Freud and Wellsby, and several prominent alienists. Slowly Ian was learning the basis for this new profession of his.

Strangely enough, he found that what he did to make her happy made him, if not happy, then at least content. Pleased with himself for the first time in years. Andrew was making great strides, and in truth, Ian had never been so proud of anything or anyone as he was of the boy.

And Lara. Sweet, guileless Lara was more of a comfort to him than he would have thought possible. For hours they sat together, sometimes reading, sometimes drawing, sometimes saying nothing at all.

On the outside, Ian's life looked to be improving. But everyone in Lethe House knew the truth.

They understood his moods, his depression, his overwhelming sense of loss. His need for Selena was a living, burning, growing thing inside him. It brought him out into the darkness every night, too weak to stand, too lonely to cry. Missing her. Oh, God, missing her . . .

"Take care of her," he prayed to the God who'd given him so much and taken even more away. "Take care of her."

Autumn came to the settlement on a cold, soughing wind.

Elliot glanced at the washhouse. Again.

The squat white building rose up from the already dying grass, its white walls a stark contrast to the searing blue sky. Multicolored leaves lay scattered across the lawn, in airy heaps at the bases of the trees. Soon they would be gone, swept into big wooden baskets and carried away.

Through the clear windows, he could see Sister Lucy's back. As always, she was hunched over the trestle table, ironing.

He strained to catch a glimpse of his wife—*just a look, Lord, just a look*. Tomorrow, he knew, Agnes and Lucy would begin their rotation in the kitchen, baking pies, and he would be denied even the simple pleasure of seeing her during the day.

He clutched the wooden ax handle in sweaty hands and repositioned the piece of wood on the chopping block. In a single swift, sure motion he swung the ax and split the wood in quarters.

He tossed it onto the growing stack of firewood and paused, wiping the perspiration from his brow with his bandanna.

God help him, he glanced at the washhouse again.

He tried not to think of Agnes, knew it was a sin to dwell on memories of her so often, but he couldn't help himself. She had changed so completely since her return. Each day she seemed a paler and paler imitation of the woman he'd seen at Lethe House.

She was trying to fit in. She walked straight and tall and had learned to speak quietly, if at all. She carried herself with an elegant grace and seemed to be serene.

But Elliot knew her too well to be fooled. She was failing. The grace and serenity were a fragile cover. A layer of glittering ice on a dark, turbulent pond. When she'd first returned, her moods had been childlike and obvious, from giddy laughter at a raindrop's beauty to a teary-eyed sadness at the death of a turkey. No more. Now her moods were flat and even, unvaried by anything, unleavened by curiosity. Nothing here intrigued her or captivated her. She sat at the family meetings like a colorless ghost, almost smiling, making eye contact, but never really seeing anything. She never complained, never argued, never disagreed.

And never laughed.

Bending, he grabbed another thick, round log from the pile. When he picked it up, he saw a single white flower, struggling to grow wild and free in the shadow of the matted, broken grass behind the woodpile.

It reminded him so sharply of Agnes. He remembered last week's union meeting, when he'd stolen a few precious moments with her, speaking softly while the others watched.

I want flowers in my room, Elliot. I miss the flowers. . . .

He'd been so devastated by the wistful sadness in her voice that he couldn't think. He'd answered by rote, mumbling that flowers were not to be grown for their beauty. Such an ornamental use would be 'contrary to order.' Roses were grown only to be used in making rose water, not for their scent or their beauty.

Oh, she'd said with a half sigh. *How sad.*

And it was, he realized suddenly. Sad not to enjoy the beauty of a flower. Sad that God would demand such a thing when He had created the beauty in the first place.

He bent and plucked up the flower. It looked delicate and impossibly fragile in his big, rough fingers.

Across the street, he heard Lucy say, "I'll be right back, Agnes. We need more lavender water."

Elliot's gaze shot to the washhouse, to the open door.

He didn't think, just moved. With a quick sideways glance each way, he hurried across the street and ducked inside the building, closing the door quietly behind him.

Agnes looked up from her ironing. There was a moment's surprise on her face, and then it was gone, replaced by a dull acceptance. "Hello, Elliot."

Lord, how she had changed. He remembered in a flash how she'd looked at Lethe House, coming down the stairs in the worldly dress, her pale shoulders so creamy and soft-looking, her eyes sparkling with happiness. For the first time, he wondered how she'd been injured. How desperate had she been to leave this place? Desperate enough to run into a moving carriage?

He brought the flower up, handed it to her. "I don't want you to miss the flowers."

She stared down at it, and the dull, glassy look in her eyes melted away. "It's white," she whispered.

For a second, just a second, she was the woman he'd seen at Lethe House, breathtakingly beautiful and filled with emotion. She took the flower, brought it to her nose and inhaled deeply. A slow, hesitant smile curved her lips.

"Thank you," she said.

He stared at her in silence, not knowing what to say, what to do.

She looked up at him. "Do you ever think of leaving this place?"

For a second, he almost said yes. Then reality rushed in, pulverized the feeble hope. He remembered what it was like out there, how people treated a huge man with a disfigured face. "I ... I have a tough time in the world."

"Johann told me that the world was a cold, cruel place. It must be true if a gentle man like you is treated badly."

"You were the only one," he said softly, surprised to hear himself speak. He hadn't meant to voice the thought. Heat crawled up his cheeks.

"The only one what?"

"The only one who never ran from me. Never held this face against me."

She gave him a sad smile. "Then you knew the wrong people. No one at Lethe House would have cared."

He sighed. Lethe House again. "Maybe."

Her gaze dropped to the flower in her hand. "Did you ever want children?"

He drew in a sharp breath. *Children.* So many nights, as he lay in his lonely single bed, he'd thought about the children he'd never have, the grandchildren he'd never raise. Long ago he'd named the invisible children, dreamed of them, but those visions had finally collapsed in on themselves, devastated by the weight of their own impossibility.

And now, as he looked down at Agnes, he dreamed of them again. He'd give anything, even his immortal soul, to hold a child of hers. He'd always yearned for a child, one whom he could hold and kiss and shower with all the love he'd hoarded for a lifetime.

It hurt to think of it, so he stopped, pushed the memories away. "It was not God's will."

She snorted and looked up. "It is always God's will to bring babies into this world. God did not force you to choose celibacy." She moved closer. "You should have made a baby with me, and if I would not, then you should have found a woman who would."

He stumbled for a response. "But my face—"

"Your face is not who you are, Elliot." She leaned toward him, tilted her chin up. "A child cares more about his father's heart than his face."

Elliot stared down at her, feeling oddly out of place, as if his whole world had suddenly tilted to the right and left him scrambling for balance. "You've changed, Agnes."

He'd said the wrong thing, he knew it instantly, though he couldn't imagine what the right thing would have been. She drew back. "Have I?" She sounded tired again.

A silence descended. He looked at her. She looked at the flower in her hand.

In the distance, the supper bell rang.

She sighed and set down the flower. "Like cattle, we go now to eat."

Before he could respond, Lucy rushed into the room. She skidded to a stop at the sight of him and bobbed her head. "Brother Elliot."

He nodded curtly—the proper thing to do. "Sister Lucy."

Agnes lifted her head and gave him a wan, lackluster smile. "Good-bye, Elliot."

Once again he thought of Lethe House and how vibrant and alive she'd been there.

Chapter Twenty-six

❦

The whole family was gathered in the meetinghouse for the weekly union meeting. Outside, the October night was coated in darkness and drenched in rain. Occasional cracks of thunder rumbled through the bloated gray clouds, spit out bolts of lightning.

Selena tried to care about what was going on around her, she really tried. As always, there were men and women sitting on benches across from each other, talking in quiet voices, their bodies held a rigid six feet apart. Every now and then Brother Matthew led them in a subdued song, and occasionally they would dance—in two separate lines, going two different directions, but still, it should have been fun.

She watched them, smiling if they smiled at her, and knew that they were trying in their own strange, silent way to make her feel welcome. Once, it might have worked. If she'd awakened here after her injury and come to life around these God-fearing people, she probably would have accepted their religion and its celibate discipline without question. And she probably would have been happy. They were good, caring people.

But it was too late for Selena, she saw that now. For a brief time, too brief, she'd looked out a clear window on a bright and shining world, a world filled with beauty and poetry and promise. Now that window had been closed, locked tight, and the world she was left in was painted in shades of pious gray. She knew the colors were still here—blue sky, white clouds, gold sun; the colors still existed, but she didn't care about them anymore, barely saw them. Before, she'd seen the world through so many eyes—Johann's, Maeve's, Andrew's, Lara's, and Ian's. Each one of them offered her the gift of the world, sifted through their souls and their experiences.

No more.

Her gaze moved around the room. It took her a second to realize that she was looking for Elliot. They spoke rarely if at all, and yet she'd come to care for the big, life-beaten man. He was always watching out for her, protecting her in that strong, silent way of his. She remembered the flower he'd brought her last month, and she smiled.

Somewhere a door creaked open and the dancing came to a sudden halt. Utter silence descended through the meeting room.

Eldress Beatrice moved into the room. The crowd parted instantly to allow her access, and Selena suddenly wondered if the eldress was ever lonely. Beatrice lived up in a big house with only another eldress and two elders for company. They were always separated from the others so that their impartiality wouldn't be compromised.

Across the room, Eldress Beatrice caught Selena's gaze. The older woman beelined through the now silent crowd and stopped directly in front of Selena.

"Sister Agnes, I have come to speak with you."

Frowning, Selena rose. "Yes, Eldress?"

"Come with me."

A sinking feeling pulled at Selena's insides. They knew about Elliot's visit to the ironing house. It was forbidden, of course, for them to speak for more than fifteen minutes without Beatrice's permission.

Selena followed Beatrice across the room. At the corner, Lucy shot her a worried look and Selena gave a little shrug. She couldn't help thinking about last month, when Sister Joan had been caught speaking to her husband. All of the Believers had been drawn into the meetinghouse unexpectedly. When they were seated, Sister Matilda, a frail, innocent-looking old woman who'd been a Believer since childhood, rose and spoke in a sharp, clear voice. *There is one among us who has need for humiliation.*

Eldress Beatrice had asked Sister Joan to stand. *In what way, accuser, is Sister Joan guilty?*

Sister Matilda had answered immediately. *Sister Joan has broken the faith by speaking to Brother Winston without permission. I accuse her of tempting the brother into sinfulness.*

One by one the Believers had risen and cried out, "Woe, woe." Just the single word, over and over again, until it was deafening in the wooden-walled room. Sister Joan began to cry, begging, pleading for forgiveness.

Finally, when the cries were so loud, Selena couldn't stand them anymore, someone called for silence, and it came, suddenly, sharply, sweeping into the room.

Sister Joan fell to her knees, her head bowed.

Let us pray, Believers, for Sister Joan's redemption.

Selena swallowed hard, fighting a rising panic as she followed Beatrice down the women's hallway and toward the front door. Was this how it began?

She didn't know if she could handle such humiliation right now. God help her, she had no reserves of strength, no core from which to draw.

Beatrice pushed through the closed wooden door and stopped on the small porch, beneath the overhang. Rain slashed all around them. Wind howled down the deserted street, whipping the dead, blackened leaves into a frenzy.

Nervously Selena twisted the small, lacy kerchief that was required to be in her lap during union meetings. "Y-Yes, Eldress Beatrice?"

"There has been an accident. Elliot was out with several of the men yesterday afternoon. I am not entirely certain yet what happened, but I believe the brothers accidentally trespassed on someone's land. The world," she said softly, "doesn't accept such accidents by our kind very well. Elliot was shot. The doctor believes he is dying."

"Dying?" Selena's legs seemed to give way. She reached out, steadied herself by clutching Beatrice's rail-thin shoulder. "I must see him."

"He's being well taken care of, Sister. It isn't proper—"

"I must see him."

Finally Beatrice nodded slowly. "A short good-bye would not be so worldly." She cocked her head to the left. "The infirmary is the building just beyond the herb house. Before the sisters' workshop."

"Thank you." Selena meant the simple words from the bottom of her heart. With a quick nod, she yanked up her cotton and worsted winter skirt and ran down the leaf-strewn walkway. Rain pummeled her, wind slashed at her face.

With every step, every breath, she prayed that she would not be too late. She didn't completely understand death—but she knew that once a person died, you never saw them again. Knew that the body was buried beneath a mound of cold, cold dirt.

Please don't let that happen to Elliot. . . .

She could not imagine those loving, compassionate brown eyes closed forever.

She tore up the infirmary steps and pushed through the double doors, hearing them smack hard into the walls as she skidded to a stop. Her breath came in great, burning gasps, and she bent over, trying to breathe. Rain plunked from her clothing on the floor, puddling at her feet.

"My goodness, a most non-Believer-type entrance," said a quiet, gentle voice.

Selena straightened, found herself in a large room,

with white walls and polished wooden floors. A squat black stove sat in one corner, sending waves of welcoming warmth into the room. Three small, wooden cradles lay against one wall. Beneath a bank of multi-paned windows were four narrow beds. Beside each bed was a four-legged table, heaped with white crockery pitchers and cups and instruments.

Elliot lay in one of the beds, his face as white as the sheet tucked lovingly beneath his chin.

"Oh, Elliot . . ." She brought a cold, shaking hand to her mouth and tried not to cry. But all she could think about was the flower he'd brought her.

A stoop-shouldered old man with snow white hair and round spectacles pushed away from his desk and walked toward her. "Hello, Sister Agnes. You have permission to speak to Brother Elliot?"

"Yes." The word was small, broken.

"Go ahead, then."

Selena forced her wobbly legs to move. At his bedside, she pulled out a chair and sat down. "Elliot, can you hear me?"

The doctor shuffled over to the bed and stood on the opposite side. "He can't hear anything, Sister. He's been sleeping on and off for almost twenty-eight hours. They brung him to me right away, but there wasn't nothing I could do except dig out the bullet. There's already a hint of inflammation. He's in God's hands now."

"God's hands." She repeated the words dully, leaning over Elliot. He lay as still as she imagined death must be, his breathing shallow and labored.

"I'm gonna go get me some buttermilk. Would you like some?"

"No."

The doctor stood by her for a minute, then turned and shuffled away.

She stared down at Elliot, knowing he could hear her in there. Praying he could. She began talking to him in a quiet, reassuring voice. She had no idea what the words meant, or if they meant anything at all. She just talked.

Finally he stirred.

She scooted forward, grabbed his big, scarred hand, and pressed it to her cold, wet cheek. "Elliot?"

His eyes fluttered open, his breath released in a ragged sigh. "Agnes."

Her relief was so sharp, so poignant, that she almost cried out. She leaned toward him, tenderly brushed the messy hair from his face, and stared into his watery, bloodshot eyes.

And saw love.

He tried to smile. "Heard Doc talking. Says I'm dying."

"I will not let you die."

Very slowly, he reached out with his good hand and touched her cheek, a feathery, gentle touch that was over too quickly. "I should have left you with him." He sighed, his hand fell back to the bed.

"Do not speak of the past, Elliot. Think of the future. You must get well."

"I don't think I want to get better, Agnes." A phlegmy cough rattled his chest. At the movement, he grimaced in pain. "If I die, go to Lethe House. Ten miles past Craigdarroch Point. Anyone . . ." He coughed again. "Anyone in Alabaster will know the way."

"Elliot—"

He squeezed her hand hard and drilled her with a pleading look. "Promise me."

She didn't know what to do, what to say. "I promise."

He breathed another heavy sigh and relaxed. "Good."

She edged off the chair and carefully sat on the side of the bed. Trying to smile, she gazed down at him, touched his scarred, puckered flesh and felt the heat from his fever. She felt sick at the thought of losing him. This big, loving man with the sad, sad eyes, who'd never done anything but love her. "I will not leave you, Elliot."

His eyes slid shut, his breathing melted into a slow, rhythmic tide. "I love you, Agnes," he whispered.

"Elliot?" She leaned closer, feeling the first cold brush of fear. Was this death? A quiet lapse into a restful sleep. Had the words released him? "Elliot?"

She felt a hand cup around her shoulder and squeeze reassuringly. "He woke up?" the doctor asked.

Selena turned to him. "Is he . . ."

The doctor touched Elliot's wrist, then shook his head. "Not yet. See? His chest is still moving. He's breathing."

Selena's shoulders sagged with relief. "Thank God."

"But it won't be long now. A couple of days, maybe, before the infection kills him." He stared down at Elliot, wincing at the sight of the scar. "Maybe it's a blessing. Brother Elliot has been in pain all of his life."

"A blessing?" Selena repeated the words. At first she was incredulous, and then, slowly, she became angry. "A blessing?"

The doctor shrugged. "Children in the world used to run from him, screaming. Did he tell you that? Even here there were people who crossed the road to be away from him. As if that damned scar was the mark of the devil. Why, once I saw—"

"Can I take him to a worldly doctor?"

The doctor frowned. "*Can* you take him? What do you mean?"

"I mean the rules. Will Elliot still go to Heaven if I take him to a worldly doctor?"

A quick smile quirked the doctor's mouth. "We call in worldly doctors all the time, but—"

Selena jerked to her feet and spun around. "I shall be back in forty minutes with a wagon. Make him ready to move."

"But, Sister Agnes—"

She smiled. For the first time, she felt a flash of hope

for Elliot. She knew there was one man who might be able to save her husband. "Perhaps I am God's hands, Doctor. Make him ready."

Ian was in the parlor, sipping coffee, reading Henry Cunningham's latest treatise on the treatment of female mental disorders. Johann and Andrew were on the settee, sharing pages of last week's *New York Times*. The last time Ian had seen Maeve, she was spouting Shakespeare and reprimanding her stuffed owl for cussing. The now familiar sound of hammering was a dull, echoing reminder that the asylum's addition was nearly complete.

Maeve flitted across the room, one arm bent dramatically across her chin. "To thine own shelf be true." She paused suddenly and cocked her head. "Someone's coming."

Johann looked up. "I believe Laertes has the next line."

Maeve's arm fell to her side. "No. Someone is *really* here." She traipsed out to the entryway, her diaphanous cape trailing behind her, and peered through the window beside the front door. "Oh, my."

"Kind of late for a delivery," Ian said without looking up from his papers.

"Ian," Maeve said softly. "It's Selena."

Ian felt a rush of hot hope, even went so far as to lean forward in his seat before he realized the truth. Maeve had "seen" Selena a dozen times in the last few months. Slowly he resettled himself in the chair. "That's nice, Mother."

Andrew leapt to his feet and raced to the door, pushing Maeve aside so that he could see out the mullioned window. "Oh, my gosh."

The boy's voice, whispery and filled with awe, brought Ian to his feet in a rush. He looked at the two people, pressed side by side at the little window, their noses pushed against the glass, and felt a stirring of honest hope. He looked at Johann.

Johann put down the newspaper and rose. "Could it be?"

Ian was afraid to believe it. Even more afraid not to. He walked to the door, and with each step, his unreasonable hope grew. With a shaking hand, he reached for the cold brass knob and turned it, sweeping the door open wide.

The winter night was shadowy and dark. Moonlight reflected off the layer of new frost that clung stubbornly to the blackened, dying grass. A wagon was parked in the drive. Great plumes of breath shot from the horse's nostrils.

A wraithlike shadow sat on the wagon's front seat. It turned, spoke to the driver in a quiet, subdued voice. "They will help me carry him in. Thank you."

Her voice, so familiar, washed over him. "Selena?" he whispered, his knees weakening. The loneliness left him in a rush. *She was home. Sweet Jesus, she was home.*

She turned to him then, and in the pale moonlight he saw her face, cloaked as it was by a huge, black cape. "Ian." That was all she said, nothing more, just a whisper that was his name.

Maeve screamed, "Selena's home!"

Edith and the queen and Lara rushed down the stairs, shouting, arms waving, skirts flapping. All four women and Andrew hurtled down the stairs, tugged Selena down from her perch on the wagon and enfolded her in a huge, laughing hug. Everyone was talking at once.

Ian stared out, feeling oddly anxious. Something was wrong. She'd said his name, but not the words, not the phrase he ached to hear from her lips. And why wasn't she beside him, clinging to him, smothering him with her sweet kisses?

Johann came up beside Ian, stood beside him in the open doorway. "You haven't moved," he said.

Ian couldn't answer past the lump in his throat. He felt achingly, obviously, vulnerable.

Did she still love him? The question came out of nowhere, sharp and painful. In all this time, all these months, he'd imagined her pining away for him, as lonely and depressed as he was.

But maybe he'd been wrong. Maybe this Elliot truly had been her love for twenty-two years, and her time with Ian was just a pleasant interlude. . . .

"Don't torture yourself, Ian," Johann said, "though I know how much you enjoy it."

He turned to his friend. "What if—"

Johann dismissed the fear with a wave of his hand. "What ifs are for writers and children."

Finally the jabbering crowd grew quiet. One by one, the inmates peeled away from their goddess and filtered back toward the house, until only Selena stood at the wagon.

Ian stood there, waiting, his heart hammering, his throat painfully dry. She stood stiffly, her hands clasped nervously at her waist, her voluminous cape billowing gently around her ankles. Her face was a pale—too pale—oval amidst the darkness of the hood, her eyes wide and mysterious.

He leaned infinitesimally forward. Now she'd speak, now she'd say the words he needed so desperately to hear. *I've come home, Ian.*

She moved toward him, her booted feet crunching on the stone path. At the base of the steps, she stopped, and he thought—crazily—that she was afraid to come any closer. "My husband," she said softly.

He nodded. *Yes. Tell me you've left him.*

She pointed weakly back at the wagon. "My husband is wounded. He needs your help, Ian."

He froze. Everything about the moment—the hope, the dreams—everything shattered at her simple words.

She blinked up at him, unsmiling, her hands coiled at her waist. She knew how she was hurting him. Damn her, she knew what he needed right now, and she said nothing. Did nothing.

The minute drew out, breathless and poignant, and no one moved or spoke. Then Andrew directed the driver to start unloading Elliot. Johann raced down to help, but Ian couldn't move. He just stood there, his insides broken, staring at Selena.

There weren't even tears in her eyes. She, who cried when a flower died, was dry-eyed now.

He forced his gaze away from her. It hurt too much to look at her and he turned his attention to the wagon. As if released, Selena hurried to help Johann and Andrew. The three of them carried Elliot on a stretcher up the steps.

Ian stepped to the side. "Take him to the empty bedroom on the second floor."

The crowd funneled up the stairway and dispersed at the top, turning to the left and disappearing. All that was left of her was a trace of scent, completely foreign. Lavender, he realized dully. When had she begun to smell like lavender?

Ian remained at the bottom of the stairs, unmoving, unbreathing, until he was alone and the stairwell was dark and empty once again. He wondered for a second if he'd dreamed it, if he'd risen from his chair and looked outside and really seen nothing at all except the frost on the lawn and the pale scythe of the moon. She couldn't be here, couldn't have looked him in the eye and not cried and said quietly, "My husband is wounded." As if nothing else mattered, just her husband.

"Ian," Maeve yelled from the top of the stairs. "Get up here."

Woodenly he began to move. He went to the study and retrieved his medical bag, then slowly climbed the stairs.

The bedroom was wreathed in darkness and filled with people. "Everyone out," he said in a dull voice. "Only Andrew and Johann and . . . Selena can stay."

No one argued. Maeve shepherded the others outside of the room and shut the door behind them. Andrew busily set about lighting the lamps. Within moments, the room was thick with haze and smelled of smoke. Wavering golden light swept the darkness into cobwebby corners.

Ian walked over to the bed, where already Elliot lay atop the sheets and blankets. His half-scarred face was the same color as the grayed linen pillowcase beneath his head. He was bare-chested, and Ian noticed that the same burn that marred his face and hand had eaten down his side as well. Bandages wrapped his shoulder and part of his chest; the fabric was stained brown with blood.

"What happened?" he asked.

"He was shot."

"Bullet still in there?"

"No. The doctor said he dug it out."

Ian nodded, but didn't look at her. He didn't dare. Not yet, not while the pain was so fresh and raw. "Idiot doctor probably used his fingers to dig out the bullet—after gardening, no doubt. Take off the bandages."

Andrew scurried to the bedside and gently peeled the stiff bandages away from Elliot's body as Ian examined the injury. The ragged wound was ringed by flesh that was already an angry red, and a greenish pus pooled in the opening. "It's infected," he said quietly.

Selena came up beside him. He felt her presence, and it took all his strength not to turn to her and take her in his arms. Instead he stood there, not looking at her, looking down at the man who'd taken everything from Ian, taken his very soul.

"Ian." She said his name in that quiet, throaty voice of hers—God, how he'd missed that voice.

He waited for the softness of her touch, the gentle pressure of her fingers on his arm. But she made no move to touch him.

"He is a good man, Ian. He does not deserve to die."

"Doesn't he?" Ian heard the ugly bitterness in his voice and he cursed himself for it. But he couldn't stop it.

"Can you save him?"

I don't want to. Again, so ugly, but he couldn't help himself. He wanted to let Elliot die. Now, tonight. Just move back and do nothing and let the old man die.

Elliot's death was Ian's only chance for a life, and he knew it, had known it the second he looked in Selena's eyes. Her decision hadn't changed. If Ian saved Elliot's life, Selena would leave Ian. Again.

"Ian?" she prompted.

She put a wealth of meaning in that one little word; he felt her expectation, her trust, like a weight against his lungs.

He swallowed hard, wishing—oh, Christ, wishing a million things. All pointless, all impossible. Wishing Elliot had died on the way, that he'd been shot in the head, that there was no way to save him. But mostly he wished he'd never promised Selena to be honorable.

Yet, only in doing his best, giving his best, was he worthy of the woman at his side. And he'd rather die than let her down.

He closed his eyes and tried to prepare for what lay ahead. Breathing deeply, he leaned forward and touched Elliot's fever-hot brow. At first all he felt was the damp heat. Then the images came, spinning deliriously, one after another, until Ian felt weak and dizzy. They came so fast and were gone so quickly, he could only focus on a few of them.

A dirty, dark-haired girl pawing through a garbage can . . . a group of men in somber brown garb sitting on narrow benches . . . a white flower . . . Selena wearing a dull brown dress, walking in a silent row with other women, her head drooped forward . . . Elliot standing before her with the same white flower.

He got emotions with the pictures: an aching love, a staggering regret. *I'm sorry, Agnes. So sorry.*

And the strangest thing of all—a thought, loud and clear and filled with razor-sharp pain. *Go to him, Agnes . . . promise me. . . .*

A headache shot across Ian's eyes, lodged in his temples. He squeezed his eyes shut and tried to concentrate on exploring the wound, only that. The hole from the bullet was small and ragged, a black spot oozing poison from just beneath the collarbone. It had missed the heart and lungs.

With treatment, Elliot would live. Without treatment, he would die.

Selena stood beside Ian, still silent. She didn't say anything, and he knew she wouldn't. She would just stand there quietly and wait, believing in Ian more than he'd ever believed in himself. Believing in him with all her heart and soul, knowing he would do the right thing.

He sighed. "Get me the carbolic acid, Andrew, lots of it. It's in the herb room in a big black jar. Johann, go to the washhouse and get some clean, dry sheets. We're going to need new bandages. Tell Edith to start boiling water and bring some up here."

Andrew and Johann ran from the room; the door banged shut behind them.

Slowly Ian turned to look at Selena.

She stood beside him, close enough to touch, close enough to kiss, and yet there was a stiffness to her that kept him away.

"I knew you would do the right thing," she said softly, giving him a sad smile.

"I know you did."

The stiff, awkward words made no sense. It wasn't what they should be saying to each other right now.

He gazed down at her.

She broke eye contact and looked down at her husband.

Ian forced himself not to move, not to touch her. *Did you miss me, goddess?* He wanted desperately to ask the question, but he didn't dare. He didn't think he could bear her answer.

Finally she turned, looked up at Ian for a long, long time.

And the silence broke his heart.

Chapter Twenty-seven

~⟨∞⟩~

Selena stood in the corner of the bedroom, huddled in the shadows, watching Ian battle to save Elliot's life. Sounds reverberated through the air—the *ping* of steel instruments hitting the metal tray, Elliot's quiet moans, the labored gusts of Ian's breathing, the harsh timbre of his voice as he snarled orders to Andrew.

The tension was so thick, it was palpable.

Over and over again, her mind replayed images of her return, coming always back to the first time she'd looked at Ian, the first time she'd said his name. It had taken everything she had inside, strength she hadn't even known she'd developed, to remain silent.

The images remained, stabbed deep into the tender region of her heart. Oh, Lord, what she had asked of him, both in words and in silence. *Save him, Ian. Save him so I can leave you again.*

It still hurt, hours after she'd done it. She wanted to go to Ian now, slip her arms around his waist and bury her face in the soft lawn of his shirt, to breathe in the familiar scent of him, feel the silky softness of his hair through her fingers. But she was afraid, so afraid, that if she touched him—just once—she'd fall apart. And this time there would be no recovery, no strand of hope that would sustain them both. This time she knew the life that honor required of her, and it was only half a life. She wasn't sure she could do it again, wasn't sure she could climb into that wagon and leave this warm, loving place and return to the village.

In fact, she was certain that she couldn't. Yet she must.

And what if Ian saw the truth in her eyes? It would kill him to know that she was unhappy in the Believer village, to know that she'd left his arms for a sterile, regimented life. She could never tell him about her life with Elliot. Never.

Ian peeled off the thin rubber gloves he'd worn to clean Elliot's wound and dropped them onto the blood-stained tray. "I've done all I can. Now it's up to him."

Across the bed, Selena looked up. He saw a flash of pain in her eyes, raw and mesmerizing in its intensity. Then she quickly dropped her gaze, stared at her own hand, wrapped so tightly around Elliot's big, scarred one.

Though the room was full of people, it was eerily silent. Each of the inmates stood stiff and motionless, their gazes darting from Selena to Elliot to Ian and back again. They'd crept back in, one by one, to stand in proximity to their goddess. But none of them, not even Johann, had dared to speak in the last few minutes.

Ian watched Selena, saw the stiffness in her shoulders, the defiant tilt of her chin, the way she kept squeezing Elliot's hand.

It hurt, all of it hurt, the soft murmur of her voice, the pale creaminess of her skin, the tired resignation in her eyes. Something about her was different; it had bothered him all evening. Every time he drew back from his patient, he'd looked at her, kept hoping she'd look up and meet his eyes, but she never did. Finally, after a while, she'd let go of Elliot's hand and backed into the shadowy corner.

All it had taken to draw her back was a whimper of pain. Elliot's agonized moan slipped into the room and she followed it, surging toward him, murmuring soft nothings, smoothing the sweaty hair from his brow until he stilled again.

Now Elliot was quiet, the wound was clipped and cleaned and soaked in carbolic acid, the bandages were new.

"He needs to rest," Ian said.

Now, he thought, *now she'll look at me. . . .*

She nodded and drew a chair up to the bed, sitting silently beside Elliot, her gaze downward. Maeve went to Selena, touched her shoulder, and Ian saw the tiny shudder that moved through Selena at the contact.

"I'll stay with him," Maeve said, and Ian could have kissed his mother for her thoughtfulness. "Edith will make you something to eat. You're too thin."

It was a long time before Selena answered, and when she did, her voice was throaty and raw. "I have not slept in two days."

Maeve bent down and kissed Selena's cheek. "I know how it is to be so scared." She pulled up a chair and sat down beside Selena. "Ophelia wasn't smart, that's certain. Although it was most romantic. Have you seen the oranges?" She took Elliot's hand in hers and scooted forward. "So, Herbert, how are you today?"

Selena got slowly to her feet. For the first time, Ian could see the exhaustion in her face, the purplish shadows beneath her eyes, the tiny network of lines that bracketed her mouth. The hooded black cape seemed to swallow her, leaving only the pale, pale oval of her face.

"I think he wants a watercress sandwich," Maeve said, looking around. "Edith?"

Selena backed away from the bed. Ian had saved Elliot's life; she knew it as certainly as she knew anything. He'd saved Elliot, and soon she would have to say good-bye again.

Again.

Her family stood there, watching her. She knew they felt the awkwardness she had brought with her, and it confused them. She was not the same Selena who had left here; they didn't know how to treat her.

She wanted to tell them she'd missed them, wanted it so desperately, she felt sick, but she couldn't do it. The words, such little words, would open a dangerous door.

She turned slightly and looked at Ian, saw the pain in his eyes. She was killing him, hurting the man she loved with her silence. "Thank you," she said, knowing it wasn't enough, not nearly enough.

"That's it, Selena?" The words were ragged-sounding, harsh. "After all this time, you come back here and say thank you to me for medical assistance. For *medical assistance?*"

She felt fragile in the face of his anger and pain, so fragile. The strength, the resolve, the honor—it was all falling away from her. She searched deep in her own soul for something—anything—to hang on to. "What would you have me say?" she whispered.

Ian looked as if he'd been slapped. Then he crashed a fist through the medical instruments on the tray, sent everything clattering to the floor. "Out!" he screamed.

The family scattered like ants, scurrying to the door, disappearing.

Selena blinked up at him, trying to think of something to say, but there was nothing, nothing.

"Pick up your toys, dear," Maeve reproached him softly.

Ian lurched around the bed and grabbed Selena's wrist, his fingers punishing in their grip. Without a word, he spun toward the door and strode out of the room, dragging her behind him. In the hallway, the crowd gasped and parted.

He led her stumbling down the hallway and through the entryway, out onto the darkened porch and beyond into the rainy night. Across the grass, down the drive . . .

Oh, no, she thought as the moon garden came into view. *Not here. Oh, Lord . . .*

Finally he spun around and stopped, staring down at her through angry, pain-darkened blue eyes. Rain slashed at his face, wind whipped his too long hair. "What would I have you say?" he hissed. "Jesus, Selena . . ."

"Ian, don't."

"Don't?" He took her by the shoulders and pulled her to him. Her head snapped back at the force of the movement, her hood fell away, exposing her face to the cold rain. "What would I have you say?" He said the words again, only this time they were swollen with sadness. "How about 'I know there's no future for us, but I still love you'? Jesus, Selena. Look at me, touch me, something. . . . Tell me you love me."

She squeezed her eyes shut, unable to look at him. If she did, oh, God, if she did, she'd start crying and ruin it all.

How long could she keep her need for him in check? Another day, another minute, or not even that long? She wanted him so badly, needed to feel his arms around her, needed to breathe the masculine, familiar scent of him.

For a beat of her heart, she remembered his bed, their bed, their love, and a blushing heat crawled up her ...s.

"...elcna," He said her name, whispered it, and she let ... low, breathless moan.

...owly, not wanting to, but unable to stop herself, she opened her eyes. He stared down at her, barely breathing, his mouth drawn in a hard, straight line. But it was his eyes that destroyed her. So blue, so sad . . .

If she leaned forward just a little, tilted her chin, he would know how much she wanted him, how desperately she still loved him. He would take her, right now, amidst the frozen flowers and the dying grass, in the garden that smelled of the last white chrysanthemums. And she would let him. God help her, she would let him.

I shall be honorable, Ian.

"Ah, Selena, you're killing me." He seemed to deflate. The anger left his eyes, his breath released in a ragged sigh, his shoulders rounded. His hold on her eased, melted into gentleness.

He looked beaten, so sad and utterly without hope, and suddenly she couldn't stand it anymore, couldn't stand his pain, or her own. She loved him, loved him more than life, and she couldn't hurt him anymore. How could she ever have thought she could?

"Is it gone so quickly?" she murmured, reaching up, brushing the moist hair from his eyes. "Already you worry that I do not love you?"

It took him a moment to answer, and when he did, his voice was hoarse. "I don't know what to think."

God forgive her. "Then feel," she whispered.

His hands slid down the wet wool of her cape and circled her waist, drawing her close, so close. She tilted her face up and pressed against him, finding warmth through the wet layers of their clothing. Overhead and all around, the sky blustered and blew, sending raindrops splashing down their cheeks.

They came together for a wrenching, passionate kiss that tasted of sweet raindrops and bitter desperation. She clung to him, whispered his name, moaned her surrender, and knew suddenly that she'd never had a choice, not really, not in the face of this.

He drew back, gazed down at her greedily. His fingers moved across her face in disbelief, touching, stroking, memorizing. He pulled the starched white cap from her head, let it fall to the ground.

"Ah, Selena," he breathed, "I've missed you."

"I've missed you, too, Ian. So much . . ."

He clung to her, stroked her wet hair from her eyes and rained kisses on her forehead, greedy, hungry kisses that seared her cold flesh. She curled into his arms and let him hold her, pressing her body tightly against his, drawing strength and comfort. It felt right, so right to be in his arms. She closed her eyes and dreamed—of the future they would never have, the children she would never bear.

"Selena." He said her name so quietly that for a moment, she thought it was the wind. She waited for him to go on, but he said nothing, and the silence hurt her in a way that no words ever could.

Very slowly, she opened her eyes and gazed up at him. Rain splashed his face, slid down his cheeks in zigzagging lines. "There is one thing left for you to teach me, Ian."

He took her face in his wet hands, held her with infinite gentleness. "What's that, goddess?"

"Teach me to live without you."

Behind him, lightning snaked across the sky, exploded in a brilliant white flash above the trees. He drew her into a fierce, desperate hug. Rain fell all around them, battered their skin and soaked their clothes.

"I can't, Selena," he said in a broken voice. "I can't."

She felt his words, hot and moist and whispered, against her ear. His warm tears slid down her throat, mingled with the freezing rain.

She forced herself to look up at him. His beloved face filled her vision, made her ache with need and want and love. She lifted a hand and held it flat, watching the raindrops land like stones on her palm. "God is crying for us."

Ian didn't smile. "The son of a bitch better be."

Elliot woke in a strange place. An unfamiliar bed. The room was big and bright with sunlight. And messy. Clothes and trays and bandages lay scattered across the hardwood floor, heaped over the backs of chairs. The window was pushed wide open. A crisp, sea-scented breeze fluttered the sheer white curtains. Beside his bed was a small, blue-painted nightstand that boasted a pitcher of water, two cups, and a thermometer.

The memories hit all at once. *A gunshot . . . searing pain . . . clutching his chest and pitching to the frozen ground . . . Agnes, screaming her name, holding her hand . . . the doc, saying Elliot would die, a blessing, really . . .*

He jackknifed to a sit, and at the movement, pain exploded in his shoulder. He clutched the wound, felt the bumpy ridge of bandages, and sank once again into the comforting pile of pillows.

Agnes, he thought. *Where are you?*

As if in answer to his silent question, the bedroom door opened and Agnes appeared, carrying a tray of food. Tantalizing scents floated through the room, made his stomach grumble in response.

She moved toward him, and her dress alone told him that they weren't in the village anymore. Not that he needed such proof—the room itself, and its clutter, were answer enough.

She was wearing a beautiful bronze dress that reflected all the red and brown highlights in her eyes. Her hair was down, flowing in waves around her pale face. She looked exquisitely, vibrantly alive.

She smiled brightly. "Good morning, Elliot."

He ignored the burning pain in his chest and struggled to sit up. "Hello, Agnes."

She put the tray on the bedside table and sat down, scooting her chair in close to the bed. "You must be hungry."

He glanced at the food—fried potatoes and sausage, buttered biscuits with jam, and a steaming cup of coffee. *Coffee.* The forbidden brew smelled so tempting. "I am."

As she prepared a plate for him, spread jam on his biscuits and salted his potatoes, he couldn't help staring at her. She looked so young and beautiful and happy. "Where are we?" he said at last.

She flinched at the question. Slowly she put down the salt shaker and turned to him. "We are at Lethe House,

Elliot. I did not know anyone else who could save your life."

"*Ian* saved me?"

She nodded. "He is a great doctor."

Elliot watched her. Was she truly as innocent as she appeared right now? Did she not understand what this Ian had done, how he had ruined his own life by saving Elliot's? "He must be. How long have we been here?"

"Three days."

Three days. And already she was blooming again, already this place had made her happy. He'd had twenty-two years to make her happy, and he'd failed. Over and over and over, he'd failed. And Ian did it in seconds.

He stared up at her. "You should have let me die." He said the words softly.

She leaned forward, pressed a warm hand to the healthy side of his face, the side that could feel the gentleness of her touch. "You know me better than that, Elliot."

"You'll go back with me again?"

She didn't blink, but he saw the way her jaw tightened, the way her fingers clenched in her lap. "Of course. You are my husband. My family."

He didn't understand. This wasn't the old Agnes, wasn't really a woman he knew at all. She was so strong, so honest, so honorable, and she had the biggest heart he'd ever known. He believed that she thought of him as her family, and the belief fortified him.

Family. That's what he and Agnes were, what they'd always been. The two outcasts, together against the whole world. Only now, she had another family. He could feel it in this old house, hear the murmured voices of the people downstairs. This was her family now, and he was just a useless has-been, a part of her life that should be over but wasn't. "Agnes, you hate life in the village. I know you do."

"Hate is too strong a word. I do not hate it, nor do I hate the people."

"Then what?"

"I simply ... die there. I cannot tell you why."

He knew he ought to release her, now, before he lost his nerve. She deserved so much better than a broken-down, scarred old man with nothing to offer. She deserved children and light and laughter, all the things he might once have given her, but now never could. It was too late for them, there were too many moments lost.

Suddenly the bedroom door opened.

And a breathtakingly beautiful woman appeared in the opening. She was a small woman, no taller than Elliot's shoulder. Strawberry blond hair lay piled in a loose coil atop her head. She paused uncertainly, her fingers resting on the doorknob. He remembered her suddenly—Ian's mother. "I—I don't mean to intrude. . . ."

Agnes beamed at the woman. "Do not be absurd, Maeve. Come in." She turned to Elliot. "Maeve sat here with me the past two nights."

Maeve glided toward the bed. "Good morning, Elliot. You may remember me. I'm Maeve." Her voice was soft and sweet, like a lullaby.

He couldn't find his speaking voice.

"Selena," Maeve said, "go rest. You look like a cadaver."

"Oh, no, I should not—"

"I'll stay with Elliot," Maeve said.

Elliot felt a rush of pleasure at Agnes's response. Even here, in this wonderful old house, with Ian a few footsteps away, she chose to be with Elliot. "Go ahead," he said with a smile. "I'll be fine."

Agnes kissed his scarred cheek, then left him alone with the beautiful woman named Maeve.

He stared up at her, unable to look away. She was lovely, with her pale skin and hazel eyes, and curly red-gold hair that shone like reflected sunlight. What must she think of him, this fey, vibrant beauty? He twisted slightly, tried to press the scarred half of his face into the pillow.

"Now, why are you sinking down into your pillow, Elliot? You can hardly eat that way."

"You don't have to stay."

At first she looked offended, and then she sighed quietly. Her shoulders rounded and her hazel eyes turned sad. "You want me to leave. I suppose Selena told you about me."

Elliot frowned. "No. I just . . . just figured you'd want to leave."

She laughed—a high, clear sound that was lighter than the winter air. *Christmas bells,* he thought suddenly, and wondered where such a worldly thought had come from. But it was true, her laughter reminded him of the long-forgotten sound of Christmas bells. "Then leave the figuring to someone else, Elliot. You're no good at it."

The melodious sound of her voice mesmerized him, made him forget—for just a second—that he was big and clumsy and horribly scarred. "You're beautiful," he whispered, stunned to hear the thought slip from his lips. Immediately he was ashamed.

A smile tugged on her mouth. "Really?" She brought a pale hand to her chest. "No one has told me that in years."

He couldn't imagine such a thing. "Me, either," he said with a self-deprecating laugh.

She stared down at him, her gaze steady and frank. "But you're a very good-looking man."

He frowned. Was she making fun of him? He couldn't tell. Those hazel eyes were so honest-looking. "You . . . you aren't disgusted by my scar?"

She laughed again, but the sound was softer this time, had a sad edge. "You haven't seen my scar, Elliot. And believe me, it makes that little mark on your face seem like nothing."

"Little mark on my face?"

She smiled. "You know, in some cultures—or is it fiction? I can't recall—anyway, *somewhere* people think scars are badges of honor on a worthy soul. I wouldn't mind a little physical scar myself. It would be better than my problem."

He shouldn't ask so personal a question, but her remark seemed to invite such familiarity. Slowly, feeling as if he were inching down a thin, thin branch that could snap at any second, he asked, "What's your problem?"

"I'm . . . mad."

"You mean angry?"

"No. Mad, like tomorrow I might not recognize you. Any second now, I could begin a debate with the bedpost or eat the paint. Mad. Insane." She tried to smile.

He could see the sadness in her eyes, and the shame. Two emotions he recognized well. "And the day after that?"

"The day after, I could be as sane as you are. Or I could believe I'm Sigmund Freud himself. There's no telling." She gave a trilling, brittle laugh. "Of course, you can ignore me on those days. It won't hurt my feelings a bit."

"Don't."

She drew in a sharp breath. "What do you mean?"

"I've lived with this face for forty-nine of my fifty-six years, Maeve. I know you get used to people rejecting you. You come to expect it. But it never stops hurting. You spend your whole life looking for someone—just one person—who sees past the scar."

Tears filled her eyes. Their gazes met, and in that one unexpected moment, he saw that they understood each other, understood and accepted. It had never happened to him before; never had he shared his pain with another with such honesty, such blatant weakness. And now that he had, he felt an almost magical sense of awe. As if sharing the horror diminished it. Or perhaps two people simply carried the burden more easily than one.

Chapter Twenty-eight

There was laughter coming from somewhere.

Elliot peeled back the warm, heavy blanket and gently eased to a sit. The pain in his shoulder was still there, a low, thudding drone, but it was bearable now. The sharp, biting agony of the past few days was gone.

He flipped back the coverlet and got awkwardly to his feet. The thick flannel nightshirt he'd been given strained across his chest and pinched his arms as he walked to the window.

Outside, it was a beautiful early winter morning. Sunlight pierced a high layer of haze and glittered across the steel gray sea. A layer of sparkling snow dusted everything.

Directly in front of the house, on a large patch of scuffed snow, people clad in heavy cloaks and hats and mittens played croquet. He recognized the players—Agnes, Johann, Andrew, and the woman they called the queen. Another old woman stood huddled in a thicket of trees, gesturing wildly to no one. In one corner, by herself, Lara sat on a tree stump, playing with a pair of rag dolls. And Maeve danced and swooped and somersaulted, a stuffed raccoon clutched in her arms. Only Ian was missing.

The chattering sound of their talk drifted upward, peppered now and again with laughter.

Elliot drew away from the window before he was

seen. With a sigh, he leaned back against the cold wall and tried not to dwell on the scene below.

He'd searched for a place like this all of his life. Once, years ago, he'd thought he'd found it in the Believers, but now, as he stood here amidst the faraway laughter, the truth was painfully obvious. A family was not a community of people who believed in a common cause; it was not raising children by groups or sleeping in sterile rooms with members of your own sex. It wasn't orderly and tidy and self-contained.

A family was what he saw on the snow-covered lawn. A big, messy, laughing group of people who cared for each other.

The thought hurt, so he pushed it away. He walked stiffly to the heavy oak armoire and opened the carved, mirrored doors. Inside, his clothes hung from brass hooks. He struggled out of the too tight nightshirt and slipped on his old woolen pants and linen shirt. By the time he was finished, he was winded and his chest ached.

He sat down until the pain passed, then he got to his feet and walked slowly to the door. There was something he needed to do.

Ian stood at the open parlor window, watching the party on his front lawn, listening to the laughter. Every nuance of sound, every giggle or cry or yowl of mock hurt, was a knife that drove into him. He wanted to be out there with them, pretending everything was normal, but how could he? How could he look at Selena and feel anything but a yawning despair?

Behind him, the door creaked open. Footsteps shuffled slowly inside. There was a pause, then slowly, a masculine voice said, "Dr. Carrick?"

Ian's breath caught. A sharp pain lodged in his chest. He schooled his face into an impassive mask and slowly turned around. Elliot stood in the doorway, his head hung low, his suit wrinkled and still stained with old blood. He looked ancient, beaten.

Good, thought Ian with a surge of bitterness, but even as he felt the emotion, he lost it. Elliot wasn't triumphant or boasting or cocky. He was just an old man who'd loved a special woman for a very long time.

Ian walked to the sterling silver tea and coffee set and poured himself a steaming cup of coffee. "You're up," he said into the quiet. "How do you feel?"

"Alive."

Ian nodded. It felt as if he should say something, do something, but he couldn't think of what it could be. Short of groveling before the old man, or killing him, Ian had no recourse. "Your wound is healing nicely."

"It feels better. Thank you."

"Hmmm," Ian said with a nod. Then he waited.

They stared at each other. The silence increased, felt uncomfortable.

Finally Elliot took a shambling, limping step forward. "I came down to thank you for saving my life."

"I'm a doctor."

He took another step, and looked up at Ian. "Why did you do it?"

Ian took a sip of coffee before answering. "I didn't want to."

"I don't suppose you did."

Ian took another long drink of his coffee, peering at Elliot over the gilt-edged rim of his cup. "There's a long answer, but I won't bore you with it. The short answer is, I saved you because she wanted me to."

"But you knew that if I lived—"

"I knew." Ian set down his cup of coffee and moved toward Elliot, searching the old man's face, trying to find . . . Hell, he didn't know what he was searching for, what he could find that could make a difference. *Go to him, Agnes.* The words of the vision came back to Ian suddenly and he wondered what they meant. "She says you are a good man," he said softly.

Elliot released his breath in a heavy sigh. "I wish that were true."

Ian stared deep into the man's eyes and slowly put out his hand.

Elliot didn't look away as he reached out, clasped Ian's hand in his. "Thank you again for saving my life, Ian."

Ian winced. His hand caught fire, the headache burst behind his eyes. Images rammed into his mind with the force of a blow. *Selena standing in a room full of people, separated and alone . . . a closed door, a single bed . . .* And the thoughts: *She loves you, Ian, and I love her.*

Ian yanked his hand back. For a second he felt nauseated by the headache, and then gradually it passed. He tired to smile at Elliot, but couldn't quite manage it. "Did Selena tell you about my . . . gift?"

"No."

It hurt, that simple little denial. He wanted somehow to be the focal point of their conversation, wanted his name to batter Elliot's consciousness the way Elliot's battered his.

Again the silence fell, awkward, heavy.

Finally Elliot spoke. "I guess we'll leave tomorrow."

Ian flinched at the unexpected words. *No,* he thought. *No. I'm not ready. . . .*

But he'd never be ready, and besides, his feelings didn't matter at all.

"Tomorrow," he said dully, wishing there were something he could say, some way to change what couldn't be changed.

Elliot looked up, snagged Ian's gaze for a second, then looked away quickly. "I think I'll go rest again."

"Could you . . . bring her back sometime?" The words were out before Ian could stop them. He looked at Elliot's pale, frozen face and knew that he shouldn't have spoken, shouldn't have asked the pathetic question.

"I don't think I could."

Ian wished he had the strength to nod. To shore up and act like a man even though his insides were dissolving. But he didn't. It took everything he had inside him to just stand still and not scream. At last he said all that he could say, and it wasn't enough. Not nearly enough. "Be good to her."

Elliot nodded in response, and then he left the room.

Selena checked in on Elliot around one o'clock and found that he was still sleeping. She pressed a quick kiss on his cheek and left him. Back in her own room, she stripped out of her soggy woolen dress and stockings and re-dressed in a pair of Andrew's black woolen pants and white linen shirt. She was just about to go see Ian when someone knocked on her door.

"Come in," she said.

The door opened and Maeve stood in the opening, wearing a pale mint green muslin dress and heavy black cape. "Follow me," she said with a grin.

Selena slipped her hand in Maeve's. "Where are we going?"

"Close your eyes."

Laughing, Selena did as she was told, and Maeve wrapped a heavy strip of black silk across her eyes, tying it tightly. Then Maeve led Selena down the hallway and down the stairs.

They came to a stop. "Maeve—"

"Surprise!" voices yelled out.

Maeve whipped off the blindfold, and Selena found herself standing in the parlor, with her family all around her. Dozens of apples lay scattered about the room, on the windowsills, the furniture, along the floorboards. Each apple held a single candle, their flames a hundred bright dots of gold against the tapestried walls. The pungent smell of apples and smoke filled the room.

All were dressed in their Sunday-go-to-meeting clothes. Lara wore a white lace gown with a big red velvet bow at her waist, the queen a regal purple satin gown, and Edith's pudgy body was wedged into a frothy confection of red and green silk. Ian and Johann and Andrew all wore black pants and coats with stark white shirts.

"Oh, my . . ." Selena said, drinking in the sight of them, memorizing this moment. Every nuance, every sound, every sight.

Ian strode across the room, held his bent arm out to her. "Milady, we would like to invite you to sup with us."

She gazed up at him. He looked heartbreakingly handsome in the evening clothes, his gold hair brushing against the black wool, his flame blue eyes sparkling. Her heart picked up its beat. "What are we doing, Ian?"

He shook his head, and she saw the flash of sadness that darkened his eyes. Then it was gone. "Today is not a time for questions or sadness."

She understood suddenly. "Tomorrow," she whispered.

He nodded.

She slipped her arm through his and clung to him, pressing her cheek against the soft wool of his coat. "Yes," she whispered. "Make me forget tomorrow."

Johann picked up a golden wicker picnic basket, Lara swept up a handful of toys, Andrew picked up a violin, and Maeve grabbed a jug of wine. All talking at once, they crowded out of the room and walked across the crisp, snow-covered lawn, their feet crunching through the thick layer of frost on top.

They got halfway across the lawn and Selena stopped dead. She spun around and looked at Andrew, realizing for the first time that he was outside. In broad daylight.

He grinned at her. "Hi, Selena."

She pulled away from Ian and ran for Andrew, throwing her arms around him, knocking him to the ground in her exuberance.

Snow fluttered up around them, landed in tiny white

flakes on Andrew's jet black lashes and melted into silvery droplets of water. "I am so proud of you," she whispered.

Tears glazed his eyes. "Thanks, Selena."

After that moment, the day took on a magical quality. Selena and Andrew got back to their feet and held hands as she walked back to Ian.

Without a word, Andrew let go of her and rushed on ahead, laughing and chattering with the crowd as they melted into the darkness of the forest.

Selena stood at Ian's side, staring up at him, loving him more in that instant than she'd ever thought possible. "Ian-God," she breathed, knowing she didn't have to say more.

Smiling, he slipped his arm around her and drew her close. Talking quietly, they followed the family through the forest and out to the ledge of the cliffs. Below, the sea was a crashing white foam against the gray granite.

They spent the day together, clustered on a soggy woolen blanket, throwing rocks into the sea, playing catch, eating the cold, succulent food that Edith had prepared.

Gradually the pale sun sank into the distant gray haze that clung to the horizon. The keening cry of the seagulls gave way to the moaning whimper of the evening wind. A shadowy comma of moon appeared in the distance.

One by one, the crowd dispersed. Johann got cold and went inside for a straight shot of bourbon; Lara and Edith and the queen went back to get warm; Maeve went back to see Elliot; and Andrew just disappeared without a word.

Selena lay on the wet, icy blanket, snuggled close to Ian. They were both freezing cold, but neither one of them wanted to leave. The word *tomorrow* kept sneaking back, winding itself through words unspoken, thoughts unvoiced. With each passing moment it felt heavier, closer.

She stared up at the sky, listening to the squawking chatter of the shore birds and the whispering cant of the breeze. The sea was a steady thrumming that washed across the rocks. "It was a wonderful day," she said. "Thank you."

"He says he's taking you home tomorrow," Ian said.

Home. For the first time, Selena heard that single word as something cold and hard and just a little frightening. So different from the way it should be. *Home.* It should be light and love and warmth. She glanced at Ian, saw her pain reflected in his eyes and knew that she should say something to console him. But there was nothing.

"I can't think of a way to stop him," Ian said at last into the growing silence. "The fever's gone, the infection is nearly gone. Any doctor could finish the job."

Selena closed her eyes. Despair washed through her, colder than the winter air. A sudden, desperate longing came with it.

She couldn't stop pretending, not yet. No matter how hard it was, she couldn't let go of the fairy tale. Reality would come soon enough, and it would hurt. Oh, God, how it would hurt . . .

All they had was make-believe, the fairy tale was more real than the truth that they had nothing. Words, dreams, touches—they were what Selena would take away from here, and she refused to stop dreaming simply because it hurt.

She nestled closer to him, trying to feel him against every inch of her body. For one bright, razor-sharp instant, she fell into the fantasy, saw the life they could have led, the love they could have shared, and though it hurt—sweet Lord, it hurt—it also soothed and warmed her. "Madelaine," she whispered.

He stroked her hair. "Madelaine, what?"

"That's what I would have wanted to name our daughter."

He stilled. "She would have looked like you," he said softly. "I would have made her life a living hell."

Selena sat up, twisted to look down at him. Her wet hair snaked across his chest. She didn't understand what he meant, but the understanding wasn't the important part. What mattered was the moment, the memory they were making. She remembered what it had felt like at the Shaker village, how she'd wished she'd let him spin the dreams for her. Now she would let him talk forever, because she knew that his words were gifts that could be opened again and again when she got lonely. It was the words that would stay with her forever.

"What do you mean?"

Ian crossed his arms behind his head and stared up at her. "You don't know about courting. But if some man tried to steal a kiss from our daughter . . ."

"You would probably lock her in her room."

He brushed a strand of hair from her mouth and tried to smile. The wobbly failure made her want to cry. "Only for the dangerous years. Ten through twenty."

At his quietly spoken words, the fairy tale fell apart, left Selena with nothing to cling to, nothing to believe in. The words weren't enough, the memories too weak . . .

She would never see him smile again, never feel the gentleness of his touch or sleep in the safety of his arms.

"Oh, Ian . . . it hurts so much."

His forced smile faded as he gazed at her through pain-darkened eyes. "I know, baby."

A soft, gentle snow began to fall, pattering on Selena's hair, catching on her nose and eyelashes.

"Selena." He said her name so quietly that for a moment, she thought it was the wind. "I haven't asked you this before. . . ."

She squeezed her eyes shut, knowing what he would ask. It was the question that hung between them always, resting like granite on her heart. *Could you stay?*

"Do not ask it, Ian," she said. "There is no point."

He stared up at her for a long time, saying nothing, then a soft, curving smile shaped his lips. "I'm proud of you, goddess. Now, let's talk about something else, for God's sake. We haven't much time. Tell me about your life—the real one, the one you're going back to. Every time I touch Elliot, I get these images of you in strange clothing, walking in lines with other women. I want to know what you do every minute of the day so I can imagine you—"

"No," she said too quickly. "I do not wish to spend our time speaking of a past that does not matter."

"If we don't talk about the past, what do we talk about? There is no future."

She leaned down, kissed him slowly, thoroughly. "We have what we have always had, my love. Dreams and memories."

"Ah, Selena . . ." He took her face in his wet hands, held her with infinite gentleness. "It hurts to dream with you."

Tears stung her eyes. "I know," she said in a trembling voice. "But it's all we have."

The next morning Selena stood at the armoire, staring at herself in the mirror. What she saw made her feel queasy, unsteady on her feet.

The dark russet wool of the Shaker gown covered her from throat to foot. Already the tender flesh of her throat was chafed by the high collar. Slowly she buttoned the unadorned kerchief around her throat, straightened it so that the "indecent" outline of her breasts was completely hidden. Braiding her hair, she wound it into a tight bun at the base of her neck and pinned her white, starched cap in place. The ruffled edge framed her face and covered the flyway curls that grew along her forehead.

She made her bed, carefully tucking the heavy blankets in, smoothing the white sheet hem along the top.

Her fingers lingered lovingly against the cotton, feeling the softness one last time.

One last time . . .

She waited for the hot sting of tears, but this time they didn't come.

Forcing her chin up, she straightened and headed for the door and went into the hallway.

The house was quiet, too quiet.

She descended the stairs slowly, her booted feet creaking on the worn wood. Everyone was waiting for her at the bottom of the stairs. Elliot stood by the door, hat in hand, as alone in a crowd as a man could be.

The minute she reached the bottom, the crowd surged around her, crying, talking softly all at once, saying their good-byes in harsh, throaty voices. She hugged each one in turn, clinging as long as she could, and then she drew back.

Ian turned to Elliot. "May I say good-bye in private?"

Elliot squeezed his eyes tightly shut and nodded.

Ian walked up to her, his every footstep a blow that seemed to strike her heart. Gently he took her hand in his and led her through the front door, out onto the silent porch.

In front of them, the wagon sat in readiness on the drive. Behind it, the world was still and white.

He took her in his arms and held her closely. She clung to him, melting into the strong, familiar warmth of his body, wondering if she'd ever be this warm again.

"Someday," he breathed, drawing back.

She gazed up at him, this man who was her rock, her lifeline, the other half of her soul, and she couldn't think of a single thing to say.

What was left? Every hello they'd ever said had really meant good-bye.

* * *

Elliot stood awkwardly in the foyer, wondering if he'd given them enough time—if enough time existed for the kind of good-bye they were saying.

Maeve came up to him, put her thin, pale hand on his arm. "I will miss you, Elliot. I miss you already."

He looked down at Maeve and was wretchedly ashamed that he'd brought sadness and heartache into her home. Of all the people he had known in his life, this small, quiet woman had accepted him the most freely. "I'm sorry, Maeve."

Her eyes glittered with unshed tears. "I know you are. Take care of our Selena."

His throat felt too tight to speak. "I will."

She smiled. "And take care of yourself. Do that for me."

He nodded and reached for the door, opening it quickly. Ian and Agnes stood on the porch, locked in a tight, desperate embrace.

When he stepped onto the porch, they slowly drew apart. Agnes gave Ian a last, lingering half smile and came to Elliot, slipping her arm through his.

Together, silently, they walked down the sagging steps and across the soft layer of new snow. Still silent, they climbed aboard. Elliot took the cold, flat reins in his gloved hands and urged the horse forward.

The wheels whined in protest and slowly began to turn, crunching through the snow.

For a long time, Elliot couldn't bear to look at Agnes, and when he finally did, he wished he hadn't. She sat hunched and shaking, her chin tucked protectively into her chest. They hadn't gone more than fifty feet from the house and already she was beginning to wilt.

It broke his heart to see her pain.

She was the only real family he'd ever had, this wife who wasn't a wife, had never really been a wife. They weren't lovers, not in the physical sense of the word, and not even in the emotional.

It was amazing how the realization freed him. For the

first time in years, maybe forever, he understood how he felt for Agnes. She was his family. His friend. She had always been there for him; even after he brought her to the sterile world of the Believers, she'd always been there. A stolen look, a little wave, a tired smile. She'd always been his rock, comforting and anchoring him by her very presence.

But what had he been to her? Her protector, her savior. Not her husband, never truly her husband.

He loved her, certainly. But not the way she deserved to be loved. Not the way Ian loved her. Elliot had never felt honest sexual desire for her—or if he had, it was so long ago, he couldn't remember. He wanted her for the same reason she wanted him. So they wouldn't be so alone in the world.

Only she wasn't alone anymore.

The driveway forked up ahead. One road led to the huge, iron-scrolled gates, which now were silvered with frost. The other led back to the house.

Ian leaned against the porch stanchion, his arms crossed tightly on his chest, his mouth drawn in a taut line. Watching her leave him. Again.

The world was quiet, still, with only the low soughing of the wind to punctuate the clip-clop of the horse's hooves.

He stood stiff, straight, afraid that if he moved, if he even blinked, he'd run after her, fall to his knees beside the wagon and beg her to stay with him.

Marry me, Selena. Marry me because I'm selfish and unenlightened and need you so. . . .

He squeezed his eyes shut, not ready to remember yet, wondering if he'd ever be ready to remember.

His life spiraled out before him, endless days and longer nights, and yawning, desperate loneliness. Children he wouldn't father, kisses he wouldn't feel.

"Jesus," he moaned, fisting his hands. He'd never

known a man could feel this sharp a pain and keep breathing, keep living.

"They're coming back," Maeve said softly.

Ian's head snapped up. He opened his eyes.

The wagon had reached the curve in the driveway and turned left. Back toward the house.

Johann pulled away from the door, moved toward the steps. "Holy shit."

They stood there, Andrew, the queen, Lara, Maeve, Johann, and him, breathless and waiting, hoping. But no one said a word.

The wagon pulled up in front of the house again and stopped.

Ian pulled away from the post, took a step forward before he stopped. He looked up at Selena, sitting there, her back straight, her cheeks already pink from the cold, sparkling air, and thanked God that she was back. Even if it was only for a second.

Elliot set the reins down and climbed out of the wagon. Crossing behind it, he went to Selena and helped her down, then he led her back toward the house. The crowd parted wordlessly, leaving Ian alone at the top of the stairs.

Elliot led Selena up the steps and came to a stop in front of Ian.

Elliot drew in a deep breath, then, very slowly, he took Selena's cold hand and placed it in Ian's.

"Ian," he said in a soft, steady voice. "I give you my wife to be yours. All I ask . . ." Tears filled his eyes, fell in streaks down his face. "All I ask is that you love her and make her happy. I cannot do it anymore."

Ian felt a rush of emotion so powerful, so intense, that his knees went weak. He squeezed her hand tightly, too tightly. He looked down at Selena. She was crying quietly, but she hadn't looked at him.

"Elliot—" Selena whispered, a stricken look on her face.

Elliot gave her a heartbreakingly tender smile. "We are not truly husband and wife, Selena. We never were."

"But . . ." Her voice broke. She looked at Ian, her eyes filled with a mixture of tears and love and awe.

Elliot leaned down, kissed her cheek. "Be happy, Selena."

He pulled his hand away from Selena's and left it in Ian's, then started down the stairs.

For a second, Ian was too stunned to react. Then he pulled her into his arms, crushed her in his embrace. She clung to him, whispering his name over and over again, as if she couldn't believe they were together.

Finally they drew apart, and he stared down at her. "I love you so much," he said in a cracked voice. Such little words, so small, to express the pounding, aching emotion in his chest.

Tears puddled in her eyes, slid down her pink cheeks. She gave him a trembling smile, then cast a sad look at the old man walking away from them. "It is not right," she whispered, and another tear fell.

Ian looked at Elliot, watched the man crunch through the new snow toward the wagon, his whole body hunched in defeat.

And suddenly Ian understood. All of it made sense. God had demanded the best from all of them—Selena, Elliot, Ian. Each of them had to dig deep in his or her soul and find the honor, the love, the truth.

In finding the goodness in themselves, they'd been redeemed.

"You're right," he said softly. Squeezing her hand, he led her down the steps and across the snowy yard. "Elliot!" he called.

The big man paused just before boarding the wagon and turned back. His eyes widened in surprise as Ian and Selena moved closer. He pulled the floppy hat from his head and crushed it to his chest. "What is it?"

It took Ian a moment to find the words. He wanted

just the right ones, but in the end, he couldn't find them. So he simply said, "Stay."

Selena gasped, smiled up at Ian—so painfully beautiful, it took all his willpower not to crush her against him.

Back on the porch, Maeve let out a scream and came running down the steps.

Elliot looked from face to face in obvious confusion. "You're just being polite."

"No," Ian said.

Selena squeezed his hand, then let go, moving toward Elliot. "I told you once that you were my family, Elliot. I believe this is what families do. They grow. One person at a time, one day at a time, they grow and change and stay wondrously the same."

Elliot touched her face, a fleeting, emotional gesture. "There's no Agnes anymore," he said quietly. Tears filled his eyes again, and he seemed unashamed of them. His mouth curved in a tender smile. "You're offering me a family."

Family. Ian heard the reverence in the word, and it moved him. This big, scarred man had wanted what they all wanted, what they'd all found when only they'd opened their hearts.

Elliot could nod right now and it would be done. He could release Selena, release himself from their past. Together, they could all create the future.

It was so simple, so incredibly simple. Selena had been right from the very beginning. The world came down to choices, simple, straightforward choices.

"Elliot," she said in that soft, throaty voice, the one that always mesmerized Ian. "You belong here with us."

Maeve moved up beside Elliot, placed a small hand on his huge shoulder. "Stay, Elliot."

Elliot looked up. Above the women's heads, he stared at Ian, flashed him a last, silent question.

Very slowly, Ian nodded.

A grin broke across Elliot's big face. "I'd like to stay."

A whooping holler rose from the crowd and they surged forward, shaking Elliot's hand, patting his back. Welcoming him.

Selena turned to Ian then, and he knew that if he lived to be a hundred, he'd never forget that moment. That look of shining, brilliant love in her eyes.

She moved into the circle of his arms. He held her, felt her melt against him, and knew that this time it was forever. He closed his eyes, heard the distant rumble of the sea, the ebb and flow of the horse's breath, the murmuring of voices in the background. Somewhere a gull cawed, and it sounded like the cry of a newborn babe. God's exquisite symphony.

Slowly he opened his eyes and gazed down at her, loving her so much, it hurt. "Ah, goddess," he said in a thick voice. "I can hear the music at last."

Epilogue

〜❦〜

They say that the old mansion on the isolated coast of Maine still stands, waiting for a loving, restorative hand to bring it back to its former glory. Trees and underbrush have crept across the once-shorn lawn, winding slick, green tentacles around the peeling porch rails. A thousand white wildflowers grow stubbornly amidst the weeds, their fragrance a sweet reminder of days gone by.

No one visits the old asylum anymore, no one has in years. The many children of Ian and Selena flew from the nest long ago, scattering like dust in the wind, raising their children and their grandchildren in other, more modern places.

But every now and then, the locals creep through the weeds to gaze at the old place, and even now, more than a century later, the house of the broken windows welcomes them. Over the years, more than one person has claimed to hear laughter. Some say it is the wind, others the restless spirits of the lunatics who once lived here.

The children know, though, and the grandchildren, too. This wild, lonely house by the sea is like no other, haunted not by demons or sorcerers or evil, but by the memory of a passionate, undeniable love.

For when the night is dark and the tide is low and the wildflowers glow like scattered diamonds across the blackened yard, the sound of laughter lingers in the air. And the lovers hear it as they stand along the desolate shore, waiting for the moon.

Dr. Bloom waited patiently for an answer.

Meghann Dontess leaned back in her seat and studied her finger-nails. It was time for a manicure. Past time. "I try not to feel too much, Harriet. You know that. I find it impedes my enjoyment of life."

"Is that why you've seen me every week for four years? Because you enjoy your life so much?"

"I wouldn't point that out if I were you. It doesn't say much for your psychiatric skills. It's entirely possible, you know, that I was perfectly normal when I met you and you're actually *making* me crazy."

"You're using humor as a shield again."

"You're giving me too much credit. That wasn't funny."

Harriet didn't smile. "I rarely think you're funny."

"There goes my dream of doing stand-up."

"Let's talk about the day you and Claire were separated."

Meghann shifted uncomfortably in her seat. Just when she needed a smart-ass response, her mind went blank. She knew what Harriet was poking around for, and Harriet knew she knew. If Meghann didn't answer, the question would simply be asked again. "Separated. A nice, clean word. Detached. I like it, but that subject is closed."

"It's interesting that you maintain a relationship with your mother while distancing yourself from your sister."

Meghann shrugged. "Mama's an actress. I'm a lawyer. We're com-fortable with make-believe."

"Meaning?"

"Have you ever read one of her interviews?"

"No."

"She tells everyone that we lived this poor, pathetic but-loving exis-tence. We pretend it's the truth."

"You were living in Bakersfield when the pathetic-but-loving pre-tense ended, right?"

Meghann remained silent. Harriet had maneuvered her back to the painful subject like a rat through a maze.

Harriet went on, "Claire was nine years old. She was missing sev-eral teeth, if I remember correctly, and she was having difficulties with math."

"Don't," Meghann curled her fingers around the chair's sleek wood-en arms.

Harriet stared at her. Beneath the unruly black ledge of her eyebrows, her gaze was steady. Small round glasses magnified her eyes. "Don't back away, Meg. We're making progress."

"Any more progress and I'll need an aid car. We should talk about my practice. That's why I come to you, you know. It's a pressure cooker down in Family Court these days. Yesterday, I had a deadbeat dad drive up in a Ferrari and then swear he was flat broke. The shithead. Didn't want to pay for his daughter's tuition. Too bad for him I videotaped his arrival."

"Why do you keep paying me if you don't want to discuss the root of your problems?"

"I have issues, not problems. And there's no point in poking around in the past. I was sixteen when all that happened. Now, I'm a whopping forty-two. It's time to move on. I did the right thing. It doesn't matter anymore."

"Then why do you still have the nightmare?"

She fiddled with the silver David Yurman bracelet on her wrist. "I have nightmares about spiders who wear Oakley sunglasses, too. But you never ask about that. Oh, and last week, I dreamed I was trapped in a glass room that had a floor made of bacon. I could hear people crying, but I couldn't find the key. You want to talk about that one?"

"A feeling of isolation. An awareness that people are upset by your actions, or missing you. Okay, let's talk about that dream. Who was crying?"

"Shit." Meghann should have seen that. After all, she had an undergraduate degree in psychology. Not to mention the fact that she'd once been called a child prodigy.

She glanced down at her platinum-and-gold watch. "Too bad, Harriet. Time's up. I guess we'll have to solve my pesky neuroses next week." She stood up, smoothed the pant legs of her navy Armani suit. Not that there was a wrinkle to be found.

Harriet slowly removed her glasses.

Meghann crossed her arms in an instinctive gesture of self-protection. "This should be good."

"Do you like your life, Meghann?"

That wasn't what she'd expected. "What's not to like? I'm the best divorce attorney in the state. I live—"

"—alone—"

"—in a kick-ass condo above the Public Market and drive a brand-new Porsche."

"Friends?"

"I talk to Elizabeth every Thursday night."

"Family?"

Maybe it was time to get a new therapist. Harriet had ferreted out all of Meghann's weak points. "My mom stayed with me for a week last year. If I'm lucky, she'll come back for another visit just in time to watch the colonization of Mars on MTV."

"And Claire?"

"My sister and I have problems, I'll admit it. But nothing major. We're just too busy to get together." When Harriet didn't speak, Meghann rushed in to fill the silence. "Okay, she makes me crazy, the way she's throwing her life away. She's smart enough to do anything, but she stays tied to that loser campground they call a resort."

"With her father."

"I don't want to discuss my sister. And I *definitely* don't want to discuss her father."

Harriet tapped her pen on the table. "Okay, how about this: When was the last time you slept with the same man twice?"

"You're the only one who thinks that's a *bad* thing. I like variety."

"The way you like younger men, right? Men who have no desire to settle down. You get rid of them before they can get rid of you."

"Again, sleeping with younger, sexy men who don't want to settle down is not a bad thing. I don't want a house with a picket fence in suburbia. I'm not interested in family life, but I like sex."

"And the loneliness, do you like that?"

"I'm not lonely," she said stubbornly. "I'm independent. Men don't like a strong woman."

"Strong men do."

"Then I better start hanging out in gyms instead of bars."

"And strong women face their fears. They talk about the painful choices they've made in their lives."

Meghann actually flinched. "Sorry, Harriet, I need to scoot. See you next week."

She left the office.

Outside, it was a gloriously bright June day. Early in the so-called summer. Everywhere else in the country, people were swimming and barbecuing and organizing poolside picnics. Here, in good ole Seattle, people were methodically checking their calendars and muttering that it was *June, damn it.*

Only a few tourists were around this morning; out-of-towners recognizable by the umbrellas tucked under their arms.

Meghann finally released her breath as she crossed the busy street and stepped up onto the grassy lawn of the waterfront park. A towering totem pole greeted her. Behind it, a dozen seagulls dived for bits of discarded food.

She walked past a park bench where a man lay huddled beneath a blanket of yellowed newspapers. In front of her, the deep blue Sound stretched along the pale horizon. She wished she could take comfort from that view; often, she could. But today, her mind was caught in the net of another time and place.

If she closed her eyes—which she definitely dared not do—she'd remember it all: the dialing of the telephone number, the stilted, desperate conversation with a man she didn't know, the long, silent drive to that shit-ass little town up north. And worst of all, the tears she'd wiped from her little sister's flushed cheeks when she said, *I'm leaving you, Claire.*

Her fingers tightened around the railing. Dr. Bloom was wrong. Talking about Meghann's painful choice and the lonely years that had followed it wouldn't help.

Her past wasn't a collection of memories to be worked through; it was like an oversize Samsonite with a bum wheel. Meghann had learned that a long time ago. All she could do was drag it along behind her.